A Northern Light
in Provence

A Northern Light in Provence

A NOVEL

Elizabeth Birkelund

BALLANTINE BOOKS
NEW YORK

Published in the United States by Ballantine Books, an imprint of Random House, a division of Penguin Random House LLC, New York.

Hardback ISBN 978-0-593-72221-3
Ebook ISBN 978-0-593-72222-0

Printed in the United States of America on acid-free paper

randomhousebooks.com

9 8 7 6 5 4 3 2 1

FIRST EDITION

Book design by Barbara M. Bachman

Title page and part title art by John Eric Oberbeck

For my sons and belle fille

I.

Home

Oqaatsit ataasiinnaat
naammanngillat.

—TRANSLATION FROM
THE GREENLANDIC:
ONE LANGUAGE IS
NEVER ENOUGH.

Chapter 1

FROM THE WINDOW OF THE TOP FLOOR OF THE OLD SEA CAPTAIN'S house, Ilse Erlund gazes at the flat sword of sky and the steely sea, dotted with icebergs. She looks through the binoculars hanging on a shoestring around her neck. A glowing blue ice sculpture tips, rotates, and drifts past. With its trail of mist, the form resembles a skeletal ghoul, indifferent to all but its cavernous-eyed pursuit of the sea, the sea, the sea—and freedom from its ice-bound form.

It's midmorning and high tide. In a few moments, the prone silt and rock craggy headland, on which Ilse's sea captain cottage rests, will liquefy into silver froth. Ilse is concerned about the stability of the four stilts that support the house, especially after the lightning storm last night when she'd spent much of the flashing, wind-howling hours tossing with fear that the cottage, and her in it, would fall into the sea. Even on sunny days, the house and her clothes smell of mildew.

Malu, Ilse's mother, says it's Ilse's imagination, that houses don't wobble back and forth. Of all people, Malu, who has the most Inuit blood in the family, should trust her daughter's perceptions. In the Inuit culture, all things, living and inanimate, have souls, wobbly houses included. But Malu is a practical practitioner of life.

Jann, you would believe me! Jann, Ilse's brother, born just eleven months before she was, her almost-twin, the youngest and best soccer player in Greenland. He'd been awarded MVP every year since he'd been drafted at seventeen years old by the Polar Teddy Bears, Greenland's national team.

This next iceberg looks like an escapee, its arms extended behind, as it slips between sheets of black ice and snow-covered floes. Fleeing from what? Ilse removes the binoculars from her neck. She could play the "What does the iceberg resemble?" game all day. Back to work—or rather, back to her everyday affordable getaway, peering into the narrow interstices, no, not between icebergs, but between words and punctuation marks to decipher other worlds, other people, other ways of life.

Ilse Erlund is a Greenlander who translates French texts into Danish or English, or both.

"Don't ask why," she tells her fellow Greenlanders after informing them about her profession. A look of confusion, followed by "French?" is a fair response. The more typical reaction is a few noncommittal words or a giggle. The relatives on Ilse's mother's side of the family are more opinionated. Those are the ones who regaled the young Ilse with Inuit myths and now consider her a traitor. Great-Aunt Jôrîna even warned Ilse that by gazing too eagerly at another culture she was risking the wrath of the Moon Man. Ilse suspects that her parents worry that she'll hightail it out of town as soon as she has enough money to travel—and they're right. Her parents are from the generation that still considers exiting a settlement taboo: if one person leaves, the community is weakened.

Can Ilse help it if she has a natural ear for languages? She'd learned English, thanks to her mother who spoke it to her at home—Malu's grandfather was a cartographer from Liverpool who charted North Greenland, previously terra incognita, and then stayed and married an indigenous Greenlander. Thanks to Malu's fluency in English, she was awarded one of the most prestigious jobs in Greenland, that of a well-paid postal worker.

Danish is Ilse's father tongue, also spoken at school when she was growing up. Most Greenlanders speak it. Fa's (*Far* is "father" in Danish) family immigrated to southwestern Greenland from Denmark in the early 1900s to set up logging posts—that's when there were still forests on that part of the island. Since then, Fa's family has married into Greenlandic families, so Ilse also speaks the local *kalaallisut,* which became the official language in 2009.

But being trilingual wasn't enough for the then twelve-year-old. That was Ilse's age when a certain perfume-wearing, high-heel-boot-sashaying Madame LaRoche arrived to teach French in Ilse's school.

Love at first hearing.

This morning, Ilse Erlund is struggling with her first love. Despite her preternatural ability to translate words from one language into another, the French expression *faire la grasse matinée* is not coming easily. The phrase appears often enough in the novel by Zoë Gaudet that Ilse is convinced the French author thinks the words constitute the purpose of life.

"To make a fat morning" is the literal translation. In the context of Gaudet's novel about a philandering woman who swings from lover to lover like a monkey from tree to tree, the expression has erotic implications.

"Enjoy a lazy, postcoital morning" is hardly sexy, Ilse says to herself. The Anglo-Saxon language is many things, but a romance language it is not. For a richer verbal transmigration, English would have to languish topless on the pebbled beaches on the Mediterranean coast, or step among sunflowers in the dusty fields of Provence, or at the very least bite into a tranche of crusty French bread. And that would be only the beginning.

Ilse suspects, after fifteen years in the translating business, that *faire la grasse matinée,* like so many other French expressions, is culturally impossible to unlock in its original, delicious sense.

Ilse's best-kept secret to those in her business, shhh, don't tell her French publisher, is that she has never stepped foot in France! *You* try paying for the extortionate round-trip airfare from Greenland to Iceland to France, she often rationalizes, and then the lodging, food, and drink, with the paltry salary of a translator.

Her friend Troy Belke, otherwise known since middle school as Beluga (kids can be so cruel), tells her that money is a poor excuse, that travel is cheaper than ever these days, and the reason she's never crossed the seas is that she's afraid.

Afraid of what? Finding out that she's an imposter, that she has no more right to be translating this love language than converting a Greenland sled dog's bark into words? That she has miles and years to go before she can even *begin* to understand the French culture, and that one day she'll be found out and be forced to quit this work that sends her imagination soaring, and resign herself to working as a tour guide out on the Tasermiut Fjord, explaining glacier melts to ice-cream-faced kids?

It is a shameful truth that at thirty-five years old, Ilse has never left Greenland. But that doesn't mean she doesn't love living on the largest island in the world and one of the least populated. Where else could she witness the dazzling dance of northern lights on the darkest nights of winter and find herself awestruck over and over again by the telltale spouting of a humpback whale and its dramatic flip of tail as it dives into the deep? Even as an adult, she loves to clamber over the coastal mussel-strewn boulders and rocks—geologists say they're 3.9 billion years old—and trek up ice-capped mountains for panoramic views in every direction. She still weeps at the beauty of the spread of purple Arctic flowers and white Boreal cup lichen that carpet the terrain in early summer.

Landscape? Seascape or skyscape perhaps. "Icescape" would be the more apt word. Eighty-two percent of her country is covered with a silky frozen cape, in some areas in the middle four miles thick. But now the garment is shrinking. Hourly, the ice is calving, breaking off into ice-filigreed cathedrals and frozen sea creatures, many of which she sees from her window. Even the ice tongues, the floating platforms of ice attached to glaciers, are thinning. No wonder the earth's sea level is rising every year. She'd recently read a statistic that the island is losing 277 gigatons of mass a year, and when she looked up "gigaton," she found out it equals one billion tons!

Many Greenlanders who'd traveled, like Beluga, returned to this self-governing province of Denmark, boasting that nowhere else on earth can you feel so close to nature, nowhere else does every view offer a glimpse of infinity. After one extensive leave-taking, Beluga had even waxed poetic, unusual for him, and that's why Ilse remembers it so well: he'd said that only in Greenland on a moonless winter's night could the sky hold a billion trillion sparkling diamonds, and on a summer's midnight could it shine like pearls turned into iridescent powder. Others, when they were away, complained of the "Polar Spell," an unclassified anxiety that dissipated only when they returned to the treeless icy expanses and lichen-slick cliffs descending into fjords.

Beluga liked questions, and Greenland, he said, was a place where every question raised another question. But Ilse liked answers. And she was beginning to have had enough of the unresponding measureless sea and troposphere—enough to make her long for dry land.

Thanks to the Internet, Ilse office-chair-travels round-trip to France most days of the year. She knows the latitude and the longitude of the 212,935 square miles of L'Hexagone by heart and can recite the names of the rivers, mountain ranges, cities, and many towns. And although she has not scrambled to the top of the Eiffel Tower or walked in the footsteps of Diane de Poitiers at Château de Chenonceau or skied down the French Alps, hey, she's read about all these things, including how French women stay thin and still eat dessert (small plates and discipline).

Somehow, she's been able to pull the wool over her French authors' and her editor's eyes, and even the reviewers who'd given her translations top reviews.

"She's invisible," they write.

Translating may be the only profession in which being imperceptible is laudable. Luckily for her, that part is easy.

Ilse will ask her French colleague, Bea Fugue, who translates from English to French, the reverse direction from Ilse's work, for help with *faire la grasse matinée*. Ilse met Bea several years ago at Ilisimatusarfik University in a class on "The Importance of the Human Translator in the Future." Now friends, they often call each other when stuck in translation.

But Bea and she don't share the same views about their work. Bea insists that translating is as much her creative work as the author's, that her completed translation is as much an original as the source material. Ilse is a purist; in her view, the best translators surrender to the creativity of the author, slip indelibly under their skin in a kind of transmutation of energies.

"That's provocative," Bea had responded.

"I'm not talking about sexual energy, Bea."

"What other kind of energy is there?"

The French!

Their word duels continue something like this:

Bea: As a translator, I must project.

Ilse: No! Rather, you must *protect*.

Bea: A translator should become.

Ilse: *Succumb.*

Bea: Overcome!

Ilse: Be faithful!

Bea: To yourself.

Ilse: To the *author.*

Despite their different approaches, both women agree that their daily challenges are the *untranslatables,* words that resist adaption—brand names, clothes, objects, clichés, puns, bad syntax, alliteration, assonance, rhyme, rhythm, and most of all, argot, the colloquial coinages, arbitrarily altered words and original expressions that become part of a working language.

"Move over, Minou." Ilse tickles the white spot under the neck of her mostly black cat who likes to lounge on her warm computer keys.

"Are you enjoying a *grasse matinée*? You were out awfully late last night."

Had *Ilse* ever slept into the late-morning hours with someone, legs interlocked after making love all night? Could she help it if she, a fisherman's and a postal worker's daughter, was an early bird, and her best working hours occurred in the morning, even during the Great Dark, the four-month winter plunge into nighttime?

On second thought, Ilse won't ask Bea for help. Bea loves to tease Ilse about her uptight Nordic heritage. The last time Ilse asked Bea a loaded translation question, what *really* constituted French kissing, *un baiser langoureux*, Bea had burst out laughing, exclaiming, "You people in Greenland, rubbing noses instead of tongues!"

Bea should know better than to make fun of the *kunik*, the affectionate nose nuzzles usually shared only between parents and grandparents and their children. A responsible, professional translator is in a perpetual pursuit of nuance, and achieving nuance takes nimbleness. But Bea translates fast-paced detective novels.

Ilse mouths the phrase, *faire la grasse matinée*, as she rubs her fingerless-gloved hands together and checks the Internet's English-French dictionary for the various meanings of the word *gras/grasse*.

Un rire gras: a coarse laugh.

Une peau grasse: greasy skin.

En caractères gras: in bold letters.

Du lard gras: fat lard.

Foie gras: delicious . . .

It's too cold to concentrate! She's tempted to turn up the heat, but she can't afford to amp the thermostat higher than sixty degrees.

So she does what she always does when stumped: she skedaddles down the sagging wooden stairs, throws her waterproof jacket over her brother's tattered gray Shetland sweater, slips on her insulated rubber boots, and tops her outfit off with her dented leather rain hat. She pulls the warped front door open, shoves it shut, and starts to walk. Her outing is a pilgrimage of sorts, her mission to clear her mind so she can slay the untranslatables in work and in life.

AFTER MONTHS OF WIND-BATTERING, spirit-draining winter weather, a pale glint of sun skims the line of clouds in the distant, flat coastal horizon. Thank goodness it's March 19th, and tomorrow is the spring equinox, when daylight is three magical hours longer than in February. As a child, Ilse would record the arrivals of sunrises and sunsets in a journal to mark the progressing days. As an adult, she finds that the dark days pass faster when she doesn't acknowledge them.

Ilse takes the path along the shortest peninsula of the five wetland fingers that stretch from the palm-of-hand-land out to sea.

"Oh, look!" She jumps over a miniature clump of fuzzy green leaves and stops to examine it. "A patch of prepubescent Arctic bell heather! And you, the tiniest insinuation of pink saxifrage. You have a few months to reveal yourself, but I know you're under there. Tomorrow *is* the first day of spring!"

Just the other day, her father was saying that the spring snowmelt was happening earlier compared with only a few years ago, that the four oldest trees in the country, planted down south in Narsarsuaq by a Dutch botanist in 1893, were waking up, and there were fresh, green sprigs on trees that had been sleeping for the last two centuries. It's treeless where Ilse lives, that is if you don't count the barely visible miniature forests growing underfoot. She sidesteps to avoid a spread of unripe crowberries. She'll have to wait until August before picking the tiny black berries for her mother, who is known for making the sourest crowberry jam in the settlement.

Sled dogs yap and howl, sensing her footsteps. Here's the part of her walk that she dreads, jumping from rock to rock, just far enough away from the dogs shackled by long chains to boulders along the path. They're especially yappy today, probably because of the spring air.

"No, you don't!" she shouts at one lurching toward her. She steps away to avoid his toothy jaw.

Gulls fly overhead without flapping: the wind is their wing. Their calls feel urgent, as if they're warning that time is running out, and the plovers look like waves as they ruffle-skirt the shore.

Usually by this time on her detour, Ilse would have come up with a translation solution, or at least part of one, and would have scribbled it in the small notebook that she carries in the pocket of her slicker. But this morning, no word-gifts emerge. Nothing but the sea rushes in, ripple by ripple, translating the land into its frothy language.

The tides extend and retract. It's as if the sea is breathing, and without realizing it, Ilse is calibrating her breath to its long scratchy inhalations and foam-spumy exhalations. When the tide comes in, the spit of land disconnects and becomes an island; when it goes out, Ilse's home is on the mainland. They say people who live on the specks of tidal islands off Greenland are of two minds: they are social when the sandbars join them to the mainland and misanthropic when they are set apart. Only a Greenlander with Danish blood—she can thank Fa for that—would choose to live apart from the already small, concentrated settlement of Oqaatsut as she does. In her country, solitude is thought to be a form of failure.

But Ilse doesn't care; she prefers the solitary life.

She'd better turn back to her cottage. If she doesn't, in a matter of minutes she'll have to surrender, like this little tip of land, to the sea, to the sea, to the sea. On some days, mostly in this gray twilight season of wet winter-spring, when her cottage is pounded by frigid gales and currents, and when she misses her brother desperately, the sea feels as though it's beckoning to her, as it does now. Over the years, she's learned to shut her mind to it.

Yes! She touches the two ten-krone coins in her slicker pocket, enough for a cup of coffee. Though she knows that Val will offer her one for free. A little social hour at Tipsy's, Val Barker's coffee shop, with its steamed-up windows and a few local friends, will do her good. She has not encountered a person in three days.

That is, if you don't count Mr. G. He's the ghost the previous renter had warned her about, and why the monthly rent for the old sea captain's cottage is so cheap. Mr. G runs up and down the stairs nightly, and Ilse must yell in her firmest voice, "Move on now!" from her bed to get him to go bother someone else. "Denying the existence of a ghost will only make it grow bigger" is a Greenlandic proverb. She keeps a bowl of sea-softened stones and silver mussel shells at the top of the stairs as an offering to the ghost. Soon she will be gathering purple saxifrage for him.

Tipsy's is a fifteen-minute hike from the pinky peninsula, the rocky path now two inches under freezing water. She stops to watch a sea otter floating on its back, paddling with its hind legs, and sculling with its tail. Now that it's mating season, the gulls and qaqulluk honk and croak louder than normal. Mussels shine like sparkly necklaces along the black rocks.

She hears a set of crashing booms in the distance, like gunshots—it's the ever-present sound of ice calving, breaking off the glacier. Will these be the sounds at the end of the world? Will the opposite of the Big Bang be the exploding blast of the last remnant of the glacier thundering into the sea?

She wishes she'd grabbed some lip gloss on her way out the door in case Beluga shows up. Beluga is too modest and humble to demand to be called by his given name, Troy. He's thinner than he was in school, and taller, at six feet, five inches. Maybe if he happens to be at Tipsy's, which is doubtful at this midmorning hour, Ilse will surprise him and everyone else there, and say "Hello, Troy."

Chapter 2

"WELL, LOOK WHO THE TIDES BROUGHT IN," SAYS VAL, SITTING solo on a twirl stool at the counter, a white mug of coffee between her hands. "I had a feeling you'd be in today."

She always says that. Val has a dark complexion, green eyes, and a small mole on the left side of her mouth that draws your attention to her full, curving lips. She is descended from the Saqqaq, the earliest of the ancient Arctic peoples who settled from 2500 B.C.E. to 800 B.C.E. on the southeastward Inland Ice Sheet, where some years back archaeologists found animal and human bones, wood carvings, and a few pieces of leather. These days, coastal erosion and higher sea levels are making mush of such ancient grounds. History, evaporating before Greenlanders' eyes.

Val was a classmate of Ilse's up to seventh grade, when Val dropped out, along with half the grade to support their families and be "purposeful," as Malu called it. "Porpoise-full," her brother would tease. Jann was the only one who could joke with formidable Malu, their no-nonsense mother who sorts mail for the 4,671 residents of Ilulissat, if you include Ilse's cat, who receives mail from Bea, Ilse's translator friend in Paris. Ilulissat, Greenlandic for "iceberg," is 186 miles north of the Arctic Circle. It's where Ilse grew up until she left five years ago to live in Oqaatsut, a remote settlement of thirty-five inhabitants, a half-hour boat ride north.

Val, the first and only person in Oqaatsut to open a coffee shop (prior to Val, the communal all-purpose Pilersuisoq store sold coffee and cake), wears an electric blue scarf over her head that she ties under her chin to control her thick, black, wild curly hair. She says her ancestors wore their hair like fur coats, and this would be entirely plausible to anyone who has seen Val's extravagant tresses.

"Sure, why not," Ilse says after Val pulls the green bottle of Brennivin schnapps from under the counter. "I'm sleepwalking as it is this morning."

When Ilse woke in the middle of the night, agitated by the storm and the unrelenting challenge of translating *faire la grasse matinée,* she'd had to remind herself, as she has on many occasions, that a text is inert, not a feral animal stalking her to get the words right.

"You stumped on a word?" Val asks as she pours the schnapps into the coffee.

Ilse says the phrase in French.

"Not in frog language, Ilse. Give it to me in Danish, English, or Greenlandic."

A gust of damp cold whips into the coffee shop.

"I'd like to hear it in French."

It's Beluga's voice, deep and low. He ducks under the doorframe and pulls the door closed behind him. The cold stands suspended around him.

"You have a way of appearing out of nowhere," says Val. Her teeth glint in the sudden dash of sun from the window.

Beluga removes his wrinkled felt hat and sits on the stool beside Ilse. His knees have a hard time fitting, so he sits sideways. As Val turns to walk the gauntlet between the two counters to the kitchen at the back of the hut, Ilse notices Beluga's eyes fastening on the bow of Val's white apron, tied just so, around her backside. Seconds later, Val returns, places a mug on the counter in front of Beluga, and bends lower than she had for Ilse to retrieve the schnapps bottle. Her red beaded necklace makes music with the counter.

"How about a little extra pizzazz for you this morning, Beluga? And a refill for you, Ilse?" Val pours the clear liquid into Beluga's mug without waiting for his response. Ilse covers hers with her hand.

"Thanks, Val, but I've got a full day of work ahead of me."

Beluga has trimmed his beard since the last time Ilse saw him, and the angles of his square jaw look sharper.

Ilse had dated Beluga during the summer they both turned sixteen. They had kissed and done pretty much everything but, until Beluga left school in the middle of the following school year when his father, a former professional heavyweight boxer, began to lose his mind. When his father died a year later, Beluga supported his mother and two sisters by training and working as a commercial pilot at Air Greenland. He installed radar sites, and sometimes he ferried planes to Europe. Taking advantage of the fact that Greenland is a country with only ninety-three miles of roads, of which only fifty-six are paved, five years ago Beluga took out a joint loan with three other pilots to purchase a DHC-6 Twin Otter, a plane that can be fitted with skis, floats, or normal landing gear, and became a private pilot. He spends most of his days airborne, flying people and supplies from town to town. He's often gone for weeks at a time.

Beluga doesn't boast about his Norse ancestry as others do here in Greenland, but there is no doubt of his peripatetic DNA. But he is more skyfaring than seafaring. His work has taken him over almost every inch of Greenland, and into Europe and Asia. On one trip, requiring several fuel stops along the way, he delivered a tenth-century bronze sword found buried under layers of silt near Upernavik to a wealthy Athenian. He has hauled stuff to customers in Istanbul, and even to Cyprus, from where he brought Ilse a dusty white rock that she holds from time to time to imagine the warmth in such a place.

When Ilse was in high school, and Beluga was no longer being educated, he accused her of talking down to him, even though he was the one spending time in the air. She blamed him for resenting her, and they had slowly drifted apart. Then she began dating one of his cousins, and he was involved in a serious five-year relationship with Maritha Ignatiussen, a misty-eyed classmate of hers, daughter of the

Lutheran minister. He and Maritha broke up when her family moved to Iceland.

Ilse gazes up at Beluga, and their eyes meet for a moment. His eyes often look sluggish, as if he's just woken from a winter's nap. It isn't fair that he has such long black lashes. Hers are thin and spiky.

"Beluga, since when did you learn French?" asks Val, now leaning on the counter a few inches away from him.

"Ilse and I had the same French teacher. She lit the fire under Ilse, but she put the fire out in me."

"That teacher snuffed the fire out of herself," says Val. "So I heard."

"The first loss of my life," Ilse says. "That was before the other earth-shattering, me-shattering one."

Val turns quickly to Ilse and pats her gently on the shoulder.

"Okay," says Ilse, pushing her coffee mug closer to Val, "a little more."

Val reaches for the bottle under the counter.

"That woman wasn't meant for this part of the world," says Beluga; his eyes shift downward as if in respect. He is so decent, Beluga.

Ilse cannot see out the steamy window.

"This should send you a few good words," Val says as she pours.

"Counting on it."

"Who's the author? Anyone famous?" asks Beluga.

Val slides a plate with a large piece of confection-sugar-dusted *kalaallit kaagiat*, the Greenland national coffee cake, in front of Beluga.

"Just out of the oven," she says.

"This author is just out of the oven, too. I'm guessing she'll be famous. She thinks that plot is a male machination, that it's anti-thought, so her novel is a series of scenes of people talking, concentric circles that wrap around one another. The idea is that each time you go around, you catch another glimpse of yourself, even if it's by the tail. I'm having a tough time trying to get underneath her language. Or for that matter, getting on top of it."

"That sounds sexy," says Val, fingering her beads.

"It's provocative, it's true. In an interview that I saw with her, she said that we're so confined within the context of our lives that we'll never truly experience freedom. Her hope is that her writing will stand apart from her as an unshackled, independent being of sorts. She thinks the book she's writing knows more than she does."

"Now you've really lost me," calls out Val, heading toward the kitchen.

"Here comes Duggan," announces Beluga.

Beluga's knees brush Ilse's as he twists to greet the newcomer. How did Beluga know it was Duggan? Ilse can barely see out the salt-streaked windows.

Duggan is another large man, bigger widthwise than tallwise. He wears a yellow slicker, black rubber boots that cover his knees, and a green knit hat pulled down over most of his gray, wiry eyebrows. In addition to owning and running the biggest commercial fishery in the town of Ilulissat, he's the area's unofficial mayor. He is Ilse's father's age, sixty-nine, and has white whiskers mixed in with red ones, which make it look as if he's had a slurp of crowberry juice. His long gray hair is tied in a ponytail, rather a donkey tail, a remnant from his hippie days, and Ilse suspects that he wears his hat inside Tipsy's to hide his bald spot.

He's a friend of Beluga's, but then again, everyone is a friend of Beluga's.

"Just the man I was looking for," Duggan shouts out, addressing Beluga. "Samuelsen needs you today. I told him I knew where to find you."

"Will anyone in this place let me finish my coffee without asking me for something?"

"I haven't asked you to solve my word problem," says Ilse.

"Give it a few more minutes."

Duggan hangs his slicker on one of the hooks by the door.

"Ilse, nice to see you," Duggan says, eyeing the schnapps bottle on the counter as he squeezes into the stool on the other side of her. "The coffee-schnapps ratio looks mighty impressive today."

"It's Monday. A kick start to the week," says Val, returning to the counter. "The usual, Duggan, no sugar, no milk?"

"No liquor either. I don't know how you three get any work done."

"This *is* my work," says Val, hip-swaying in an exaggerated kind of way back to the kitchen.

"We're all working here," says Beluga. "We're helping Ilse find the right words for a French expression that she's translating into English. Come on, Ilse. Set the scene."

Val slides the filled coffee mug along the bowling-alley-like counter to Duggan without spilling a drop.

"She has the touch, she does!" yells Duggan. Despite his huge potato-man ears, Duggan is losing his hearing.

Val shows up at the counter opposite them with two small plates of Danish sponge cake, places one in front of Duggan and the other before Ilse. Too bad they aren't the recipients of the fresh-out-of-the-oven *kalaallit kaagiat* that she'd given to Beluga. Val has established a hierarchy of deliciousness depending on the customer.

"We're waiting," says Beluga, tapping his large fingers on the counter. Val leans her elbows on the counter, revealing the tattoo of an anchor at the base of her neckline.

"Okay, the scene," Ilse begins. "The sun is melting like caramel into the room. A transparent curtain blows lazily in the light breeze. It's late morning, no, rather, midday. The lovers are entangled, legs, one over the other, after a night of . . . of—"

"How much have you had to drink, Ilse?" yells Duggan.

"Duggan, don't interrupt just when it's getting good," says Beluga.

"The couple has slept through the morning after a night of lovemaking," continues Ilse. "The French say all of that in four words: *faire la grasse matinée*. Anyone here have four words to say the same thing in English? Or Danish—or Greenlandic, for that matter?"

"In Greenlandic," says Val, her hands at her narrow waist, "we'd say it in one word."

"Tell us," says Ilse.

"*Equisimaarput* means sleeping arm in arm as lovers."

"It sounds exquisite, but your word doesn't take into account the timeless morning spent together," says Ilse.

"It's too early in the morning for this kind of talk for me," says

Duggan, standing, mug of coffee in hand. "I'm late as it is. Beluga, when should I tell Samuelsen that you're free? Or maybe you want to hang around here all day waiting for the caramel sun to melt?"

"Tell Samuelsen I'll be there in half an hour. No, give me forty minutes. My outboard needs a new spark plug."

"Spark plug?" Val says winking at Beluga. "Ilse, how do you say *that* in French?"

"Thank you, Val." Duggan plunks his empty mug on the counter along with a few krone bills and stretches his arms into his slicker. "Ilse, you haven't been to visit your parents in a while. Your father was grousing about it the other day."

"I thought when I moved to this tiny settlement up the coast people in Ilulissat wouldn't know my business."

"Your ma says she can see your house from her attic window."

"She has the eyes of a hawk. Duggan, do you know that I'm thirty-five years old?"

"Getting on in age, Ilse. I wouldn't go around announcing it."

"It's old enough not to have your mother snooping on you. Anyway, *you're* not afraid to say your age, are you?"

"Proud of every winter I've made it through." He pulls his gloves out of his slicker and looks surprised to have found them there.

"Exactly."

"All I'm saying is a visit to your parents wouldn't hurt you none."

"Correction: it does hurt when they tell me that I'm wasting my life—"

"Can't help you there," Duggan says as he opens the door and slams it shut, but not before letting a heavy draft of cold air slip into the cozy hut.

Minutes later, Duggan's ruddy face appears again.

"Ilse," he yells out, "You said you're thirty-six?"

She turns on her stool. "Thirty-five."

She should have lied and said thirty.

"Thirty-five," he repeats, half his body now in the doorway, his ash-gray eyes glaring under his wiry brows. "And you're—"

"Living on my own, supporting myself, doing what I like."

As soon as she'd said it, she knew the words "doing what I like" would come back to bite. Around here, doing what you like is equivalent to saying you don't care about anyone else. She's been holed up in the sea captain's house for too long.

"There's doing what you like"—here it comes—"and then there's doing what's expected of you."

"Either come in or out," Val shouts from the kitchen. "It's spring, but you're letting in the dead of winter!"

"Ilse, pay them a visit," Duggan yells into the room, then slams the door again.

"Pay a visit," repeats Ilse under her breath. "An appropriate phrase, taxing you for being born."

Oqaatsut is definitely not far enough away from Ilulissat. Uummannaq, about one hundred miles to the north, would have been better, but there's no Tipsy's in Uummannaq.

"Val," Ilse calls from her stool, "may I pour myself another round? I owe you for this one."

"Go for it!" Val calls out.

"It's on me," says Beluga, rounding the counter before Ilse can. He moves swiftly for a large man.

When Val returns, she does a little shimmy with her shoulders, a little cleavage reveal, then follows Beluga around the corner of the counter and perches on the stool next to him.

"Ilse," Val says, leaning into Beluga in the direction of Ilse. Val smells of schnapps and coffee and something else sweet. "You're scaring away my customers with your French talk. People around here don't want to hear another way of saying something. Between people speaking Greenlandic, Danish, and English, isn't life complicated enough?"

"Speak for yourself, Val," says Beluga. "I was enjoying hearing about the French midmorning sun on naked bodies, the warm breeze moving the curtains slowly, back and forth, back and forth."

Beluga waves his large hands to imitate waves.

"Nice, Beluga!" Ilse trills. "Now you know why I love what I do. You get to be somewhere else."

"I don't want to be anywhere but here," he says, winking quickly at Val. He lifts his hat and stands, his hand now on the door latch.

Ilse prepares herself for the next blast of cold wind and for the empty feeling she gets when Beluga leaves.

"This should take care of Ilse's Tipsy portion," he says, dropping two hundred kroner on the counter, with a wink to Ilse.

Tipsy's is well named for the overflow of schnapps and tips.

"I'll be back later, Val," he says. He dons his hat, opens the door, and, looking back, dips his head a little as he says goodbye. It's a humble gesture that he's repeated for every goodbye since elementary school. He shuts the door quickly behind him.

"I like it when he shaves his beard close like that. He's got a good chin," says Val, scooping the yellow bills into her apron pocket.

When she was eighteen, Val Bakatvaal took off with Jake Barker, a pilot in the Royal Danish Navy, and moved to the Thule Air Base. After seven years, she returned south to Oqaatsut with a new name and Caroo, her seven-year-old, bright-blue-eyed daughter, and set up shop.

"He sure likes your *kalaallit kaagiat*," says Ilse. "Did you notice how he gobbled every last crumb?"

Val twists her stool to face Ilse. "You know, and I know, that I'll only ever be a substitute for you."

"People grow out of their childhood sweethearts, Val. We were sixteen."

"I don't know why you never went for him. He's not bookish enough for you, I guess. You speak his language, but he doesn't speak yours?"

Ilse sips her coffee and gazes out the window, which is clearer of condensation now that the heavy-breathing men are gone. In the vista ahead, a dirt path forks one way down to the dock and the fishing boats that travel back and forth to Ilulissat, and the other to a coastal-rock-hopping trail, curving in the direction of her captain's house.

"Yes, we're too different."

Val twists her stool to face Ilse.

"If it's okay with you, Ilse, I'll happily pick the leftovers off your plate."

"Val," she laughs. "You know you don't need my permission!"

Ilse notices the mole beside Val's lips, and despite her laughter, an unexpected, unsettled feeling rises in her stomach as she imagines Val and Beluga kissing.

"Caroo is crazy about him," Val says. "The other night, he played hearts with her for hours—you know, the card game. Now I want him to play hearts with me."

Val stands and peers out the window. She's nearsighted but only wears her glasses when she's in the back-of-the-hut kitchen, out of sight of her customers.

"I thought so," she says. "It's the phalanx of Qannik brothers. Better get the musk ox sizzling. They'll want at least four pieces each."

She loosens the blue scarf on her head and reties it, tighter this time. Ilse closes her eyes to erase the vision of Beluga's fingers stroking Val's luxurious hair.

"Donny Qannik is my true love," Ilse says, sighing. Donny is the youngest of the five brothers, the one who has Down syndrome.

"*Now* you tell me! Lucky Donny!" says Val, on her way to the kitchen.

"True love." Ilse swirls the words around in her mouth as she savors the last sip of coffee-schnapps.

"Thank you, Val," she calls from the door, leaving her two-krone tip and donning her slicker and leather hat. "See you tomorrow night at the party!"

Val throws herself a birthday party every year and sets up a paying bar, so she cashes in when the night's over. It's a win-win situation: the more drinks her friends buy, the happier she gets, and the better the birthday. Most of the residents in Oqaatsut show up.

"Happy matinee or whatever your love-sleep is called," Val yells from the kitchen.

Love-sleep.

Not bad.

"Love-sleep," repeats Ilse, outside Tipsy's, as she zips up her jacket and pulls her hat over her brow.

It has started to rain.

BEFORE SHE GOES TO bed that night, Ilse writes the French phrase on a sheet of paper followed by a question mark and leaves it on her desk. Sometimes it works, this invocation, offering words like a sacrifice to the altar of her desk. During the magic and mystery of the night, the spirit of the phrase may be revealed.

Chapter 3

BLAME THE FRENCH TEACHER.

That's how Ilse's parents explain their daughter's strange choice of vocation. All that education, and she gets paid less than a schoolteacher, and much less than a postal worker!

Teaching in the local high school was the typical job for a young woman who graduated from Ilulissat's high school and Ilisimatusarfik University in Nuuk, Greenland's capital. When Ilse informed her parents that her exciting new job involved translating French novels into English and Danish, they looked at her as if she was speaking another language. And she was. No wonder translating was easy for her: she'd been trying to define and explain her world to everyone around her for as long as she could remember.

Malu is right: it was the French teacher's fault.

Melody to her ears was Madame LaRoche's velvety voice on that first day of French class in seventh grade. It was by a twist of fate, *une torsion du déstin*, that's what Madame called it, that Madame found herself the first French teacher in the Ilulissat school's sixty-year history. Madame with her hennaed hair and black eyeliner that extended out from her eyelids would not have endured five minutes teaching French to a bunch of fishermen's brats if it weren't for the allure of Douglas McNare, whom everyone called "McSnare." Ilse had spotted him on several occasions with his curling, buttercup-colored locks, a physical trait unusual for her country, outside school, waiting for Madame. On the day of summer break, he met Madame after class with an armful of *niviarsiaq,* the national flower of Greenland. He must not have realized that white nettle shoots were interspersed among the bright pink blossoms. How they must have stung!

Seductive were Madame's words and the way she spoke. Her accent was like the train of a long formal gown that she whipped around when she turned a corner. Ilse remembers thinking on that first day of French class that she wouldn't mind hearing French as she lay dying.

According to Malu, Madame hijacked their daughter's mind from "What Mattered," and filled it with the incalculably irresponsible belief that another world was out there. Then Madame proved her mother's disdain right by killing herself.

MALU AND FA'S HOUSE is a murky, watery yellow, the color of urine. In the eighteenth-century colonial era, the wooden houses sent up from Scandinavia as timber kits were color-coded so that people knew where to locate things quickly: the hospitals and medical centers were painted yellow; churches, schools, and ministers' and teachers' homes were red; green was for engineering and auto repair shops; blue was for anything fish-related; and black identified the police. Nowadays, residents paint their houses any color they wish, which makes it all the worse that her parents chose urine-yellow voluntarily.

Maybe Ilse can solicit Beluga and his pals to paint her parents' house a fresh, bright blue. The house hasn't been repainted for at least three snow-sleet seasons, and here, most people touch up their houses with bright colors yearly. During the darker months, especially under strings of light lacing the roofs, the brightly painted domiciles are often the only cheerful aspect of the landscape.

Her parents' home, and hers growing up, a long rectangle with small, narrow windows set too high to see out of, was originally a bright-blue-painted whale blubber storehouse. Like the other buildings on the slope of the town tilting to the harbor, it is bolted to rock. The two windows above the front door resemble eyes that now squint down at her.

There's the familiar scent of rotten eggs, the result of throwing wet coal in the potbelly stove combined with the scent of a seal hide drying on a rack just outside the front door. Ilse hears the familiar static din of crowds cheering from the television inside. No doubt Fa is watching, or rather pretending to watch, the Polar Teddy Bears match against the Falkland Islands that Theo Qannik told her about the week before at Tipsy's. Everyone is rooting for Norsaq Mathaeussen, the lead scorer. *Jann, everyone would be cheering for you.*

Ilse pauses before she opens the door.

"Oskar, Ilse is here!"

Malu's hearing is as good as her eyesight. Could she really detect the crunch of Ilse's boots on the melted-snow-mud slop that covered the wooden walkway up to the house? Or had Malu been standing on a stool looking out the window?

Malu opens the door as Ilse turns the handle.

"Duggan said you'd be coming today," Malu says as she gives Ilse a bony embrace.

"I never told Duggan—"

"Good thing you listened to him." Malu turns and heads into the kitchen, as if Ilse is late to a business meeting there. "Your Fa has been asking after you for weeks. What you do in that old house with water up to its knees I don't know. Great-Aunt Jôrîna didn't scare you enough with tales of Qalupalik!"

As a child, Ilse had made friends in her imagination with the Qalupalik trolls, who according to Inuit legend carried away children who wandered too close to the shore. Ilse even admired their long hair, green skin, and blue fingernails.

It's cozy-warm inside her parents' house. Theirs is one of the few houses left with a coal-burning stove. Most people have installed electric heaters, but Malu refuses to pay the government for heat she can outsource herself. That and water. Fa carries their fresh water in a canister from the local shed just down the wooden walkway or else in a large bucket after a day fishing on the fjord.

"Malu, we've talked about this. I like my home surrounded by the sea."

"You call that place a home? You look like you're dressed for an ice floe crawl. How many layers are you wearing? And how are you ever going to meet anyone way out there, living by yourself?"

Fa doesn't see Ilse as she approaches, but when she takes his hand, he lifts his face, and she notices a sigh of relief pass through his body. Ilse's father, Oskar Erlund, has sun-browned skin, creased with wrinkles from years in the sun. A large dark sunspot around his right eye makes him resemble a bulldog with an eye patch. Because he is severely myopic, he's often squinting, especially on a sunny day. His cheekbones are high and wide, and Ilse likes to think she inherited them from him.

When he's not looking at a soccer game inside, Fa is out on Disko Bay, fishing for cod, halibut, or Arctic char, but mostly halibut. Lately, he's begun to wear a funny, small-brimmed canvas hat that keeps the sun off the top of his head. Ilse had once referred to the hairless spot as his halo, to which he'd responded, his eyes in their chronic squint, "Talk in my language, now, Ilse, will you?"

Fa's nature is sullen, but Ilse remembers that when she was younger, on occasions usually accompanied by drink, he would respond to a joke with an unexpected deep howl of laughter. He rarely guffaws or smiles inside the house, where futile frivolity is against Malu's rules.

"Troy Belke would have been a fine choice for you, Ilse Erlund," Malu calls out as Ilse sets the card table with the stained basket-weave mats of her childhood and the small, square paper cocktail napkins that Malu has hoarded through years of summer visits to Akiki, the ice cream shop in town.

Here it comes, Malu's "the clock is ticking" harangue.

"He's built himself that nice, new, insulated house," she says, now following Ilse around the table. "I've never been inside, though I've been waiting for him, we all have, to host a *kaffemik*." A *kaffemik* is a Greenlandic traditional community gathering at a host's home to celebrate big and small occasions, birthdays along with everyday firsts, like the first day of school or even a child's first fish caught. Spiked coffee and the national favorite cake, *kalaallit kaagiat,* that Val bakes so well, and a bevy of other cakes are served.

Why does Malu insist on keeping the fourth chair at the kitchen table? Ilse moves it aside to face the wall. She changes her mind and places it next to Fa in front of the soccer game. *There, that's better.*

"There's a short supply of men around here, Ilse, and good men, even more limited."

Ilse collects three beer mugs hanging on hooks on the kitchen wall.

"Yes, Troy Belke would have been a fine match," Malu repeats. "He's strong-boned and with all the sense of the world, but no, you were too good, too proud, with all that education in your head, for him, and now that he's back from Copenhagen, you've lost the chance again." Beluga had spent most of the previous year in Copenhagen.

Ilse escapes Malu and kneels next to her father's chair. She takes his large, crusty hand in hers.

"Val Barker's got him tied around her pinky finger!" Malu shouts over the soccer game. From where she sits, Ilse can smell the steamy *suaasat,* the stomach-warming broth made with barley and seal meat.

"Malu, that's not new news," Ilse calls out.

"Bobby Inuksuk was another one, but he married the Larson girl, and now they've got four babies! Ilse, get the bread and take the beer and frozen crowberries out of the ice shed. I saved some ice cream for you."

Ilse realizes that most of her parents' friends in the community have several grandchildren. But Ilse has a full life with a large extended family: she cohabits with hundreds and thousands of words, not to mention their adjectival and adverbial aunts, uncles, and cousins. Her kin is engaging, even intrusive, and bursting with infinite variety; it would be small-minded to want anything else. She is as complete as she ever could be.

"Let's eat in front of the game," Ilse offers for Fa's sake.

"No, you don't," calls out Malu as she ladles the soup into the bowls.

Fa rises slowly, and Ilse takes his arm. As they walk to the table, Ilse has the fleeting memory of dancing the *sønderhoning,* a Danish sailor's reel, with him as a child. The dance was supposed to suggest a ship riding the waves. Those were the days when Jann was among them.

"*Kasuutta!* Good health!" says Ilse, lifting her mug. She desperately wants to cheer up Fa.

When Malu starts in about the teaching position at the high school with the new headmaster who is recently widowed, Ilse interrupts.

"Malu," Ilse says. "Doesn't it feel good when you see a book in the library with my name on it? 'Translated by Ilse Erlund.' Doesn't that make you proud?"

"Who goes to a library these days?"

Ilse cups the bowl with her hands. The *suaasat* is deliciously soothing.

"Useless places, libraries," Malu continues between bites of the bread. "The last time your fa and I went to the library and saw a book with your name on it, it was a children's book, and your name was so tiny, I had to ask Yura Nuniq for a magnifying glass. Your fa couldn't see it even with the glass. You think that makes us proud, to have to use a magnifying glass to see our daughter's name in print?"

"I still get paid royalties for that book, small ones, but it's something."

"Children are the only ones who should bother reading, that is, until they can be made useful. If I could, I'd take all those children out of the library and put them to work in the post office, helping me lift boxes."

Malu is the fastest sorter in Greenland Post Office history. For the last seven years on the first Saturday of June, she has won, hands down, the sorting contest at the annual Post Office Day Fair, hosted by Upernavik, a town that relies on Air Greenland for its mail. Malu knows every four-digit zip code in the country and most overseas codes well enough to recite them backward, which she does when she's washing the dishes.

Malu is tall and lean, and her hair is mostly silver, but there are a few tresses that still shine a crow-blue black. When Malu tilts her head down and to the right, as she does when she's at her headquarters at the sink, and when she's not screwing up her eyes in scorn, which she does most of the time, she resembles the beautiful young woman in the photograph that her father keeps on his bureau.

It has started to rain again, or is that sleet? The three look up at the ceiling as the rain pings the flat aluminum roof. A deluge may require Ilse to stay over. Only a few months ago, she could ask Fa to take her home in his outboard, but now, Malu says he can hardly find his way to the harbor. Ilse doesn't own a skiff; she'd caught a boat ride down in a trawler belonging to one of Duggan's fishermen.

Dinner is a short affair. Fa mutters some excuse and leaves the table to return to his chair and the game. Like many Greenlanders, Fa has never been a talker. Extreme cold creates silence. And hunters and a fisherman like Fa know that animals and fish can hear everything from far, far away.

Fa began to lose his eyesight around the time that Madame left them and took to the sea. That's how Ilse refers to Madame LaRoche's passing—as if she'd walked into another element. It just happened to be death. Ilse liked to think she died not out of despair, but out of possibility—for infinity.

Ilulissat was affected by Madame's unexpected departure almost as much as the town had been thrown off by her stunning arrival. After Madame's foreignness wore off, and that took a few years, adults and children alike swam to her like carp to homemade doughballs. She gave Ilulissat some swag, something to boast about other than its icebergs—and for Ilse, a reason to dream.

It was when Jann died a year later in a motorcycle accident that Fa's eyesight deteriorated completely. From then on, it seemed to Ilse, his severe myopia was deliberate, as if he'd willed himself not to see anymore. Jann fell to his death when his motorcycle, borrowed from a teammate for a onetime ride before the Greenlandic Championship, collided with a ready-mix truck carrying concrete on Road S39, a mile outside the capital. Strong bones of an athlete, crushed to crystallized dust. Bone dust to earth dust.

Ilse had been the one to identify him. Malu refused, and Fa was destroyed enough as it was. The team captain paid for Ilse's two-and-a-half-day roundtrip ferry ride to Nuuk. The Inuit people believe that human souls leave the body and go to an underworld that is warm with abundant food, but when Ilse looked at Jann in the drawer at the mortuary that the unibrow undertaker opened for her, even in Jann's crushed state, he seemed fully in his body. Only his face was uncovered, and she could see that his slightly open lips had the same intensity they had just before he scored a soccer goal.

She'd placed his favorite Nike Zoom Air cleats, a gift from the prime minister of Greenland, beside him. Her heart burst out of her chest when she told him to sprint out of death and come back to her. She didn't care in what form.

Come back to me, Jann.

Crooner was the name on the side of the concrete truck. Had Jann been lulled to death?

She had researched, like she did everything, the local history of S39, the longest tarmac road, at 3.8 miles, built in Greenland's history. Before it was dubbed S39, it was known as Prayer Road, probably a reminder to say prayers before driving it. Prior to that, it was the Prairie Path.

As in all things, the original words had been lost in translation.

In the first years after his death, Ilse joined Malu in blaming Jann. He knew better than to ride a motorcycle when he was a novice, on a wintry-mix slippery morning down in Nuuk when early spring fog can drop like a wall out of nowhere.

Which made some people who knew him wonder: had his accident been a death wish? It is an acknowledged fact that everyone in Greenland knows someone who's killed himself. But Jann had everything in front of him! Maybe it was *because* he had everything in front of him. He was planning to marry Annita Kristendatter that summer; Annita, who hung on him like a marsupial. Three months after the accident, she moved to the United States. It was a good thing since no one could look at her without crying.

Malu had returned to the clockwork routine of her life, but Fa had not recovered the color in his face or in his life. Unlike Malu, who was the express mail of feelings, Fa kept his life inside him.

"Your fa is very low these days," Malu is saying. "It's hard when all you see is darkness, inside and out."

For once, Malu and she agree on something. Ilse's cellphone lights up. It's Duggan, offering her a ride back in his trawler the following morning at seven-thirty. Duggan is like a second father. He and his wife, Mary, have no children. Because they've lived less than fifty feet away from the Erlunds for the last thirty-six years they're as close as family. Like the Erlunds, most of their relatives settled in Southern Greenland, too distant to visit.

At the end of the second half of the game, the Polar Teddy Bears are losing. Ilse follows Fa out the back door to fetch a bag of coal. Sheets of rain shimmer in the light from the single bulb hanging from the shed. A dog howls in the distance. Another joins in. Now it's a chorus of howls.

"Fa," Ilse says, as he bends to pull a sack of coal from the pile. "Did you know Madame LaRoche well? It's six years ago tomorrow, that she . . ."

Fa turns quickly and raises his hand. His face is a shield except for his mouth that makes a twisted shape that she's never seen before.

"You loved her like everyone else did in this town, didn't you?"

She can hear Malu in the kitchen, scouring the pots from dinner.

He lowers his hand, and his face relaxes. He closes his eyes and nods.

"Was there . . . more between you two?"

He turns his back to her for the bag of coal.

"Fa?"

She takes his free hand.

"Fa?"

When he faces her, his unseeing eyes tell her everything.

"I'm sorry, Fa. I'm so sorry. Does Malu know?"

He nods again, his eyes downcast.

No wonder Malu despised her daughter's choice of profession or anything French. In an irrational world, after time passes, some things become intelligible.

At the back door, Ilse whispers, "But Fa, Mr. McNare?"

"Fa?"

His mouth is contorted in that twisted position again.

"Your mother is calling you."

Fa and Madame LaRoche! Madame in her red silk scarf and her snow-soaked black leather high-heeled boots, with her father, in his oversized fishing overalls and neoprene boots coated in oil? But Fa was handsome in his strong, quiet way. Is this why the French teacher took a special interest in Ilse, why she bequeathed her red silk scarf and her taffeta curtains to her, why she housed Ilse during her university years in Nuuk? And Ilse had thought it was because she demonstrated a talent for the French language! So focused on her own accomplishments, she'd seen only a part of the whole.

She recalls the many times that Fa had visited her over the four years that she had lived with Madame. By that time, Madame had moved from the Ilulissat high school to teaching at Ilisimatusarfik University. Whenever Madame was free, day and night, she coached Ilse in French. Fa would take the ferry to Nuuk and stay over for days at a time, sleeping on the sofa in the front room. Ilse remembered thinking at the time that it was odd, her thrifty father spending his savings on the two-day ferry ride, breaking from his fisherman routine in Ilulissat, but decided that he missed her, his daughter!

Jann must have known. Not long before Madame's death, he and Fa had had an argument, one of those that neighbors can hear, like the Nielsens, fifty feet away. Despite Ilse's pleading with Jann, he refused to tell her about it. While Jann remained resolutely silent, Fa proved stone-wall impenetrable. As the air cooled between father and son, Ilse gave up her discovery mission as she did certain untranslatable words. Occasionally, like most unresolved things, the untranslatables would bubble up and bother her when she least expected it.

Her father didn't need better eyesight. She did.

She steps away from the shelter of the coal shed, the cold rain in her face.

"Oh, Fa, we were both in love with her," she says, hugging him.

"What are you two doing out here in the rain?" It's Malu. "Digging for coal?"

Fa lifts both hands as if caught by the police.
"Does it hurt?" she asks her father as they go inside.
"What?" He looks at her with his bleary blue eyes.
"Your eyes," she says quickly. "Do they hurt?"
"No, my daughter," he says. "I don't feel a thing."

Chapter 4

DUGGAN DROPS ILSE HALF A MILE FROM HER HOUSE AT THE dock near the Oqaatsut Gravel Company. The aluminum building and the towering gravel heap beside it are the last outpost of civilization before the descent into the sea-riven rocky mud path to Ilse's cottage.

Who needs to visit the Great Pyramid of Giza when you can admire this massive gray triangle, an unannounced wonder of the world? The Oqaatsut Cultural Centre, if there were one, could charge admission to witness this mountain of jagged scree reaching to the sky. If it were her company, she'd name it the Giza Gravel Company.

Oren Sorrell, the oldest son of Jacob Sorrell, had taken over the business from his father, but anyone who knew the family, and everyone in Oqaatsut did, was aware that it was Eva Sorrell, the younger sister of Oren, who ran the place. She was only seventeen, but she could calculate the square footage of anything just by eyeballing it, be it an iceberg, a whale, or a crescent beach shore a mile away. Theirs was one of the few enterprises along Greenland's western coast, not counting the fishing export business that survived the 2008 recession, and it was run by a teenage girl.

Fortunately, a year before Ilse moved into her rental, the Sorrells had exhausted rock blasting in her area, and the site serves now as a storage and sales operation. Eva Sorrell recently made a deal with Beluga to be the sole transporter of gravel from this site to the company's customers. Beluga uses his utility task four-wheeler and plane to move the gravel, but if crushed rock is needed up north, he subcontracts with his friend, Akumik (the name means "go with the wind"), who runs a dogsledding outfit a few fjords away.

Ilse waves goodbye to Duggan, then stretches her arms out horizontally to feel the wind push against her. Her vapor breath is like the fog forming across the half-frozen, half-rippling sea on her right.

It's begun to rain again, and before she knows it, her leather hat and hair are drenched, and the water is running down her legs into her boots. By the time she reaches home, her feet will feel like blocks of ice.

She checks her phone for the time. Ten o'clock. She has a call with her French editor at eleven o'clock, three o'clock French time. She rushes along.

Where are you going? the a cappella long hoary throat of the wind asks her.

"I'm going home," she shouts out.

You're thirty-five years old, and where are you going in your life, silly?

Silly is the sea speaking.

"Jann, where am I going?" she asks the clouds, trying to make out the image of her brother in the moving white shapes. "The clouds are swift, but not as fast as you."

Did you know where you were going, Jann, she says inside herself, *when you drove that killer motorcycle on that fog-blinding morning? You, with your fast reflexes and your keen eyesight?*

Do you know where you're going, Beluga? she types into a text message to him. Beluga always comes up with an answer, and he's the only one who won't think she's crazy for asking. He already knows she's crazy. She presses send, then regrets it. He may think she's being nosy about his budding relationship with Val.

She searches the whitecaps for a sandbar to take her south to the Labrador Sea, then across the North Atlantic to France. If there were a natural submerged shoal from here to there, she wouldn't have to pay for the airfare. It's not such an outrageous idea. She'd read about deposits of sediment that rise like mountain ridges from the ocean floor. She could be the first to discover the underwater range that extends from Oqaatsut to Calais. She would call it the Oqaatsais Pass; that has a nice ring to it. On second thought, it should be named after her: the Erlund Pass.

Around the next bend, a series of short waterfalls froth and gush. In the five years since she's walked to and from her cottage, Ilse has never seen or heard such a rushing outpouring. Is it because she's never paused long enough to notice, or is it because the glaciers are calving and thinning at an accelerated speed? Spring should be full of hope, not thoughts of the demise of the planet. She, like most Greenlanders, has a love-hate relationship with spring. While it heralds the approach of sun-filled days, there's too much glacier melt, too much sleet and rain, too much leaking, mildew, and mold.

Ilse thinks of Duggan's comment about her age. She lives in a small cottage teetering on stilts at the edge of the sea in a small settlement, on a small spit of land, that for a few hours a day is separated from the mainland by the tides. Malu and Fa had chosen the perfect name for her. Switch the *l* and the *s*, and Ilse would be called Isle: a small self-isolating island.

She shakes her head to throw off the image of herself as a loner for the rest of her life and starts running along the mud-slick coastal path to escape her runaway thoughts. *If I don't get out of here, I'll end up like Madame LaRoche.*

But hey, it's not such a small life! She talks to Paris, sometimes daily! Who in Oqaatsut or even Ilulissat could make such a claim? When she's not decoding French into English, she's researching, analyzing maps, and reading histories and biographies that will help her reimagine France in another language. Her lively imagination that feeds her dreams of one day traveling to France is her weapon against despair.

There it is: her ash-colored shoebox of a captain's house on stilts, surrounded by the sea, with its chipping, faded cobalt blue front door that Ilse had painted within days of moving in. She'd been inspired by a photograph of a house in Provence. Patches of black plastic poorly nailed down to cover the leaky high-pitched plywood roof flap rapidly back and forth in the wind. Will the house take flight?

The broken picket fence with its hanging-off gate is a welcome sight, as is Minou, lounging on the front doorstep in a sliver of sun-gleam that is now poking through the round rolls of pillowy clouds. *Weather, you're a trickster this morning.* Ilse removes her dripping wet hat.

"Houdini Minou, you slipped out the back door on your own again, didn't you?"

Note to self: The back door needs to be secured with a hook and eye. Next note to self: The front door desperately needs repainting.

Things fall apart quickly up here above the polar circle, where weather knocks continually on the door, or rather, it bangs, crashes, thunders. Her parents and most people she knows spend a large proportion of their lives fixing yesterday's damage. Most houses in the area are either bolted to rock or raised three or four feet above the rock on pillars. The piles supporting her dwelling are plywood, and the last time she checked, her cottage was only two feet above the swirling swells.

Beluga offered to replace the wood stilts with concrete for the fee of the equipment and his men's hours, but the owner had declined. Clearly, her landlord isn't concerned about the sinking house. No matter, the worst of the winter is over, and her rent is the best deal in town. Mr. G aside.

A buzz from her phone, a text from Beluga.

Isn't every day a where-am-I-going day?

Beluga tends to respond to questions with questions. It's a cop-out.

"Meow," Ilse says to Minou.

She and Minou speak pretty much the same language.

She plucks a wad of stringy black seaweed from the muddy strawberry plants Beluga had set in the granite speckled soil as an experiment inside her gate a few years back. They did produce six strawberries one particularly warm year, but most of the plants have washed away.

Grasse matinée.

"That's the problem, Minou," she says as the cat gets up and waits for her to open the door. Ilse pets her until she purrs.

"*C'est ça le problème, Minou,*" she says as she shoves open the front door. *When was the last time I basked languorously in sheets bright with midday light? When was the last time I dozed, leg over leg, arm over arm with a lover?*

"Brrrrr. It's freezing in here."

She kicks off her muddy boots and pulls off her socks. She hops up and down to get the circulation back in her feet. On with her thick wool socks that Malu had knitted for her last winter. She fills the kettle with water, lights the gas on the stove with a match, and holds her hands over the flame.

Yes, Ilse has had lovers: Max Møllner, and a sprinkling of others, and oh yes, Teddy Olafson, lovely, kind Teddy, but who lacked what was it—oomph, an excitement about being alive. Max had that in spades.

She'd probably been overimpressed by Max's success as an eco-entrepreneur. He traveled the world with the Oceanic Patrol. Love-making, hmm, was it that good anyway? It seemed they were finished as soon as they started. Though she sprinkled their nights together with verbal *I love you*s, he barely murmured the words to her. That should have been the first clue. Six years was a long time to be with someone and still not know them. Had he ever cared to get to know her?

The teakettle is whistling. She pours the hot water into a mug with her favorite Mariage Frères black tea that Bea sent her from Paris. (Bea says she'll start a tea company if the translating thing doesn't work out financially.)

What she and Max had, or so she thought, was *un grand amour*, a concept that Madame LaRoche had introduced when talking about Douglas McNare or, now that she thinks of it, it could have been Fa. Hard for her to imagine—but maybe? And look what happened to Madame. Drowned herself in love and then in the sea.

Why not blame Madame LaRoche, as her mother did? At twelve,

Ilse drank the potion. At thirty-five, she's skeptical. Most of the people around her have nice lives and little loves. They seem content—enough. Or is it? Enough?

Fa and Malu rarely exchange a kind word or gesture. Did they ever love each other, even for a moment?

Minou meows.

"Minou! Yes, yes, breakfast is coming. Forgive me! I was doing it again. I was thinking about love."

Chapter 5

ILSE CHECKS HER WATCH. SHE HAS JUST ENOUGH TIME TO SLIP in a quick call to Zoë Gaudet. Émile Moreau, Ilse's boss at Éditions Elsevier and Zoë Gaudet's editor, forbids translators to communicate with authors without his permission. But this morning, Ilse is feeling rebellious. It would only be a quick question: would the author please explain *faire la grasse matinée* in her own words in French. To hear the author say the words aloud would reveal so much. Ilse has simmered in the sauce of Gaudet's prose long enough to know that Gaudet considers invisibility a violation of the human condition. So why should Ilse remain invisible?

Gaudet had written her phone number on the first page of the manuscript—perhaps for her translator, for Ilse! It's four hours later in Paris. Ilse taps the numbers on her phone. One ring, then a second one. Someone picks up, then clicks off, someone who doesn't want to be bothered by an unidentified caller.

Ilse will have to remain invisible—for now. A grinding sound interrupts her thoughts. She turns to the window facing west. A yellow bulldozer in the distance is pulling through the curdled, muddy flats. The clouds stalk the bright vehicle.

"What are you doing?" she wants to yell out the window. "Don't take any more land away!"

With the Arctic ice melting, over the last few years, the government has been excavating Greenland's buried treasures of iron, ore, lead, zinc, oil, even diamonds and gold for exportation. In the process, who knows how many thousands of transverse lady beetles, Arctic weevils, thin-legged wolf spiders, and other underground land fauna have been uprooted.

Enough procrastinating. Ilse rushes to the other side of the room to check her hair and to recite for the umpteenth time the two-line speech she's prepared for her video meeting with Émile. She knows her Parisian editor well enough to suspect that he will try to bribe her with another project if she can deliver Zoë Gaudet's novel a month before her due date. He does this before every deadline.

But this time Ilse has her own plan—to request a higher rate per word. In the five years since she's worked for Émile, she's never requested a raise. She will also tell him (not ask) that she now charges an express rate, two times the price per word for manuscripts with an expedited deadline.

The last time she and Émile spoke, he'd complimented her, saying she was one of the few translators he could trust to capture his authors' style as well as meaning. So many translators these days had no imagination. The ones who did thought they had the right to create their own version of a work (like her friend Bea). Her ability to intuit an author's intentions and express them, while remaining invisible, he'd told her, was her special gift.

"Émile," she says aloud, taking her seat in front of her laptop, "I may be invisible on the page, but in life, as you're about to see, I'm unmistakably visible! Thank you, Zoë Gaudet!"

ÉMILE MOREAU IS WEARING his signature ironed black dress shirt with unbuttoned cuffs. His face has an orange tinge this morning that makes his blue eyes appear brighter. Does he use self-tanner? Or is the color off on her screen? Ilse has never met the man; they conduct their meetings virtually. She enjoys watching the balletic way he moves, raising his hands behind his head, tilting back his chair, tipping his head in this direction and that.

Ilse has thrown on the only jacket she owns. It's navy, and she thinks it makes her look professional. He can't see her shirt that hangs below the jacket, or her gray sweatpants, or her thick red socks.

She and Émile speak mostly in French, but when Émile occasionally slips into English, the lilt in his voice and slight slur of his accent transform the most ordinary words into luxury items.

He has just asked Ilse to send the translation of Zoë Gaudet's novel in two weeks, a month earlier than the deadline in her contract. Just as she had predicted.

"Ilse, are we on the same page? I'm assuming we are."

Another thing Émile does with regularity is to supply answers to his own questions. Ilse guesses that he could carry on a conversation with himself for hours.

"I realize there's a lot under the surface of Gaudet's novel," he continues. "That's why I gave you the job, my deep-sea-diver translator." (She'd been called a "deep-sea diver" by one of her reviewers.) But translating Gaudet was more like building something from the ground up. Every word she added was part of the scaffolding for the next word, and so on. In a recent nightmare, the structure, with so many walls within walls of words, came tumbling down.

"I'm going to need more time, Émile. The translation still doesn't have the feeling of being born in English yet."

"The English are too stuck up to birth someone as sensual as Zoë Gaudet. Darling, perfection is a dream we wish for, but in the end, never want. Approximation is what I'm after. Resemblance. But you translators are never satisfied."

"Dante forgot to add the translator circle to his *Inferno*."

"Ilse, I need the translation *tout de suite*."

Now is the time to take her stand.

"I hope you've got a good title?" he asks.

Titles are Ilse's nemesis. They're supposed to whet the appetite of the market, but they also must be true to the work.

"*Call of the Siren,*" she says, trying not to lift her voice at the end of her answer, as if she's unsure. If Émile balks at this one, she's ready with another title: *Don Juanita*.

"Not bad, but not quite right. Send me a list of other options."

"I have—"

"On another note," Émile interrupts. "You don't happen to have any experience with the Provençal language, do you? Of course you do."

"Yes," she says too quickly. "A little," she adds. In fact she doesn't know one word in the Provençal dialect, although she remembers listening to a radio program from the Provence region. The accents made it impossible to understand. "Why?"

"If you get Gaudet to me in two weeks," he continues, "I'll offer you a gift that you will thank me for, for years to come. I need another translation."

He raises his foot onto his desk. She hates when he does that. *Put your foot down, Émile!*

"It's a book of collected poetry by one of our national treasures. Some call him the last living troubadour of Provence. It's hard to believe he's never been translated into English. I'm guessing that the reason is that many of his words and expressions are in Provençal, and the British and U.S. publishers shy away from translating these dialect languages. That's where you come in."

"Poetry?" Ilse interrupts his monologue.

She has never translated poetry professionally. First, it doesn't pay; second, it takes much more time: every word weighs. Lastly, she has very little experience with it.

"As you'll see when I send this over, the poems appear easy to understand, but they're never simplistic. A critic has written that the mind reads them the first time, the heart reads them the second, and the soul the third. Since you've been working hard on Gaudet's extremely nuanced novel, I've decided that you're primed for this—that is, if you send me the Gaudet in two weeks. They say this book of poems is the poet's swan song, and we all—well, Daphné in particular—thinks it will have legs in the American and English markets."

Daphné Solenz is the publisher of Éditions Elsevier, and Émile's boss.

He removes his foot from the table and then bobs up and down in his chair.

"A little in-house gossip for you: Daphné's daughter, who you remember is half American, is marrying the son of said troubadour this summer on the island of Nantucket. Daphné wants the American edition published by the wedding, to which, by the way, I've been invited."

"The plot thickens," Ilse says.

"Daphné will be giving your English translation as a party favor to the four-hundred-plus guests, mostly people in the book business, reviewers, and such. Also, she's planning to launch an extensive advertising campaign in England and in the U.S., unusual for a collection of poetry, that will put you on the map in the global translation market. I know you haven't done much—"

"Just at university, years ago. I prefer—"

"I can assure you, Ilse, that after Gaudet, this will be a piece of cake."

Émile loves to use idioms, especially American ones.

"You said she wants it before the wedding?"

"French pub date is next week, March thirtieth." Émile taps on his laptop. "I've just sent you the glowing prepub reviews. Daphné has it from a source that our troubadour is going to win the Prix Mallarmé this year. As you know, it's one of our oldest and most prestigious awards for poetry, which is another reason Daphné wants an English translation published ASAP. For you, Ilse, this could be *the* translating job of a lifetime. We need to publish the English and U.S. editions on August tenth, since Daphné's daughter's wedding is the following week. But you, Ilse Erlund, must be concerned with only one date, and that's the deadline I'm giving you right now, Monday, June fourth. Please engrave it on your forehead."

"The U.S. will publish it that quickly?"

"Given the personal relationship of our publisher to the poet, we're accelerating the project. To expedite the English-language publication, Éditions Elsevier is commissioning this translation, and the American publisher is reimbursing us. So, Ilse," he asks in English, "are we on the same page?"

She pauses.

"I believe we are," Émile continues. "You're the only translator I can trust at this moment to do our Provençal poet justice."

She's heard Émile's sweet talk before.

"I'm also," she says, "the only translator whom you could ask to deliver a book of collected poetry with such a short deadline."

"Artificial intelligence will do it within milliseconds."

"Touché. How many poems?"

"Only . . . eighty."

"*Only* eighty?"

"Ilse, I'm doing you a favor. I'm giving you a reprieve after the mental marathon of Gaudet."

He's peering into the laptop camera. It is rare to have Émile's full focus. He's often gazing down into his phone, or his eyes are twitching on the screen as he reads incoming emails.

"I've been meaning to ask you for an increase of my hourly rate," Ilse says, "especially for rush jobs like this one."

"You call two and a half months to translate a book of poems a rush job?"

He tilts his chair back, a slight smile on his face. Émile relishes the art of negotiation.

"As you know, Émile, for poetry translation"—she'll speak his language—"every word is a note in a complex melody. You've got to convey the right tone, rhythm, and meaning to sing the song."

"I knew it! You're already on the right track," he says. "Troubadours' poems were sung."

"I'll send you Gaudet two weeks from today," she says in her deepest voice, "and will take on the troubadour for double my normal fee. That will be my rate going forward. Also, I'll be charging ten percent more for projects that need to be expedited, like this one."

Ilse rises from her desk, crosses the room quickly. Out of sight from the laptop camera, she looks at her face in the mirror. She has just said the words "double" and "ten percent more."

"I'll talk to Daphné about it today."

That's it? You mean she could have asked for this a year ago and made enough money then to upgrade her phone and maybe have some kroner left over to replace the rotting window frame that her stingy landlord refused to pay for? She places her hand on the windowsill to stop the chilly airflow.

"I'll send you the first-pass pages of the poetry collection by the end of the day. In the meantime, I'll be expecting Gaudet as discussed."

"You'll receive the Gaudet once you confirm the rate change in writing."

He can be squirrelly, Émile.

She holds her breath.

"Ilse, I think translating Zoë Gaudet has changed you." Émile seems rather proud of the new "her."

She does not respond. Gaudet would not have.

Ilse hopes the Gaudet spell lasts.

Before Gaudet, Ilse was willing to accept the blurry boundaries of life. It wasn't uncomfortable for her to find multiple meanings, not only for words, but for her relationships with others. Since she's been in the world of Zoë Gaudet's novel, and perhaps because she'll be turning thirty-six this September, she's begun to realize that this laissez-faire attitude has been a way for her to not take responsibility.

She's begun to crave definition.

"Émile—" She catches him before he exits the screen. He likes to sign off with the last word.

"What's his name? The poet's?"

"Poet."

"Yes, his name?"

"That's what he calls himself: 'Poet.'"

"Émile, his name, please."

"Geoffrey Labaye."

Within seconds, the screen goes dark.

Chapter 6

Celebrating her raise the next morning, Ilse swirls Madame's red silk scarf over her head. Along with the pink rose-patterned taffeta curtains that Madame LaRoche had bequeathed to Ilse at her death, she had given Ilse this large red silk square. Ilse had always told herself that she would wear the scarf the first time she stepped on French soil.

When would that be?

Bea had once told her (and she said it in French, which made it sound that much better) that a heart has three functions: to pump blood, to feel, and to desire. Ever since she'd heard the French language so many years ago, her heart's desire has been to go to France. What did the philosopher Lacan write? Desire is a lack, but desire lacks nothing. Something like that. How many times had she told Jann that they would go to *la belle* France together? But then he'd left her.

She'll wear Madame's scarf to Val's birthday party at the coffee shop tonight.

Last year at the end of the party, when it looked like the moon and the sun were facing off in a battle for brightness, and the sky had that very pale shade of purply pink, the color of thistles, Ilse had found herself sitting in Beluga's lap in one of the plastic chairs outside the coffee shop. They were exhaling clouds and laughing, pretending they were spouting whales. They had drunk too many Tipsy Reindeers, Val's lethal combination of Kahlúa, rum, and her signature schnapps. When Ilse rose from his lap, Beluga had given nothing away, not the slightest emotion.

Looking back on it, Ilse remembered experiencing, in that moment on Beluga's lap, a fleeting sense of feeling complete. But Beluga wasn't interested. And also, Beluga was part of this life and would always be. She wanted another kind of life, to be translated into another world. Madame LaRoche, it *is* your fault!

She pulls on her reliable black pants. She's gained a few pounds over the winter—she always does—and these pants are the only ones that aren't a squeeze. March 24 and it's still windy and chilblain cold. It might rain. It always might rain at this time of year. Why bother looking at the weather app on her phone?

White dress shirt. Nope. Too much like her teenage waitress uniform at the Café Iluliaq. She'll wear her red sweater with the pompoms on the sleeves. Festive. A bit tight at the chest. Too much hot chocolate. Oh, who cares? She got through another Arctic winter.

Wrapping Madame's red scarf around her neck twice as she'd seen Bea do on a recent face-to-face call inspires a thought. Since asking for a raise had proved so easy, why not make her next bold move and insist on a paid trip to Provence so the poet himself can help her with the difficult Provençal vocabulary? She'd heard it called "triangulation," when a translator works with a native speaker to get as close as possible to the original.

She's on a roll, after all.

She scoots upstairs from her bedroom to her top floor office and opens her laptop to compose the email. Courage!

Émile,

The only way that I will be able to do justice to France's last troubadour is to meet the poet in person and to stay in the region for a week.

She deletes the words "a week," and types instead "two weeks." Brrrrr, it's so cold up here even with a sweater and scarf.

A dialect is not only a different language; it's an entire culture. I can assure you that the translation will benefit enormously.

Sincerely,
Ilse

Émile is right: translating Gaudet has been transformational.

"Let's see what Émile says to that!" she says to Minou as she dips down to pet the cat.

She pulls her hair into a ponytail: too librarian. Clips it on top of her head: too Disney princess. She brushes it to the side: it will have to do.

When Ilse places Minou's food in front of her, the cat looks up at her in disdain.

"Fine," Ilse tells the cat as she grabs her jacket. "I know you don't like my hair this way. Eat some juicy mice while I'm gone, will you please?"

T. S. ELIOT WROTE about "Midwinter Spring," or was it "Midspring Winter"? She can't remember. Lately, Ilse has been trying unsuccessfully to unmemorize the lines from "Little Gidding," words that she identified with and loved during her senior year at university but now dampen her spirit, especially with this excessively rainy spring.

Sodden towards sundown . . .
soul's sap quivers . . .
This is the spring time, but not in time's covenant.

T.S. must have visited Greenland, where there are endless "sodden towards sundown" days in their mud-slushy winter spring.

Now, she recalls the lines.

Midwinter spring is its own season
Sempiternal though sodden towards sundown,
Suspended in time, between pole and tropic.

It *is* midwinter spring! Ilse loves poetry and loves memorizing it, but that doesn't mean she likes to translate poems *or* knows how! In the one poetry translation class she'd taken at Ilisimatusarfik, one of the assignments had been to translate "The Drunken Boat" by Arthur Rimbaud from French into Danish. What a struggle it had been to incorporate rhyme and meter and keep the meaning intact. Impossible! She would have failed if not for the nuanced suggestions of Madame. At the end of the term, Ilse wrote an essay arguing that poetry is technically untranslatable, that a translator's only poor option is to create another form, entirely separate from the original. And what translator is a poet? Certainly not Ilse!

Damn! She'd forgotten to ask Émile whether the Provençal poet wrote in rhyme. Few contemporary poets use rhyme, but then he is the last living troubadour of Provence.

Almost stepped in a deep puddle. That could have been a sinkhole, one of those fissures in the sediment that fill with water in the spring and suck you in. Last year, Ollie Olson fell in one, and luckily, someone heard him hollering for help and hauled him out with a rope just in time. Especially at night, her walk to Tipsy's requires concentration. In the milky light of the moon, the land ahead of her looks craterlike.

She stops.

"Hoot, hoot, hoot, good evening to you, too! Are you a tawny or a bull-horned owl? Or maybe a short-eared one? No! You're a snowy owl. Reveal thyself!"

She closes her eyes. Jann would know. He recognized most bird calls.

"Now that I've paid adequate attention, forgive me, great horned owl.

"And you—on guard!" She addresses the scuffling, shuffling in the brush beside her. Through the mist, she spies a buck with curved antlers, a doe, and two fawns. It's a family of reindeer. They stand as motionless as she does. The eyes of the fawns shine in the flicker of revealed moonlight.

"Sorry to disturb your sleep," she says, and continues on her way.

Goodbye, moon. Rain has begun to fall in dense solid sheaths. Good thing she skipped the mascara, and why had she even bothered with the lip gloss? She'll arrive soggy and red-nosed. Makeup is ridiculous in Greenland. Somehow, Val manages with her black kohl eyeliner, and Madame LaRoche never appeared in class without her red lipstick and rose-gold eye shadow intact.

Ilse has been jumping puddles successfully in the dim light, but her feet are wet and cold. The wind chill whips through her jacket.

Nothing that a good shot of whiskey can't help.

She spots Lump Terret. The mound of earth was formerly a castle. An exaggeration: it was actually a fort. Folklore has it that at one point, Erik the Red ruled the world from this berth. Centuries of battles against time and weather have converted the fort into a clump of dirt.

Nature always has the last word.

The pulse of rock music blends with the banter of voices. Ilse hesitates in the shadows of the local fitness building. To get inside Tipsy's, she must pass through the gauntlet of men outside the door. They will look her up and down as she passes, and she feels insecure as it is. Wouldn't it be wonderful to be like the audacious female protagonist in Gaudet's novel, caring not whether she's beautiful but only if she's independent.

Ilse's not in the mood for small talk. All she can think about is the troubadour poet and her email to Émile. Will he grant her heart's desire? *Please, Émile. Fly me to France!*

She smells cigarette smoke. Someone has strung up colored Christmas bulbs around the windows. Nice touch, but thankfully, it's March, not December. It will be humid inside and will smell of beer. She can hear the creaking of the temporary snap-lock vinyl floor under the tent beside the hut. The dancers are making Tipsy's tipsy.

Now is the decisive moment: Ilse can turn about-face and saunter happily back the way she came, hooting to the owls on the way. It will be cozy in her kitchen beside Minou and the wood-burning stove. No one will notice that she's not there, except for Val—and Donny. She imagines Donny's big eyes searching for her in the crowd. This weekend, she'll ask him to walk with her along the coast to the north of her cottage where she frequently spots fin whales. She and Donny will play their game of running along the skirt of the incoming tide, pretending that the froth in the waves is the sea laughing with them. But often, Ilse suspects that it's laughing at them.

And to make it up to Val, she'll attend the *kaffemik* that Val's cousin, Saki, is hosting tomorrow afternoon. The good thing about a *kaffemik* is that you're only expected to stay for ten or fifteen minutes, enough time to sip a coffee, enjoy a few slices of cake, tell a story, and then depart so that someone else can take your place. When an entire community gathers in one person's home, you have to be conscious of how much space and time you take up.

When she sees Tim Tuqquk, one of Duggan's fishermen, on the porch, that does it: she reverses direction and slinks away. Tim is the only bachelor in town other than Beluga, but he's closer to her father's age than Ilse's. His long white hair makes him look like a wizard. At last year's dance party, he wouldn't leave her side. Yes, she thinks, Oqaatsut is *trop petite*. But it was hard enough to depart Ilulissat, the town where she grew up, let alone imagine leaving Greenland.

Now it's sleeting. Freezing cold darts sting her face. Ilse begins to run along the narrow path. She quickens her pace when she hears a nearby crack of thunder and sees a dazzling bright dash of zigzag lightning. It's a relief when she spots the small yellow light outside the front door of her cottage.

After Ilse's shower (thank goodness there's hot water), she dons as many sweaters as she has over her long nightgown and hops into bed with her laptop. No word from Émile. She stays up most of the night scouring the Internet for Geoffrey Labaye, who she discovers lives in Belle Rivière, one of the designated "Plus Beaux Villages de France." In the sallow light of morning, she prints and pins the images of vineyards, hilltop villages, lavender fields, and *mas,* the French word for "farmhouse," around her bed.

More thunder.

"Minou, come back!"

The cat has dashed from Ilse's lap and has disappeared under her bed.

Chapter 7

It's several days later, and Ilse has given up on Émile responding to her over-the-top request for a trip to France. She's about to start typing another email to him to remind him that she exists, when, hello, an email from him pops up on her screen. It begins with a complicated array of numbers and names.

What?

It's an itinerary—Greenland to France! She closes her eyes. It's not possible. She skims the email.

It *is*!

She jumps up from her desk, picks up Minou, and dances around the room. "Minou, Minou, I'm going to France to meet the last living troubadour of France!"

Minou scampers out of her arms and down the stairs.

"Thank you, Émile! Thank you! Monsieur le Poète, whoever you are! You are my ticket to France!"

She runs to the window. She opens it and yells to the gulls and the passing clouds, "I'm going to France!"

Wait until she tells Malu, who never misses a chance to disparage her choice of vocation. Even Bea will be shocked.

Back to her laptop, Ilse reads the details of the itinerary:

DEPART: Monday, April 30, 15h14, Icelandair, Ilulissat Airport
ARRIVE: Monday, April 30, 20h45 Keflavik International Airport
OVERNIGHT at Aurora Hotel at Reykjavik-Keflavik Airport Terminal

DEPART: Tuesday, May 1, 6h04, Icelandair, Keflavik International Airport
ARRIVE: Tuesday, May 1, 10h30, Paris Charles de Gaulle Airport

DEPART: Tuesday, May 1, 11h45, Air France, Paris Charles de Gaulle Airport
ARRIVE: Tuesday, May 1, 13h15, Nice Côte d'Azur Airport

HERTZ CAR RENTAL, Reservation Number: 30K499

La Cigale Bed & Breakfast, Route des Moines, 84220, Belle Rivière, France
Upon arrival, contact Madame Madeleine Hugot 33.6.84.60.81.41

RETURN: Tuesday, May 15, 12h55, Air France, Nice Côte d'Azur Airport

The date of her departure from Greenland is, eerily, the day Jann left the earth.

Three flights to arrive in Nice! An overnight at an airport hotel in Reykjavik! She knows how extravagant this trip is. She's calculated the cost a million times before. And that was without the airport hotel or the bed-and-breakfast in Belle Rivière or the rental car.

Rental Car?

Thanks to Malu and the carefree postal truck driver who preferred hunting and fishing on sunny days to delivering mail, Ilse learned to drive before she was the legal age of eighteen. During a summer break from university, she'd driven the mail truck around Ilulissat for fifteen weeks (completing translation work after the morning delivery) while the official driver was on paternity leave. It was good money, despite having to live with her parents.

She rereads the itinerary.

Two paid weeks in France, everything included? She will never underestimate Émile Moreau again.

Ilse,

This is an unusual bonus, the first I've awarded a translator, and ma chère, not given lightly. Daphné and I have decided to indulge you because of your record of excellence at this house for the last five years, your willingness to meet our deadlines, and the challenge you may meet with the Provençal vocabulary. This is going to be a high-priority book for us.

As much as I would like to meet you and Monsieur Labaye in the Luberon Valley, my schedule is too complicated to pop down south—and due to this extremely extravagant expense allocation, I'm not able to offer you a short stay in Paris. We'll save that for next time.

You should know that after reading a sampling of works by many translators, Geoffrey Labaye has approved our selection and is looking forward to working with you.

Bien cordialement,
Émile

The last sentence worries. So far, she's been able to hoodwink Émile. But she has the unsettling feeling that the moment she opens her mouth, a poet, attuned to the syllabic feet of rhyme and meter, will detect her secret—that she's never been to France—that she's a fraud!

Émile has attached the first-pass pages of the poet's work. She presses print. Her friend Bea calls Ilse extravagant and a Luddite for preferring to read manuscripts on paper, but part of the joy of her work is the feeling of the pages in her hands. She also likes the flexibility of taking the manuscript with her on walks into different settings under different light. She removes the pages from the printer and sits down to read the opening stanza of the first poem in the collection.

L'Amour Provençal

Je ne l'ai pas, mais elle m'a.
I have her not, but she has me.
Elle est dans la tombe, au-delà de la mer,
She is in the grave beyond the sea,
Elle est dans le tombeau haut dans le ciel,
She is entombed in the sky,
Je ne l'ai pas, mais elle m'a
I have her not, but she has me.
She rankles mind, bends shape,
Blinds me in her never-ending light.
I have her not, but she has me.

Thank goodness! He's a troubadour, but a contemporary one. Émile is right: the poet's short phrases are a relief from Gaudet's dense, intense prose.

But wait. The next two stanzas are completely incomprehensible. They are written in a language of which she has no knowledge.

She looks out the window at the sea, and the sea looks back at her.

Provençal! How can she possibly do justice to this poet's work, she with no knowledge of a language steeped in the context of centuries of culture? What hubris she'd had to think she could make this work! She thinks of her mother's grandfather, the cartographer, who arrived at the unknown territory of Greenland to interpret and record its geography. She, like him, must create a map, a sketchy version of what already exists.

She locates Levy's *Petit Dictionnaire Provençal-Français* on the Internet. The wind whirs and whistles outside her window. She grabs a blanket to wrap around herself.

"Here we go," she says aloud.

THE LAST TIME ILSE flew in a plane she was sixteen. It was during her school's winter break, when she was earning a few kroner in her mother's post office's sorting room. Jaken Jenkins, second-in-command to the chief post officer, who called himself the "King of the Skies," had offered Ilse a ride in the Cessna 208 twin-engine seaplane on his regular mail route north. Malu refused the offer.

But one brilliant sky day when Malu was out on an errand to restock packaging tape, Jaken asked Ilse if she wanted to know what it felt like to be a bird. Within minutes, Ilse was sitting beside him in the cockpit ready for takeoff.

How her heart exploded out of her body at the mounting speed of the plane and the thrill of leaving the land as they punctured the ice-blue sky. How fearsome and fierce was the feeling of freedom, of soaring above the ice-blanched terrain, far from the pestering minutiae of everyday life. They coasted on air drafts and through cloud wisps, and the ride felt as soft as floating among down feathers.

And when they had done the job of landing and taking off from the frozen glaciers and ice-ringed inlets of three towns including Qaanaaq, one of the northernmost settlements in the world, and on their way home had spotted two musk oxen banging horns together on the snowy tundra, Jaken Jenkins took his hands off the controls and told her to land the plane beyond the massive Ilulissat Icefjord, then to fly-float backward into the Ilulissat harbor!

Ilse never said a word about the flight. But not long after, and Ilse knew it had to do with Malu finding out, Jaken Jenkins, the King of the Skies, was demoted to an office job in Tasiilaq on the eastern coast of Greenland.

And that was the last time Ilse Erlund had left the earth.

2.

Provence

When the good Lord begins to doubt the world, he remembers that he created Provence.

—FRÉDÉRIC MISTRAL

Chapter 8

ILSE ERLUND, WRAPPED IN MADAME LAROCHE'S RED SILK SCARF, takes her first whiff of *la belle* France. Outside the airport terminal, the air is warmer than any warmth she has ever felt. She wants to slip off her clothes right there in the middle of the airport walkway and let the sun touch every square or not-so-square inch of her body, especially all the crevices that still carry the cold.

"Breathe, skin," she says aloud. *Take in this tepid teacup air while Malu is sitting cross-legged on the sorting room radiator, wearing her winter uniform with long underwear and lined wool socks.*

She texts Malu and Val to let them know she's arrived, then removes her sweatshirt and ties it around her waist. Her phone pings. It's a message from Madame Hugot, the proprietor of Le Cigale, instructing her to park her car near Belle Rivière's war heroes monument at the center of town and to call her from the nearby café, Le Cercle Républicain. The text also informs Ilse that Le Cigale is overbooked, and Madame is "kindly" offering her accommodation in her nearby home for a reduced price. Ilse has little choice but to tap *D'accord. Merci, Madame.*

The air smells like car exhaust and jet fuel. She squints to minimize the glare of the sun bouncing off the metallic rip of hundreds of vehicles zipping back and forth on the highway near the airport exit. In the country of Greenland, there are more sled dogs than cars.

The sky isn't the stark, glacial blue that feels like it holds you at gunpoint at home in Oqaatsut. Here, thousands of miles south of the Arctic Circle, today at least, the sky is a pale blue dipped in yellow, tipping back in a rocking chair and smiling. A row of green fireworks, bursting high up in the sky, lines the highway. She hadn't believed the photographs: there really are palm trees in France! It's hard to believe that a tree can grow so tall unimpeded by the forces of that she-god called weather. Here everything is so verdant, compared to the stark, ice-chilled home she left two days ago.

"Jann, for the first time in my life," she says, addressing the wisps of clouds above, "I know where I'm going! I'm here! And I know where I'm going!"

She says this before she tries to locate the Hertz sign in a vast rental car parking lot nestled inside a six-lane, two-directional highway.

How will she find it, let alone cross such a busy road? She must have missed the signs to an underground crossing. She decides to take her life in hand and dashes across one highway, then another, horns beeping, and into the never-ending parking lot on the other side. Her hand trembling, she continues to press the remote unlock button on the key fob, hoping this will help her identify the car.

"I know where I'm going. I know where I'm going," she repeats to herself as she zigzags around the enormous lot. *How hot it is in the baking sun!*

Half an hour later, ready to give up and return to the kiosk inside the airport, she spots a light blue Peugeot, blinking at her. When the woman at the Hertz desk, how chic she was with her red-and-blue scarf double-tied and knotted around her thin neck, said the car color was "*ravissante*" with her *je ne sais quoi* extravagance, Ilse could not refuse. But the color is not that "*ravissante.*" It's faded blue, and the car is tiny.

Whatever the case, she's in.

This car's interior in no way resembles that of the mail truck or cars she's driven in Ilulissat. For one thing, there's no place to insert the key. Deep breath. After following a how-to video on her phone, Ilse finally manages to start the car and navigates it to the exit sign.

Egress blocked. She tries another way around and finds herself at another dead end. No one told her that she'd need another translation degree to exit an airport parking lot.

She rolls down all the car windows. Let the French air in. Who cares if she spends the next two weeks in the car park? So what if the passenger-seat window does not roll up when she repeatedly presses the up arrow?

Another wrong turn? She thought she'd exited the car rental area a few minutes ago. Instead, she's made a circle and is back at the entrance.

She surrenders. She'll use the navigation app to exit the airport terminal. She taps "Belle Rivière" on her GPS app, noting her phone's diminishing battery life. Émile must not have requested a rental with a navigation unit because of the added expense. And the compass Beluga had given her so long ago at her high school graduation is in her carry-on bag, now in the trunk of the car. It was Beluga's father's compass, engraved with his initials. The note that accompanied the gift was written in Beluga's chicken scrawl: *If you get lost, I will be your True North.* He'd given it to her years after they'd broken up, even though they were both in different relationships. Ilse suspected it was one of the few things Beluga possessed from his father, and several times she'd offered to return it.

She checks the time: 2:45 P.M. French time, 10:45 A.M. Greenland time. She imagines Beluga and Val at Tipsy's, knees grazing as they sip schnapps-infused coffee.

Ilse finally exits the terminal parking zone.

Keep your sleepy eyes on the road. Oh no, another inexplicably complicated toll booth ahead. At the last one, unable to find the slot for her credit card, she'd held up a line of irascible French drivers. One man had jumped out of his car and yelled words she thankfully couldn't understand.

She's going the speed limit, but it feels as if she's flying. And this highway is as wide as an airport runway! The only highways she knows in Greenland are the winter snow–covered fjords, where dog sleds are the swiftly moving vehicles.

What are those small groups and couples doing at tables along the route? After a few more glances, Ilse realizes that these people are picnicking. What—in the breakdown lane? It's three in the afternoon, and the French are enjoying lovely lunches wherever they happen to find themselves. Fresh baguettes and *saucisson,* a chunk of cheese, perhaps a cornichon or two. Ilse's driving too fast to spot a wine bottle, but she's sure there's one on every table.

She searches one-handed in her purse for the sliced-cheese-and-lettuce sandwich she'd bought at the Reykjavik airport. She bites into her soggy lunch. To the French, this sandwich would be a disgrace, as is the state of her carry-on luggage, an embarrassment of a roller bag made of gray, dented plastic. She'd borrowed it from Mary, Duggan's wife.

She drinks in the muted, sunbaked pastel colors of the landscape and towns she passes, the terra-cotta rooftops against the indolent blue sky, the pale yellow wildflowers, and the upright purple blossoms of some amazing unknown-to-her plant lining the highway meridians. She almost crashes into the car in front of her as she turns to look for a second time at a swath of trees with enormous trunks covered in brown and beige camouflage-like bark. She's read about these trees, *les platanes,* otherwise known as London planes, planted by Napoleon to provide shade for his marching soldiers. Although his troops would not have benefited much from the shade of saplings, had the emperor envisioned the future elegance of these iconic tree-lined roads?

Three hours later, there it is, the sign for Belle Rivière! Ilse gazes up at the ancient village, sitting high on a ridge of bleached limestone rock.

Instead of heading straight and upward into the village, she finds herself winding along a sandy driveway. She's done it again; she's taken a wrong turn. It looks like an approach to a castle in a fairy tale. Bordered with lush trees that form a canopy over the road, the drive forks sharply to the right thanks to an immense tree in the middle. She's never seen such a gracious being! In the area where she lives, there are a few stunted and spindly gray leaf willows, and a sprinkling of dwarf birch trees, but mostly low-lying grassy shrubs and red and green stem mosses—*nothing* with this tree's height or wingspan. The tree must be hundreds of years old, and no doubt was given precedence when the owners designed the driveway.

She will exit by following the path a full circle around the tree and hope to regain the correct road that leads to the village. To do this, she has to pass in front of a large white manor house, half covered in an intricate design of red vines, sprouting green in places. Beside the house is a vineyard, stretching what looks like miles beyond her view. *A real vineyard!* As she curves around the front of the house, oh dear, she sees a man walking toward her. She slows the car to a stop.

While there's no private land ownership in Greenland, she's read about the century-old skirmishes over property lines in France. This man has every right to upbraid her for trespassing. She's almost at his front door.

"*Bonjour,*" she says, trying to imitate Bea's sonorous French accent. Her voice shakes. This is her first encounter with a French person in France other than the Hertz rental personnel.

"*Excusez-moi, monsieur,*" she says to him across the open passenger-seat window. He's a dapper, older Frenchman, wearing a loose white shirt and a straw hat with a white feather tucked in the ribbon. He could be a movie star from a classic French film.

She prepares herself for a Duggan-like scolding.

Instead, his face opens the way the sky clears after being covered by clouds. He smiles as if he knows her.

"*Vous cherchez le centre du village,*" he says.

She nods.

She's one of endless lost tourists that this man must endure.

"*Prenez à droite, puis encore à droite et vous y arriverez.*" Two rights, and she'll find it. His accent is different from Émile's, and Bea's. He speaks more slowly than the Parisians, articulating his vowels as if feeling each one of them.

"*Merci!*" she calls out, as she continues out the long driveway. She wishes she could have taken a photograph of the man's face. He is someone who, in her meager experience, seems to have lived a good life. A good life in France could mean so many different things.

Following his directions, she drives, spiraling higher and higher up the giant calcareous rock hilltop, passing one sloping vineyard after another. At one point, she stops to examine a crumbling stone wall, which she guesses is a portion of the leftover ramparts she'd read about that protected the village in ancient days from the Visigoths, and perhaps even a few of her Norse ancestors. Narrow, upright houses, most adorned with pale blue shutters, occupy the space between the broken-down wall and the road. At the plateau of the hill, she spots the bronze war memorial. She parks next to it, locking the car despite the open passenger window.

She glances at the names on the war memorial: *Pierre de Cler, Luc Blanchard, Jean Prévot, Ciprian LaCroix* . . . Ilse imagines the mothers, fathers, wives, children, and sisters of these men, their only solace the moments when they could forget. Forgetting must have a secret pact with death: to ease the pain, as it has helped ease hers. But like so much else, forgetting is illusory and temporary.

What? There's a Geoffrey Labaye on the list of commemorated soldiers lost in World War I. That's the name of her poet!

She is already claiming him as hers.

Ilse listens for the river of Belle Rivière. On this steep, rocky cliff, how could there be a river, let alone a creek? She sniffs the air. It's as if someone has sucked all the moisture from it. No damp, musty, earthy, tangy, pungent scent of mold and mildew, wet socks, rotting wood walls, and seaweed, nothing to which her nose is accustomed.

She recalls the story Fa had once told her in a rare garrulous mood about a prosperous Thule settlement near his birthplace that was built on a dried-up riverbed and that several decades later was washed away when the river reappeared, gushing in a torrent that took every edifice downriver in one fell swoop. His teaching points: observe and respect nature and its patterns; what was once a river may be a river again; be wary of where you put down roots. She had not exactly heeded his words, and she knew that Fa had grown tired of pestering his daughter about the seaside cottage she had rented following Jann's death.

But she's only renting! And she has views of gleaming icebergs constantly changing shape before her eyes. That and the sparkling Disko Bay with breaching humpback and fin whales and playful seals. And on any given winter night, she has front-row seats to the theatrical northern lights. All that for only fifteen hundred kroner a month!

She texts Madame Hugot to let her know that she's arrived. On her way down the sloping road, she passes two restaurants. People are sprinkled here and there at tables on the terraces of each of them. Five forty-five in the afternoon: cocktail hour in Belle Rivière. The tinkle of glasses and the lilting French voices are music to her ears.

There it is, on the right: Le Cercle Républicain. It must have once served as a political meeting place. Or perhaps it still does. The narrow door at the slant of the hill off the main square is easy to miss. She trips on the uneven steps.

Don't smile, she tells herself. From their online face-to-face meetings, Bea had warned her northern colleague to contain her emotions when first meeting the French. Their culture, she'd said, is protective and defensive, and that's the reason why they rarely smile when greeting strangers, and why in their language, they often use double negatives to express affirmations. *Ce n'est pas mal* means "it's good." They've been through more wars, plagues, and famines than a Greenlander can imagine.

But hadn't the gentleman whose driveway she had mistakenly entered smiled at her—a total stranger? *And* a trespasser?

Inside Le Cercle, three men stand pressed to the bar. Two wear painter's overalls; the other sports a blue jacket and the iconic black beret. They're drinking a smoky, yellow liquid from tall glasses. White plastic tables and chairs are scattered randomly on the other side of the bar. At the back of the room, the sun blazes through French doors that lead to a balcony.

She reads *Le Manifeste du Cercle Républicain* on a poster tacked to the wall opposite the bar. In bold letters, at the top of the framed document, is the motto *Un pour tous, tous pour un.* One for all, and all for one. Good thing Ilse hadn't sat in one of the chairs and expected wait service.

A woman, whitish-haired, with a tanned face and vertical lines down her cheeks, pops her head up from below the bar.

"*Oui?*" she says, her eyebrows pinching together.

Ilse has interrupted her.

"*Bonjour, madame.*" Ilse tries on her most deadpan face. Oh no, her voice is wobbling. "*Je voudrais un café au lait, s'il vous plaît.*"

In one volley, and with a loud clatter, the woman produces Ilse's coffee in a white cup on a saucer, along with a tiny white slip, the bill. Now the woman is tending to the three men, pouring what's left of a bottle of liquor into their glasses. The woman says something to make the three men laugh, and there it is, a wrung-out smile from her, followed by a deep, husky laugh. To be on the receiving end must feel like winning a prize.

"*C'est à moi,*" says one of the men before the others have time to pay for their drinks.

Ilse takes her coffee cup and saucer to the threshold of the postage-stamp-size balcony and stops short, her cup rattling on the saucer.

No way! She had greedily gobbled up photographs of the Luberon Mountains in her research of the area, but the images did not reveal what she sees now: up front, a patchwork of terra-cotta rooftops in various angles and configurations within the village's stony ramparts; next, a valley of vineyards in different shades of green intermingled with wheat-colored fields, and beyond that, the Luberon range. Le Petit Luberon, a solid rectangle shape tapering down on the right side in a dragon's tail, is a color that she has never seen or dreamed of before: the blue of the sea, but on a mountain!

When she peers over the edge, she almost falls into the nearby plastic chair. It's a vertiginous drop to the narrow, curving cobblestone path below. A deep, green gorge separates the balcony from the limestone cliff on the other side, on which she watches the silhouettes of cars and trucks approaching the village. But wait, what was just a few minutes before the sea-blue color of the Luberon Mountains is now lavender.

She is bedazzled.

She sips her café au lait and pinches herself.

"Jann," she whispers. "I have arrived."

Chapter 9

A TALL, SLENDER WOMAN IS WALKING HURRIEDLY FROM THE interior of Le Cercle in Ilse's direction. She looks fortyish and is wearing a red apron over a calf-length denim dress. Madame Hugot. Must be. Is Ilse so obviously *l'étrangère,* the foreigner? Does she look that different from everyone else?

Madame is busy squinting, sizing up the woman from the Arctic who will be sleeping in the extra room in her home.

"Mademoiselle Erlund?" The woman's voice is the frayed end of a kite tail.

Ilse rises. Without another word, Madame about-faces. This must be Ilse's cue to follow. She brings her coffee cup and saucer to the counter and places her euro, plus a tip, on the counter. She searches for a parting acknowledgment from the steely face, now at the far end of the bar.

Nothing.

No time to linger. Ilse follows Madame Hugot's dash down the lopsided steps onto the alleyway that she had noticed from the balcony. A gutter grooves the edges of the cobblestone passage. Madame turns the corner, and Ilse, not far behind, finds herself, what? Stepping onto a terra-cotta roof? It *is* a roof. They're treading on loose terra-cotta roof cylinders that shift and clatter as their feet scurry over them.

This must be a shortcut.

The breathtaking view again. A cavernous gorge opens before them with the backdrop of misty mountains, their lavender color now tinged with green. But Madame does not stop to gape at the view. Clink, clink, clatter, clatter. The inhabitants below must be able to hear them.

Madame, in her brown espadrilles, is not making as much noise as Ilse in her thick-soled sneakers. Maybe this is why the French wear espadrilles, so they can run along rooftops. Ilse must get a pair as soon as possible.

A black cat slinks across the rooftop, then another. *Jann, did you see that?* It's obvious that the cats are accustomed denizens of tile vaulting. Their black fur against the orange terra-cotta of the roofs in the bright afternoon sun sends an electric charge through Ilse. If her phone weren't dead, she'd be snapping photos. But no, she wouldn't. She doesn't have time to stop.

The figure ahead of her has just leapt from one roof to another. Madame is as lissome as the cats. Ilse stops short before the two-foot gap in roof lines. Maybe Belle Rivière is the home of the last living troubadour of Provence and the notorious daredevil of Provence. Ilse takes a breath and jumps. Who would have thought that on her first day in Provence, she'd be scampering across rooftops and leaping across thirty-foot drops?

It reminds her of the times when she would sneak around the rocky outskirts of Ilulissat, following Jann and his coterie of pals. But she's out of practice. She's lost Madame Reckless again. There she is, sliding down the sloping edge of the roof to a winding path below. To the right of this passageway, the exterior of a limestone cave shines golden in the afternoon sun. Ilse later learns that this grotto once housed a makeshift chapel, where country dwellers brought those dying from the plague for last rites.

"This is the parking spot for your car," Madame announces to the breathless Ilse after they climb up a rock-strewn hill to a small flat slab of green grass, "but don't expect to keep the tourists off it. I guard mine with my life."

How strange to have to defend this small rectangle, barely large enough for her tiny car! Ilulissat has plenty of space for parking. More people own boats than cars, and most of the cars on the few roads are owned by companies and are shared. And Oqaatsut, well, there are no cars in Oqaatsut.

Up a few steps, Madame turns the latch on an arched wrought-iron gate. They cross a terrace, just big enough for three metal café chairs and a table and planters of the same overflowing purple flowers that Ilse had seen along the highway on her drive from Nice.

What? Ilse looks up to see that the house, if you can call it that, with windows on the first and second floors, is set inside a limestone cliff. She has read about troglodyte dwellings, cavities dug into the soft stone, where people live the way they did in the fourth century B.C.E., protected from the extreme elements of summer and winter. But most of these habitable caves are located in the Loire Valley. Ilse had never dreamed that she would see, let alone *stay* in one here in Provence. Surely Malu would appreciate the way the landscape is put to good use.

The door color, a muted pastel blue, is a far cry from the lurid blue that Ilse had painted on her cottage door in an effort to copy the French *joie de vivre*. Hers is a poor translation.

Madame plunges her hand into her apron pocket and out comes a key, which she uses to unlock the door set into the cliff.

Once inside the cliff, Ilse is greeted by the overwhelming smell of garlic, onions, and tomatoes, accompanied by sizzling sounds. Madame dashes through the sunny front room furnished with carved wooden chairs, a glass coffee table, and a small television on a stand, into the kitchen where she is now stirring the noisy ratatouille. No wonder they had hustled back to the house: the pan on the gas stove has been on a low simmer.

Ilse need not have worried so much about her conversational French on her first meeting with Madame. She has not been given the opportunity to speak.

A small, round wood table is set for four, each place decorated with a terra-cotta plate; beside it, a red-and-white-checked cloth napkin rolled into a wooden napkin holder; and next to that, a short glass. A baguette lies at the center of the table. The sun alights on yellow flowers in a blue ceramic vase on the counter. Red-and-white-striped curtains frame the two bright windows. Everything feels welcoming, soaked in intimate happiness. Might Madame have set such a pretty table to welcome Ilse to Provence?

Leaning over the cast-iron skillet, Madame tastes the tomato mixture with her wooden spoon. She pinches salt from a miniature white bowl and releases it into the pan, twists the oversized wooden pepper grinder, then turns off the burner and wipes her hands on her apron.

"*Oui,*" she says, as she opens what looks like a broom closet door.

She gestures for Ilse to follow her up the curving stone stairs that land in a bedroom. The first thing Ilse notices in this sun-dappled room painted orange is a desk facing French doors. Two white towels hang over the back of the desk chair. A sink occupies one corner of the room, a stained oak wardrobe the other. On the back wall, a twin bed with a carved wooden headboard juts into the center of the room.

All she needs; all she will ever need in a lifetime.

All business, Madame crosses the room to open the French doors onto a small Juliet balcony. Ilse joins her there to see a view of the descending valley, a mosaic of different shapes and hues of vineyard and farmland. In the distance, Ilse glimpses a snow-capped mountain that reminds her of the jagged peaks of Ukkusissat, the mountain that Ilse could see on clear days from Madame LaRoche's apartment in Nuuk.

"Mont Ventoux," Madame says to answer Ilse's pointing finger. "That's not snow at the top, but bare limestone," she continues in an unusual flush of words. "We call it Bald Mountain. You will see the peak only on clear days like today."

Ilse can count on Madame to lower her expectations. She crosses the room to touch the cool, irregular wall that is the mountain cliff as it curves over the bed. Can the tiny, raised form be a fossil of an oyster shell, a previous guest of Belle Rivière? She inspects it, her nose up to the wall, and feels the skin tingle up her back.

In her early school days, Ilse had dreamed of becoming a geologist. The quarryman who worked in a strip mine behind their house in Ilulissat spoke to her after school of mantles, bedrock, drifts, shifts, cores, crusts, cinders, molten magma, and igneous metamorphoses. She spent hours drawing these things, imagining the churning life at the bowels of the earth. It was only later in high school that she realized that she was more interested in the exotic-sounding words than in the things they described.

This fossil could be one hundred million years old, late Jurassic period, when the soils were this same kind of calcareous, lacustrine clay. Lacustrine. A divine word.

"*Oui, nous vivons dans une montagne.* Yes, we live inside a mountain," says Madame, as she tries to pry open the wardrobe with her house key. She seems to start every sentence with "*Oui,*" which perhaps is a way to tell the world that she already knows everything. She nearly falls when the door swings open. It hangs open due to the slanting wooden floor.

"*La clé,*" she says, handing Ilse the key. As if Ilse owns anything worth stealing.

No dilly-dallying: the ratatouille must be watched. Madame leaves the room.

Ilse guesses she's supposed to follow Madame down the stairs again, and nearly bumps into her at the bottom as Madame opens another door in the kitchen, even narrower than the door leading up to the bedroom. Neither Beluga nor Duggan would fit through it.

It's the WC.

Ilse nods, but Madame has already turned her back to tend to her skillet.

"*Pour se laver?* To wash?" Ilse asks.

Madame's face is a question mark.

Ilse pantomimes washing under her arms. Vulgar, yes, but illustrative.

"*Oui, l'évier,*" she says after a few seconds, impatiently pointing a finger up the stairs. Of course: the sink.

Ilse mimes washing her hair.

Madame shakes her head and sighs in the way that older people do when they consider how spoiled young people are these days. To think that this ingrate temporary tenant would ask about washing her hair! To her, Madame Hugot is a woman of few words, but Ilse can already hear her gossiping about the new boarder to her friends.

"*Le spa est dans le village, mais c'est payant.* The spa is in town, but you must pay for it," she says, sipping the simmering tomato liquid.

In what is left of the afternoon, Ilse moves her car to the precious parking spot and her clothes into the wardrobe in her room. Since no dinner invitation from Madame is forthcoming, which is a disappointment, Ilse explores the village.

The most imposing buildings are the citadel-like Saint-Firmin Church, named after the patron saint of healing, and the château, the fortified castle built in the eleventh century. The château was used through the years as a prison, warehouse, and boys' school and now houses the local cultural center. The remnants of the ramparts and these two structures, towering above all else, are convincing proof that this hilltop village must have protected its residents from the rampages of rival neighbors over the centuries. As Ilse explores the cozy *rues* that wind serpentine through the village's interior, she tries to discern each street's personality. It's part of her Inuit heritage to honor the soul, even of a dead-end road.

Two *boulangeries* face off against each other on either side of rue du Four, road of the oven. She chooses to enter the bakery with the window that displays five baskets of different kinds of baguettes. Inside, she smells a sweetness she'd never expected of bread. An interior window reveals a bread machine, a metal octopus that churns the dough. In her research, she'd read that for a *boulangerie* to sell a *tradition* baguette, it had to be baked on the premises. She decides to buy her most typical French accoutrement at this shop.

Down the rue Neuve, past the butcher's shop, with its life-size plastic bull's head above the door, Ilse bites into *le quignon*—the crunchy end of the baguette—and stops in front of a hat and espadrille shop. She is simultaneously delighted by the tasty crisp crust of the baguette and by the spectacle of the many different-colored espadrilles. No doubt about it: she will choose the lavender. Too bad the shop is closed.

In the tourist whatnot store, she buys postcards that she will send to

Malu, Fa, Val, and Donny. She mills around the aisles of scented soaps, maps, coffee mugs, and guidebooks. She won't leave the store until she inhales the twelve sample bottles of room spray with appealing names like *fleur d'oranger, eau de patchouli, violette impériale,* and *citronelle.* How can she have lived thirty-five years and have never heard of or imagined room spray?

Without a doubt, she's never smelled so many delectable things in a day. At home, it seems she's always sniffing for things gone wrong: mildew in her clothes, seawater in the basement, gas leaks from her stove.

Only when Ilse locates La Poste, the square, squat building with no charm in a village that explodes with it, does she feel at home. And because she's feeling suddenly hungry and exhausted from the sleepless flight, the long drive, and the excitement of her arrival, Ilse decides to have an early dinner at the empty La Crêperie de Maman across from La Poste. After she eats a *galette au saumon fumé* served with *crème fraîche,* savoring every bite, she plugs her phone's power cord into an outlet and taps Malu's number.

"It's true," Ilse responds to her mother. "I could have called you sooner. But I did text you to let you know that I'd arrived safely."

To elicit guilt, Malu chills the tone in her voice like one does with a good white wine.

"I've been sick with worry about your drive."

"It was overwhelming at first, the highway is huge. There are so many cars here, thousands of them, you wouldn't believe it. And Malu, the colors here, I've never set my eyes on so many different hues, tints, vibrant sun-warmed shades that change by the second or faster than that, with the light. The light is the driving force of this place—"

Malu interrupts.

"Yes, I know, Malu, the iceberg blue, and the northern lights, but everything has a warm sun-filtered tint here. I've never seen so many different variations of green in the landscape. My eyes are still adjusting. Now I know why so many artists are inspired by this area."

This kind of emphatically positive talk can make her mother irritable. Then again, Ilse can't describe circumstances as too distressing, or Malu will hands-on-hips say, "I told you so."

Unthreatening boring is what Malu stomachs best.

"What's that sound in the background?" Ilse asks.

"The shredder."

"What are you shredding?"

"The mail of the gone astray."

"Since when do you call them the 'gone astray'?"

"Since forever, that's since when."

"And you shred their mail? How long after they've—"

"What do you expect us to do with it? With only me and my aching back and a few other workhorses in here and all these *damn* boxes?"

No use pursuing a lost cause, especially when Ilse is in paradise.

"How's Fa?"

The waitress returns to the room and takes a long look at Ilse's grocery-store-bought sneakers with no brand.

"Exactly as you left him. That's how he is."

WHEN ILSE ENTERS THE Hugots' kitchen later that evening, two teenage children, engrossed in open laptops at the kitchen table, glance up and smile tentatively at her. Monsieur Hugot, a bald man with thick-rimmed square glasses, Ilse assumes he's the husband, closes his newspaper and stands to greet her with a "*Bonsoir,*" then resumes his seat and newspaper. Madame is where she always is, in front of the stove, stirring. It is a sweet family scene, reminiscent of her own, when Jann and she would sit on the stools at the kitchen counter, tackling math problems, while Malu prodded a stew simmering on the burner. Jann knew all the answers before Ilse picked up her pencil. Jann!

That night, Ilse snuggles under the thick cotton sheets and light comforter and inhales the dry, thyme-scented air from the open French doors. Unfamiliar sounds, Monsieur's deep bass voice, Madame's shrill one, the son's monotone and the daughter's barely audible, gentle one, rise through the floorboards and slide under her door. What a relief not to hear the wind-slapping tarp on her roof in Oqaatsut, or the yapping and howling of hungry sled dogs, or to be listening warily for Mr. G's nightly scamper up and down the stairs.

A cat mews on the street outside.

Oh, Minou, I hope you are well.

After much consideration, Ilse had asked Val to house her beloved cat. Beluga travels too much, and Malu and Fa are out of the house most of the day.

Ilse jumps out of bed, crosses the room, and opens her charging laptop. In the hubbub and excitement of her preparation, departure, and arrival, she suddenly realizes that she'd left the *faire la grasse matinée* phrase untranslated in Gaudet's manuscript. She'd been hoping to call Ms. Gaudet again before she sent the completed translation to Émile. But Ilse hadn't gotten up the gumption the second time, and then she forgot. She's surprised that after all this time, Émile hadn't caught the omission. *Émile, you're slacking off! Why did you torture me for that early deadline if you haven't even read the translation?* Or, horror of horrors, perhaps he'd translated the phrase for her. Doubtful. If he had, she wonders if he'd pondered the connotations for as long as she had. Whatever the case, now she'll have to notify him. *Damn.* She could have buried an uninspired version into the prose, and Émile would never have noticed.

Excuse the omission. Please use the words, she types in an email to him, *"late-morning sleep-in."*

It's unnuanced and unsexy, a dull and boring substitution for a phrase that imbues the text with a luscious, sensual subcurrent. Too bad Ilse has chosen a profession that involves brutal daily compromise.

Dissatisfied, she returns to bed. From where she lies, she can see gently twinkling stars out the open French doors. They seem distant, unlike the ones at home, where the swaths of firedust appear so close you feel you can touch them. An older woman in her settlement boasts that she can read by the light of the stars, and even sometimes by the reflection from the stars on the ice.

Ilse hears talking, then a twitter of laughter somewhere down the street. She brushes away what feels like granules of sugar on her forehead. Then more. She switches on the bedside light. Sand, the same color as the wall, speckles her pillow. She brushes it from her hair, her face, her neck, and her arms.

It's the limestone cliff wall! It's shedding. The wall dust sparkles in the light. Madame should have told her about this, or at least have supplied her with goggles. Ilse wonders if this happens to every room in the house, or only to the boarder's bedroom.

Chapter 10

BEFORE ILSE LEAVES HER ROOM THE FOLLOWING MORNING, her first full day in France, she stands with her eyes closed, and the French doors open, reveling in the pampering warmth of the sun and the slight breeze. It seems unfair that some people live in such a luxurious climate, while she and others shiver beside windows with no insulation, their feet in two layers of socks.

With Monsieur Hugot's help, she returns her rental car to the Hertz dealership in Coustellet, the town below Belle Rivière. The car is too expensive to keep, and Madame Hugot tells her that she won't need it as Monsieur Labaye's house is only a short walk away. On the way back from Coustellet, Monsieur drives his Citroën as if he's a Grand Prix driver, speeding around every curve. Holding on to the grab handle for dear life, Ilse asks if Monsieur has a meeting that morning, but he declines to respond. Perhaps it's rude for her to ask. Ilse has a feeling that she will be spending much of her time in Provence calibrating the moods and manners of the French. It's another form of translating.

Émile has arranged for her and the poet to meet for lunch at the Renaissance Café, one of the restaurants she'd passed the day before on her way to Le Cercle Républicain. After that, she would be on her own.

The goal she sets for herself for this first meeting is to listen for the poet's tone and the pitch of his voice, to watch for the directions in which he pulls or pushes the language in his speech. A translation instructor had once urged her to grasp not only the author's intentions for the work, but also the intentionality, their *orientation* in the world.

But she's jumping ahead.

First, she must understand the poet's dialect. Second, she'll try to speak French as if it's her first language, well, okay her second, or maybe even her third, but not her fourth.

This is the first time she's ever met the author of a work she's translating or has translated. It had always been enough to inhabit a writer's world through the portals of words. If allowed the time, the words osmose like tea leaves diffused in hot water, and she gradually senses her subject's heart and the feelings beneath the words.

She hopes that these in-person meetings with the poet will benefit the work and not hinder it. What if she dislikes this man? What if he is arrogant, heir as he is to a vocation dating back to the Middle Ages? What if her feelings about him affect the words she chooses to place over his words?

She's wearing white capri pants, her short-waisted blue denim jacket, and Madame's red silk scarf. Too bad those lavender espadrilles, or any espadrilles that she'd seen in the shop the day before, were not available in her size.

She pitter-patters as gently as she can, via the roofs, to the center of the village, the way Madame had shown her, crouching down in places to get her balance over the loose tiles, stopping to gaze at the cloudless horizon and the Luberon mountain range in the distance and to snap photographs. She lowers herself down from the roof onto the cobblestone path that leads to the main street.

By now, Ilse has skimmed a few of the poems in the collection, which she's noted is dedicated to Inès. Is she the poet's wife, his muse, his lover, or all three? Geoffrey Labaye is called the "Last Living Troubadour of Provence" for good reason. Émile had warned her of a "sprinkling" of Provençal words, but Ilse would say there's a drenching of words and expressions not only in the unfamiliar dialect but also in the disused courtly language from the twelfth century. Many of the words have their roots in Arabic and Spanish, both of which are foreign to her. She will need every bit of time that the poet can give her during these two weeks.

Just like all twelfth- and thirteenth-century troubadour poems, Labaye's are about love in all its forms: adoring love, grieving love, erotic love, the renouncing of love, apologies for love, and the anguish and loss of love. There are also debates in dialogue form about the nature of love.

Last night, before Ilse turned off her bedside lamp, she had struggled, using her new 387-page companion, Emil Levy's *Petit Dictionnaire Provençal-Français,* through Labaye's "love lost" poem titled "No Sap Chanter Qui So No Di," poorly translated by her as "No one can sing where no melody is." After she'd read the poem, staring up at her shedding cliff wall, she found herself wiping her tears, feeling the sting of loss, the blow of the deprivation of her brother and that of the beautiful Madame LaRoche, the decline of her father's eyesight and his diminished happiness since Jann and Madame died, and the march of days since then that had left her father, and also her, in a vacuum of acute aloneness.

She turns a corner and hears someone singing an archetypal French romantic melody accompanied by the organlike sound of an accordion. Madame had told her that today is Belle Rivière's market day. The music is now blanketed by the blur of voices and activity. Around another corner, to her surprise and delight, she discovers a world brimming with color and movement. Shoppers with straw baskets crowd the streets, mulling around food stands abundant with produce. The scene is out of a movie! The full-throated musician sings, "*Parlez-moi d'amour.*"

Yes, please speak to me about love!

She is early for lunch, so she meanders among the shoppers, trying to look as casual and experienced as the French. Big-boned, big-footed, and tall at five feet, eight inches, she stands out in the crowd. But no one seems to notice her; they're too busy examining the cheeses and *saucissons* and everything else piled high on stalls. Ilse gravitates to the fruit stand with its display of plump cherries, strawberries, raspberries, blackberries, and apricots. The fruit that is not local is marked with handwritten signs naming their foreign origins: melons, though not yet ripe, hail from Cavaillon, cherries from Apt, and the origin of the small, shiny strawberries is Carpentras. She's never seen so much fruit in one place. The vegetable stalls are loaded with red and yellow cherry tomatoes; root vegetables of all colors; red, green, and orange peppers; radishes, beans, and an array of lettuces. She's never seen so much fresh produce! And nothing is as expensive as a head of romaine lettuce that costs 124 kroner at the Super 1 Supermarket just outside Ilulissat. She takes photographs of the overflowing bin of black and green olives. The sparkling tapenade resembles caviar.

Oh, and the *saucissons*! Every kind imaginable is on display: dried sausages mixed with pistachios, figs, garlic, mushrooms, olives, pepper seeds, truffles, even lavender. With the supply ship from Copenhagen arriving in Ilulissat only once a week, and to Oqaatsut once every other week, this abundance is hard to fathom. The vendor, a woman in a green silk scarf and matching apron, offers Ilse a slice of the *saucisson à l'ail*. Garlic. Ilse has never tasted anything so simultaneously savory and sweet, but *alors*, now her breath will smell like garlic before her important lunch. Next to the profusion of *saucissons* is a stall with cured meat, premade *poulet à la plancha*, stuffed Provençal tomatoes, tartines, and sandwiches. And to think that this village has this gustation celebration every Wednesday!

From afar, she smells *savons de Marseille*, soaps handmade in Marseille, each with different scents and colors. At the table, she reads the labels: *Bergamote*, *Rose Écrasée* (Crushed Rose), *Jasmin*, *Muguet* (Lily of the Valley), *Lavande* (Lavender), *Violette*, *Chèvrefeuille* (Honeysuckle), even something, she chuckles, called *Fanny* soap. When she asks about it, the woman behind the stall tells her it's named after a play by Marcel Pagnol about his love for a woman named Fanny. *Bien sûr*. Everything here is about love. Next week, she'll buy soaps for Val and Mary. If she has enough euros by the end of her two-week stay, she'll buy Malu one of the colorful tablecloths that dance in the breeze.

She listens to the way the shoppers talk to the vendors, calling them by their given names. They politely ask, don't touch, wait patiently.

The cheese stand is her favorite. Rectangle, triangle, round, and rolled, the goat cheeses are ash-colored or creamy yellows, and whites. The rounds of *chèvre* with a *petit* sprig of thyme pressed into the center are small masterpieces. As are the cylinders and balls, wrapped in a chestnut leaf and tied with raffia. She inhales the earth-farmy, rich scents.

She photographs the spice table with its many bowls of different-colored and unique-smelling condiments. Sniffing, without cheating and looking at the scrawled notes on each, she can identify only the curry, rosemary, and thyme. Wait, the *monsieur* behind the goat cheese table has just smiled at her and is approaching her, her specifically. He offers her a napkin with a small piece of cheese on a cracker.

"*Merci,*" she says. He smiles, bows, and returns to his stall. He's wearing a blue-and-white-striped shirt. Of course he is!

To be a part of such a swirl of color and activity, a connection to a time and a place—Ilse feels giddy with joy.

The terrace of the Renaissance Café is packed. Still a few minutes early, she waits beside a small statue of the Virgin Mary tucked into a niche near the entrance of the restaurant. Two fresh white lilies must have just been placed beside the statuette. At their meeting time, twelve-thirty, Ilse summons up the nerve to ask the maître d' for the table of Monsieur le Poète, which is what Émile had suggested she should call Monsieur Labaye. A waiter in black pants and a tight-fitting light blue shirt looks not into her face but down at her sneakers, before leading her to a table for two at the center of the terrace under the shade of a *platane*'s leafy, extended branches.

Has her host chosen the center of this bee's hive to enliven their talk, to distract her from him, or else to ease any awkward silences? Ilse glances at the menu in chalk on a blackboard propped against a branch of the tree: wild mushroom soup, country pâté with cornichons, *tarte aux oignons, escargots à la Bourguignonne, moules frites, poulettes, steak au poivre*. He has invited her, but the prices are tourist expensive. The preset menu of an *entrée* and a *plat principal* costs twenty-eight euros. Leave it to *la belle* France: they force you to enjoy a first and second course. Dessert is an added expense.

She takes a deep breath. What if Monsieur le Poète thinks her French isn't good enough to merit translating his work? Émile had told her that he'd apprised the poet about her lack of familiarity with Provençal, but knowing Émile, he'd probably told his client that her knowledge of the dialect was a little rusty. What if she and Monsieur dislike each other on first meeting? What if he grows impatient with her questions? His time is valuable. Every minute that he spends with her he could be composing original work.

It is five minutes after the appointed time.

What if the last living troubadour doesn't show?

Ilse strains to overhear the couple's conversation at the next table. English! Ilse guesses that the woman is American by the way she smiles and seems to be conversing so freely.

At the entrance of the restaurant, Ilse recognizes the older man wearing the straw hat with the feather tucked in it, the man who'd kindly given her directions when she was lost the day before. Belle Rivière may be just as small as Oqaatsut.

She smiles at him in the distance before she realizes that—he's heading for her table.

No way!

Monsieur le Poète?

He must be the Poet!

Her poet.

Chapter 11

"MADEMOISELLE."

Ilse stands and receives an air kiss on either cheek and a third one on the first cheek.

Their first meeting, and three kisses? In her country, even people who know each other shake hands in greeting.

"*Vous êtes surprise,*" he says, bowing and removing his hat. He places it on the table.

She's a little discomposed by the kisses and by the fact that she'd met this man by accident the day before.

"Yes, I didn't . . . I didn't expect . . ." she says in French.

"If you've read any of my poems, you'll know that I don't believe in coincidences."

She should have read all his poems by now.

He sits after she does.

Monsieur le Poète is an attractive older man, and tall, maybe six feet. Émile had told her that he was seventy-four years old. He looks thinner than the man she met yesterday, slighter, his cheekbones more pronounced. He gives her the impression of someone who was once larger than life but now is less in voice, and body, and face. He has a peppered white mustache and a closely clipped beard, not unlike the way Beluga has been shaving recently. His mostly white hair is brushed back and hangs over the collar of his loose white shirt in a kind of rakish way. The outfit is topped off with a short black vest, the expected garb of a Provençal poet, or so she imagines. His eyebrows are the shape of a seagull in flight.

"You did not realize that there is a plan beside your own?" he says, his eyebrows rising. Now she feels at home: many Greenlanders, like Fa, talk mostly with their eyebrows.

Is he speaking slowly and drawing out his vowels because he knows she needs time to understand him, or is that the Provençal accent? His voice, that salty, warm one that she remembers from yesterday, sounds today as if it's infused with melancholy. Slightly purplish, small pouches under his eyes look as though they hold tears.

She hesitates.

"We were meant to meet," he says.

"We were," she says, with a little smile, as if he's joking.

Their waitress is thin, wiry, with dark brown hair cut short at her chin, and her eyes are lined with kohl, drawn half an inch to the outer side of her lids, not unlike the way Madame LaRoche wore her eye makeup. Having ignored Ilse during her wait, she's now making a beeline to their table. Bzzzzzz. The waitress's white apron is bordered with frills up and down the straps, which flutter when she moves. The look is fetching.

The restaurant is more alive, if that's possible, now that this charming, elderly man is in it.

"*Monsieur Labaye,*" the waitress says, her voice in a curtsy, "*que puis-je vous apporter aujourd'hui?*" What may I bring you today?

Clearly, he is a regular.

"May I tempt you with a Ricard?" Monsieur le Poète asks Ilse with a tilt of his head.

A flirtatious Frenchman, even in his seventies. He glances at Madame's red scarf around her neck. Maybe to avoid her eyes. He must notice how awkward she feels, so much bigger and taller than any of the other women, a pretender who speaks the language but has not dwelled in it. Maybe he will write about her today, about the way she has tried unsuccessfully to wrap her scarf like a Frenchwoman would.

"A Ricard?" she asks.

"A local favorite, it's an anise-and-licorice-flavored aperitif created by a certain Marseillais, Paul Ricard. It would be important for your translation of my poetry to taste this drink."

From watching U.S. TV shows, she is certain now that the accents at the next table are American. It's a relief that she's not the only *étrangère*.

"*Oui?*" he asks her.

The waitress waits on tiptoes.

Ilse would already have had her first schnapps-infused coffee at Tipsy's by this time of day.

He raises two fingers to the waitress before Ilse finishes her nod.

"Tell me: you've never been to Provence, let alone France, yet you translate French into English," he says.

It's not an accusation, she would be sensitive to that. Like his poetry, it's a simple assertion that is more exploratory than opinionated.

But how did he know?

Not even Émile knows, or at least she thought he didn't. It would be outside Émile's imagination to even consider that she'd never stepped foot on the land of her source language. And if Émile suspected it, he certainly would not tell one of his authors. If his boss, Daphné, knew, she would never have agreed to have her daughter's future father-in-law's book translated by her.

Ilse avoids the Poet's searching eyes and reaches for her water goblet. *Hand, stop shaking!*

"It's true" is all she has the courage to say.

His seagull eyebrows lift to fly.

Suddenly she feels sad, as if for her whole life, she's been looking out the window and not being where she was supposed to be.

"And you are here now to translate me."

He looks at her in a curious, serious way, as if open to the idea.

"To translate your poetry," she says.

His eyes speak of culture, history, literature, and poetry. They are wise eyes, but mostly, they are kind and empathetic.

Thankfully, the drinks are delivered, along with a carafe of water.

"*Le menu?*" the waitress bee says.

Ilse follows the Poet's gaze to the blackboard. The scent of thyme and rosemary. And then a musky scent. It's the perfume of the woman at the next table, not the American, but a middle-aged woman at the table on the other side of them. She's wearing a crisp white blouse, embroidered with bright blue flowers. She has curved, dark eyebrows, and whatever perfume she is wearing is intoxicating. Sweet and spicy, and thick enough to linger. *Diabolique*, the French would say.

A perfume that makes Ilse think of *faire la grasse matinée*!

Monsieur le Poète tilts his head to know her answer.

Ilse had studied the menu on the Internet the previous night. She chooses *la soupe aux poireaux* and *la salade au saumon*. He makes a comment to the waitress that Ilse does not understand. It's his accent, vowel sounds that she's never heard voiced before.

He pours water from the carafe into their glasses, transforming the inch of yellow liqueur inside into a milky white concoction. Will it taste like licorice?

"*Salut*," he says, raising his glass.

Rather than chink glasses robustly as they would at home, Monsieur le Poète dips his head and gazes into her eyes. She mimics his toast with a nod of her head. She's such a copycat.

The elixir is licorice delicious, and the taste brings back the memory of the long red and black strings of it that her father would buy for her and her brother when they were young. She can blame the licorice for the fillings in her molars.

"I suppose I'm a translator too," he says, still slowly, "my mission, to convert the base metals of people's feelings, thoughts, and lives into gold. Poetry as alchemy; reflection, into refraction."

His voice is a series of undulating hills, rolling up and down.

"*Je ne sais pas comment vous le faites*," she says. I don't know how you do it.

"The goal is to enter through the heart. Sometimes if I'm lucky, I rearrange the furniture in there."

He has just done that to her. In the short time she's been with him, she feels strangely at ease, something she has not experienced since her arrival—perhaps even months or years since her arrival.

"It can take a lot out of you," she says, "to move all that psychic armament."

"*Absolument!* It's an enormous energy drain." He laughs, tipping his chair backward, and she follows his gaze to the underside of the white umbrella. The moving patterns of the leaves of the plane tree above are mesmerizing.

"To get the readers to believe in us, we poets must use disguises, take on personas, lie and cheat, play mind games."

He's smiling, with a mischievous turn of his head, a glint in his eyes.

"You're playing mind games with me now! It was my understanding that a poet plunges deeply inside himself, then breaches with the truth. It's we translators who are the imitators and manipulators, the liars. We're the ones who slip on the masks of others."

While at first she had difficulty with his accent and the length of his sentences with the arcs of his voice, now she understands more than just fragments. And her speaking French is coming a little easier now. She has hardly spoken since her arrival.

"You *knowingly* impersonate; we rascally devils don our personas in secret."

She throws up her hands and laughs.

"I still don't believe you," she says.

"By the time you finish translating my work, I guarantee that you'll see the manipulation."

The soup course is served with a buzzing flourish.

"*Bon appétit,*" he says to Ilse, and nods to the food.

She wonders if he will continue to use the formal *vous* to address her for the next two weeks. Of course, she will wait for him to be the one to switch over, if he ever does, to the more familiar *tu*. The *tu* invites intimacy, while the *vous* maintains a guarded distance. Such calibration of relationship is embedded in the French language. The Danish sometimes distinguishes between the informal *du* and the formal *de,* but over the last century, the *de* has been mostly discarded. It makes life so much easier.

"Do you often meet the authors you translate?" he asks.

As he lifts his spoon, Ilse notices a gold wedding band on his slender left ring finger. He tilts his spoon away from him as he dips it into the soup, then sips delicately from the long side of the spoon, instead of gulping it down from the front.

"You're the first," she says. "Most publishers aren't willing to pay the price for travel, and also I think many, like mine, believe it can make the work more difficult."

"Comment?"

"The idea is that being on the outside and being required to use one's imagination is the key to getting inside. Also, meeting the author can take the translation in directions that aren't part of the author's writing. Many people believe it's best to let the words speak for themselves."

"Then, *mademoiselle,* or is it *madame?*"

"*Mademoiselle,*" she says.

He nods and seems to look at her a bit more intensely.

"Then, *mademoiselle,* you're on a dangerous mission."

She wonders if the mission would be less dangerous if she were a *madame.*

She mirrors his laugh and his soup-sipping.

"Precarious for sure."

"You may lose your way now that you've met me." He winks in a flirtatious way.

"I'm most afraid of losing my way in the thicket of your Provençal dialect. Levy's *Petit Dictionnaire Provençal-Français* may not be able to help me out of the weeds."

"Haha!" he laughs. "I'll be your guide, like Virgil for Dante through Purgatory and the Inferno. And I will lead you to Paradise, but like Virgil, I cannot enter there."

"That's when you'll take on another persona."

"You catch on quickly," says the Poet, tipping his head to one side, then taking another spoonful of soup.

This is so much fun!

"Other than to translate a fragmented language that flourished in the High Middle Ages, tell me the real reason you're here," he says, now serious.

He's waiting for her answer, but it's as if he already knows: that she was restless and needed to break free from place and time.

She sips her Ricard, then laughs uneasily. It's a false laugh, and she suspects he hears the artifice.

Now he's laughing, but she's not sure why.

She has the childish desire to hide under the table. When she glances around, she notices that the couple at the next table are looking over at them. Monsieur le Poète turns and tilts his head in their direction. It's a courtly gesture, a greeting from afar, like a nobleman to his people.

"Whatever the reason," he says, finally, "I hope we make your time here worthwhile."

"Conversely, I hope my visit is worthy of *your* time."

He turns his head, then looks at her out of the periphery of his eye, as if he doesn't believe her.

Of course, his time is more worthy than hers. Ilse feels undeserving of most things in life. Six years with Max Møllner reinforced the feeling.

A party of six is being seated at a nearby table. This group looks so fully as if they belong here, which they do, as does Monsieur le Poète. In their sense of ease, they define the French expression *être bien dans sa peau,* being comfortable in one's skin, a sensation that Ilse certainly does not know well. She closes her eyes to savor the taste of the soup and to identify an unfamiliar ingredient. Fennel? It's not unlike the taste of the Ricard.

"You've planned your arrival well," he says. "May is the symbolic month of troubadour love. 'When the days are long in May,' " he sings, then says, "Forgive my voice, but as you know, all troubadours sing their poetry."

And there, in the middle of the chatty, thronging Renaissance Café,

Monsieur le Poète leans forward and begins to incant in a soft, melodic voice,

> *Sweet the songs of birds afar,*
> *And when I choose from there to stray,*
> *I bring to mind a love that's far . . .*

"It's a riff by Jaufre Rudel," he explains in his lilting voice, "a troubadour who lived in the mid-twelfth century and was famous for developing the theme of *amor de lonh*, love from a distance. According to legend, Rudel put *amor de lonh* into practice: learning from returning Crusaders about the beauty of the countess Hodierna of Tripoli, he journeyed to meet her. When he finally arrived on the shores of Tripoli, sick and fading fast, the countess, who had gotten wind of his love for her but had never met him, is said to have hastened down from her castle and cradled the dying man in her arms.

"*Oui*," he adds. "*L'amour, c'est fou*, love is crazy."

She nods but feels that she doesn't know enough to agree or disagree. All she knows is that it is poetry, being with him.

"Every breath of this Provençal spring air will bring you closer to enlightenment. *Per solatz revelhar.*"

"Help!"

"To wake delight once more."

His face brightens as she laughs.

"If I knew Spanish or Arabic, it would be easier."

"Inès, my wife, grew up in Morocco. Her *jadda*, her grandmother, sang and spoke to her in Arabic, and Inès did the same with me. Inès was a brilliant musician: she played the oud, the parent of the European lute. She taught me the songs she knew, and when she forgot the words, I would supply new ones in Provençal, which she understood. Eventually, I became her singing Scheherazade, devising new lyrics to keep our love alive night after night."

He looks around. The waitress is beside their table within seconds. She replaces their soup bowls with the salads, then departs.

"I'm grateful that your poetry doesn't rhyme."

"It *should* rhyme, but I'm more focused on the role of rhythm. Most troubadour melodies are notated with neumes, which, unlike our musical notes, offer no indication of rhythm. The rhythm of many of the twelfth-century sung poems was the drumbeat of the military."

"I have a lot to learn," she says. "This morning, I stumbled on the word *Solelhós*."

"So-leel-oh-s," he pronounces slowly. "It means sunny. It refers to the weather but also to a person's disposition. I can see that the word describes you."

"Because of the warming light in this place!" she says, but she really wants to say *Because of you*. She's reflecting this man's seeming joy to be alive.

She removes her notebook from her knapsack and scribbles the word. With this one translated word, she might be able to justify her trip to Provence.

"Another thing I should mention . . ." she begins.

She was not going to tell him this! Now it's too late.

"I've never translated poetry, that is if you don't count some clumsy attempts in a class at my university long ago."

He leans back in his chair, and she can't read his expression.

"My publisher must really value my work. He sends me a translator who has never stepped foot in France, who doesn't know a word of Provençal, and who has never translated poetry. I'm not sure if this is a joke."

She's given away too much! Her French gig may yet be just that, a short-lived performance.

"You said we were meant to meet each other," she tries. "Also, my publisher doesn't know the part about my never having been to France."

His seagull eyebrows descend, his face solemn.

"I've done some research of my own, Mademoiselle Erlund. If the reviews of your work are verifiable, I'm in good hands. I don't speak much English, but my reading in the language is not bad. I read your last translation, the novel about the small-town tailor who falls in love with a client for whom he's sewing a wedding gown. I was intrigued by your ability to stay close to the text, and, as far as I could tell, to channel the author's tone, and most importantly, infuse the text with the author's depth of feeling. Unless that was *your* depth of feeling!"

She smiles. "Both of ours, I like to think."

"And your spoken French is quite remarkable for someone who's never been in this country before."

"As preparation for your work, I've been trying to read Bernart de Ventadorn," she says. It was her airplane reading. "It's the edition with the Provençal on the right side of the page, and the French translation on the left." De Ventadorn was a famous twelfth-century Provençal poet who lived at the court of Eleanor of Aquitaine.

She pauses to watch his eyebrows lift.

"It hasn't been easy," she adds.

"I wouldn't have believed you if you said it was. Forget the words. If you can get the rhythm of de Ventadorn, then we're in business. I wonder if you've heard this ditty by him. I will sing it in Provençal first, then in French."

He leans forward in his chair, and she turns her ear to him. He takes a deep breath, closes his eyes, and begins to sing.

> *May she have the courage*
> *to have me come one night*
> *there where she undresses*
> *and makes me a necklace of her arms.*

The couple to their left smiles at him, and the waitress, nearby, looks as if she is about to swoon.

"No, no, please don't!" he says, opening his eyes wide. "I hear you translating me in your head. Step away from the literal meaning and listen for the rhythmic structure of the song: the pitch, the tone, but most of all, the feeling."

Not only is her poetry education paltry, but she has no musical education. She'll never be able to transport this man's harmonic compositions onto a page.

"In my work and in that of all troubadours, sound always claims priority. If I'm truly descended from the troubadour Geoffrey Labaye, these poems should be sung. Sadly, no one trills these days, not even warbles, barely hums. I don't understand why our culture has made us feel ashamed to share such a vital part of ourselves. Why speak when we can sing?"

She nods and closes her eyes as he starts singing again. When he stops, she opens her eyes. She has understood nothing, but what she's heard has touched her core. It's as if she knew the meaning without comprehending the words.

"There, that was better. I could feel the stillness in your mind, and the openness. Don't berate yourself for not recognizing the actual words. If you offer each of my poems such mental silence, they will speak to your heart. The troubadours reached people through music. My goal is to reach people, not with words, but with the *feeling* of words."

She nods.

Émile! This work will be much more challenging than tiptoeing around Gaudet's well-placed word-mines.

"Yes, you're entering another world. There were troubadours in my family as far back as the eleventh century. Sometimes I think I may be a reincarnation of one of them."

"The last living troubadour." She hates that she's just said these words. It makes it sound as if he's going to die soon.

"I do have a son."

"The heir?"

"Sadly, he's not interested in anything to do with me or his heritage. He's chosen another path, one that is centuries ahead of mine. I'm the one in the wrong century."

"They lived where you do now? Your ancestor troubadours?"

It's a habit of hers, to change the subject when the conversation becomes uncomfortable.

"Yes, in the same house. Every generation since has occupied it, but sadly, I'm not sure about my son. He has broken . . ."

In her former life, she would have completed his sentence. But she waits, as she has noticed this man does with her. It's a new way of conversing, letting each word be heard, weighed, and balanced, then allowing for the possibility of a new thought to emerge.

"With tradition," he says, finally. "Inès told me to leave him alone, that he's a new soul, unlike she and I, who are old souls—"

"Ah, Geoffrey!"

The booming voice surprises her. When she looks up, a large man with a wide smile lighting up his tan face approaches their table. He has a gap between his two front teeth, and he's wearing the iconic blue-and-white-striped cotton sweater, dark shorts, and blue espadrilles.

The Poet stands.

"Georges! *Quelle surprise!* Georges, I would like to present Ilse Erlund." The Poet opens his palm in her direction. "This is the woman who has been sent to us to translate my gibberish into fine English."

Georges kisses her three times. Is this the village custom, or do all the French do this?

"Georges is my cousin."

"God help you, translating this man," says Georges.

"I'm easily assimilated," says the Poet.

"Only if the translator has a rich range of emotions."

They both look at Ilse. She may be a deep diver when translating fiction and nonfiction, but poetry may require a richer emotional understanding.

"*Mademoiselle,* don't listen to my cousin! Georges, take my seat," says the Poet, offering his cousin his chair.

"No, thank you. I can't stay," Georges says. "This man strings together words that convey absolutes. The emotions are buried so deeply inside the lines that sometimes you feel them days, even weeks or months later. No, I won't take a seat. I'm here to tell you that Hervé and I are counting on you for a game later this afternoon. You've been too much of a recluse."

"I'm working. Another afternoon."

"You can't refuse. We need your fire drive this afternoon."

"Not this afternoon, another day."

"We'll lose without you."

"Then lose without me. It's not the end of the world."

"Lose a game of *pétanque*? How can you say such a thing? If it isn't the crushing devastation of a lifetime to you, it is to me!" says Georges. "I'm sorry to interrupt your lunch." He bows to Ilse. "I'll get you next time!" Georges shouts out as he walks away.

"My wonderful cousin." The Poet's expressive eyebrows knit together, and he clears his throat. "Where were we, yes, the house, my son. My son has decided to live his life elsewhere," he says.

The Poet could have let that interrupted part of their conversation evanesce. He must wish to talk about his son.

Ilse nods.

"He may break what is left of my broken heart."

What was all laughter and light is now dismal and dark.

Ilse sips the Ricard and lifts her face out of the shade of the umbrella to feel the sun.

They had not ordered espresso, but as if on cue, the waitress is now beside them, placing the daintiest cup Ilse has ever seen in front of each of them.

"And a *tarte Tatin, s'il vous plaît,* just one, for the young lady. There's a poem in my book about a *tarte Tatin,* so it's required tasting. Now that I think of it, you should taste every word before translating it. The challenge is to make sure the words stimulate your palate as much as each forkful of this forthcoming *tarte.*"

Ilse has been so focused on the Poet that she hadn't noticed the departure of many of their fellow lunchers.

"*Et voilà.*" The waitress surely has wings hiding under her frilled apron.

"Why don't you come to my house tomorrow after lunch, around three o'clock, with your first volley of questions. You know my address from yesterday, but whatever you do, please don't walk via Route 7. The cars and trucks will run you off the road. There's a shortcut if you take the château's tunnel to my house. If you have time after our lunch now, I'll show you the way, à la Virgil . . ."

The *tarte Tatin,* a concoction of apple custard, baked apples, and crust, melts in her mouth. She knows after a few bites that a translated word will never come close to tasting so good.

—

AS SHE AND THE Poet walk to the tunnel, Ilse looks for the view of the blue Luberons. There it is, and here she is—in France, having had her first meal with a French person! Not only has he understood her, and she him, but her French has begun to feel more natural. Her endless listening to French podcasts through the days and nights must have helped.

She'd read that people change according to the language they speak. She likes herself better in French. She's somehow more bold, more interesting. She feels more alive.

Chapter 12

Walking through the dark tunnel under the grounds of the château to the Poet's house is taking more time today than it did when he showed her the way yesterday. Ilse checks the time on her phone. It had taken roughly fifteen minutes, but today, she's already been underground for about twenty-five. The Poet had told her that many of the chambers in the passageways carved out of rock were originally quarries used for building materials, and subsequently served as wine cellars for the château. This explains the musty scent of resin, the sour aroma of old wine, and the random barrels that she now notices in corners with her phone flashlight. She touches the slightly moist wall on her left. She must have taken a right turn too soon. She's hopeless with directions.

No phone service down here.

She feels panic rising in her stomach.

What if her phone flashlight goes dead? For the second time on this trip, she wishes she'd brought Beluga's compass with her. And what difference would that have made? She has no idea which direction she should be going. Ilse's imagination stirs, picking up bits and pieces of horror-story detritus as she walks. She'll be stuck in the tunnel for days. She'll have to scavenge for anything the mice have left, maybe even the mice themselves, and smash open one of these century-old wine casks to quench her parched throat. The Poet was joking about Virgil, but she may really need him to guide her out of this *Inferno*! After a few days, he'll send out a search party. People will find her dead drunk or just dead. She walks faster, her hand on the rough cave wall to guide her.

She recites aloud from the *Inferno.*

> *In the middle of the journey of our life,*
> *I found myself within a dark wood,*
> *where the straightway was lost.*

Dante would probably be horrified by the translation.

Ah! There's the oak barrel that the Poet had pointed out to her yesterday close to the start of their walk. She takes a deep breath. She realizes she's circled back to where she'd begun.

Where am I going?

She's tempted to exit the cave tunnel where she entered and walk the heavily trafficked Route 7. Get hit by a car or lost in a tunnel. She thinks of Jann, summons up her courage, and marches forth into the darkness again, this time carefully trying to recall every turn. For Jann's sake.

Ten minutes in, she spies the edge of daylight.

Yes! Thank you, Jann, you are my Virgil!

Once outside in the glorious sunlight, she takes the worn path through the hayfield that the Poet had shown her. She follows the line of cypress trees that leads to his house.

His address is 9 rue Myrtle. Of course the number of the Poet's house is nine, Jann's favorite number.

A view of the Luberon Mountains appears around the next corner, and Ilse thinks of herself two days ago when she arrived lost yet again, and so nervous. How different a person she is already. Her lips are forming around different words; her eyes are adjusting to different lights, colors, and faces. She's still anxious and jittery, but she's in a foreign country twenty-five hundred miles from her own and speaking another language!

She passes a vineyard on her left. The vines are as tall as she is, but the grapes draped inside are still green. When she squints at the rows of wires holding up the vines, the curved branches form a kind of script. They're like notes on a sheet of music. Vine language!

The vineyard is bordered by tall grasses and red poppies, hundreds of them. She's tempted to run through them, to lie down and share in the crimson glow of them.

Translate me into this color!

Beluga, you're wrong. There is more in the world than the wide expanse of the Arctic sky and the glossy icebergs that inhabit the coast like prehistoric beasts, and yes, okay, the majestic whales that vault from the sea and sprout fountains. There is more! Here is an enchanted land with mountains the color of lavender, endless warm days, and a profusion of red poppies blushing in the breezes. Fa and Malu, you who have never left Greenland, I wish you could see this!

And it occurs to Ilse that for all these many years, she's been living in a box that she and others have created for her—to be safe. Safe in a sea captain's house eroding gradually from the rising tides? *Her* form of safety took the guise of isolation. It was easy to be invisible in the pallid landscape of the Arctic. But in this sunny place, with this older but lively French man of letters, she feels as if she is undeniably eye-catching. It's as though she's breathing in color for the first time in her life. Can this be so, that all it took for her to find herself was to get out of the self-inflicted confines of her home and country?

In a story she'd read as a child, a girl digs to the other side of the planet to discover that everything there is upside down. Well, here everything is right side up. Upside down is where Ilse came from, especially when on a midwinter evening the moon shines from below, reflected on a sheet of ice.

Ahead of Ilse is the white stucco manor house with pale blue shutters that she'd seen on her first day in Belle Rivière. It is flanked by two outbuildings. The roof of the main house is a darker brown terra-cotta, not the orange-reddish color of the tile roofs that Madame Hugot, the witch in espadrilles, likes to fly over.

Another line of soldierlike cypress trees guards the residence on the left side, and a field of daisies borders the sandy path that is the driveway on the right. The drive is separated by that tree with the massive trunk that Ilse had admired on her first mistaken encounter with the Poet.

Ilse doesn't think of herself as a tree-hugger, but she's tempted to wrap her arms around this enormous trunk's wide girth. In this place, it's as if nature wants you to embrace it. *Touch me, smell me, taste me, listen to me, witness me.*

In contrast, nature in Greenland is formidable: it wags a finger at you, like Malu does. Watch out, a storm is brewing. Beware, the water's rising in your basement. Prepare, the wind will crash through your windows. Most people who dwell so close to the Arctic Circle live in fear. And for good reason. *Damn!* She hadn't remembered to nail plywood over the windows before she left. But she'll only be gone for two weeks, and it's May, for heaven's sake! Duggan would be reminding her that hurricane-force gales, the *piteraq,* have been known to wreak havoc through June.

She resists the temptation to photograph the Poet's house; she doesn't want to appear the nosy tourist who's never seen anything in her life, which is the truth.

She's half an hour late, thanks to the lost-in-the-cave detour. She sprays the lavender *eau de toilette* that she'd bought that morning on the insides of her wrists.

The front door is ajar. No doorbell. No knocker. When she raps with her knuckles, the door opens wide.

"*Monsieur?*" she calls, stepping into a large stone foyer. In the adjacent living room, three sets of tall French doors open onto a terrace and a view of lush green landscape beyond. The furniture in the room is covered in sheets. A life-size portrait of a woman occupies the left wall. She has long blue-black hair, enormous glossy mustard-brown eyes, and quite red lips. The artist has captured the intensity of her face, in the eyes mostly. She wears a floor-length, colorful, patterned abaya, a Moroccan shift.

This must be Inès. Will she be coming around the corner to greet Ilse?

A sudden burst of barking startles Ilse, and she turns to see one, two, three, four dogs on the threshold where the French doors connect the terrace to the living room.

An alarmingly large all-black mastiff groans, then barks in staccato. Now a collie and two smaller dogs join the cacophony of snarling and baying.

"It's just me," she says, stilled.

Any North Greenlander is used to aggressive husky-type dogs. Even so, this mastiff is a dog she'd imagine as one of Sherlock Holmes's hounds of the Baskervilles: robust, with a big square head, short muzzle, drooping jowls, and enormous paws. The four dogs continue to make a racket but have not stepped past the terrace threshold.

"*Arrêtez!*"

A deep voice in the distance.

The mastiff whines. The other dogs whimper and quiet down as the Poet enters the room from the terrace. Like a circus act, each of the dogs jumps onto a sheeted piece of furniture and settles down.

"The door was open," she says.

He greets her with his three cheek kisses, then twists in the direction of the portrait.

"I see you've had a glimpse of Inès, or rather, Inès has had a glimpse of you."

"It's a powerful portrait," Ilse says.

"She's the woman of my poems, the inspiration for everything I've written or have been . . ."

He gazes down at his worn red espadrilles. He shakes something in his pockets.

"I'm sorry," he says, facing away from her to the French doors.

Had Inès died recently? It's too rude to ask.

Seconds later, he looks up at her. "This happens from time to time.

Let's go into the garden, where I've prepared some refreshment. There's a slight breeze, which is the beginning of the mistral. I'm afraid it will bewitch us for the next three days, but it can also last more than a week."

The night before, she'd researched the cool, northwesterly wind that gusts through southern France along the lower Rhône River Valley toward the Mediterranean. Called "*le vent qui rend fou,*" the wind that makes one crazy, the mistral can reach up to fifty-six miles per hour, she'd read. It blows strongest and lasts longest in the transitions of the seasons. Belfries in hilltop villages in this area are constructed open to allow the powerful gales to pass through without resistance. And farmhouses are built to face south with their backs to the wind.

Ilse follows the Poet to the terrace and up a few stone steps to a grassy area under an olive tree. Directly under the silvery leaves, a square table is set with a white tablecloth, fluttering in the breeze. Behind the perch of table and three metal chairs is a vineyard, and beyond that, the ever-present backdrop of the Luberons, whose folds mimic those of the tablecloth.

How wonderful! A black cat lounges lengthwise on the table, its size occupying half the surface. Beside the now-stirring cat is a silver tray with a bottle of Ricard, two tall glasses imprinted with a fleur-de-lis inside a shield, a pitcher of water, a bowl of grapes, a glass carafe of coffee, two small espresso cups with saucers, and two thick, white cloth napkins. A handful of poppies and daisies in a blue ceramic vase holds down a small pile of paper.

"Please excuse Chou-fleur," Monsieur le Poète says, as he pulls out a wrought-iron chair for Ilse. "We're disturbing her favorite afternoon napping spot. Mine too, though I choose to lie on the grass, over there." He points to a shaded spot on the other side of the olive tree. "Sometimes, I escape into the middle of the vineyard where no one can find me, that is, no one except the vintner and his workers, but they only show up later in the summer."

Chou-fleur means "cauliflower" in English, though the cat, who could be Minou's French cousin, is entirely black. Chou-fleur purrs loudly as Ilse strokes her.

When the Poet sits, the dogs surround his chair, except for the smallest dog in the pack. He's reddish brown, and he's now biting at the hem of Ilse's skirt, which she pulls down with each gust of wind.

"What are their names?"

"Mastiff, that's his name, is the lion, and also lion-hearted; here's Ronsard," he says, pointing to the collie. "She corrals the group, and this is Carenza, very serious and sensitive. She's named after one of the first women to write Provençal verse in the Middle Ages. One of Carenza's poems begins with a nun addressing her, '*Na Carenza al bel cors avinen,*' Lady Carenza of the lovely, gracious body.

"Something makes me think that Carenza comes from the Basque territory, and that's where she left the secrets of her past. The one who likes your skirt, we think, is the youngster of the pack. His name is Orang-outang, but we call him Tang for short. Inès and I found him, a scrawny, starving, thirsty puppy on one of our mountain walks, and we could not stop him from following us home. Now look at him, he's a veritable bullfighter. It seems your skirt is the *muleta*."

The Poet moves the vase with flowers and his papers to the side of the table.

"I disturbed your writing," she says.

"Does a butterfly disturb a flower?"

She laughs.

"May I ask what this one is about?" she says, pointing to the top paper.

"About, about, about, I should write a poem about the word *about*. My poems aren't about anything." There's a slight edge to his voice. She hadn't meant to upset him. "They're reflections of the light, the sounds, and shapes around me. The law of reflection says that the angle at which a wave of light touches a surface equals the angle at which it is reflected. In this way"—and he looks up at the sky—"I am the echo of the sky, and the passage of the clouds, the contours of those mountains, of you here, now. The other day, on my way to visit a friend out of town, I noticed that a school bus had stopped by a cemetery down the road. Had a child asked the bus driver to visit the graveyard? Had the driver stopped along his route to pay his personal respects to someone? The juxtaposition of the bus filled with noisy children and the quiet serenity of the cemetery have changed the shape of me for the rest of my life."

A fluff of clouds sheathes the sun in the soft blue sky.

The Poet strokes Mastiff under his hanging jowls, then gazes at her.

"And you, I can see"—he nods his head—"you're reflecting someone . . ."

The cat stretches out, and the breeze blows one of the cloth napkins off the table. She catches it and places the Ricard bottle over it. She pets Chou-fleur.

He waits for her answer.

Who is this man? Has she ever encountered anyone who seemed to intuit her thoughts, or at least guess at them? Let alone anyone who was curious enough to try? Jann sometimes did, but he was her brother, and anyway, she and he were parts of the same being.

She could say she was thinking about Minou while petting Chou-fleur.

She relents.

"I was having a word with my brother."

"How long has he been away?"

"Five years."

She pictures the way Jann's face braved each day, the way he loved their parents more than himself, how he made Ilse feel like she belonged. To him, to life.

"He was thirty-one years old." She wonders if he has aged, or whether he's thirty-one years old for eternity.

Hold it together, Val would be telling her. *This is a business meeting.*

The wind whistles in and around the wrought-iron table legs and swirls the white cloth. The Poet's eyes on her face make her want to burst into tears. If she starts, she may never stop.

"My wife died five years ago today," he says slowly, each word as if it is a flower that he is placing on her grave. He grips the edge of the table and looks into Ilse's eyes in a way that makes her blush. "But for me, she's not up *there,* not that she doesn't deserve to be, well, maybe she doesn't." He looks down at the rippling tablecloth.

"I'm sorry," she says. Her words come out like empty things.

"To answer your earlier question, the poem I'm writing is about what is at stake when you give your heart to another."

What is at stake.

Tang is chewing her skirt. It's the only skirt she's brought, and she can see that the dog has already poked a hole in it, front center, with his sharp fangs.

"Tang, stop!" the Poet says. Mastiff growls.

Tang trots, tail wagging, to the Poet.

"I've given you the choice of a glass of water, a Ricard, or an espresso. Maybe you'd like all three? Simultaneously?"

He nudges the bowl of grapes closer to her. A pair of small scissors rests inside the bowl. Made especially for cutting grapes?

"Thank you," she says. "Water is fine. I can serve myself."

He pours the water to the rim of her glass with a shaking hand, then clips off a twig of grapes with the petite scissors and places the small bounty beside her glass. At her home, they pull off grapes with their fingers.

She's never eaten a grape that tasted so sweet.

"Thank you for lunch yesterday," she says. "It was a wonderful welcome to your . . ." She wants to say *life,* but says instead, "To Belle Rivière."

"*Avec plaisir.* Now, shall we start?"

She removes the manuscript from her bag and chooses a page on which she'd found more than a few impossible-to-translate Provençal words. She's embarrassed by the number of question marks she'd scrawled over the type.

She reads the title: "Inès, you left me." How could she have picked this painful love poem on the anniversary of his beloved's death?

He glances at the poem, upside down, and sighs, then smiles. The puffiness under his eyes that was blue is now gray, like a shadow.

"You have chosen well," he says.

How cruel it is of her to make this man revisit the pain that had caused him to write, possibly to exorcise himself of it in the first place.

"We can choose another one to start, especially . . ."

"We are on this earth to feel. That is the only thing we're required to do. So be it."

Chapter 13

"I MAY NEED A LITTLE RICARD BEFORE WE BEGIN," ILSE SAYS.

"Now you're speaking like a true Provençal."

It's the following afternoon at three o'clock, and today the mistral is blowing even stronger than it had the day before.

"After you drink this, you'll be thinking like one. Georges won't like it, but I'll join you. I have only an hour before my cousin will drag me away to *pétanque* practice. A week from this Saturday, we're playing our most competitive rival. You're welcome to come watch a bunch of old men toss metal balls. I'm known as the firebrand, but Georges is the one with the gentle, silvery finish."

"I'd like to come."

He pours an inch or so of the Ricard into each glass, then adds water.

"To you, Inès, wherever you are," he says, raising his glass to Ilse's, then sipping as she does.

Such a bright, sparkling blue are his eyes!

The Ricard coats her throat. While schnapps girds your belly against the cold, this liquor makes her feel inclined to dream. At this moment at home, she'd be shivering by the window, switching a mug of hot black tea from one hand to the other to warm them.

"I don't think I've heard conversational Provençal since I've arrived, not even between you and your cousin," she says as she places the pages of his poetry onto the table.

"True. Our beautiful age-old dialect is disappearing, and with it, its humanity, culture, and identity. About a million and a half people, mostly elderly who live in rural areas, speak a version of Provençal in their daily lives. Maybe about five million can understand and speak a few basic phrases. Provençal is one of these languages on its last legs, like I am."

Ilse is proud that Greenland claimed Greenlandic as its national language when it was on the brink of submersion into Danish.

She follows his eyes to a yellow bird alighting on a trellis in the vineyard. When he returns his eyes to hers, he smiles brightly. Just as he'd told her that the school bus in the graveyard had changed the shape of him, she wonders if seeing the brilliant yellow bird perched on a trellis has done the same. Maybe he would write a poem about it that afternoon. For a few moments, they listen to the bird's trilling.

She pets Chou-fleur with one hand, and with the other tries to keep Tang from chewing on her skirt.

"So which translating challenges do we have on the menu for today?"

She points to one of the many underlined Provençal words that she has not found in the dictionary.

"Ah," he says, as if with relief. "*S'amarzis* is to turn bitter." She makes a note in the margin.

"And this one?"

He sighs and leans back in his chair. "The phrase is complicated, especially for the French, which is why I decided to use the Provençal version. *Tan am midons e la tenh car* is 'I fear and cherish her so much.'"

He closes his eyes, takes a deep breath. "I hadn't realized that this translation work would affect me this way," he says.

When he opens his eyes, he touches one of many drooping poppies in the blue vase.

"Wildflowers are happiest tilting to the sun and dancing in the breezes of an open field," he says.

A mistral-swept cloud passes over the sun again, and she and the Poet are in the shade.

She waits.

Come back, Poet. Come back.

He takes a sip of the Ricard, then sits up straight.

"But of course, you've come to me at exactly the right time in my life. Come on! Let's go."

Expression by expression, he explains the words that Ilse has underlined, and the poems begin to take shape and meaning. But English can never replicate the flowing Provençal sounds of these words. How to transpose the music of one language into another? It's like telling an inanimate object, like a chair, to dance.

"Find the music that resides under the notes," he says out of the blue.

What does he mean? She feels almost ill with incomprehension.

"You are capable of this, Ilse; I know you are."

He's reading her despair.

"In the translations that I've read of yours, the parts that I could understand," he continues, "I've been impressed by your sensitivity to language. You have a way of keeping the door ajar for the written word to open and blossom. I think it's because you know—intimately—the life of an indigenous language, and ultimately, it's why I chose you as my translator."

She reads the next poem to herself while he sits back and sips the Ricard. She roughly translates the parts she understands.

You gave me your hand in life
But not in death.
I would have disobeyed
'til death do us part,
and beguiled the stars
with you for eternity.
But no, now you
Doze, a lizard on

A hot, hushed wall,
You incubate in your tomb.

Come back to me
Even if only
to sing a lullaby
when I am dying.

Would Ilse ever feel this passionately for another? She'd thought she loved Max, but then he became a stranger. Take that back: he was always a stranger.

The Poet empties his glass of Ricard.

"When I read your poems, like this one," she says in a hesitating voice, "I feel envious of a love as profound as this."

She would never be so open with anyone at home, not even Val. Perhaps it's his age, or the fact that they come from such different places, or that she's only visiting for two weeks.

His eyes follow a swallow swooping in waves above the rows of vines, then settle on hers. His look is not one of pity but of something like reverence, that she could have been so bold as to say this to him.

"My son has said the same thing. In fact, he's said it on several occasions. You are here for only a short time, but there are ways to open one's heart. In my experience, it has to do with listening, but first to yourself."

She wipes the space over her lip, where she perspires when she's nervous.

"Speaking of listening"—she changes the subject—"one day, may I record you singing one of your poems, so that when I'm back in Greenland finishing the translation, I can try to be true to your resonance, to the sound of you?"

"*Bonne idée,*" he says.

Phew, back on safe territory.

"Perhaps not today, as my voice is a bit wobbly. But another time."

She leafs through the dog-eared pages to ask more questions. It's hard to see the text underneath her scribbled questions, comments, and highlighting.

"Translating involves a lot of false starts," she says to excuse the messy margins.

He has taken a page from her stack and doesn't seem to like what he's reading. "I never hit the mark on this poem," he says. "*Voilà*, here's the one that I will read for your recording another day. It is titled 'Bruised—' "

Mastiff barks and dashes across the terrace, stopping at the French doors. The other dogs run after him, making a racket, but Chou-fleur looks up at Ilse as if to ask, *Do I have to go?*

The Poet glances at his watch and stands. It's Georges, galloping awkwardly across the parterre. Ilse had not noticed his limp the other day.

"You can see why I retreat into the middle of the vineyard."

The Poet calls off the dogs.

"Time to go, firebrand cousin!" Georges calls out as he approaches the table.

"It's not time yet!" the Poet yells back. "You said four o'clock!"

"*Bonjour, mademoiselle.*" Georges, now at the table, bows deeply. "I'm sorry to interrupt, but I must take my cousin away." He's breathless. "We must practice and strategize, cousin. Isseee, is that correct?"

"*Oui.*"

He pronounces her name like Donny does. Oh, Donny! Pronouncing the combination of letters in Ilse's name also proves challenging for the French.

"The game against Goult is eight days away. Goult is our most competitive adversary, and Po, here, is our secret weapon."

"Po?" she asks.

"Yes, Po," Georges says. "The whole village will be watching. I've just been told that they're planning a celebration around our victory. For the honor of our village, we must be champions. Please excuse me, *Isseee,* but this is more important than anything having to do with poetry."

"Surely not more important than a poem called 'Bruised Appetite'?" says the Poet.

"I realize your poems are critical for saving souls, but what we need right now is to lift the spirit of Belle Rivière. We'll do that by winning."

"I'll meet you at the square after I change clothes."

"*Allez!* I'll give you twenty minutes while I rustle up Hervé. *Au revoir, Mademoiselle Isse.* When we win, I hope you'll translate the results for the world." He jogs lopsidedly to the French doors, then turns back with his wide, gap-toothed smile.

"Aie!" he cries out as he smacks his head on the side of the doorframe and disappears into the room beyond.

Ilse collects her notes and pages and places them into her knapsack.

"Will you forgive me," the Poet says, "if I'm tempted to call you Île? As you've just heard, *Ilse* is difficult to say in French. A poet cannot help himself: you seem more like an Île than an Ilse to me." *Île* is "island" in French.

"You may call me whatever you like," she says. She won't mention that at home in Greenland, she'd been taught that islands, mountains, hills, even a single rock can be offended if you call them by a name of your choosing in passing. It's not a good idea to attract nature's attention unless it's extremely important.

"I will call you *Île du Nord,*" the Poet says as he walks her to the path in the direction of the tunnels under the château.

Island of the North. With three French words, *Île du Nord,* the Poet has translated her into his language.

Chapter 14

THIS AFTERNOON, ILSE RECORDS THE POET SINGING "BRUISED Appetite." The combination of his singing voice and the steady buzz of bumblebees in the nearby honeysuckle blossoms makes for an orchestral symphony.

They've started at five o'clock this afternoon instead of the usual three o'clock because the Poet had a meeting with the vintner to discuss introducing ladybugs, a natural predator for aphids and other unwanted vineyard pests.

Ilse is holding her phone under the Poet's chin, recording his voice as he sings. She's so close, she can feel his breath on her face. She closes her eyes. What? When she opens her eyes, he is kneeling and lifting his hands to her. She blushes, almost believing that he is singing the song specifically for her. The words he's chosen seem strangely suited to her. One of the refrains even includes her new nickname. He's a conjurer, the Poet.

"It's as if you wrote that song especially for me," she ventures.

His face brightens, or is that because yet another cloud has been sent farther south by the mistral?

"You caught me! Singers of tales must think on their feet. As you can undoubtedly hear, I'm out of practice. But since you've arrived and have been demanding all kinds of things from me, including my voice, I've begun to sing more frequently again."

"I wish to hear you sing every day, then," she says.

He darts his twinkling eyes at her.

"Beware of what you wish for, lest it come true."

He has used the more familiar *tu*.

She smiles at him, but the moment when their eyes meet is too intense, so she looks down at Tang and strokes the pup's short, coarse fur.

Not for long. Mastiff is barking, and Tang and the two other dogs take off in the direction of the house. Jean-Pierre, dapper in his tilted black beret, is making his weekly Saturday visit, Ilse learns, to exchange two bottles of his cousin's red wine with two from Domaine Labaye. Jean-Pierre's cousin, Étienne, is a vintner at Domaine Saint Hilaire, the vineyard on the other sloping side of Belle Rivière.

If it were her first day in the Poet's world, she might have asked why he and Jean-Pierre don't exchange a case at a time, but by now, she understands that the visit and the banter about the weather and viticulture are more important than trading bottles.

"Jean-Pierre, you're late today." The Poet rises.

And this is the Poet's life: Georges pops by several times a week to talk *pétanque*, Jean-Pierre comes around to exchange bottles of wine, and through the week, there are other village visitors, all welcome, all convivial, all friends.

"I hope you've brought me the 2016s," the Poet says, after introducing Jean-Pierre to Ilse. She remembers reading his name and title, *Président*, at the bottom of the Manifesto of Le Cercle Républicain.

To Ilse, the Poet says in an excited voice, "You must experience the scent of *muguet* in Étienne's vinegar of that year."

"Vinegar?"

"Our little joke. Jean-Pierre, have a seat!"

Jean-Pierre holds up his two bottles with a sly smile. "And I hope *you've* pillaged two of your 2012s." To Ilse, he whispers conspiratorially, "Best year for truffles, perhaps ever." He smacks his lips.

Before she knows it, Jean-Pierre has opened the 2016 Saint Hilaire with the wine opener on his keychain, and the Poet is toasting *les muguets,* lilies of the valley, of which he says Ilse is one. Then he turns to her and sings so gently they can barely hear him. It's a song in Provençal.

"It's about a cluster of bellflowers crowning a young woman's head," the Poet whispers to her.

Jean-Pierre's small brown eyes open wide as he looks from the Poet to Ilse. She feels her face warm. A few minutes later, the three are laughing and toasting again, this time to truffle hunting, Jean-Pierre's favorite sport.

"And to my truffle-sniffing dogs!"

Jean-Pierre departs gleefully with his two bottles of Labaye 2012.

Because the Poet says the devilish mistral has cleared the skies, he invites Ilse to join him, that is, after they complete a few more pages of translation, for a "Sunset Ricard" at La Trinquette, one of his favorite restaurants in the village. Ilse had had to look the word up to discover that *une trinquette* is the metal triangle attached at the bow of the boat that keeps the staysail upright. The Poet's friends Laurent and Chloé own and run the restaurant. During the off season, they enjoy sailing a small skiff on the Mediterranean.

By the time Ilse and the Poet arrive on the small terrace on the second floor, the sunset over the Luberon Mountains is a fiery red melting into a rueful orange.

Choosing coffee instead of another Ricard—Ilse is already under the influence following the afternoon wine tasting—Ilse offers to help Chloé, who misses these magical sunsets because she's downstairs, taking care of customers' dinner orders.

"*Non, non,*" Chloé calls out, after declining Ilse's offer. "*Profitez du coucher de soleil!* Take advantage of the sun that's going to sleep!

Ilse loves how the French say *coucher de soleil.* In Greenlandic, sunset is *unnuk,* a declarative and simple "no sun."

Pascal, owner of the restaurant Le Teston, across the way, joins their cabal for a sunset *apéro,* aperitif. Pascal wears his hair in a ponytail and has a small gold hoop earring in one ear. Here comes another man. He has thick brown eyebrows, long sideburns, a sharp chin. The Poet leans in her direction to tell Ilse that he's the village butcher.

"Raymond, *un Ricard*?" Chloé asks.

Raymond nods.

What transpires among these people gathered for sunset is like a riff in jazz where it's unclear who will show up, which and how many instruments will be playing, what the subject will be, and how long it will continue. There's no agenda, only fluidity, spontaneity, and possibility, the joys of friendship. It's not unlike a *kaffemik* in her country, but there, the whole community shows up!

Monsieur and Madame, the parents of Pascal, arrive, three kisses, three kisses, even to Ilse. Someone jokes about the basket of bread that Monsieur is carrying, that the baguettes are *ancienne*, not *tradition*, which Ilse has learned, are crisper than the chewier *anciennes*. Pascal's father is laughing, insisting that the *anciennes* are for Pascal's restaurant. He pulls out the one *tradition* baguette, which is for his and Madame's dinner that night.

The discussion turns to the *pétanque* match, a week away.

Of course!

The game is not the local pastime that Ilse had imagined. According to the poster pinned up next to the Manifesto in Le Cercle, the winning team will compete in the qualifying rounds for the World Championship, organized by the International Federation of Pétanque held in the Bois de Boulogne in Paris.

Laurent lifts his hands. "Our match, next Saturday evening, is the biggest night of the year in our small village." He and Chloé are offering one-time-only take-out Brie and ham sandwiches for the spectators. Ilse claps her hands in excitement. Luckily, her flight back isn't until the following Tuesday.

"It's an old man's game," the Poet whispers to Ilse.

"How can you say that when my daughter plays it," says Pascal, who'd overheard. "A group of her friends and she play after school in the square against the boys. The girls call the boys 'fannys.' '*Ils sont fanny!*' 'Fanny,' " Pascal turns to explain to Ilse in French, "is the word for the player who scores no points."

"It's up to you, Po," says Laurent, "to put the Gloating Goults in their place. I hope you've been practicing. When you're on, you're our best player."

"When I'm *on,*" the Poet says, bowing his head. "Don't worry. Georges is the best *pointeur* on the team." To Ilse, he boasts, "Georges can toss the ball closest to any *bouchon,* no matter what distance."

"We're counting on *you,* Po," says Chloé, smiling at the Poet from the doorway.

"Chloé's going to take the night off," says Laurent.

"The pressure's on." Po takes a sip of the Ricard. "Île du Nord, here, has never seen the game played."

"Not possible!" the taciturn Raymond says, turning his chair to Ilse and opening his eyes wide. He downs the last of the Ricard and leaves five euros on the table. Shaking his head, the Poet returns the euros to Raymond.

"*Celui-ci est pour moi.*" This one is on me.

"When I watched it for the first time as a kid," Laurent continues, "I wondered what all the fuss was about: a bunch of old men on a patch of dirt throwing a ball. It takes time to catch on to the subtleties of the game, the personalities, the strategizing, the hand-eye skill."

"Maybe you can import the game to Greenland?" says Laurent.

"Your *boule* would be a small chunk of ice," says the Poet.

"We already play soccer on ice," says Ilse, laughing.

"Even elderly men?" asks Pascal.

"Maybe not the very elderly." Given her country's harsh landscape, the wise elderly stay close to home.

"I find it hard to imagine your icy world," says the Poet.

"Don't listen to him. He's lying," says Chloé, now joining them. "Po, you could whip up a poem about a *boule* made of ice in seconds. Let's hear it before the sun sets and before our first customers arrive."

The Poet raises his forefinger to his chin.

"Let's see . . ." His eyes are livelier than they'd been just moments before, lit from inside, and eager for an unfurling.

La boule de glace
vole à travers
la terre gelée d'Arctique . . .
Personne ne peut l'attraper,
sauf le soleil,
qui la fait fonder,
ou l'enfant,
qui la lèche
Et puis sourit.

The group claps their hands.

"*Impeccable!*" shouts Laurent.

His poem is about a scoop of ice cream that flies across the Arctic shelf, and no one can catch it except for the sun, which melts it, or else the child who licks it and then smiles.

"Which is it, the sun, or the child's tongue?" asks Pascal.

"Which do you like better?"

Poetry by popular consent.

"I root for the sun," says Laurent.

"And I prefer the child," says Chloé.

"I agree with Chloé," says the Poet.

Ilse would keep both in the poem.

After the sun sets and dims their world, Ilse walks with the Poet back to the entrance of the tunnel, where he embraces her with his three goodbye kisses. His eyes twinkle as he twists for a last glance at her before heading into the dark.

Ilse had never imagined that she would experience such joy here in Provence, spending time with a person who relishes words as much as she does. Provence is her new love; its people, the Provençals, are her second love; and yes, the Poet is her third love. If a body can know more than a mind, her body feels at one with this world. It's as if she's a vine, belonging among many in a large thriving vineyard. She can thank the Poet for introducing her to his way of life, his friends, and most intimate of all, to his language.

On the way back to the Hugots', Ilse passes Raymond on the street.

He's loading the plastic boar's head that had been mounted above the door of his butcher shop into his van. Ilse rushes over to help his daughter, who's having difficulty hoisting a large package into the van.

"Monsieur, que faites-vous?" Ilse asks.

"On ne peut pas gagner sa vie dans ce village," he says. One can't make a living in this village.

But Belle Rivière is supposed to be the perfect village. Where else in the world would you find a butcher shop that's also an art gallery? Raymond and his wife, Simone, support local artists and artisans by selling their sculptures and paintings of bulls, boars, cows, pheasants, and other such livestock.

Raymond tells Ilse that their destination is Apt, half an hour away, where there's a larger local population.

"Apt is a town, not a village," he says, frowning. "Too bad it's not as beautiful."

That night, Ilse asks Madame Hugot at her sink headquarters about the butcher.

"It's the secondary homeowners," Madame says, narrowing her eyes. "They've bought up all the houses in our village, but they come here only twice, sometimes once a year. The full-time population is shrinking, and our local businesses can't survive without them. Look around at the hilltop villages. The designation 'Les Plus Beaux Villages de France' is destroying us. We've become seasonal tourist destinations. Pretty soon, the *boulangeries* will move out. And then we'll be a museum."

Paradise is in the process of becoming lost.

Chapter 15

"SHALL WE GET TO WORK?" THE POET SHOUTS FROM THE threshold of the balcony of Le Cercle Républicain.

It's Sunday morning. She hadn't expected to see him today. Le Cercle must be part of his Sunday morning rounds.

Sitting with her *café allongé*—she thought she'd try another type of coffee—in the corner of the small balcony, overlooking the splendor of the world, she's been thinking sadly of her return flight back to the Arctic north in only nine days. There's a chill in the air this morning, and she shivers at the thought of the frigid damp Greenland spring.

Daily coffee gallantry is lovely to witness. The Poet is placing euros on the counter to pay for his and probably everyone else's espresso. In this *bar tabac*, it seems as if the customers rarely pay for themselves.

The Poet is the heart of Le Cercle, and Le Cercle is the heart of this village. Here, his loyal compatriots sustain him, nourish him, laugh with him, and he does the same for them. He's approaching her table, carrying a cup of coffee and a plate of two croissants. Despite the forever-golden sun, his face looks pale.

"I thought you create in the morning, and we word-wrestle in the afternoon," Ilse says, standing to greet him.

During their three-cheek-kiss embrace, there's an instant, as the

Poet moves from one cheek to the other, when their breaths intermingle. But then it's over, and of course, she thinks she's imagined it.

The French! Or is it the Poet? Is he wishing to take their relationship beyond a professional one?

"What keeps an old man old is the inability to change," he's saying. "I'm thinking that working with you in the morning light will inspire me to be creative in my afternoon lulls. If it's all right with you, I'd like to try it."

"*C'est mieux pour moi*. It's better for me."

"I knew you'd use those exact words! Look, I've written them down." He shows her the small square paper napkin upon which her French words are written in his script. He must have scrawled them at the bar when he spied her on the balcony.

"I'm predictable," she says, "and you're a magician."

"A little guessing game I play with myself. To see if I'm still tuned in as a human."

"You're challenging me to be unpredictable."

"Please don't change, Île du Nord. Stay exactly as you are." He shoots her an intense glance under his seagull eyebrows.

"I used to know who I am," she says, "but lately, I'm not so sure." As Ilse was becoming more versed in the Poet's language, she had the feeling that a part of herself that had been closed off was slowly opening. It was as if he was, meeting by meeting, expanding her set of five senses to include many more.

"Look into my eyes," he says suddenly, with an intense look. "Our conception of ourselves is often unclear, but deep down, we know who we are. Sometimes, all we need is for another to confirm our colorful splendor."

Six years of Max's coldness was somehow more comfortable.

"No. Really stare into my eyes."

His eyes are the sea on sunny, freezing days in Oqaatsut.

"Now tell me your name."

"Ilse Erlund." Her voice wobbled.

"Keep looking into my eyes. Now say your name again."

"Île du Nord," she says firmly.

She closes her eyes and feels a tranquility spread like a warm blanket over her body. So that's who she is.

"Now that we've cleared that up, do you happen to have your work with you?"

"Always," she says. "Predictable once again."

"You see, you do know who you are."

She loves to watch his eyes turn into crescents when he laughs.

She dips into her knapsack and removes the five poems that she'd chosen the night before for today's translating work. Oh no! He's looking down at her ugly black-and-white sneakers.

"These are for you," he says, pointing to the croissants.

"I can't eat two. One is for you."

"I have no hunger these days."

"I will give you some of my hunger," she says. She pulls off a bit of croissant, and as she eats it, it flakes in crumbs onto her lap.

His loud laugh surprises her.

"It's easier to eat a croissant like this," he says, and he takes a bite from one end of the second croissant. She smiles and copies him.

"It's a miracle to have this little balcony to ourselves. It may not last long. This morning, we can see the spread of Cavaillon and the outline of the Alpilles. *Allons-y.* Let's get started."

She's grateful for his wish for expediency. In what time she has left, how can she possibly catch this world in her net and then set it free in a different form?

She won't admit to Émile that some of the expressions that confuse her aren't Provençal but simply French. Over the last few days, she's had the sinking feeling that no matter how long and how much she studies French, she'll never be able to grasp the supple and nuanced language of a local. How could she have chosen a profession in which, despite relentless searching for parallels, no absolutely true equivalents exist? Thankfully, the Poet doesn't seem to mind.

In the poem titled "The Water Jug," in which a woman fails to balance a jug of water on her head, Ilse has underlined the phrase *yeux bordés d'anchois.*

"Eyes rimmed with anchovies," he says. "A favorite of mine. It means to have red-rimmed eyes, due to fatigue. Just look at mine, and you'll see."

His eyes do look a bit redder than normal.

A couple makes their way to the table next to theirs, and the Poet watches as they rearrange the chairs to look out at the view. The way they've suited up nicely for the day makes Ilse think they're not from Belle Rivière. The locals often look as if they've rolled out of bed. She detects a German accent.

"Where were we?" he asks, looking down at her pages.

She points out *être couvert comme Saint Georges.*

"Nice one. I included that expression for my cousin. The phrase means to be dressed like St. George in his heavy armor in preparation for killing the dragon."

"You mean killing the other team in *pétanque,*" she says.

He claps his hands together. His eyes are sparkling again. "You're catching on, Île du Nord!"

"This Provençal line, *farai un vers de dreyt nien,* pops up in several of your poems."

"It's a poet's prerogative to repeat himself, especially if he's in his seventies. As you know, most songs have refrains. This one means 'I've composed a song without meaning.' To me and my troubadour ancestors, as we've discussed, meaning is of lesser value than the pitch or tone of the melody."

The woman at the next table holds her pearl necklace up to the view as if to see if it reflects the purple color of the mountains. This place makes people look at life through different lenses. The receding morning mist in the valley now reveals the upper crest of the wave of the Luberons.

"And this one? *Mout jauzens me prenc en amar?*"

"The theme of so many troubadour poems: 'Great is the joy that I grab hold of in love.' "

As she scribbles in the margin, she's thinking that words belong to this man as if they are part of his body. When she's alone with her work at night, sometimes she feels the need to give her translated verbiage a good rousing to get the blood flowing or to place a flame under an expression to heat it up. Ultimately, every word she chooses to replace one of his must be as vibrant as the Poet is—and worthy of him.

"I feel like a gardener, and you're supplying me with fertilizer to nourish the words and make them flourish and grow robust."

"Very good, *ma traductrice*," my translator.

Please repeat those words: ma traductrice.

"I can tell you this because I'm an old man," he says, his voice gentler than when lancing the words in translating mode, "Île du Nord, your presence is making *me* flourish and grow robust."

She blushes. Everything inside her feels warm.

"You're being true to your troubadour self," she says.

A deflection.

He frowns. A lock of hair has fallen over his brow. "I'm not being true to anyone but you."

Tears gather at the back of her throat.

Don't cry, she tells herself. The woman behind the bar, Ilse had found out from Madame Hugot that her name was Carole, is watching from inside.

He's nodding.

"Please don't deny me my feelings. You're so fresh and open, and even though you don't know it, so true to who you are. It's as if you've dropped down from one of those feathery cumulus clouds over there, especially for me."

She follows his gaze to the clouds.

"So what kind of translator are you really, Île du Nord?"

Will he touch her hand that rests on the table beside her pen? He's looking at it as if he's tempted.

No. Instead, he gestures with his chin to the half-eaten croissant on her plate.

"I haven't given you a chance to finish your breakfast," he says.

"Only if you eat yours," she says, picking up her croissant.

"You need more nourishment than I," he says, "especially as you adapt our Romance language that spends so much time indulging and luxuriating in the ineffable, into the more blunt and earthy Anglo-Saxon."

She can breathe again. They're back on the safe terrain of work. The mist is gone from the valley, and the pale lavender mountain stands revealed in full sun.

"A well-known translator, David Bellos," she says, "believes that in our work, *everything* is effable."

"Surely, you don't agree?"

She hesitates, then thinks of *la grasse matinée.*

"We poets, especially, use spaces between words, pauses, to try to convey a deeper meaning that words will never be able to capture."

And then Monsieur le Poète begins to cough. He pushes his chair out to stand, and still coughing, turns away from Ilse toward the view.

"*Ça va?*" she asks, beside him.

He can't seem to stop. With a trembling hand, he brings a wrinkled white cotton handkerchief up to his lips.

"I get this cough," he says in chunks of words, trying to clear his throat, but his voice clogs, "when the mistral is here. There, that's better. I have the ineffable feeling"—and he coughs again into his handkerchief—"that the mistral will torment us for another few days."

Ilse runs to fetch a glass of water. Carole is no longer behind the bar. From inside, Ilse hears the Poet continuing to cough. She slips behind the sacred territory of the bar and fills a glass with water from the tap.

Carole appears.

"*Et alors!*" she roars in her raspy voice.

"Monsieur le Poète." Ilse points to him.

The woman with the pearl necklace is standing, offering him her glass of water.

Carole frowns.

"*Allez, allez!*" she says, shooing Ilse to the balcony.

The Poet takes the glass from Ilse with a shaking hand, while holding a handkerchief to his nose. His face is flushed, his eyes red and watery.

"Thank you. This kind woman has also offered me hers." Ilse notices the empty glass on the table. He coughs again, then sits down hard on his chair. Ilse sees Carole's concerned face at the door of the balcony.

Ilse and the Poet remain in silence for some time. His eyes are closed. The poet, composing himself.

"Shall we walk back to your house?" she asks when he opens his eyes and looks at her.

"Yes," he says hoarsely, turning to gaze at the view, then back at her. "The sun is filling the deepest folds of the Luberons." He moves his chair out from the table and stands. "I'm surprised Carole hasn't thrown us off, or else sent Jean-Pierre, the president, to do her bidding. We're taking up valuable real estate on a Sunday, at prime time no less."

A couple looks hungrily at their table from the balcony's interior door.

On their way out of Le Cercle, the Poet places a short stack of euro coins on the bar and thanks Carole.

"Stay out of the mistral," she says to him, motherly kind.

He nods and laughs, then coughs, handkerchief up to his lips. His breathing is heavy.

"I'll walk back with you," Ilse says.

"Thank you, Île du Nord, but I'll accept your company only to the tunnel. I have composed some of my best poems alone in those dark corridors, and I feel a few coming my way."

At the tunnel's opening, he brushes her cheek three times with kisses as he does, then steps a few feet from her and bows.

And she curtsies. She never knew she possessed this gesture in her vocabulary of movements. She watches his white shirt pass through the shadows of the grotto three times before he is gone.

Please get home safely, Monsieur le Poète. Please.

Chapter 16

FROM FAR AWAY, ILSE CAN SEE THE POET STANDING AT HIS FRONT door. It looks as if he's been waiting for her for some time. He must sense her anxiety about the numerous Provençal expressions and words still to be addressed.

He's wearing navy trousers and his uniform of a long white poet's shirt and a shorter black vest. She's surprised to see white whiskers on his cheeks and chin. His face is gray, and the patches under his eyes look puffier than yesterday. He looks as if he could use some fresh air.

He opens his arms to welcome her inside the house, then takes her hand. His hand is cool despite the warmth of the day. He guides her past the worktable under the olive tree toward the vineyard.

"We're starting with a walk today," he says.

At the edge of the rows of vines, he lets go of her hand to remove his sandals. "It feels good to go barefoot after a sloggy winter. Those sneakers of yours must be hot."

She's about to defend her sneakers. They have never made her feet feel hot, but then again, it's rarely warm in Greenland.

He slips off his sandals, and she her sneakers. Seeing their shoes lined up next to each other fills her with an unexpected sense of contentment, something she would imagine shared by old partners in life.

His feet are tanned, with pale, clipped nails, while her feet are lily white.

The Poet bends his arm so that it forms a triangle, and as if it's a square dance, she places her hand inside the shape. He is walking with a slight limp, and she adjusts her pace to his as they enter the grassy path into the vineyard. Her bare feet have never felt anything so soft and springy in nature!

They duck around curling sprigs and buds of leaves that shoot out from the horizontally trained arms of the vines. Under the vines, she spies clusters of the dangling green grapes, shiny from the morning dew. The air is fresh and smells of spice and wet, fertile soil.

"Because we had a few surprisingly frigid cold spells this year, our Grenache harvest will be late. The good news is that cold weather ensures a uniform grape size and a strong and lusty taste. Marie-Violette, my friend from the village, has brewed a fresh pot of coffee for us, and she's even brought it out for me to my special spot. Only she, the dogs, the harvest workers, and now you know of this place."

He had not mentioned Inès. Nor his son.

He stumbles a bit, as if sensing her thought.

"Are you feeling a little . . ."

"Yes, weak in the knees today. But don't tell Georges. He will go *catatonique* if he suspects I am anything less than a firebrand for Saturday's match."

"Should you be checking with your doctor?"

"Not you too! Georges won't stop asking me that question. Carole knows best. It's the mistral. I'll be my fiery self by Saturday."

The vines are denser and taller the farther they advance inside the vineyard.

He trips on a branch in the path, and she uses all her strength to catch him and hold him up. She grasps his arm tightly now.

This is a sudden change from the Poet's seemingly unshakable composure when they met less than a week ago at the Renaissance Café. Does the mistral have such an adverse effect on people?

"I've considered dying in the middle of this vineyard," he says suddenly. "It would be nice to imagine my blood mixing with the makings of wine. Grand Cru Geoffrey Labaye. Perhaps the sommelier would describe it as rhapsodic."

She laughs gently, but it's not funny.

He leads her left, then right, and then left again, and it reminds her of her first ramble in the dark tunnel under the château. The Poet seems to favor secret, circuitous ways of getting places.

They are now in the thick of vines, and it feels like being in the swell of a large ocean. All she can see is the expanse of blue sky above them. The vines muffle the leaf-rustling whirr of the mistral that was so evident when they were near the house. It's oddly quiet now, and hotter, and she is grateful to be barefoot.

"Forgive me if I talk of death," he says, stopping. "I want to make it my friend . . . so when it comes, I can take it by the arm just as you took mine at the beginning of our walk, trusting me to guide you."

He stares ahead of him, but it's almost as if he does not see.

"Inès spoke a lot about death. She was born in death, or rather through it. Her mother died because of birth, and every day I was with her, or so it seemed to me, Inès flirted with it—death—then crashed headlong into it."

He veers off the path, and she follows, attached to him, to fasten a stray vine back to the wire trellis.

"How did it happen?" she asks. "That is, if it's not too painful to talk about."

He stops walking to look at her, as if to make sure she really wants to know. Then he nods, and they continue on the path through the vines.

"It was a Porsche convertible, red, of course. A former lover offered it to her. We only had the old truck at the time. When I told her to refuse such a gift, she became obsessed to have it, and then it appeared one day with the man in it. I heard them laughing in the driveway out front. I ran to the window. He was older than I, Italian, with a mustache, and of course, handsome. He had large, brown, wet eyes, not unlike a Labrador's. When he finally left, after, to my shock, a long kiss on the lips, she took the Porsche for a drive, and when she returned her eyes were wild with glee as if she had experienced something I would never be able to grasp. After that drive, she never lost that almost feral, desperate look in her eyes. I considered crashing the car myself to get rid of it, but she did that fine on her own, a year after it and the Italian arrived."

How tragic. The Poet lost his beloved in a crash like Ilse had. She can find no words to respond.

"Voltaire said the secret to being a bore is to tell everything about yourself. Come on, we're almost there."

"I lost my brother in a motorcycle accident," she says.

He turns toward her suddenly and hugs her, and rather than feeling awkward, it's as if he's brought her into a safe resting place where no harm can reach her.

"You see," he says, still in the hug, "we didn't meet by coincidence."

They separate when they hear Mastiff baying close by. That must be him and the other pups rustling in the leaves in the row of vines behind them.

"*Un sanglier!* A wild boar!" the Poet yells, pulling her back and close to him, as a stocky, gray-brown pig with tusks dives onto the path three feet away from them.

Ilse has seen polar bears at close range, but nothing with tusks like these. The boar is in the middle of the path staring them down.

"Hold my hand, keep your eye on him, as we slowly back away," the Poet says in a calm voice, as they step quietly backward into the vines behind them.

Here comes Mastiff, baying and snarling and charging the wild pig! The boar dives at the dog, aiming his sharp prongs, but Mastiff leaps out of the way. When the three other barking dogs arrive on the scene, the boar plummets back into the vines in the direction it came. Mastiff and the dogs follow it, baying and barking.

Ilse is shaking. The Poet continues to hold her hand as he wipes his brow with his other hand.

"*Sangliers* are whip-fast, but Mastiff will herd this one safely away from the vineyard. That boar, I think it's the same one, wreaked horrendous damage last winter. I don't want to know how many vines were uprooted before Mastiff got wind of him. Let's keep walking. There must be a breach in the Le Mur de la Peste."

"Le Mur de la Peste?" she repeats.

"A seventeen-mile stretch of seven-foot-tall dry stacked stone walls, built in 1720 to prevent the northward spread of the plague. The wall took around twenty years to build but kept the plague out for only seventeen months. A portion of our vineyard is bound by this wall. One day, I'll show you a tower where the sentinels stood on guard."

She hears more rustling. Phew, it's just the wind in the vines.

"My sister, Agnès, has been telling me that we need to install an electric fence around the vineyard, but I've been resisting. An electric fence around this grand old vineyard? The ghosts of my relatives would be up in arms. Who knows, it could even change the taste of the wine! Let's not tell Agnès about our spontaneous *sanglier* meeting today."

"Are they dangerous?" That one looked vicious.

"Only if they feel threatened, like this one, by Mastiff, and then by us, in its path."

The Poet has increased his pace, and his hand grips hers firmly.

"Jean-Pierre calls it the 'Plague of Pigs.' Destroying our century-old vines! Most truffle hunters, like Jean-Pierre, use dogs these days instead of wild pigs to ferret out the truffles. That boar that nearly skewered us looked like a crossbreed of wild boar and domestic pig. The hybrids are difficult to train. The government will pay a small fee for the damage to the vines with the money they collect from hunter license fees. But money can't replace a seventy-five-year-old vine."

A left turn here, a right turn, then another right. Ilse has lost track of the way.

"Carenza!" the Poet calls out in a raspy voice, looking around them. "Just a few weeks ago, I lost her in this vineyard."

"Carenza!"

The spotted mutt, larger than Tang, tears through the vines. You can see the ripple of her bones as she moves. The Poet stops, out of breath.

They walk a few more steps.

"By the way, why do you think that she's from the Basque territory?" She'd been wanting to know since the first time he'd described this dog. "Is it because you recognize the accent in her bark?"

He laughs. "It's true, you can tell everything from a voice. Hear that?" He stops. She's guessing that his stopping is a way to catch his breath.

She listens.

She hears wheezing in his breath.

Bird calls.

"They're duet-calling. There. Above." He points.

Two small brown wrens perch on the post of the vineyard trellis beside them.

"It was popular among eighteenth-century Japanese poets, this kind of call-and-response poetry. Do you know it?"

This man is so esoteric. She shakes her head.

"A poet composes three lines, and the other poet starts his poem with the last word of his friend's poem. Sorry, generally, these poets were men. The women were probably whispering the words into their ears."

Mastiff continues to bark, but the sound is farther away.

Finally, it is quiet. The Poet is dragging his feet and leaning on her a little. If he were to fall and break a leg, she would never know how to find her way out of the twists and turns, slopes, and dips of this endless vineyard.

They climb a small hillock, and from there, not far away, towering above the vines, she sees a landmark: it's a tree, and it must be fifty feet tall. It's even taller than the tree in the middle of the Labaye driveway that she'd wanted to hug.

"My friend, the cork oak." He answers her unspoken question. "During harvest days, in the midday heat, grape pickers seek rest under the cork's shade."

He separates from her and bends slowly to sit on the edge of the hill. She can tell that he's grateful for the rest.

"This is the last of a forest of them. Generations of ignorance. Before the Labayes planted vines, this land belonged to a cork forest.

A cork tree like that one can live over three hundred years and can be harvested over fifteen times in its lifetime. Every nine years or so, these grand specimens were stripped of cork. We've let this tree enjoy its retirement years, which is why its trunk is gray and not red and bare."

She sits beside him, leaning back on her hands. It's a miracle of a tree.

"Cork oaks, like the Iberian lynx, the noble cat that used to prowl these grounds, are now almost extinct. I take extra care with this tree. I found a description of it in the daily records of Gregory Labaye during the wine blight in 1863. He wrote, 'The massive cork is still with us, thank God Almighty.' This tree has been beloved by many long-dead Labayes.

"Gregory, the *arboriste* in the family," the Poet continues, standing up slowly, and now pulling her up gently with both hands, "was possibly more important than any of my troubadour forebears, yet he was the outsider. There were tales of him loving trees more than humans. I've inherited this trait: I can't go for many days without the company of trees."

How would the Poet survive in her tree-barren Arctic?

"Here's a like-minded confession," she says. "When I first saw the huge tree at the front of your house, I had this distinct desire to hug it."

"I knew we were knit from the same cloth!" he says with a guffaw and a tap on her shoulder. "We humans receive deeply needed sustenance from trees."

Gravity hastens their pace down the hill. They walk in silence almost sleepily along a path through a denser incubation of vines.

"You've told me you live on an island alongside the largest island in the world," the Poet says finally. "Well, here, Île du Nord, is my little island in the sea of a vineyard."

The passage opens into a round clearing, surrounded by rows of vines stretching out in five directions like a star. At the center is the enormous cork tree, its gray-black, knotty trunk so wide it would take four people to embrace it. Whitish fringe, on its exterior sprigs, flutters in the wind. Under the tree's lowest branch, she sees a small table and two chairs.

"Do you hear it?"

Where it had been still and quiet inside the layered embrace of vines, this clearing vibrates with the sounds of leaves fluttering at a high-pitched hum.

"That's the mistral whistling through the leaves of the cork. When I spend a long time here, this tree sings ballads to me. You can tell she's a female by the clusters of black drupes in the leaves. There, you can see a few up there. As you are learning, I make nothing up: it's all already here." He leads her to the table.

"Please, have a seat, Île du Nord," he says, bowing.

He struggles a bit to pull the chair out for her. The dogs settle around the Poet's chair, except for Tang, who, tail wagging, stands beside her.

Set before her is a tray with a dainty pink floral trim, and on it, a metal coffeepot, a small white ceramic milk pitcher, two white cups with saucers, two matching white bowls, two silver spoons, a basket covered with a napkin, which she guesses hides croissants, and a yellow bowl, filled to the brim with bright, shiny strawberries.

"I picked these strawberries for you at midnight last night," he says, puffing up his chest.

Bliss is strawberries, picked at midnight, and eaten under the shade of a cork oak in a secret garden in the vineyard.

When the Poet pours the coffee, he spills a few drops on the white cotton napkins on the tray. He lifts the small milk pitcher—he knows by now that she loves the fresh milk here—but this time, his hand slips, and the milk splashes onto the table.

"*Quelle horreur,*" he mutters to himself.

"Allow me," she says, standing to mop up the milk with her napkin.

Now she's certain. The Poet's symptoms are more serious than anything caused by the strong dry wind of Provence. He is much frailer today. When they return from this walk, she'll find a way to contact Georges or at least tell Carole about his condition. He needs to be checked by a doctor.

"Please, go ahead," he says, nodding.

She has never thought to ask permission to sip from a cup of coffee, but with this man, in what feels like a sacred place, every action and gesture merit a kind of thoughtfulness and humility.

"Tang, leave Île du Nord alone. Tang seems to have taken as much a liking to you as I have."

She reaches down to pet the dog.

"And taste these strawberries, or all my efforts to please you will have been in vain."

She spoons the berries into one of the white bowls and tastes. What sweetness! *Jann, are you tasting this?*

"Do you have one where you live?" he asks, leaning forward as if the question should be a secret.

"*Pardonne-moi?*" It feels good to use the more familiar form.

"A hiding place."

She hesitates.

"I suppose . . . my house is my hiding place. If you want to see me, you have to jump over swirling waters in the summer or cross black ice or fall in snowdrifts in the winter. The sea surrounding my house is my version of a moat."

No one, except for Donny, drops by these days, and she smiles to think of him maneuvering the gate that's now off its hinges.

"Well, you are garrisoned, aren't you, Île du Nord? Why do you make yourself such an unapproachable island?"

She takes a deep breath, gazes up at the long, twisted branches in the tree above her, and finds a triangle of blue sky.

"I'm a patient old man."

"I've never been very social," she says.

He looks away. He's not satisfied with her answer.

"I suppose," she starts, placing her damp, wind-swept napkin under her saucer, "it's because of my brother, Jann, the one I told you died five years ago. Of course, it's not his fault. Or maybe it is. *Jann, it IS your fault*. Just that when he died, my life stopped, or at least, it felt as if it did. It seemed that I didn't deserve life, since he no longer was able to enjoy it. That, and I didn't feel the desire to live without him. Without really being conscious of it, I sequestered myself, died his death with him. And, up to the time when I arrived here, I've been living in a way that I imagine it must feel to be dead. And alone."

This vineyard sanctuary must have conjured such words from her. Or else it was him, this man, who brought them forth.

The Poet sips his coffee and gazes upward into the tree. Is he searching for the sky between the branches like Ilse had? Or is he glimpsing something more infinite?

A firefly flitted by:
"Look!" I almost said,
but I was alone.

"A haiku by Taigi, an eighteenth-century poet. I feel your aloneness. But then you and I meet, and I don't feel so alone."

She feels like leaning over and kissing his cheek, but she doesn't.

He places his cup down and nods at her. There's so much quivering movement and wind swishing in the leaves above her.

"Five years ago," he says, wincing and touching his chest, "both of our lives, as we knew them, stopped."

After Jann's accident, she had actually tried—unsuccessfully—to pull out a Dead End sign on a road in Ilulissat so she could stick it into a crevice in the rock in front of her rental cottage. What was the meaning of life when the most beloved person on the planet dies for no good reason, a random slip on a slick road on a foggy day?

"But," she begins, resisting the tears, "you hardly seem lonely here with your friends surrounding you."

He nods. "I go through the paces of a life, but grief hangs on me like these worn pants. Your presence is helping me to shake it off. I'd like to do the same for you."

He tilts his head and looks at her from the corner of his eyes.

"You are, Monsieur le Poète. You are," she says, nodding. "Over the last few days, I've had the feeling of emerging, as if from a chrysalis."

He smiles and nods as if he knows this.

On her way home that evening, she wonders if the price of her emergence is the Poet's decline. What if her constant plea for explanations is exhausting him, like drawing water from a well? He should be spending his precious hours writing poems and not consoling her about her brother's death or teaching her translations that a native French speaker would know by heart.

She stops by Le Cercle to tell Carole about her concern for Monsieur le Poète. Carole insists it's the mistral, *le vent des voleurs,* the wind of thieves, that's robbing Monsieur of his health. She tells Ilse that she will talk about it to Georges when he comes in for his afternoon Ricard. But, she says, shaking her head, Monsieur Labaye is *"têtu comme une mule,"* he's as stubborn as a mule, and she turns away to retrieve an espresso cup for the man in a red beret who has just arrived, most probably one of the many friends of Monsieur le Poète.

ALONG WITH THE MISTRAL, spring has picked up momentum. In the eight days since Ilse arrived, everything seems to be blossoming. The lilac bushes near the front door of the Poet's house fill the living room with a fragrant, heady scent, and the fields that were green with a bright trimming of red poppies are now a full dazzling crimson.

Word lover that Ilse is, in the last few days, she has begun to get the hang of the simple words of the Provençal language. In the tunnel, on her way to the Poet's house, she has even begun to sing the lines from the Poet's poems in Provençal to any old tune she can think up. It feels liberating to hear her voice echoing underground.

Today, there's movement in the house, birds flying in and out, building nests. Thank goodness the Poet appears livelier today. Maybe Carole was right, and the mistral had only temporarily sapped his strength.

"I wish my son were here with us," he says on his way to the table. "I would like him to meet you. I mean, you to meet him. Both ways.

"You have arrived from the land of midnight suns," he continues, "and not coincidentally, long ago, I nicknamed my son 'Midnight Son.' "

"Why that name?"

"As a child, he cried every night at the stroke of midnight, and up until a year ago, which is when we last spoke, he was still waking at the minute of *minuit*. He says he does his best work at that time. Inès used to call him her little bat. I'm a lark, trilling all morning long. Inès was an acolyte to the afternoon. She preferred the tapering light of day, reminding her of the veil-like gossamer glow of afternoons in Morocco, the country where she was born and where I think she yearned to be for our entire married life. Our family comprised a lark, an owl, and a sun-loving lizard."

Jann and she were larks.

"Frey, that's my son's name, short for Geoffrey, is an engineer. He assembles artificial intelligence to support the underserved. He gets his heart from Inès. As you are learning from me, poets are selfish, searching the world to nab sparkly things to beautify their work. Frey is part of a team that builds AI to plumb the depths and access water and transport it to arid places in the developing world."

"That's noble."

"Funny you should use that word. I realize that he's helping to save the world, but I confess to thinking that his motivations are more ignoble than noble, that he's chosen this work, which is the extreme opposite of anything that we, the Labayes, represent, to shoot arrows at his old father. Of course, this is a purely solipsistic view."

Ilse wants to yell out, *He's alive and you're alive. Don't waste time. He could die any day, and then how would you feel?*

Something bangs on the other side of the house.

"That's the mistral having its way with the shutters, telling me to shut my mouth! I haven't forgotten that dozens of incomprehensible Provençal phrases need to be migrated into your language. What do you have for me today?"

He rubs his hands.

She points to *Lo tems vai e ven e vire*.

"Time comes, and goes, and runs away."

Chapter 17

WHAT'S THIS? A TEXT FROM MONSIEUR LE POÈTE. IT'S SATURDAY, the day of the much-touted *pétanque* match between Belle Rivière and Goult. The Poet is asking Ilse to postpone their work session that morning until four o'clock in the afternoon, after which he'll drive her to the village square.

She's surprised by her disappointment. She doubts that the Poet and she will get much work done in the pregame afternoon, and she still has pages and pages of Provençal expressions that need to be dismantled and reassembled. But her disappointment isn't really about her work. She will miss the Poet's company this bright morning. And his gentle voice, and the way he laughs at her, and the way he taps her hand ever so gently to scold her, or to congratulate her on taking greater risks to render words shaped by sound.

Over the last few days, when he escorts her to and from the tunnel, he walks so close to her that she can feel his body's warmth, and when he talks, his breath on her cheek and her neck. Sometimes he looks longer into her eyes than she feels is comfortable. And always, she casts her eyes down, knowing his feelings, and wondering about her own.

Ilse often counters his attentions by pointing to another incomprehensible phrase. But what she really doesn't understand is what is happening between her and this older man. What is this uncharted territory that she would call "happy to be in the presence of each other"? What is the translation for that in French? In Provençal?

When she arrives that afternoon, the house is strangely quiet. The dogs no longer bark at her, but, hello, here's Tang, biting at the hem of the sundress that she splurged on at Belle Rivière's Wednesday *marché*. The dress is white with red roses that match the color of Madame LaRoche's silk scarf. She has a feeling that Madame would approve.

The other dogs follow Tang to greet her. Mastiff has taken to licking her neck when she bends down to him. This time, Chou-fleur is part of the welcoming committee.

"Chou-fleur, *bonjour*! You make me miss my Minou." She calls into the living room. "Monsieur?"

"*Voilà*, Île du Nord, I'm here," the Poet says, emerging from the kitchen, carrying a small tray of two cups filled to the brim with spilling coffee. He places the tray on the desk in the living room as he greets her with his three-cheek kiss. He's wearing his white poet's shirt, but it looks too big on him today, white linen pants, and a light blue linen scarf tied around his neck, just so. She has noticed that he has been dressing with more flair over the last few days. His face is still pale, but maybe it's because he's wearing all white.

"I need this coffee for the match," he says. "I'm feeling extremely slothful today. Despite that, look, I've frothed the milk for you. Froth from the sloth."

At the table under the olive tree, they sip the coffee in silence. She can't stop thinking that her magical sojourn here will be over in four swift days, really two, if you don't count today and Tuesday, which is a travel day. Just as she's been able, recently, to replicate the rhythm in her translations, she and the Poet have created a cadence to their days. She's become accustomed to starting her work mornings in the presence of this gifted, gentle man, drinking the smooth bittersweet-tasting French coffee and listening to his voice mixed in with the rustle of the silver olive leaves above their heads. She's already looking back at her time here in Provence and yearning to return.

At their worktable, Ilse asks for help with *De fin'amor son tot mei penamen.*

"Île du Nord, that's too easy for you, but I think you ask because you wish to hear me say it to you. 'On true love, are all my thoughts bent.' However, in this case, I would add"—and he looks into her eyes—"On true love *and you,* are all my thoughts bent."

He speaks in a kind of breathless voice.

"I like today's version much better," she says, smiling into his eyes.

He takes her hand. "I won't let you go!"

"And I won't let you let me go!"

"That's better, *mon* Île du Nord. That's better." He grabs at the shirt at his chest.

"Are you okay?"

He nods, letting go of his shirt.

"*Monsieur,* are you well enough to play this afternoon?"

"*Ça suffit!* No more calling me *monsieur.* It makes me feel old, and you too young. Please call me Po. My sister is the only one who insists on calling me Geoffrey, the given name of generations of trespassers who claim this land as their own. In your literary travels, you may have run across Li Po, the eighth-century Tang dynasty poet and the well-respected translator for Emperor Xuanzong. He and his friend Du Fu exchanged poems about nestling against tree trunks and listening to the winds in the pines, just like you and I like to keep vigil under this loquacious olive."

"*Très bien,* Po," she says. She likes how it sounds in her mouth: *Po.*

When he closes his eyes and holds out his hands, palms up, she places her hands in his.

"There, that's all I needed: I have stolen some of your glamorous youthfulness, and more than that, some of your affection."

And she thinks back to how she'd been plucking out the gray hairs in front of her office mirror in the sea captain's house. Since she's been in France, she feels younger than she has ever felt, possibly in her life.

He almost drops the cup when he picks it up, spilling coffee on his black vest.

"Let me," she says, rising to wipe the dark spot on his black vest with her napkin.

"It won't come out," she says after a few minutes, as she removes herself from that intimate proximity.

"You're right. It won't come out," he says in a sad kind of way. "*Merci.*" He bows from his waist, as she returns to her chair.

And he recites,

Le ciel sans teinte est constellé
D'astres pâles comme du lait . . .
Ayant décroché une étoile
Il la manie à bras tendu . . .

The sky without a stain unmarred
Is studded with milk-white stars . . .
Having unhooked a star
He proffers it with outstretched hand . . .

"It's from the poem 'Twilight,' by Apollinaire. I offer you, Île du Nord, what's left of my burning star."

"Thank you," she says, tapping his hand lightly, the way he often touches hers. "I think the firebrand should rest now and save some of his burning star for the game.

"Po," she adds.

He nods. "You can tell that I'm distracted."

When they stand, she lifts the tray of coffee cups before he can. His cup is still full. Maybe he will drink the coffee in the kitchen when she is not there to witness his shaking hands.

In the living room, at the first step of the stairs, the Poet grips the banister's crown finial so forcibly that she can see the whites of his knuckles. He tells her that he'll meet her downstairs in thirty minutes.

And this is the firebrand of Belle Rivière?

Back at the table on the terrace, Ilse fiddles with a few more words in the next poem. But she can't focus. She's relieved that they'll be seeing Georges soon. He may be better than Carole or her at convincing his cousin to go to the doctor.

She closes her laptop and waits for Po in the Inès-portrait-dominated living room. She looks at one of the many silver-framed photographs on the desk between the two large French doors. In one of them, the Poet and Inès, cigarettes in hand, are facing each other, laughing. How young they look, the Poet with long, dark locks, and Inès with dancing eyes. Inès is livelier and more enticing in the photographs than in the staid, solemn painted portrait. In the photograph, a little boy, she hadn't noticed him at first, gazes up at the couple as if wanting to get in on the laugh. Behind this photograph is another framed one, a close-up of Inès. It's rare to see such a serious expression in a photograph. Her brown, kohl-stenciled eyes stare unflinchingly into the camera. She looks as if she knows something that the observer doesn't suspect, and she doesn't care if she's been found out.

A letter and a ripped envelope are tucked under the frame.

What elegant script.

Before she realizes it, Ilse is reading the first line.

"*Mon père*. My father."

Ilse looks up the staircase, cocks her ear. Nothing.

"*Nous ne nous sommes pas parlé depuis un an*. We have not spoken in a year."

She reads on: "But I have not changed my mind or my heart."

Footsteps. The dogs charge ahead of Po, Tang in the lead. Ilse slides the letter back under the picture frame and leans against the desk.

"Ah," he says, from the landing above.

He's seen.

"I was going to put that letter away this morning," he says, "but something made me leave it there. Perhaps . . ." He descends the stairs slowly and hesitates on the bottom stair, gripping the finial for stability. "Perhaps, I wanted you to read it."

He's holding the straw hat with the white feather tucked in it, the one he wore that first day and in the Renaissance Café the second time they met. How she loves that hat. In his other hand, he clutches a small black leather bag that she guesses contains his metal *boules de pétanque*. His black pants are loose, but his black collared shirt fits him well. It has a small flame on the right front pocket. Firebrand! He's wearing his faded red espadrilles.

She kneels to pet Tang and Mastiff. Ronsard, the collie, herds Carenza into the grouping. Po steps off the stair.

"I disapprove of my son's fiancée. I asked him to wait a year before getting married. That year is now up, and the wedding is scheduled for August. He's marrying my publisher's daughter. They met at a poetry reading of mine a few years back." He shakes his head, takes a deep breath.

"My editor told me about it," says Ilse, moving toward him.

He nods.

"His fiancée is a tigress," he says. "I've met her three times. That was enough."

"Her mother, my boss's boss," says Ilse, continuing to stroke the dogs, "needed me to expedite the translation in time for her daughter's—and your son's wedding in the U.S."

He sighs, looks away.

"I'm glad the wedding is good for something."

He walks to the French doors and closes one set, then another.

"My poetry is a party favor for the wedding guests."

He walks up to her, and she stands. He's only a foot away.

"What shall I do: watch my beloved son make the biggest mistake of his life?"

She says nothing.

"This woman will crush his soul if she hasn't already. I've tried to have an open heart, but—"

Ringtones emanate from his pocket.

He nearly loses his balance as he searches his pockets for the phone. She reaches out for his arm, it's automatic, but then stops herself when he recovers.

"*Oui, Georges, je viens.* I'm coming."

He clicks off the phone.

"Since I'm running late, we'll take the car."

She's sorry to have distracted him with the letter.

When he opens the front door for her and bows as she passes, she hears wheezing in his breath. Between coughs, he tells the dogs to stay.

Outside, Ilse inhales the scent of sweet wisteria. The white stucco outbuilding with its pale blue garage doors that match the house shutters is covered top to bottom with the purple dangling flowers. After two attempts, the Poet lifts the garage door to reveal a shiny, canary-yellow Peugeot convertible. *What a racy car.* She freezes when she sees a blue motorcycle in a dark corner. It's a Honda, the kind Jann had been driving. Po opens the passenger door of the car and waits for Ilse to sweep her sneakered feet inside.

"In the old days," he says, "I would try to impress you by leaping into the driver's seat, but today, I'm taking the old man's way in."

Once inside, he reaches above her knees into the glove compartment to retrieve his aviator sunglasses. They make him look like a movie star. He guns the engine twice.

"She's still got it."

Inside the convertible, it feels as if they're on a first date. They speed out of the garage into the sandy driveway. Her hair blows in her face and around her neck, and the dust balloons behind them.

She imagines that the original thirteenth-century troubadour, Geoffrey Labaye, had a nose like this descendant's, long with a bump in just the right place in the middle, high cheekbones, arching eyebrows, and a broad forehead. In contrast, her Norse ancestors, she suspected, were distinguished by a heavy brow above their eyes. As the first Labaye composed and sang love ballads, her forebears were wearing skins and hunting musk oxen for dinner.

"Sorry for the acceleration," he yells into the wind as they turn a corner at top speed. "If I don't show up in the next five minutes, I'll be disqualified in the first round."

"No!"

"The mistral! It's still giving us a thrashing!" he shouts. "'Rough winds do shake the darling buds of May.'"

She can't see because of her hair blowing in her face.

"*Zut,* the target will go flying!" he says as he cuts the engine near the monument for the war soldiers, not far from where she'd parked on her first day. He tries to lift himself out of the convertible but gives up and pushes open the car door. He looks disappointed when she opens her door before he can get to it. They head downhill to the village square.

En route, he wipes his forehead several times with the back of his sleeve.

"*C'est le mistral qui nous rend fous*. It's the mistral that makes us all crazy. Today it's affecting my legs. They won't go where I tell them to go."

"*Enfin!* Finally!" It's a cry from the middle of the square. She counts five elderly men. Two raise their hands when they see him. One stamps his feet. The man in a red beret whom she'd seen at Le Cercle looks at his watch.

"*Allons-y*, the firebrand is here!" shouts Georges.

Chapter 18

THE BENCHES LINING THE DUSTY SQUARE ARE FULLY POPULATED. Some fans have laid out blankets on the grass. Ilse spots a bottle of Ricard and a tray of small glasses on a blue blanket nearby.

There's Carole, on the other side of the square, scowling, her arms crossed. She looks like she owns wherever she is, and everyone else is trespassing. Jean-Pierre, short next to her, holds his hand over his eyes either in a salute to Po or to block the sun from his view of the court.

Ilse hadn't expected to see Madame Hugot. Apronless, Madame wears a white T-shirt, loose-fitting jeans, her dark brown espadrilles, and the ever-present scarf that all French women wrap twice around their necks. Monsieur Hugot is unfolding beach chairs. Their children, Muette and Luc, kneel on the ground in front of their parents. A policeman and policewoman in light blue shorts, matching shirts, and black boots lean against a police car on the road at the edge of the court. This is a village occasion.

Ilse approaches Madame Hugot, who ekes out a minimal smile. Ilse feels more comfortable near the children, so she sits cross-legged next to fourteen-year-old Muette and asks for help with the rules of the game.

"Two teams, three players each: each player has three metal balls, *boules*. The first team throws, then each player in the second team throws. The team that throws or rolls their *boule* closest to a small wooden target ball, called a *bouchon,* scores a point for the round. There are thirteen rounds."

"Do they sometimes use a cork for a *bouchon*?" Ilse had read this on the Internet.

Muette's younger brother, Luc, looks over and shakes his head.

"Don't listen to Muette. She doesn't know anything."

"Shut up, Luc. I beat him in this game all the time. Sometimes they use a cork, sometimes it's a bright green plastic ball. Monsieur Labaye likes to play with a cork, but today it looks like the *bouchon* is made of wood.

"Coin toss," Muette says in a low voice as she nods to Georges and the man with the red beret at the center of the field, "is super important." She uses the English word "super."

There's Chloé, on the other side of the court. When she waves to Ilse, Ilse looks behind her, wondering if Chloé is flagging someone else. No, it's her! Ilse waves back.

It's exhilarating to be in the presence of this community, all focused on the same thing.

Ilse asks Muette about the third player, the one with the black baseball cap, on the Poet's team.

"Monsieur Gunther," she says. "Cedric won the toss."

The man Muette calls Cedric with the red beret is on the other team. He takes a baguette from a canvas bag, places it on the dirt court, and draws a circle around the diameter of it. He stands inside the circle and throws the small wooden *bouchon*. It flies about twenty feet, carried by the mistral. Gunther squats, points, and whispers to Georges and then to the Poet.

"Is that a baguette?" Ilse asks.

"Three-day-old baguette," says Muette. "An old tradition, but not a bad measuring stick. Gunther is the captain who sees three-sixty."

"And Po, I mean Monsieur Labaye?" Ilse asks.

"The shooter, the firebrand," Muette says.

"Shooter?" Ilse asks.

Madame looks over at her, her face twisted like a lemon rind in a cocktail.

"He's the best one at hitting the opposition *boules* and knocking them away from the target," Muette says. "He's the best in the area, maybe in France."

"She's exaggerating," Luc says, shaking his head.

"Papa says so. Monsieur Gunther is the strategist."

Gunther rubs his nose. Is that code? He crouches down, whispers to Georges.

The man with a red beret, Cedric, on the other team, his tanned face a sea of wrinkles, stands in the drawn circle and slowly lifts his arm behind him, his palm facing upward. He drops his arm, and with the momentum rolls the *boule*. It swivels around random pebbles on the terrain, and hello, it touches the *bouchon*.

"*Oui!* Yes!" Madame says.

The rest of the crowd does not look as happy.

Muette anticipates Ilse's next question.

"Cedric is Maman's cousin," she whispers. "He lives in Goult."

"Do the teams have names?" Ilse asks.

Muette shakes her head.

Silly question.

Monsieur Gunther slides down on his knee outside the circle to squint at the distances, then stands inside the circle and rolls his *boule*.

"You have to keep both feet planted," Muette says. "*Pieds tanqués* means 'feet stuck.' It's how the game got its name. Look, he almost lifted his foot. They're watching for that, as that would disqualify him."

"Muette, he's not going to lift his foot!" whispers her brother. "He's a professional."

The *boule* is about a foot away from the *bouchon* and Madame's cousin's *boule*. Next goes Georges: he tosses his *boule* high up and thud, it lands on the hard-packed dirt, a few inches away from Cedric's, but the red beret's *boule* is still closest.

It's Po's turn. He crouches, stands, peers over at Gunther. Gunther shakes his head, then nods at Po's lifted finger.

Po lofts. His *boule* knocks Cedric's away from the target *bouchon* and is resting where Cedric's *boule* was just seconds before, almost touching the *bouchon*.

"*Un carreau!*" cries a woman behind Ilse. Ilse looks back. Despite her gray hair, the woman who has yelled has a face and a voice that could be a young girl's. The woman smiles gently and nods at her as Ilse looks back a second time.

Ilse traces the sounds of repetitive hand clapping to Carole, across the way, whose face is stone serious. Jean-Pierre lifts a short stub of what looks like a hand-rolled cigarette to his lips. Madame is sipping her husband's glass of Ricard and shaking her head between sips.

"*Un carreau?*" Ilse whispers.

"The perfect shot. A flick of the wrist creates backspin. It's a super difficult move, but Monsieur Labaye, he's got it in his repertoire. Their team now has one point."

The teams set up for the next "end" as Muette calls it, and this time, Gunther is the one to use the baguette like the needle on a compass to draw the circle in the dirt.

As the game continues, the players perform a dance of squatting, standing, conferring, and whispering. The crowd swells.

Georges, who Muette reminds her is the *pointeur* on the team, the best one at tossing the ball closest to the *bouchon*, has successfully rolled his *boule* just an inch away. It's the team's best shot. Red-beret Cedric is now the one to blast Georges's ball from its position. As he does it, he knocks the *bouchon* away. The other team wins the point for this end.

Ilse hears a low moan behind her and turns to see the woman with the young face and gray hair, now hurrying onto the dusty court. The woman is down on her knees where a few people stand huddled. Team meeting?

"Clear the way!" someone yells out.

Now Madame Hugot runs into the gathering crowd. When Ilse hears Madame call out "It's Monsieur Labaye!" Ilse rushes forward. She recognizes his dusty red espadrilles. Po is lying prone.

"He must have fainted," she hears Madame say beside her. "It's the mistral. People are fainting right and left. His sister's calling the ambulance." The Poet's sister must be the elegant woman with gray hair who'd smiled at her.

"*Qu'est-il arrivé?* What happened?" Another worried voice.

Ilse has seen the signs of his illness for days now. How could she have let him play when she knew he was weak?

The seesaw whining of a siren sounds in the distance. Minutes later, two *pompiers* from the local fire brigade, who Ilse has learned stand in as the medical and ambulance service in the village, bolt from the red truck at the edge of the square. The crowd makes way, and before Ilse understands what's going on, the firemen are carrying Po out of the square on a stretcher. The gray-haired woman runs alongside the firemen. Ilse can only catch a glimpse of Po's profile. His eyes are closed.

"They're taking him to the hospital in Cavaillon," says Madame Hugot.

Kids are drawing circles in the sandy court with the baguette. The five players, heads bowed, their bodies deflated, pick up the *boules* and leave the court. The arrested play is like stopped time.

Chapter 19

When white butterflies flutter into Ilse's window the next morning, she wills herself to believe that this is a sign that Po is fine and has returned from the hospital. When she hears Madame's footsteps on the stairs, Ilse pops her head out of her room to ask if she's heard any news about Monsieur Labaye. Madame shakes her head quickly as if Ilse's question is impertinent.

Ilse works on a few poems at her desk by the French windows. It's midday, and she's had no word from him. She can't work; she can't think. She sends Donny a postcard telling him about the game of *pétanque*. In the early afternoon, she sends Po a text asking after his health, and whether she can bring him anything.

She wanders aimlessly around Belle Rivière, checking her phone at regular intervals. As much as she would like to believe that the mistral was the cause of the Poet's fainting, she can't stop thinking about signs of his failing health the last few mornings: the way he gripped the stair post for balance, his pallor, and his wheezing breath.

In her next text to Po, she offers to feed the dogs and cat.

No response.

She has passed from paradise into purgatory.

Later that afternoon, as she traipses over the tiles on the rooftops from the center of the village to the Hugot residence, carrying her canvas bag of baguette and cheese and wine for her dinner that night, her phone rings.

Unidentified caller.

"Île du Nord?"

A woman's voice.

"Oui, c'est moi."

Ilse places her bag down on the roof tiles and gazes out at the verdant vineyards patchworking the distant land and the pale blue mountain behind. Thankfully, the wind has died down.

"I'm Agnès, Geoffrey Labaye's sister. We're in the hospital in Cavaillon. Geoffrey gave me your number and wishes to talk to you. Here you go, Geoffrey."

Ilse hears him clearing his throat.

"Île du Nord, I apologize for not contacting you sooner." His voice is different, raspy, untethered.

"How are you?" How she has missed this tender voice, and she's only been without it for twenty-four hours.

"I fainted, but . . . will be returning soon. I realize that you're planning to leave us on Tuesday. I'm wondering if you would extend your visit, possibly by two weeks. We have a few more poems to work through."

His words are troubadour love songs to her ears.

She sees herself three sweaters deep in her office in Oqaatsut next to the window with the rotting frame. Before she left, she'd placed a rolled towel near the crumbling wood to block the chill, the sleet, and the rain. On their last call a few days ago, Malu told her that this has been one of the rainiest springs ever, and that because it poured instead of snowed at the summit of the ice sheet, seven billion tons of water were dumped. It was the heaviest rainfall ever recorded. Like most Greenlanders, Malu keeps track of the loss of ice mass.

Two more weeks before Ilse returns to her melting ice island!

Émile may agree to reimburse her for the change fee to switch flights but would have a hard time justifying paying for another two weeks of lodging for a translator. Ilse is already low on funds thanks to buying herself the sundress; the lavender *eau de toilette;* scented soaps for Val and Mary, Duggan's wife; and a red-and-blue paisley tablecloth for Malu. And she still wanted to buy a bottle of Ricard for Beluga, oh yes, and some for Val, and a leather belt for Donny and one for Fa.

"I would be overjoyed to stay longer," she says. The green in the valley below is so bright it's hard to believe. "But I'm not sure my publisher will be keen on it. Also, I think Madame Hugot has another paying guest coming in after me."

"Two weeks with Madame Hugot is too much for any sentient being," he says. "I've talked it over with my sister. You must stay with me."

"No, no," Ilse says. "I hardly . . . I don't wish to impose . . ."

"Even with all my dogs and my cat, I can't fill the rooms of the house. I suspect that Tang would be especially appreciative. Choufleur too. I've noticed that she's been sitting on your chair under the olive trees when you're not there."

Ilse hears a voice in the background.

"You would be doing us all a favor," he continues. "My sister, Agnès, '*en greu cossirier*, in great distress of mind,' the line is from a poem from the twelfth-century Beatritz de Dia, a prolific composer whom I must tell you more about—worries about me living alone . . . after yesterday."

Even from a hospital bed, Po is quoting from his endless storehouse of troubadour verse, in this case, a *trobairitz*, a female troubadour.

There is nothing on earth that would stop her from helping this man. Émile will agree to her prolonged stay if it costs him only the two hundred euros for a flight change fee—no lodging costs, and if her translation is sumptuous! It's got to be the best translation she's ever delivered. If Émile won't pay for the flight change, she'll work a second job at the reception desk at the Ilimanaq Lodge when she returns.

"Thank you, Po. This is very kind. I will consider it. How are you feeling?"

He starts to cough. Something in his throat.

"Excuse me," he says.

Oh no. Is he vomiting?

The phone clicks off.

Ilse makes her way down from the rooftops and walks along the path to the Hugots' house inside the cliff. Her phone rings again before she opens the wrought-iron gate. The same number.

"*Mademoiselle?*" Po's sister's voice.

"*Oui, madame.*"

"My brother has just told me that you're staying with the Hugot family. We can't have that! She's . . . well. We suggest that you stay at our house starting tomorrow, that is, if you can, and don't think it awkward."

Her voice has the same inflections as Po's, a similar smooth elegance, just in a higher register.

"Wait one minute, Geoffrey," she says. "Patients are supposed to be patient."

A pause. Static on the line.

"That's better," she continues. "I'm in the hallway. Though I don't yet know you, I hope it's all right, and I have the feeling it's okay to speak to you personally. Last night, my daughter gave birth to twin daughters—everything at once!—and she needs my help. Not only that: my husband's directing a play in Arles during all of this. I've phoned Geoffrey's son, and he's not sure when he can get here." A pause. Disapproval. "My brother refuses to hire anyone to help him. He's impossible. He says he's completely capable of doing everything himself. I've told him that we must employ a nurse or else ask his cousin who lives in Paris to come down to stay. He shook his head like an obstinate child at both options. And then, with that look that he gets in his eyes when he's got an idea for a poem, he came up with the idea of you. Yes, yes . . ." she says, talking to someone else. "The nurses are scooting me out of the hall. I'm back in my brother's room. He wants me to tell you that he'll cook you a soufflé every day if you stay."

A soufflé every day if you stay. She'll ask Po to make a singing poem of that.

"Okay, okay," his sister says. She must be the older sibling the way that she's taking charge of things. "He wants me to say that the grocer will deliver any foods you like, as you're the Île du Nord and must have your wild salmon daily. You must have noticed the house has not had a good clean in years, cobwebs everywhere, birds and animals coming in and out"—Ilse hadn't; the house looked perfect to her—"and all those dogs have destroyed the furniture. One minute. The cell reception in this room is terrible. I will find a better spot . . ."

Ilse hears *whish, whoosh,* a door shutting. On the Hugots' terrace, Ilse places her bag with baguette on the small table.

"Muette!" Madame Hugot's strident voice carries from inside the house.

Luc is at the entry with his bicycle. A baguette pokes out from the basket on the back of the bike. Ilse opens the gate for him, and they wave to each other.

"*Ahh, voilà,*" says Agnès. "I'm in the hall again. Mademoiselle—" She speaks in a low voice. "It's strange to be confiding in someone I don't know, but my brother is confident . . . And he lives his life like this . . . so I will tell you. We won't know for certain until tomorrow, but after the X-ray, the doctor is saying that this could be as serious as stage four lung cancer, and that we're to prepare ourselves . . ." The Poet's sister pauses, chokes a little.

"What?" Ilse cannot help herself from yelling out.

"He smoked like a chimney for most of his life. He quit five years ago. Before this hospital visit, my brother hadn't seen a doctor since he was a child. Imagine. Of course, the doctors don't know my brother, and they don't know . . . Well, anyway, Geoffrey wasn't surprised at all by this news, though of course, he may be pretending. Or it may not have sunk in. He doesn't want me to tell anyone, not you, not even his son, but of course I have told him that I'm informing you and of course, his son, another seasoned professional in the art of denial. Geoffrey insists that you are an angel sent to him, and that you have work to do together. I need someone to stay with him at the house until I can get back in a few days or until Frey, his son, comes . . . Of course, you—may I call you Ilse?—you may have other plans."

Ilse thinks of how she'd tried to rub the coffee stain from Po's vest, and he'd said it wouldn't come out.

"Geoffrey says . . . he says he trusts you. I better go back to his room. There's no need to respond immediately. He's a bit spoiled, my brother, but, but"—her voice breaks—"I . . . I . . . love him madly. I adore him. And this is such a . . . shock. Can we persuade you to stay for, and I realize this is an imposition, perhaps, two more weeks?"

"Of course I will stay."

"Thank you. My husband, Benoît, who's with my daughter right now, and I are grateful for your kindness. If you come to the house tomorrow morning—shall we say nine o'clock? I'll show you around." What was a soft, lilting voice is now the stronger voice of the older sister. "Geoffrey insists that you take the bedroom with the desk overlooking the vineyards . . ." She pauses. "I felt after spotting you yesterday—sorry, it wasn't hard, a new face in Belle Rivière stands out in the crowd, especially one with such light-colored eyes, also, my brother has been telling us about you—I felt I knew you. It's as if you are an echo of someone who's been talking to me from the future."

"The poetry gene is strong in your family," Ilse says, wiping the tears from her cheeks. A golden oriole (Po had pointed out the bright yellow bird during one of their sessions, and they'd listened to its tuneful whistling) perches on a nearby chair, then takes off.

"I'm a potter," Agnès says. "It's hard enough to hold one high-flying kite to the ground. My beloved brother sculpts words; I sculpt the earth."

THE MORNING SUN IS forging a path from Ilse's bed to the open French doors. The only way she could finally fall asleep the night before was to tell herself that Po would live out his days and prove the doctors wrong. *He can't die. He's the last living troubadour in Provence.*

She steps on the strip of sunlight that runs along the dark wood floor and pokes her head out the open French doors. Mists, like floating white ribbons, stripe the lavender Luberons.

She remembers a fragment of the dream she'd had that morning: Po was removing the life-size portrait of Inès from the wall. In the dream, Ilse remembers feeling relieved that his wife would no longer dominate his living room.

But Po would never take down the portrait, she thinks, as she watches a goldfinch loop from one cypress to another below her window. Could she be jealous of Po's deceased wife? Had Ilse really fallen in love with a man in his seventies? Theirs wasn't a physical love; it was more abstract, an affectionate, intellectual kind of love. All she knows is that she cherishes every moment they spend together.

Ilse checks her phone for a message from Émile. She'd emailed him the night before about Monsieur le Poète's invitation for her to stay in his house to finish their work. She'd decided not to mention the Poet's illness, only that there was more work to be done.

She holds her breath as she reads, then exhales. As long as Ilse meets her deadline, the publisher, Daphné Solenz, has agreed to compensate her for her business expenses and the flight change fee.

Émile had signed off saying that he expects a case of Mas de Cadenet Côtes de Provence Sainte Victoire rosé sent to his doorstep as a commission for his efforts. *Sorry, Émile,* she doesn't type back, *I don't have euros for one bottle, let alone a case of a wine with more names than I can remember.*

Her phone rings, and she answers. It's Agnès. "*Bonjour,* Ilse, we're still waiting for results from more tests, but what they see does not look good . . ." She sniffs. "They say there's nothing they can do. They're saying"—she's whispering now—"it's very advanced, that it's possible . . . that he . . . may have only a few months."

The tears are clogging the back of Ilse's throat. Can emptiness flood a person's body? She suddenly recognizes the feeling of the life force draining from her. She hasn't felt it since she'd heard about Jann's crash. Does every person whom Ilse loves have to die? Madame La-Roche, Jann, now Po?

Rather than bother anyone about dates, Ilse changes her flight to Tuesday, May 29, two weeks later than her initial return flight.

She sends an email to Émile and Val informing them of her change of plans. Val writes back to let her know that her beloved pussy (Ilse wishes Val wouldn't refer to Minou by that name) has just licked the icing off the cupcakes that she was about to serve, and that Malu has agreed to take her until Ilse returns.

Poor Minou, going to live with Malu.

When Malu answers the phone, Ilse can hear the muffled sound of her mother sorting envelopes in the background, the paper-sliding-against-paper shuffle that Ilse grew up with. Her mother is surprisingly upbeat. After complaining about the nonstop rain turning to sleet that morning, she says that Minou has been raising hell at Tipsy's because she's furious that Ilse left without her, and that it's high time Ilse returns, and that Minou will be much better off, she says, with her and Fa, and that it has brightened Fa's world to know that the cat was coming to live with them. She says this in one breath.

When she tells Madame Hugot, whom she finds watering the flowers in the pots on the terrace, that she's leaving one day earlier than planned—to stay at the Labaye house, the habitual disapproving face turns deprecatory.

"Oh *really* . . ." she says as if Ilse is a vixen who has manipulated her way into the Labaye house and heart.

For a moment, Ilse thinks Madame may be right.

Chapter 20

THE DOGS RUSH TOWARD ILSE. AS TANG LICKS HER ANKLES, Ilse hides her dented roller bag behind the door, where Agnès won't see it.

"Bonjour! Un moment!"

It's Agnès's voice, from the second-floor landing. She sweeps down the stairs. About the same height as Ilse, Agnès has her brother's eyes, but not quite so blue. Her hair is clipped up in a bun as it had been two days before, but today, strands fall in wisps around her oval face. Here's a woman who has never plucked out one gray hair. She's wearing the same brown, belted dress with a square neck that she'd been wearing two days ago at the game. How exhausted and heart-worn she must be.

"*Bonjour,*" Agnès says, surprising Ilse with a double-cheek kiss. "I've been tidying your room. Geoffrey insisted that I make it perfect."

"That is so kind."

"As you can imagine, the last two nights have been harrowing. Come, I've brewed us some coffee."

Ilse follows Agnès into the kitchen, noting Agnès's delicate, brown leather shoes.

"I don't have my brother's penchant for nicknames," she says, reaching for two cups from hooks inside an antique cupboard, "but just this time, I'll give him one: he's been an *enfant terrible!* Last night, when the night nurse went to the restroom, Geoffrey had unhitched himself from the intravenous, tripped on the cords, and the nurse found him flat out, semiconscious, on the cold tile floor."

Ilse feels a chill up her spine.

"The doctor told me before I left this morning that he won't let Geoffrey go until he receives results from a few more tests. I'll return to the hospital after our coffee and a shower, and he and I probably won't be back until tomorrow afternoon. Another night in his hospital room. I've also just learned that Geoffrey's son will be coming home within the next few days, possibly even tonight. About time." She looks away quickly.

"In that case, I shouldn't intrude. His son will look after—"

"No, no, we want you to stay," Agnès interrupts. Distracted, she spills the coffee as she pours it into the cups. Ilse helps her clean the counter. "Geoffrey and his son, my nephew, have a strained relationship. I think having you here—if you don't mind, Ilse—will soften Frey's visit. Frey is my nephew's nickname. Anyway, Geoffrey insists that you stay, and . . . I want to do what he wishes."

Something catches Agnès's attention out the window. A bird? A few minutes later, she lifts her hands to her face and begins to shake with sobbing. The dogs surround her. Mastiff whines.

Ilse stands beside her, feeling helpless. She's tempted to hug her.

"I'm so sorry," she mumbles.

"I'm at a loss. He's a national treasure," she says between her tears, "but he's also my brother and my best friend. He can't be leaving me so soon. It's too soon, too soon."

"I have a little sense of what you're feeling," Ilse says quietly. "I lost my brother."

The words came from her without thinking, and now she regrets having said them. It's selfish of her to refer to her story, her pain, when this lovely woman is suffering. And Po may not die after all, despite what the doctors say.

Agnès lifts the strands of gray hair that have fallen into her face and wipes her eyes and nose with her sleeve.

"Your brother must have been young."

Ilse nods.

"Motorcycle crash."

Agnès recoils as if she's been struck, sudden tears in her eyes.

"*C'est dévastateur.* I'm so sorry."

Agnès places her hand briefly on Ilse's shoulder.

"I was knocked out of life by it," says Ilse slowly. "It's only now, five years later, and here, that I've begun to understand how to live again."

"This place does that to people," Agnès says as she wipes her eyes with the back of her hand.

"Your brother has done it for me."

Agnès bows her head. "Most people who know him feel that way." Her voice cracks.

Neither woman speaks for some time. Agnès pulls a cloth napkin from a nearby drawer and holds it up to her eyes.

"But Monsieur is a fighter," Ilse says. "He'll outlive the doctor's predictions."

Agnès shakes her head. "He's more of a lover than a fighter. He'd rather go out loving than fighting. I'll be the one to do the fighting for him. At least I'll try."

"Your daughter—"

"Yes, Manon, she's delivered twins. Joy mixed with this anguish. What timing! My husband and the in-laws have joined forces to help. I'll get there when I can."

Agnès gazes out the window again. It's as if the view gives her solace, like a deep breath.

"Ilse, there's something about you that reminds me of my younger daughter, Muriele, who lives in Switzerland. Her name means 'star of the bright, sparkling sea,' and that's what I thought of when I first saw you."

She sniffles, dabs her eyes with the napkin.

"Muriele has, what is it, your vivaciousness, the look you have in those eyes of yours, they're pale, but so bright. I'm sure my brother has already written a poem about them."

No one has ever talked about Ilse's eyes in this way.

"Since my brother's not here quoting Shakespeare, I'll do it for him: 'The moon's an arrant thief, And her pale fire she snatches from the sun.' While other children were playing tennis, Geoffrey and I were playing catch with Shakespeare."

What a cultured childhood, so different from her own.

"*Alors.* I should be showing you around!"

Agnès opens the cupboard to reveal the bins of dog and cat food and shows Ilse the dogs' bowls, each one painted with a name. "I'm proud to say that I made them.

"Now," she continues, all business, out of the kitchen and up the stairs. "Let me take you to your room. Then, I'll take a quick shower and be off."

Ilse follows her, catching a scent of fragrant perfume. Two nights in the hospital, and this woman still smells good.

"Geoffrey's room," Agnès says as they pass the first closed door on the right side of the long corridor. "And this is yours." She opens the door on the left.

Pink light floods the room. French doors open to a balcony, larger than the one at the Hugots'. Instead of the view of the green valley, the quilt of squares of vineyard and farmland that Ilse found blissful in the Hugot house, these doors open onto the Labayes' endless, undulating vineyard, and the lavender-hued Luberon Mountains beyond.

An antique desk and chair overlook the view and the terrace below with Po's worktable. The bed with a canopy made of a faded peach-colored taffeta matches the chairs upholstered with similar fabric and flounce skirts.

"How lovely." Ilse tries not to appear as if she's never seen such a beautiful room.

"Geoffrey picked that out for you before the dreadful game," Agnès says, tilting her head in the direction of the bed, where Ilse sees a brown box tied with a pale blue ribbon. "He asked me to make sure you received it. Open it when you wish, but now I must shower and run."

"Thank you, Agnès," she tells the elegant woman, now in the hallway.

What? A pair of lavender espadrilles! She hadn't remembered telling Po that lavender was her favorite color since she'd discovered the Luberon Mountains. And her shoe size? Had he peeked into her sneakers the other day when they took their barefoot walk? She tries on the espadrilles. A little tight in the toe area, but they will stretch. She will make them stretch.

Half an hour later, from the hall window across from her bedroom, Ilse watches Po's sister depart. How high Agnès carries her head as she strides to her car. She's gathering the strength she will need when she sees her beloved brother in a hospital bed.

THAT AFTERNOON, ILSE IS word rummaging, that's what she calls it, at Po's table on the terrace, breathing in the smell of dryness, if there is such a smell. A light breeze that doesn't have the impatient fury of the mistral stirs the leaves on the vines.

Tang is by her side, looking up at her for a reassuring head massage.

"Here you go." She helps the pup onto her lap. "I'm spoiling you." Po would say there's no such thing as spoiling a dog.

The other dogs are inside, moping around on their sheet-covered couches and chairs, awaiting Po's return. Chou-fleur jumps onto the table and spreads herself onto the notebook paper and the many pages where Ilse has circled various untranslatables.

Dropping her face into the sprawling cat's fur, Ilse embraces her, whispering a prayer of well-being to Po. The house is so empty, forlorn, lacking in feeling and being without him. It's as if the world has wilted. In the poem that she's working on, Po wonders how many lifetimes it will take for him to catch up to Inès.

Mastiff starts baying, setting off a barrage of barking.

Tang's ears spring up.

"Who's there, Tang?"

Mastiff and Ronsard dart to the front door. Carenza must be out in the vineyard somewhere.

Tang leaps from her lap to join the pack. Even the lounging Chou-fleur springs from the table and zigzag scampers into the front hall.

The barking stops.

The man who walks out to the terrace does not see her. He's stretching his arms over his head as if he's waking up. She considers standing, so he'll notice her, but decides to stay seated. He's tall and slim and has dark hair that falls to his neck. He's wearing a blue jacket, a stiff, white collared shirt, and jeans: Parisian elegance. This must be Po's son.

He sees her and approaches. Tang trots back to her, tail wagging. Ilse wishes she'd stayed up in her room and were not sitting at Po's table.

"Hello," she says, standing. "I'm—"

"Agnès told me. His translator. She also told me you're something of his muse."

Chou-fleur leaps back onto the table.

The tone of his voice: it's suspicious. That's what it is.

"Hardly that. We've been working—"

"On the love poems."

He says this possessively, as if he owns the poems.

"Yes," she says.

He's a handsome man. Intense dark eyes, thick black eyelashes, to match his jet-black hair, smaller eyes than his father's. In fact, few of his features resemble Po's. The chin, and yes, the full lips are his father's. His eyes: though darker in color, they're the serious, unflinching eyes of Inès in the portrait.

"It's been over a year since I've been . . ." He's looking for another word for "home." "Back," he says.

He gazes around slowly. He's taking in the place, the smells, the sounds, the feelings.

"Will you be going to the hospital?"

She regrets her words. It sounds as if she wishes him to depart as soon as he's arrived. Or that she thinks it's what he *should* be doing.

He acts as if he hasn't heard, but she knows he has.

"Mastiff," he says, petting the dog, then kneeling to hug him. "I've missed you, Mastiff, old boy." He bends his head to the dog's chest and stays in this position for a few minutes. Ilse is grateful that she's wearing her new espadrilles instead of her awful black-and-white sneakers.

She considers excusing herself to go to her room.

"I will see to my things," he says, standing. "You're sleeping in which room?"

How to describe the most sumptuous room she's ever seen?

"The room overlooking the vineyard."

He looks up at her room.

"The best room in the house." Bitterness in his voice.

"I know this is a sensitive time," Ilse says, "and I don't wish to intrude. Yesterday, your father asked if I would stay longer, but now that you're here, maybe it's better . . . for me to leave earlier."

He doesn't disagree.

Émile will never agree to pay for another flight change fee. She will speak to Agnès about it.

"May I ask how a person from Greenland became a translator of French poetry?"

She's beginning to understand why Po and his snotty son have not seen each other for a year.

"I wish I had a more exotic answer for you, but I fell in love with your language at a tender age."

She regrets the word "tender," then wonders why she regrets it.

"Tender age," he says. Is he playing Po's game of repeating the last pivot words in the manner of the eighteenth-century Japanese poets? Of course, he is.

She doesn't take the bait.

Po's son glances down at the poem on the worktable, then up at her in a brazen kind of way. She catches a whiff of cigarette smoke.

"Well, I hope you get what you came for."

He makes it sound as if she's been stealing!

He turns and walks into the house, Mastiff following closely behind.

He's a pompous ass. Her fellow Greenlanders, and Malu in particular, would tear him to pieces.

She holds up the poem on the table in front of her, but instead of reading it for the sixth time, she is thinking that Po's son is spying on her from the hall window facing the terrace on the second floor. He's wondering what to make of the Nordic imposter.

Chapter 21

ILSE HAS SPENT MOST OF THE NEXT DAY AT THE DESK IN HER room, attempting to translate lines about the hawthorn flower, *arbor cupiditatis,* which Po is comparing to the tree of life from the Bible. According to her research, the hawthorn flower was the symbol for spiritual love in the thirteenth century, later replaced by the rose. *Damn. This is impossible.* No words that she scribbles will ever be able to encompass the rich cultural context of the Age of Chivalry.

A text from Agnès frees her from her interminable struggle. Agnès and Po will be returning in less than an hour.

Ilse throws aside her work and sails downstairs to prepare a welcome table on the terrace under the olive tree. Po would like that. She arranges a bottle of Ricard (will he be able to drink?), a carafe of water, a small bowl of black olives, and another one of peanuts. Of course, Po may want to go directly upstairs to bed.

Ilse knows that Po is near when Tang barks and takes off from her side in the kitchen. She joins Po's son in the hallway as he opens the front door. Here come the dogs! Even the independent Carenza is tail-wagging present. *Please be gentle, pups,* she says inside herself.

"Thank goodness he's not in a wheelchair," Po's son says more to himself than to Ilse as the two of them stand at the entrance hall window. "That would kill me. What am I saying? It would kill *him.*"

Po leans on Agnès as they amble toward the house. He's walking with a cane. When the dogs rush toward him, he falls onto Agnès, who stumbles under her brother's weight. She manages to hold him up as he pauses to pet Mastiff.

"Mastiff, stop worrying! I'm back," Ilse hears Po say through the open door. His voice lacks the lilt of the troubadour. He is an older man than the one who escorted her in his yellow convertible to the *pétanque* match. It's because she can't see his face, his bright youthful eyes.

"I'll be back in a minute," Frey says, leaving Ilse's side as if he's forgotten something upstairs. He takes the stairs two at a time. Frey moves as if he's bound by the outlines of his body, unlike Po where the lines are blurred between his body and who or what is around him. Po is tactile, he's always touching things, rubbing the pages of his poems with his fingers, gently tapping her hand, or embracing his friends with gusto. His face is warm, and often merry. In contrast, Frey's face is narrow, definitive, and demanding.

And yet.

Even though Ilse has just met him, she senses vulnerability underneath Frey's precision, and she guesses that his exactitude may be a shield to hide an otherwise sensitive inner essence. Is she imagining this because she wants him to be more like his father?

Po must have left the cane outside the door because he doesn't carry it into the house.

"Île du Nord!" he says, letting go of Agnès and opening his arms wide. "Thank you for being here to welcome me home." Ilse can feel him trembling as he hugs her.

"Hello, Ilse," says Agnès, after their double-cheek embrace. Agnès has that same deep way of looking at her that Po has. Of taking the time to see all of her. "Isn't Frey here?"

"Yes, he was just here. He ran upstairs."

"Frey! Your father's home," Agnès calls up the stairs. There's an edge to her voice.

"He must not realize that you've arrived," she tells her brother.

"Frey!" Agnès calls again.

The three wait awkwardly in the front hall below the steps.

"Why are we waiting inside when I see a bottle of Ricard on the terrace warming in the blue sunset?" says Po. "I haven't had a drop to drink in three days. I'm still mad at you, Agnès, for not bringing me my flask."

"Sorry, brother, I follow doctor's orders."

"Come on, Mastiff," he says without moving. "Let's go." He gestures for Ilse to walk ahead of him and waits for Agnès to take his arm.

They take seats at the table under the olive tree.

"Île du Nord, will you please excuse the interruptions to our work together? We have so many words to wrestle to the ground."

"*C'est vrai*, it's true," she says, trying to keep her voice light. Despite registering how changed he seems physically, she's relieved to be in his presence again.

Where's Frey? All three want to know, but no one is asking.

Agnès tips the bottle of Ricard and pours a thimbleful into each of the glasses except for her brother's.

Po holds out his glass. "Agnès, give a dying man his pleasure."

"Geoffrey, you're on medication. But since this is a homecoming, I suppose we can cheat a little."

Agnès pours a dash of Ricard into her brother's glass, tops up her and Ilse's amounts, then adds water into each.

"To the Luberon!" Po says, lifting his trembling glass. Ilse and Agnès lift theirs and sip.

"That's better. I'm beginning to feel alive again."

"Here he comes, Frey," says Agnès, sounding relieved.

"After the homecoming toast," says Po, under his breath.

"Father," Po's son says, walking toward them. Not a strand of Frey's hair is out of place. He has prepared for this moment.

"Son," says Po, his chin in the air. The father, too, has rehearsed.

It's the setup for a duel. Ilse and Agnès are the seconds.

"So, it is my dying that has brought you home . . . finally." Po's voice breaks, betrays his practice. He rises unsteadily, his hands resting on the table for balance.

"Father, you're being dramatic."

"I agree," says Agnès, standing. "Please, Frey, have a seat, so your father can sit down."

But Frey does not sit. The men face each other, with the table separating them.

"I'm not being dramatic," says Po. "The doctors gave me three to six months. This is my last summer, that is, if I make it to the summer solstice." He looks around him at the rows of vineyards.

"Geoffrey," says Agnès.

"Thank you for taking time away from your life, my son, to say goodbye."

"Father," the son says. "You've got enough fire in you to live a lot longer than that."

Won't Agnès change the subject, or somebody say something to pacify the combatants?

"Have a Ricard, Frey," says Agnès, finally, as she pours water into a short glass of Ricard and hands it to him.

"Thank you, Aunt Agnès," Frey says, sitting in the chair next to her.

"Did you hear about your father's *carreau*?"

"My *pétanque* game is better than my poetry lately," says Po, sinking into his chair with a sigh. "Frey, I trust you've met Île du Nord."

"It's Ilse," she says. She won't be called Po's nickname by the arrogant ass.

"Île du Nord is using her intellectual powers to navigate my Provençal vocabulary safely across the great Atlantic Ocean. When we began our work together, I thought I was the teacher, instructing this lovely student what each word meant, line by line, but now I realize, and this is the elusive, mysterious, and paradoxical beauty of life, that she is the one educating me—about my own language. Through our communion of spirits, I feel as if Île du Nord is liberating my language, turning my 'has been' words into 'might bes,' giving my work new possibility."

"Nooo," Ilse says, shaking her head.

"None of that," says Po in a reprimanding tone. "Watch out for Île du Nord: she's prone to self-abnegation."

"Father, I see you've let dogs and cats have the run of the house these days, among other . . ." Frey looks at Ilse.

How can such a wonderful man father such a beastly son?

"Why shouldn't they live here as grand as any guest?" asks Po. "If you'd come to visit this year, there would be a chair in the living room left for you."

"Father." No subject is safe.

Po empties his glass, his hand trembling wildly until he sets it down. He closes his eyes and takes a deep breath.

"Agnès, will you please do the honors?" he says, pointing to the bottle.

Agnès serves him and Ilse. Frey has not touched his drink.

"Father, you chose your life and wife. I've done the same. This is *my* life and my choice of wife, not yours."

"I never claimed *her* as *my* wife!" says Po, on the mark.

Frey narrows his eyes. Po looks up at the sky, then turns his gaze to Mastiff and scratches the dog's wobbly chin.

Po is the first to resume.

"I suppose you've delivered your message, and now you'll be departing?"

"Break it up, you two actors, with us as your audience," says Agnès. "I brought my laptop with me, not to record your drama, but because I found some old videos that I thought you'd both enjoy."

"A visit down memory lane to divert us. No thank you, Aunt Agnès."

"Don't say I didn't try," she says, returning the laptop to the canvas bag beside her chair.

"I hope I won't see this moment in your next poem," says Frey. "I'm reading it now . . . 'The son on the horizon, cold as a frozen egg yolk.' "

"Not bad, son, you could be a poet."

"The refrain of my life."

"You came home ready to fight, didn't you, even given the"—Po clears his throat—"circumstances."

"Everything for you, Father, is material for the next poem. My mother provided plenty for you to purloin."

"Even given the circumstances," Po repeats.

Ilse draws a breath.

"Frey, stop," Agnès says, standing.

"That's why you've come back: to point a dying man in the direction of hell," says Po, flushed, his tired blue eyes red with intensity. He sips his drink, starts to choke. His flushed face turns red in patches.

He stands, turns toward the vines, staggers, spits up something. Is it red?

The three of them freeze.

"I'm returning to Paris tomorrow," says Frey, standing.

"Your rancor sits heavily on me," says Po, feebly rising and facing Frey. It's a standoff again.

"Why can't you talk like normal people?" Frey says. " 'Your rancor sits heavily on me.' I'm tired of letting you escape so easily and comfortably into your troubadour doppelganger."

"What do you want me to do?" Po lifts his eyes to the sky.

"It's actually very simple," says Frey. "Accept me and my fiancée. As you know, the wedding is in a few months."

"How can you ask me to accept a marriage when I know that love is . . . absent?"

"Another poem in the making."

"Frey!" says Agnès. She takes her purse from the table and places the strap over her shoulder. "This is too much."

Po coughs again, this time into his handkerchief. Are those red spots, blood? He is so pale.

"You're sick," says Frey, "but you're still headstrong. I learned long ago that the troubadour Poet's abundant love for his paramour has no room for his child. Excuse me while I retire upstairs and call *my* paramour."

"The definition of a paramour is an illicit lover."

Frey stiffens and narrows his already narrow eyes, then turns toward the house, taking his drink with him.

"You haven't had dinner," calls out Agnès.

"'*Go: for thy stay, not free, absents thee more,*'" yells Po, his voice faltering.

"Keep quoting Milton or whomever you choose so you don't have to face yourself!" yells Frey from inside the French doors.

THE FOLLOWING MORNING, FROM her balcony, Ilse notices Frey walking along the border of the vineyard with Agnès. Mastiff and the two other dogs tag along behind and beside them. How funny that Tang stays with her in her room. At the curve of the vineyard, Frey bends, then crouches to touch the unripe green grapes under the vines. In that moment, from her window view, his face looks like a child's, full of wonder.

At nine o'clock, Po shuffles over to the worktable under the olive tree, where Ilse is waiting for him. Two weeks ago, at the Renaissance Café, this man looked in glowing good health. Now his shirt hangs on his bones like rags on a scarecrow.

He bows to her as his hello, then excuses himself from working, saying his brain is too muddled. "It's those pills," he mutters. With a shake of his head and another bow, Po declines Ilse's offer to bring a tray with coffee to his room.

After trying to work on her own for a few hours, Ilse gives up. The emptiness that stalks her at home in Greenland is at arm's distance, tempting her to be sucked into its undertow. Po should be composing poetry right now, not up in his bed, sluggish from raging cancer and drugs. In the kitchen, she can hear Agnès preparing lunch.

"Please let me help you, Agnès."

Agnès smiles up at Ilse.

"Thank you," she says, turning from the counter to retrieve her phone in her purse. "I've been wanting to show you something."

Photographs of her newborn granddaughters. "Look, this one has

Geoffrey's eyebrows," she says, and then she turns away in a quick motion, her face in the white cloth napkin.

"This is not an easy time," Ilse says.

"You may not know it, Ilse," Agnès says, blowing her nose, putting the napkin in her pocket, and turning back to Ilse, "but your being here is a great help. If Geoffrey can write poetry, I have the feeling that it will add days to his life, possibly weeks and months."

"I've delayed my flight, as you know, but still, I think Frey would prefer it if I left today."

"Frey is not making this decision. Of course, we'll take care of any fees for changing flights. But let's get through this week before we worry about the next one. Please join us for dinner tonight. I'm making—"

"*Oui,*" Ilse says before Agnès has finished saying the word *bouillabaisse.* "I've convinced Frey to stay for another day, as I must leave tomorrow morning to tend to my daughter."

Useless at work—Ilse can't glimpse one of Po's words without crying—she dons the courage of Zoë Gaudet and walks to the village to Le Cercle. Bar-side, she requests a Ricard. It's four o'clock on a Wednesday, half an hour earlier than the regulars. Is it possible? Carole smiles at her in greeting. It's a fleeting, closed-mouth smile, but it's a smile. Carole and she talk about Po and his illness, and about his son. To Ilse's surprise, Carole has only good things to say about Frey.

"He had to leave us to find himself," she says. "It's not easy to live up to the charisma and character of his father, not to mention his mother."

Carole concurs with Po about Frey's fiancée not being a suitable mate. "*Une Parisienne,*" she says gruffly, turning the tap of water on full blast to wash out the sink.

When Ilse returns to the Labaye household that evening after a long walk to a twelfth-century Cistercian abbey on the other side of the village, Po's worktable under the olive tree is set for dinner for four. As Ilse helps bring out the dinner in the hues of sunsetting pinks, it seems that some sort of stiff reconciliation has taken place between the men, most probably brokered by Agnès. Agnès and Po sit on one side of the table, and Ilse and Frey on the other.

Po uses both hands to pour the red wine before Agnès takes over. They talk of impersonal subjects: the weather, the visit of the vineyard tender the following day, and what they expect from this year's crop. Frey looks more relaxed in his jeans and navy T-shirt. Agnès is the rock of the table, making everyone feel safe and grateful, especially for her *bouillabaisse,* which is a concoction of everything Ilse loves: fennel, potatoes, mussels, clams, scallops. She tastes a dash of Ricard.

That night, Ilse scans the Internet for Caroline Solenz, investment banker, Frey's fiancée. Caroline is thirty-four years old. Her degrees and awards fill the screen. Ilse presses the tab for images, and there she is, as Ilse had imagined, tall and tidy in a business suit, her brown hair in a short, blunt cut. She has unsmiling, thin lips, elegant brows, small, intense blue eyes. She's pretty.

Ilse taps *Geoffrey Labaye, Artificial Intelligence.* "The son of Geoffrey Labaye, French poet of numerous collections of poetry, written in the Provençal dialect that reflect the era of the troubadours." About his son, he's thirty-seven years old and has attended . . . What follows is a long list of schools and universities from where he's received an even longer tally of degrees and honors. In terms of achievements, Geoffrey Labaye, artificial intelligence specialist, and Caroline Solenz, investment banker, are made for each other.

Chapter 22

It's hot this Thursday, May 17 morning, but more than the warmth of the day, Ilse is feeling the heat of her June fourth deadline. Instead of sitting in her chilly office in Oqaatsut and warily watching the dilating water stain on the ceiling, Ilse is taking cover under the shade of the silvery olive tree at Po's worktable, pulling together a very rough draft of the first half of the collected poetry.

Po has been training her ear, but she's still such a novice. The last time she asked him how to make a poem sing, he'd serenaded her with a few verses "to open her ear to the modulations and intonations." That session, she'd wiped her eyes full of tears from both sorrow and laughter.

It is as if she and Po have discovered an underground current, a place of mutual resonance, where they meet and frolic, splashing words, like water. Both know their connection is deeper than language.

Ilse plucks petite white olive tree blossoms from her laptop screen.

Now, with Po's life on the line, how can she possibly live up to his high expectations of her? Or Émile's? Or Provence's, or her own? There's so much more at stake for this translation. Now she remembers that Émile had called it the Poet's swan song, not knowing how true that was. Her work cannot be a version, a derivation, an adaptation. The words she chooses must capture the living resonance of each poem. Émile was misguided to hire her for this job. A renowned English or American poet should be translating Geoffrey Labaye, not some dilettante dissembler!

Here comes Agnès, approaching with a bag over her arm.

Agnès, please don't leave.

Agnès's face looks ashen.

"Thank goodness the mistral has left us. Geoffrey seems a little better today." She turns her face up to the sky, not unlike the way Po does.

"You too aren't blaming your brother's illness on the mistral?"

Agnès bursts into laughter.

"Oh, Ilse, thank goodness you're here. Did I just accuse the mistral?" Agnès takes a deep breath. "The doctor says that Geoffrey will have a mix of good and bad days. On the bad days, he may not get out of bed. That's when I need you or Frey to bring a tray of breakfast, lunch, and dinner up to his room."

Ilse's phone chimes. It's Émile.

"Please go ahead and take the call while I say goodbye to the dogs."

Ilse answers. Po has won the Prix Mallarmé! Ilse jots down Émile's words with a pen and pad she finds in the kitchen: "For Monsieur Labaye's steadfast devotion to an ancient French tradition, and for the grace and depth of his poetic, melodic language."

"Émile, this is great news. Yes, he's been hard to reach. Daphné has tried nonstop? Yes, I'll ask him to return her call." She still won't tell Émile about Po's illness. "Of course, I know: June fourth." She clicks off.

The pressure for the impossible "perfect" translation of the poetry of Prix Mallarmé winner Geoffrey Labaye has intensified.

"Some good news, Agnès," Ilse says, startling her. Agnès is sitting on the floor under the portrait of Inès, petting Mastiff and whispering to the dog to take care of his master.

Ilse reads aloud Émile's words.

Agnès stands, lifts her hands, then folds them together, her thin gold bracelets making tinkling music on her thin wrists.

"My little brother! I'm gratified that people care about the troubadour tradition in this day and age. This news should be life-affirming, but if I know Geoffrey, he'll say he doesn't care a fig."

Just then, Po descends the stairs, taking each step slowly. He's dressed in his white shirt, cuffs open, and loose white pants. Bare feet.

Agnès tells him that his publisher has a special message for him, that he should call her *tout de suite*.

"I don't want to talk to her."

"It's good news."

Po repeats that he doesn't want to speak to his publisher.

"It's about an award," Agnès adds, on her way out the door.

"As Dante says," Po quotes, " 'Worldly fame is nothing but a gust of wind.' "

Agnès lifts her hands in surrender to Ilse, then gives Po a kiss on each cheek, plus the third, and departs.

"What's an award to a dying man?" he says, holding on to the table in the front hall. It's as if he's on a rocking ship. "Good morning, Île du Nord." He falters a bit as if he will faint, then stands upright.

" '. . . Oh, that my tongue were in the thunder's mouth. Then with a passion would I shake the world.' "

"You're full of quotes today."

"I've been thinking that Frey is right, that I use other poets' words to distract people and mostly myself. But I can't help it. Every word I've memorized is flying in my face these last few days like a wind-whipped flurry of leaves that won't settle down."

"Maybe you're being called to write."

"My muse, indeed. But before my deadline, let's meet yours."

"Touché," she says with a fake laugh as they walk arm-in-arm to the table under the olive tree.

"I'm sorry Agnès had to leave so soon," he says. "It would be nice for you and her to be friends. She's a wise and talented artist and a loving mother and wife. She manages to balance things in her life like that olive blossom is balancing on the tip of your nose."

She removes the blossom.

"How sad that it can't stay there for the rest of the day," Po says as he settles into his chair.

After an hour of working together, Po looks drained of color. He wipes his forehead with his handkerchief.

"Lately when I try to write poetry, I feel like a lizard chasing its tail," he says. "Île du Nord, relieve me from trying to make gold out of straw! Sometimes the world just won't glitter. For a change, please tell me about your ice-bedazzled world."

She sips her coffee, takes a deep breath, and closes her eyes.

"In our country, instead of this fertile patchwork of greens and yellows, we have icy moors and fjords covered white with snow or gulls. Frosted moss clings to the rocky coastline, thick like a coat, and the brightest white things you can imagine, icebergs as big as houses appear as if from nowhere like inert, but wide-eyed creatures. On any given day, you can spot humpback whales, sometimes in pairs, rising out of the ocean as if they're pulled up by string from above. How breathtaking it is when these enormous creatures crash and splash down, giving you a flourishing goodbye with their fan-like tails. Farther up north, from a kayak, you can eavesdrop on mating polar bears and catch glimpses of the ten-foot-long spiraled ivory tusks of narwhals, our unicorns of the sea."

"Île du Nord," Po says, his eyes bright, "you're singing!"

THAT AFTERNOON, WHILE PO is napping, Ilse is trying to make sense of one of the more difficult poems in the collection. It's packed with Provençal expressions. Chou-fleur is asleep in the shady part of the worktable under the olive tree. She wishes it were Po walking toward her, and not his arrogant ass of a son.

She stands as he approaches.

"Which poem are you working on now?" Frey asks, leaning over the papers on the table.

No "*Bonjour.*" How can the son of Po, a descendant in a line of chivalric troubadours, speak to her with so little respect?

"'Perdu dans le Village des Bories.' Lost in the Village of Stone Huts."

"Please sit so I can sit," he commands.

"I feel like standing," she says.

"Okay, then stand. I'm sitting." He moves the chair slightly away from the table and takes a seat.

The coffee carafe and the two cups catch his attention.

As if she should have asked permission to fetch coffee cups and coffee.

"Is this for you and me?"

"For your father and me, rather."

"I hope you don't mind if I take my father's share?"

He says "father's share" with extra emphasis.

He pours the coffee into a cup and offers it to her.

"Please sit," he repeats. "You're making me feel uncomfortable, standing."

She takes the cup from him and perches on the edge of her chair.

"Agnès says my father is writing again, and on subjects other than the loss . . . of my mother. A tribute to you, I suppose. And yet, I hardly know who you are, and here you are, at my father's table . . ."

It's the age-old story: elderly man takes in a young girlfriend, who lusts after the family inheritance, in this case, a manor house with hundreds of valuable acres of vineyard. She's been expecting a comment like this from Po's son but hadn't prepared a response. She rereads the poem in front of her, or rather, pretends to read it.

"Interesting. You're working on one of the few poems that is about me." He looks away and up at the house.

"Really? I had no idea you starred in any of your father's poems."

"Nice repartée."

He rewards remarks that are mean-spirited.

"I appear in only a few, and in this one, I happen to play the main part."

She looks up at him.

"Perhaps I can help . . . elucidate?"

He had wanted to say "educate."

"I haven't visited the Village des Bories—"

"And you've been here for what, three weeks?" he interrupts. "You've only to walk a mere few hundred feet."

That's him: the arrogant ass.

"I've been here for two weeks and two days, and I haven't had time to be a tourist. I'm on a deadline."

He sips his black coffee.

"I was six years old when I visited it," he says, not looking up, "alone. My parents were someplace exotic, Shanghai, Madagascar, or the Maldives, who knows. The housekeeper was busy. I chased a lizard from this house into the *Village des Bories*. It's in that direction if you ever leave this house."

He points.

She narrows her eyes at him.

"People here are proud of the *Village des Bories,* a cluster of look-alike stone huts, built in the nineteenth century to protect shepherds from rain, wind, and cold weather. It's a strange, deserted place, with dried-up scrub trees and stones everywhere: stone huts, stone walls, and piles of stones from shelters that have collapsed and crumbled to the ground over the years. For a six-year-old, it was a fabulous discovery, like entering another world, the only living things snakes, lizards, and insects. No mammals, no birdsong. No sounds except a random stone falling, or the wind whirring through the cracks of rock. One of the huts that I entered had so many gaps that I decided that it was my job to replace the fallen stones.

"When I came out of the hut, it was dark. I ran in what I thought was the direction of home but ended back at the same *borie* hut."

Ilse thinks of her few minutes of terror the day she'd lost her way in the dark tunnels under the château grounds.

"Everything looked the same to me. Every hut, exactly alike. The police found me the next morning huddled in the corner of one of the stone huts. My parents only heard about it after I was found. I've always wished that they'd learned the moment I was lost so they would have suffered more, even had a sleepless night or two during their vacation. When they called from wherever they were, I told them I was fine. They returned two weeks later from their trip."

"Two weeks later," she echoes.

"That poem that you're reading is a guilt poem. My father wrote it to alleviate his shame for not returning as soon as he heard about the incident."

"Does he capture your feeling of being lost?"

"His lostness, not mine."

"The difference—"

"A world of difference. But never mind, it's his poem, not mine."

He sips the coffee. Tang whines, and Ilse bends to pet him. The other dogs surround them as if in a council. Why has Mastiff left Po's bedroom?

"Mastiff, at least *you're* happy I'm home."

Po's son leans back in the chair. Gull wings flap above them. A lost seagull?

"My lostness was primitive," he continues, "the kind when your stomach is sucked out of you, when you lack trust in yourself and the world. Every emotion, thought, and physical feeling was saturated with fear. My father captured perhaps the first few minutes of being lost, not my wide-eyed ten hours in the depths of darkness. That night I discovered a new form of aloneness, one which still terrorizes me."

She closes her eyes, experiencing the darkness under her eyelids.

"Why am I telling you this?"

"To help me with the translation," she says.

She is about to ask if he'd ever written his own poem about the experience but stops herself.

"It's probably the greatest trauma I've ever suffered, hopefully will ever suffer. Even now as I talk about it, I feel the night creeping up on me like snakes through rocks. Did you miss me, old boy?" Frey kneels to pet Mastiff.

From there, he looks up at Ilse, his intensity softened.

"I've mentioned this little trauma of mine to others, but I haven't told anyone how much it still affects me, not even my fiancée, Caroline.

I suppose it's seeing the poem that's refreshed the memory of it. Or else you have special translator powers that have triggered my emotions around it."

As he pets the dog, Frey's eyes, his taut lips, his tight shoulders seem to relax. Then he does something surprising: he gets on his knees and drapes himself over Mastiff like a cape.

In Greenland, it is well known that stroking or petting an animal is a remedy for so many things, especially the symptoms of *Perlerorneq*, the Arctic depression or hysteria in people that often breaks out in the endlessly cold spring season after the four months of Great Dark.

There's the gull again, overhead. And the birdsong of the calandra lark that Po had drawn her attention to the other morning. Po could identify most birds by the metrical composition of their song, this one by its twittering, double chirp, twittering, double chirp, its perfect repetition and refrain.

"Thinking about that poem," Po's son says, wiping his eyes and looking up at her, "proves a theory of mine."

"Yes?"

"That empathy is humanly unachievable. My father had the hubris to think that in this poem he could inhabit the boy in the stone hut during an endless dark night. He didn't get close."

Ilse takes a deep breath and puts down her coffee cup. "Your father told me that you work in AI."

"Recently, we've been working to teach AI to sympathize, which is already a great leap, but empathy is different. In that poem, my father appreciates my plight, he even sympathizes with it, but there's no way that he can experience what I did. I've come to believe that it's impossible to take the place of another in the same circumstance. And if humans can't do it, it's highly doubtful that we can teach AI."

She would disagree. Hadn't she and Po shared the intense feeling of each other's losses, her Jann, and his Inès?

Instead of quibbling, she gives empathy a try. "A six-year-old, out all night in the darkness in such an alien, foreign place . . ."

"At one point I heard voices—the housekeeper's, and others—shouting my name. Like in your worst nightmare, when I needed it most, I lost my voice. It was in the excruciating moment when they stopped calling for me, when I realized that I'd have to survive the night. That was the night that I learned how to be like one of the *borie* stones."

His black eyes are expressionless.

Neither speaks for what feels like a long time. Chou-fleur jumps down from the table, knocking over the pitcher of milk.

"Chou-fleur!" he yells.

Ilse rushes to place her cloth napkin over the puddle of milk, but not before it drips onto her lap through the crack of the table.

He offers her his napkin with a slight smile. Now that's more like the gallant son of Po.

"I've taken you away from your work." He stands. "Come on, Mastiff, let's go. Carenza, you've got to gain some weight. And Ronsard, you're perfect. Come, you three, and Tang too. We've got a lot of catching up to do. I hope I've helped your translation in some small way. Île du—"

"It's Ilse, Ilse Erlund." She'd already told him her name.

"It's an annoying habit of my father's. If he doesn't like a name, he makes up a new one to suit him, whether the person he's addressing likes it or not."

Did Po not like her given name?

"Yes, now I remember," he says, leaning over the table and looking at her for a moment longer than feels appropriate.

"Tang, come."

Tang hesitates. It's a test. Has the imposter manipulated the affection of this dog as well as that of his father?

Tang makes the difficult choice and joins Frey and the pack on the path that follows the periphery of the vineyard.

Ilse returns to her work. When she looks up an hour later, the color of the Luberon Mountains has changed from a pale lavender to a dark purple hue. The sunset is gentle tonight, as if someone pressed a warm palm against the cheek of it. All is finally still.

Chapter 23

THE NEXT WEEK PASSES IN SYNC WITH THE BIORHYTHMS OF spring across the vineyard: buds swelling and bursting, grapevines sensing the longer days through light receptors located in their green tissues, caterpillars munching on succulent leaves, weeds flowering on the vineyard floor, honeybees whizzing to collect pollen, and the sunflowers tracking the sun, all in the circadian cadence of the internal clock of nature. So too does a pattern develop in the lives of these three people, Po, Frey, and Ilse, living under the same roof overlooking the vast, burgeoning vineyard.

Frey stops saying he must return to Paris. Ilse stops saying she feels she is imposing, and both worry about Po's visibly declining health. After a morning jog, Frey works most of the day, making calls and attending virtual meetings from his laptop in the room overlooking the front drive and the huge oak and the mountains in the direction of Lourmarin, the village on the other side of the Luberon. When Ilse is not working at the table on the terrace with Po, she stays in her bedroom, overlooking the vineyards, searching for the right words to infill the translated poems with Po's insight and spirit.

During the day, when her door is slightly open, she overhears Frey talking on the phone. Sometimes, his voice has the singsong quality of his father's, and Ilse is reminded of his troubadour blood. She's also reminded that this is probably his voice when talking with his fiancée.

Ilse and Po's work sessions now last an hour and sometimes less, compared to the two-to-three-hour tête-à-têtes Ilse enjoyed at the beginning of her visit. And, Po has begun to use the cane.

She and Po are playing a call-and-response word game, to, as Po says, "warm up her mind" when Georges bounds toward them ahead of the dogs. He sits with them for a few minutes to natter on about the latest *pétanque* matches. But today, something is different: Po *acts* interested, but Ilse can tell: he's not. A few hours later, Jean-Pierre, in his black beret and with his bag of two bottles of wine, appears at the door for their weekly wine exchange. Po jokes, pulling Jean-Pierre's beret off his bald pate, protesting as he always does that he's getting the worse end of the deal, but Ilse can tell: Po is pretending. The visits matter, but the *pétanque* game and wine do not. Po has no appetite anymore for what mortals eat or drink or for the athletic games they play.

Despite this, there's no sense of melancholy in the house. Instead, in the company of the dogs at their sides or on nearby sofas and chairs, the birdsong, and swoops of birds in and out of the living room where the sparrows and goldfinches have built nests, the simple and fresh dinners that the three make and eat together, the feeling all around and inside the Labaye house is light and full of sunshine. Unless one looks intensely into the poet's tired, red eyes, or notes the pasty color of his skin, or has counted how many times he coughs day and night, it would be difficult to suspect that Po has been diagnosed with a disease from which he will never recover.

Ilse suspects that Po's good nature is the result of a new, peaceful relationship with his son and perhaps a hope for a different future for him. At last night's dinner, he toasted to "Ilse and Frey," as if they were a couple. They both smiled, but Ilse had flushed, knowing that she and Frey were aware of the deliberate combination of their names.

During recent sessions, Po has stopped tapping her hand. He no longer gazes at her with that bemused smile, his head tilted, one eye winking. She had thought, in a kind of disappointed way, that he was less attentive because of his prognosis, but now she guesses Po has another motive. And she's not sure she likes it.

AT THEIR CANDLELIT DINNER tonight, Po excuses himself early, leaving Frey and Ilse to sit quietly under the olive tree with a half-finished bottle of Domaine Labaye. The three dogs follow Po into the house, but Tang stays, as always, by Ilse's side.

"I can't understand how someone in my father's condition can appear so seemingly lighthearted. He should have been an actor. Sometimes I wonder if he'll ever take off the mask of the singing troubadour."

But that's who Po is, Ilse wants to argue. Instead, she sips the wine and gulps the night air, fragrant with a nearby patch of sweet-smelling clover. The candle in the hurricane glass wavers.

"Maybe the Prix Mallarmé has raised his spirits?" she offers.

"As I'm sure you're aware by now, my father couldn't care less about awards. He lives in another dimension."

"Do you think in that dimension he imagines that he's getting closer to meeting his true love, Inès, wherever she is?"

Frey gazes up at the dim light from the hallway window on the second floor of the house.

"Sorry to dash your notions of the troubadour's love." He moves the hurricane glass with the candle in it from the middle of their table to the side next to his wineglass so his view of her is unimpeded. She liked the candle better where it was. "I've been struggling with this question my whole life, whether someone like my father writes out of true love for a person, or from his inherited troubadour profession of praising a *symbol* rather than a person. Ronsard said himself that he didn't compose poetry out of love, but that he *loved in order to* compose poetry. The love-object doesn't even have to exist." He swirls the wine in his glass, takes a sip, and pauses, looking dissatisfied with the taste.

"Ummi was the perfect match for my father. She adored the idea of being a model for all women, the lady of divine wisdom and beauty, Dante's Beatrice, worthy of poetic glory. Maybe my father is changing his writing style of late because he's finally able to see through the charade of love conceived in the twelfth century. Perhaps he's arrived at this new clarity thanks to you, because of a certain earnest, clinging-to-the-truth quality that you have. It must be an attribute that you bring from the north.

"But it's not a heavy, serious thing, your truth," Frey adds. "It's as if it's the simplest thing in the world."

"I've always thought of myself as too serious."

He laughs. It's an easy laugh, the first time she's heard such a sound from him.

"*Au contraire,* you are *légère.* I'm going to do something that you spend many hours of the day and possibly night doing—and look up the definition." He begins reading from his smartphone aloud. "'*Légèr: duveteux,* feathery, light in weight.' The other French definitions include 'promiscuous, immoral, illegal, and free.' My comment did not include the dictionary's third-tier definitions."

"Levity as promiscuous? That's new to me. Now you can see why I love the French language: lightness becomes immoral."

He continues reading. "'*Un léger retard,* a slight delay; *blessé légèrement,* slightly injured, delicate as in perfume; *à la légère,* thoughtlessly, *plus légère, plus loufoque*—'"

"*Loufoque?*"

"Crazy."

"It sounds promiscuous to me!" she says. "I may have to Anglicize that word."

He raises his glass to hers. "To being *loufoque*!"

This surely is a different man from the one who showed up scowling at her presence. Such is the enchantment of Provence.

She laughs and lifts her wineglass to mirror his.

Instead of sipping, he tips the wine out of the glass into the grass beside the terrace.

"Not only is this wine sour, but it has the wrong color. Ummi would be turning in her grave to know that Father served this tonight."

"Really?"

"She was a colorist."

"Pardon me?"

"The best sommeliers are known to have extra taste cells, but Ummi was a super-seer. She had an eye for the most subtle differences in color. She drove the men who painted the walls in this house crazy, asking them to mix a cocktail of three, sometimes four shades of color together before it suited her taste. And it rarely did. If the hue could not express itself in the afternoon haze, or during an evening sunset, she would assemble all the cans, and mix and pour a little of this into that, and then paint the walls herself."

So it wasn't necessarily the hues of sunrise and sunset that Ilse had been admiring on the walls of the house: it was Ummi's artistry.

"Ummi thought that color shows you everything, that if the hue is right, everything will follow. My mother was a wordsmith in five languages, but I think her favorite vernacular was that of color. She would say in English, 'This color does not pass mustard.' She didn't realize the expression is 'pass muster,' and that 'muster' is a formal military inspection!"

"You're a word person, too."

"I wouldn't cut the mustard!"

Ilse laughs.

But she stops when she thinks that Ummi would not be happy with the color of Po's pallid complexion.

"Whatever colors you read about in my father's poems originate from my mother's descriptions."

That day Ilse had been working on a poem about a woman with eggplant black blue violet hair.

"Will you please excuse me?" he says, suddenly.

While Frey is gone, she tips her head back to inhale the warm night air. A bird above makes a sound, like trickling water, and she wonders if it's a nightingale. Po had told her that troubadours often wrote about nightingales who sing melancholy melodies, reminding them of their unhappiness in love. No bird who trills so sweetly would survive the frigid ice blasts of Greenland.

He's back. In the semidarkness, it looks like both of his hands are behind his back. He extends one arm out to her. Nice! He's holding a bottle of champagne with a gold label.

"This May night calls for effervescence. I found this on the table as if it were left out especially for us."

She knows who left it there.

What's in his other hand?

"Now, to open it!"

He takes from behind his back—what?—a long, curved saber.

"When Napoleon's troops passed through this area two hundred years ago, they impressed my great-great-grandmother, a young widow from the Napoleonic Wars, using this method."

Standing back, he wields the saber up and down and then around his head with flare, like a kid showing off.

She laughs.

"Île du Nord, you make me feel *loufoque*!"

She thought he didn't like the nickname that Po had given her.

He holds the champagne in one hand and with the other strikes the neck of the bottle at an angle. He slices the top cleanly off! He smiles, bows, and places the sword on the table.

"That's dramatic and also dangerous!"

"It's called 'champagne sabering.'"

She wonders how many times this man has lopped off the tops of champagne bottles for other damsels.

"Wait right here," he says. He walks quickly to the house.

She glances at her phone for the time. It's already eleven-thirty!

"I forgot the glasses," he says on his return, and he pours the champagne into two fluted crystal glasses. Then he sits, looking across at her.

In the candlelight, and in the shadow of his thick eyebrows, his eyes are blacker than usual and she cannot tell what they're saying.

"To the lightness you bring to the Labayes," he says, dipping his head to her. It's all so twelfth century—and so amusing.

"Speaking of your mother, the color purist," she says, "I admire the portrait of her."

To keep the conversation from lapsing, Ilse has just lied. She has never liked the portrait: it made Inès's character so obvious, almost cartoonish. Hadn't Frey just complimented Ilse for being truthful?

He looks away from her.

"I hate that painting," he says. "Father won't let me trash it. It's a horrible representation; it's coarse and crude. I don't know why she ever let him put it up. She always laughed that the portrait kept her in line."

The lightness between them has gone out. Why did Ms. Serious have to spoil the moment?

"She looks exotic, at least in that painting," Ilse says. Now, that *is* true.

"I never felt . . . exotic enough for her," he says, leaning down to pet Tang, who is supine on the grass.

This attractive man not exotic enough? She gazes down at Frey's wrist and wonders if his watch was a gift from his fiancée, and if there is an engraving on the underside with the words "For those who love, time is eternal."

"I felt like a disappointment to her because . . ."

"Because," she echoes softly. Po's call-and-response game.

"Because I wasn't enough."

The breeze catches a lock of his jet-black hair.

"I also know that feeling." When Jann died, she'd felt she wasn't "enough" to make up for the gaping chasm in her parents' life and that of her community. Come to think of it, five years later, she still thinks of herself as not enough. How could she ever imagine embodying even a fraction of all that he was?

"How?" he asks; he moves the lock of hair from his forehead. Now it's fallen back in place.

"My brother was a star athlete, but more than that, he was beloved by all who met him. He had charisma. People were drawn to him, couldn't get enough of him. Next to him, I was just his sister, a loner with a strange vocation. When I was with my brother, I was always more than 'enough,' and we were together all the time."

"You speak about him in the past tense."

"I lost him five years ago in a motorcycle crash."

She's said the words so many times that now they mean nothing to her.

"I'm so sorry," he says, and unexpectedly, he reaches his hand across the table, palm up, not unlike the way Po has offered her his hand. She takes his hand, smiles, then unclasps it.

They sip the champagne. It's delicious, rich, and bubbly, a perfect mix of dry and sweet. It's the best champagne she's ever tasted.

"But *you* were your mother's only child, and a son. In the Moroccan culture, surely—"

"My mother had several miscarriages before and after I was born. I grew up with more 'what if' siblings than you can count. She would talk about them as if she knew them. What if that one had survived or that one, or that one . . . I imagined her saying to my father, 'Of all those unborn children, *this* is the one we get?' The 'what ifs' became a kind of obsession for Ummi, almost a demon that possessed her. They say love is blind, but it's also deaf. She didn't hear how destructive this was to me."

He was so close to her minutes ago, holding her hand, but now, it's as if he's miles away.

"It's strange to be telling you this," he says, leaning forward and scrutinizing her with his dark eyes. "It's being home after so long or else, it's those lit-from-inside eyes of yours, reaching out to me, translating what I say into your language, into you, into your life."

He sets his glass down. "The end of my little story is that I discovered that elsewhere, in Paris, San Francisco, New York, London, Beijing, Singapore, wherever and whenever I am at work, I *am* enough."

Love doesn't know the word "enough," she thinks. It's something she's learning from spending time with Po. Which leads to her next thought of Val and Beluga in Val's round bed that one of Val's more recent beaus had made for her, and that Val had proudly shown Ilse one evening before going out. The beau had also installed the round mirror on the ceiling above the bed. The previous night, yes, now it's coming back to her, Ilse had caught a fragment of a dream of Val and Beluga in that bed. Minou was meowing, but the two of them were oblivious, and the bed began to swirl around the room, round, and round, and round, and their bodies became one body.

She banishes the thought and notices that it is dark all around them, except for Frey's face that is illuminated by the now-short stub of the candle. Has Po turned off the house lights on purpose? Is he watching from the second-floor stairwell? She lifts her glass and sips.

"It's wonderful that you've found—" she says.

"Yes," he snaps.

Ilse has taken for granted the kind and gentle way that Po lets her take time to finish her sentences.

"Caroline, like I am, is super involved in her work. Sometimes I think she's addicted to it, but it's the nature of her work, and of mine."

"She's—"

"An investment banker. BNP Paribas. She's American. BNP has offices in New York and Paris. She's been in Paris for the last two years. She's requested an extension."

"Nice," says Ilse.

He lifts his eyes to hers to see if she means it.

She doesn't.

"My father has been hard on her and on us. He's refused to come to our wedding, and now he has his wish. It looks like he won't be well enough to come."

That's cruel of him to say.

"They've met—"

"Three times. The third time, they got into an argument about the relevance of poetry. At BNP, Caroline leads a team that invests in companies with philanthropic goals. Caroline cares deeply for the underprivileged, which is something we share. She told my father that poetry doesn't do anything for the disadvantaged."

Malu and Caroline might get along. "Of course, my father defended his muse. Ultimately, I think he's afraid that when BNP is no longer able to extend Caroline's work visa in Paris, we'll live in the U.S. God forbid, a Labaye who leaves France!"

"And will you?" She's asked too quickly. As if it mattered to her! She's taking Po's side.

Frey does not answer. He gazes at the house as if he's already moved to New York City.

"Two people in love will do whatever they need to do to be together," she suggests.

He offers no agreement with her words. She sips the champagne.

"People say that you know it—when you're in love—but I think it's a myth," he says. "What is love anyway? Does anyone really know what it's like for anyone else?" He gazes at the distant darkness, then back at her. "You can't see it, can't define it. Every time you try, it disappears. My father and mother demonstrated physical love. He was always tapping her hand, circling his arm around her waist. Every photo, it's there, his arm around her. I wonder if it was all a show for the outside world. Now that I think about it, she rarely reciprocated. I've been wondering lately if they actually loved each other."

She says nothing.

"What about you?" he asks her.

He sits back as if he's ready to listen to a long tale.

"About me?" Her voice has a tremor.

"Do you have someone waiting for you at home?"

"No," she says, darn it, too quickly. "There was someone, but it didn't turn out."

Why had she stuck with Max for so long? That wasn't even close to loving.

"Obviously, your work occupies and satisfies you like it does me and . . . Caroline. The rest of life becomes almost inconsequential."

"I used to think that way. A year ago, I would have told you that if I wasn't working with words, it felt as if I wasn't breathing, but lately, this spring . . ."

She pauses. Should she tell him her age?

"Now that I'm going to be thirty-six years old this year, I have this growing fear that if I concentrate only on work, I'll be missing out."

Loose-lips Ilse!

"The biological clock," he says.

"I like to think of it more as a pivot point, the time in my life when I decide what I want to make important."

He nods slowly.

Did the mention of her age turn him, and the bubbly, flat?

"Speaking of a clock, it's time for me to say good night," she says.

"So soon? The night is young. I turned thirty-seven in March and have also taken my time with the marriage thing."

He picks up her hand, resting on the table. Her heart jumps, she blushes. It's the second time he's touched her hand that night. He leans over and brings the back of her hand to his lips.

"You have beautiful hands," he says. "Forgive me. I was being spontaneous. My mother would be proud of me."

"Hands of a fisherman's daughter."

Did she have to say that?

"And I'm the son of a man named Po."

The sound of their laughter mixes nicely.

"Good night," she says, but even as she says it, she regrets her words, and the way she is now standing and walking away from her half-empty flute and the unfinished bottle of the best champagne she'll undoubtedly ever taste.

On the balcony overlooking the terrace she spies Frey, still at the table in the shadows of the darkened vines. The moon is up now, a crescent in a Van Gogh blue starry night. She inhales the smell of the vines, the rosemary scent, an organic fertilizer. If only she could bottle this air, this place, and keep it inside her forever.

It was too early to end such a sumptuous, sweetly fragrant night. Especially after Po's elegant son had just kissed her hand. But he is affianced, practically married. It was the right thing to do: to go to bed. She thinks of Po in his room across the hall. Of course, Po had placed the champagne on the table.

Wait! She could run down the stairs, clasp Frey's hands in hers, and say, "Let's dance by the light of the moon!" And off they would go, arm in arm, one step at a time, into the darkened vineyard.

She laughs at herself and turns back toward her bedroom.

Chapter 24

On Friday, Frey invites Ilse to go with him to Domaine Labaye, a ten-minute ride away, to pick up wine for dinner that night. To drive ten minutes away to one's own wine cellar? Not in her wildest dreams!

Outside, Frey is reviving the semi-battered blue Honda motorcycle that she'd spied in the garage the day Po escorted her to the *pétanque* match. She takes a deep breath. She'd thought they'd be taking the car. *Oh, Jann, I miss you more than you know. Of course, you know how much I miss you.* She's never ridden on a motorcycle. There aren't enough roads in Greenland to justify owning one. Jann was the only person she knew who'd driven one, and that deadly bike was owned by one of his show-off soccer pals.

Seated behind Frey on the bike, she fastens the chin strap on the metallic-blue helmet as he revs the engine, and they take off around the oak and down the sandy driveway. For the first few minutes, she feels her heart beating as quickly as the pistons in the engine. But after a little time, she begins to relax, thanks to the lulling, loud grind of the motorcycle, the wind in her face, the ever-present lavender-hued mountains, the sight of a sun-whitened limestone *gîte* with pale blue shutters, a meadow of Queen Anne's lace that looks like miniature floating clouds, endless rows of tendril-springing vineyards, and a grove of *platanes* on a hill. And she realizes only after the fact that she has her arms around Frey's waist.

They pass the turn-off with the sign to the Domaine Labaye.

"We just passed the cave!" she yells out.

About a half mile farther, with no warning, Frey stops the motorcycle. On either side of the road are fields of brilliantly red poppies. He helps her off the bike and adjusts the kickstand into place with his boot. He removes his helmet, places it on the motorcycle, and comes right up close to her. He unfastens the chin strap of her helmet and lifts it off her head.

"One of my favorite places in the world," he says.

They are in the midst of a sea of red, rippling in the gentle breeze. The white blossoms of a nearby apple tree float toward and around them. It's snowing beauty.

Gazing for a few moments at the mountains, as if for strength, he turns to her and, hands in his pockets, he starts singing!

If I were brought to her stronghold,
Prisoned by her in some tower,
And daily ate my morsel sour,
Happily, I'd there grow old,
If my desire she granted me!
She should try to do no wrong:
If she made me yearn too long,
Neither life nor death I'd see:
Life for me as good as done,
While there with death I'd sadly toy.

He laughs at whatever silly expression she must have on her face. Like father, like son, the Labayes are good at serenading. She has this otherworldly feeling that this very scene could have taken place eight hundred years ago. Ilse wonders what Frey's fiancée would think about it.

"It's from a song titled 'Fortune with Her Wheel,' written in the late fifteenth century by a certain Valerius Maximus. I found it this morning in a chest of drawers in my bedroom."

"Something AI couldn't do."

"Are you kidding? A robot would sing it with Pavarotti's voice."

"I prefer your voice to Pavarotti's, and you to a robot."

"I think that's a compliment."

"You memorized it this morning?"

"Once you sing a few of these ditties, you get the hang of the words and the melodies. I used to sing these poems and others to my father before I knew what they were about. To please him."

She squints into the sun to see the mountains behind Frey. They are serenading her too.

"You are foreign to me in so many ways," he says, looking down at his boots. "For some reason, I find being with you liberating, so much so that here I am singing like an idiot with the poppies and you as my audience."

"If only there were more idiots in the world," she says.

"Let's get some wine," he says.

"Thank you," she says, "for the song and the *coquelicots*." *Coquelicot* is the deliciously fetching French word for "poppy." The sound is close to *coquette*, which is French for "flirtatious."

His smile is gentle and warm, a repudiation of the old and a fresh beginning.

"I thank *you*," he says, as he places the helmet on her head and fastens the strap for her. He looks into her eyes, this time with a kind of questioning expression. She gazes back at him but feels only confusion. Back on the bike, she takes one last look at the fields of vivid red. The sight gives a new definition to the color.

Up the sandy, winding road, the vineyard on either side, they approach Domaine Labaye, a stone building with a pitched terra-cotta roof. The same pale-blue shutters adorning the Labaye house frame the small square windows of this building. More colors to store on the palette of her mind for the rest of her life: the shiny green of the leafy vineyard, the black-green cypress, the ruddy, rustic beiges of the stone building that houses the wine, and the deep burnt-orange roof tiles, all against a dazzling blue sky. No wonder Inès was a colorist.

A blond woman in green glasses and a white apron sits at the front desk. She's gazing into her phone, which she promptly places under the desk when she sees Frey and Ilse enter.

"Monsieur Labaye," she says, standing. "Nice to see you back in the valley."

"It's good to be home," he says. "I'd like to give my friend a short tour."

"Of course," the woman says, her hand fidgeting in a drawer. She gives Frey a large ring of jingling keys.

"*Merci,* Janine," he says. His voice has changed. It's friendly.

"The electricity is out, so you might appreciate this." She lights a tall candle for him.

"There's an issue with the electricity?"

"I've called the electrician. Only the storage rooms are dark. The wine prefers the dark anyway."

"That's something my father would say."

"He's the one who said it to me." The woman smiles.

Ilse holds the candle while Frey opens a double-sealed door with one of the many keys. In the chilled dark room, the glow of the candle reveals two rows of oak barrels lining the middle of the room, a red tiled floor, and a gorgeous vaulted stone ceiling. The air is still and moist and smells slightly of mold and resin, not unlike the tunnels under the château Belle Rivière.

They pass through another room of oak barrels, then one with three massive steel tanks, and lastly a storage chamber containing dozens of racks of bottles of wine.

"Here's the best part," Frey says. "Now we get to choose. That wall houses my parents' wedding wine, 1966. They were lucky to miss the abysmally rainy year of 1965. The people around here describe the years according to how the wine tastes."

"And this year?" His wedding wine year.

"My father and Jean-Pierre say it will be one of the best vintages ever. Just the right amount of rain during the growth season, consistently warm days so far, and cooler-than-normal nights. Thankfully, no frost after bud-break."

"Auspicious," she says.

"Let's take a couple of these." He removes two bottles from the shelves, dusts off the labels, and shows her the bottles under the candlelight.

"Another auspicious year: 1982."

The year she was born! Isn't it outrageously extravagant to drink wine from thirty-six years ago on any old spring night? No wonder she adores the French.

Outside again in the bright sunshine, Frey places the wine bottles in the leather saddlebags on either side of the motorcycle. He examines his phone.

"Orders from the home front. Georges and his wife, Jacqueline, are joining us for dinner. My father wants us to buy mushrooms, two baguettes, and cheese. He must be thinking of cooking my favorite *champignons à la provençale*. If it were November, we'd go foraging for them. That forest over there is rife with chanterelles."

ON HER WAY UP the stairs after dinner, Ilse hears footsteps behind her. She turns at the top step. It's Frey. When he catches up to her, he presses her hand that rests on the railing.

"Please sit here with me," he says, pulling her hand as he settles down on the top step, overlooking the entrance hall.

She hesitates.

"Sorry, Frey. I can't right now. I must—"

"How many times have you packed, just to unpack? I wouldn't bother this time."

"What makes you so sure?"

"You love my father too much to go right now. He's hanging by a thread."

He looks at her, his eyes intense.

"You say that, and yet your father is washing dishes and carrying on a feisty conversation with Georges and Jacqueline." Banter and laughter emanate from the kitchen. Georges makes everything fun. After clearing the table, Ilse had offered to help, but Po had shooed her away.

"Tang, come!" she calls out.

"Please, Ilse."

She relents and perches beside him.

Tang trots up the stairs and settles between them.

"This is where I would spy on the annual costume parties my parents hosted," Frey says as they look down on the front hall with its pale, antique limestone floor and walls. "The costumes were outrageous. I remember one woman came as Joan of Arc, burning at the stake. She'd tied red panels of fabric onto sticks and danced around in circles with her arms moving. For me as a child, it really looked like flames. Another person arrived as the Winged Victory of Samothrace. She, I'm assuming it was a woman, but it could have been a man, made the costume out of plaster, her head was covered, and my parents said they never discovered who was underneath. One time, Uncle Georges showed up as Pan, piping on a flute. He'd covered himself with leaves and had a live goat on a string attached to his waist.

"The morning after, I'd step over people, some of them parents of my friends, some still drunk, but most sleeping, scattered around the house and the vineyard. Ummi loved a good party. My father usually retired early to bed. Sometimes, on his way to bed, he'd stop into my bedroom and find me awake. We'd listen to the drunk voices. He would often tell me a story or sing a song to me. Those were some of the best nights of my life."

She says nothing, but strokes Tang.

From where they are sitting on the top stair, they have a partial view of the portrait of Inès.

"She would have liked you," Frey says.

"But she liked the exotic."

He turns to her.

She looks away.

"Sorry to dispel your view of yourself. From where I'm sitting now, you are more than *exotique,* with the shape of your face, your high cheekbones, your almond eyes with a kind of gray lightness to them, your nose . . ."

He pulls her head to him and kisses her nose.

She freezes. He's engaged. He's having second thoughts. That, or else he's enjoying his freedom before getting tied up for the rest of his life.

"But . . ." she begins.

Po coughs as he exits the kitchen and shuffles to the terrace. Has he seen them?

"Did you notice that for the first time since I've been home, my father ate all his dinner tonight? Cleaned his plate. And even drank some wine. That was because of you, I'm sure."

She doesn't tell Frey that after dinner, she'd heard Po choking and vomiting in the bathroom near the kitchen.

"He's coming," she says, starting to rise.

"What's wrong with making my father happy by seeing us together?"

She's about to speak.

"Shhh," he says.

They hear Georges and Jacqueline in the front hall. Ilse and Frey are mostly hidden by the railing.

Georges, the personification of *bon vivant,* is laughing. Now he's telling Po to take his medicine, so he'll be able to play in the next *pétanque* match.

"As you know," Po is saying through a cough, "I'll do nothing that a doctor tells me to do. And I hate goodbyes, so don't say it. Say '*à très bientôt*' instead."

They yell out "*À très bientôt!*" as they part.

"Do you see how my father dictates how people should speak?" Frey whispers.

"He's a poet," she says. "Rather than dictating, I would say that he's lovingly coaxing words to fall into line, even if they're part of someone else's conversation."

She stands, and he rises.

"I thought of a poem the other night that expresses *la grasse matinée.*"

She'd told him about the novel by Zoë Gaudet and her struggles with the expression.

"What's that?"

"It's a poem by Meng Hao-jan, an eighth-century Chinese poet." Frey leans back against the stair railing.

"It goes something like this:

> *" 'In spring, one sleeps absent to morning,*
> *then everywhere hears the birds singing.*
> *After all night the voice of the storm*
> *and petals fell*
> *Who knows how many . . . ?' "*

"Impressive, Frey!" Had he memorized the poem for her? "I love 'one sleeps absent to morning.' " She has a feeling that Gaudet would especially appreciate this concept. "Though I'm not sure I like the idea of the petals falling."

Chapter 25

"I OWE IT TO THE POEM TO GO."

Frey looks at Ilse with a kind of horror in his face after she's informed him that she's planning to visit *le Village des Bories.*

"But, Frey," she says, "please don't think you have to accompany me."

He hesitates.

"Of course I'll go with you," he says. He detests this place. Could he really want to be with her that much?

"Frey," she says, taking a deep breath as they walk past the oak tree. "You're getting married this summer. I'm feeling that something has developed between us . . ."

"Yes," he says.

"I'm wondering if it's because we both want to please your father because he seems happy for us to be getting along. That's it, right?"

"It's more than that," says Frey. He's looking ahead at the dirt path. "I didn't see it coming. It's hit me like the *tramontane,* the wind that comes over the mountains and is stronger and colder than the mistral."

"I have an idea," she says. "Let's pretend it didn't happen. I'm leaving in three days. I'm going far away. And you're getting married."

"Please stop reminding me!"

It's a tone he might use with his underlings back in Paris in his glass office building. Imperious.

He shows her a shorter route. They cross a lane and traverse a neighbor's farm, scattering the chickens. A plump, iridescent red rooster crows.

They enter the village of stone huts. Where did the birdsong go? Within the dry rock walls that at one time hemmed in sheep or cattle, one stone dwelling after another rises in front of them like a somber funeral procession. They classify the area as an open-air museum, but perhaps they should rename it the Valley of the Dead. Crusty dried lichen drips like dirty rags from the desiccated, bone-dried branches. Skinned bark twists as if it's trying to pull away from the lifeless trees. It is almost impossible to imagine that such a place could exist so close to the immense exuberance swarming around the Labaye residence.

"It's as if the world has been forsaken. Petrified," she whispers, then wonders why she's whispering, and why she's tiptoeing.

"I told you: it's a place of nightmares. My feet feel as if they're being pulled down by the rocks."

And she feels it too, the place is dragging her down.

They walk farther inside the enclosure of walls.

"Do you mind if I go in?" she asks, stopping in front of an opening of one of the huts. "But Frey, please don't feel you have to follow me."

He nods, his face solemn. The afternoon light coming through a hole at the top almost blinds her. It's hotter inside the baking rock hut. Stones from the walls have fallen to the ground, like teeth from a skull. She sits on the packed dirt ground of the hut to imagine six-year-old Frey lost over the lifetime of a night.

His form is silhouetted in the doorway. He enters the hut and sits beside her and wipes his wet forehead.

"I'm feeling for your sweet six-year-old self."

When she looks over at him, his eyes are shut tightly.

"Hold my hand," she says. His hand is cold.

"Thank you," he whispers.

The heavy silence has shifted to reverberation, and it's now a whirring sound. It's the wind through the stones. The effect is haunting.

"Let's go," she says, starting to rise.

"No," he says, and he pulls her back toward him. He looks into her face as if examining it, then kisses her on her lips. It's a gentle kiss. He hugs her to him, then kisses her again.

"Only this," he says, his face an inch from hers, his black-brown Inès eyes, impossible to penetrate, "will erase that horrible night forever. This kiss." And his kiss is rich and luscious and makes her deaf to the eerie whispers of the wind. She tastes his tears in the kiss.

"Are you cured?" she asks, the first to pull away.

Before they rise together to standing, he looks at her in that same curious way.

Now the wind is louder, and something is brushing back and forth, almost impatiently, like a broom against the exterior stone wall of the hut. When they spill out of the hut to see what it could be, there is nothing there, no tree branch, no wild boar, no whispering ghosts. Frey circles the hut. Whatever it is must have blown or crept away. And the two hurry from the place of stones, as if driven like Adam and Eve, hiding from themselves.

THAT NIGHT, SHE HEARS Po coughing, and it seems as if the hacking will never stop. She slips on her bathrobe, fills her empty glass with water from the bathroom in the hall, and is about to knock on Po's door with it, when surprise, he opens it. He must have heard her in the hallway.

He's in a blue nightshirt, and in the faint light from the bathroom, his face is puffy and drawn. On his nightshirt, she sees several red spots of blood.

"Île du Nord, you're an angel."

He takes the water in his shaking hand, then gives it back to her without taking a sip.

His room smells stale, breathless.

"I'm not well," he says in a wheezing voice. He holds his chest, then turns to the bathroom, from where she hears him cough thickly, again and again and again.

"Let me call the doctor. Please, Po, please."

He softens as she says his name.

"No, no, I'm fine. Just a little something in my throat." He shoos her out. "Back to bed you go."

She's tempted to call Agnès immediately to report the blood on his nightshirt but decides to call her the following morning. She'll also tell Frey first thing in the morning.

It's an hour later. Po is hopefully asleep, but she is not. In three days, she'll depart, will say goodbye to Po, whom she will never see again.

She reminds herself that she is not family.

If only this bed weren't so comfortable. If only the scent out the window weren't so redolent with thyme and sage. If only the moonlit night weren't calling her to stay awake. One day she'd like to climb those beckoning, distant Luberons to determine if the scent she's now smelling originates from there. When she's in the midst of the mountains, she'll watch up close for the moment when the hues shift from pale dove gray to blue to lavender to purple. What aspirations these surroundings inspire.

A dog bays. She checks the time: three-thirty. Another dog barks at a higher pitch. At the same time at home, she'd be hearing a husky's lonely howl, then another's, and another's. Tang is beside her bed. More barking erupts in the distance. Maybe a dog is lost in the depths of the château's cave, like she was on her third day in Provence, trying to find the light at the end of the tunnel. And she had found it.

Ilse tosses to the left, away from the brightly moonlit window.

A door creaks open. It's down the hall. Maybe Frey can't sleep either. Everyone is awake in this house at three-thirty in the morning. Maybe Frey's just finished an affectionate chat with his fiancée; they've exchanged loving, middle-of-the-night mewing.

Footsteps. Not Po's. Po's are slow and meandering. These are younger, athletic feet.

It's Frey, passing her door. Down to the kitchen. Late-night munchies.

She sits up. She's tempted to join him. Her boring, beige flannel bathrobe that she brought from home hangs on the hook inside the bedroom door.

No, let him be.

A few minutes later. Footsteps again. Up the stairs. She hears him outside her bedroom door. A pause.

Her heart stops. She turns her head to listen better. Her father does that too, twists to one side to use the superior ear.

A little knock, barely audible. It could be a mouse running into a hole in the wall, or Tang changing position in his sleep.

"Yes?" she says softly.

The door opens slowly. In the darkness, a form.

"Ilse," Frey says at the door. Her name sounds silvery in his voice.

She switches on her bedside light. She wipes her eyes, pulls her hair to one side.

Frey is in a bathrobe, a long gray one to his calves, white initials on the pocket.

"I thought you might be awake," he says.

He squats to pet Tang.

"Did you find anything good in the refrigerator?"

"Nothing good. May I?" he asks, as he approaches the bed. "May I sit closer?"

"Yes," she says.

"I gathered up the courage to knock on your door to tell you that I don't think you should leave on Tuesday. Ummi was never one to hesitate before the truth. I think your presence here . . . has been beneficial."

"It's a delicate time for your family."

He moves closer to her. Very close to her. She can hear her heart beating. He leans over and kisses each cheek, then her forehead and then her lips, a gentle quick kiss on the lips.

"Am I terrible," he says.

It is not a question.

Even up close, he is attractive; his Roman nose, his curving lips, and his brown-black eyes now look warm and beckoning under his brows.

"You very well might be terrible," she says.

And everything inside her is moving.

"I'm not thinking," he says. "I'm feeling. I'm channeling my mother. She always told me that I think too much. The feeling I'm having is that I don't want to let you go."

He places his hand on the underside of her chin.

"Your chin," he says as he touches it.

"What about my chin?"

"You lift it in a way that beckons me to kiss you, and so I will." And she kisses him back. His face has night stubble on it and is scratchy. She hears the nightingale or whatever bird that is singing, *tit-tit-tit, twitter, twitter, twitter, choo-choo-choo, twitter, tit-tit-tit,* and now their kiss is deeper, probing, passionate, and hungry. She opens her eyes to see his black lashes, closed. He lifts his arm from her arm, where she's sure he's left fingerprints, to turn off the light on the bedside table, and they are in the velvety darkness of each other.

She pulls away, sits up a little, and turns the light back on.

"This isn't a good idea," she says, "you know why . . ."

He takes a deep breath, closes his eyes. The lock of hair that has fallen over his forehead and eyes reminds her of the way Po's hair falls over his. As with Po, Ilse is tempted to move the lock from his brow.

"Yes, we absolutely should restrain ourselves," he says, smiling.

"Absolutely, we must."

She's the one who finds his lips this time, and as he kisses her, she can feel him trembling. When he cups her head in both his hands, it's as if she's suspended in time. He is an arousing, sensuous kisser. Now she's the one who shifts in the bed to switch off the light. This might be him scoring his last errant kiss before his marriage, his farewell to bachelor life, and she wonders if that is okay with her, and maybe it could also be her hello and also her final goodbye, to a long-ago dream of living in France.

As he unbuttons her cotton nightgown, the one Max had given her, made of a diaphanous material with little rosebuds at the neckline, and as she opens his bathrobe and places her hands around his thin waist and feels his soft skin, and then pulls his head to hers and feels the warmth of his lithe body and the strength in his arms and legs, she imagines that the vines are gossiping.

"We can stop now," he says, looking up at her, his face shining in the light of the moon.

"Now you say that!" She laughs. "Just when . . ."

He stops kissing her and breathes into her ear. "Just when what?"

"Just when I've begun to feel and not to think."

"I'm way ahead of you," he says.

And she pulls him down again and drinks his breath smelling of vineyards in the Medoc sun and kisses his lips stained with centuries of Labaye Côtes du Rhône. His body is cool and lovely and soft, and in the moonlight that does not discriminate between colors, his skin looks as if it's made of marble. They move together, touching each other as if to make an impression on each other's skin, as the light breeze rustles the leaves of the vineyards outside her window, and as Tang changes position at the floor next to the bed, and as the dog barks, lost inside the cave in the distance, she feels complete, as if this is the way a person is meant to feel on this earth.

And when every muscle of his relaxes into every muscle of hers, and in the faint light, she sees his eyes closed, she slumbers until the rooster from the farm down the way crows once and then again and again.

"Please," he says, his voice groggy into her neck.

"More sleep," he says, and this time, she rolls onto him. And when the morning sun addresses them for the second time through the transparent curtains, she stretches her arms and legs. Arm in arm, entwined, she does not know if his legs are hers.

"Île du Nord," he says, sighing.

He pulls her head to him and kisses her nose, then her lips, then each eye, then up and down her neck and then each breast.

He touches her in a way that makes her swallow.

"I'm falling in love with you," he says.

And she thinks of their tender caressing as the ripples in the sea that lap against her captain's house on stilts in Oqaatsut, and, oh no, a little fear pops into her head, the feeling of mounting alarm that she has, of the invading sea corroding the piles that hold up her house, and the old sea captain's cottage gradually giving way, slipping into oceanic oblivion. But before she gets to the part in her imagination where the cottage is floating away with her in it, she puts her arms around Frey's neck and pulls his body down on her, and she reminds herself that she is in the Luberon, and the days here are sunny and warm, full of honeybees, and rich with the smells of thyme and sage. And he kisses her back, roughly, scraping her cheeks and chin and neck with the stubble of his beard as if he knows she is thinking too much.

When the rooster crows again, she wonders if Po is writing about her and Frey, and whether he suspects that they have spent the night together. She listens to the pattern of thrush song: a whistle in burry tones for two seconds, then a pause of three seconds, then another two-second flutelike call. Po has taught her to recognize pattern and repetition in nature. How wonderful it is for the birds to be a part of this house, how, flying in and out, they provide music and movement, and Ilse hopes that Agnès does not take down their nests in the corners of the living room as she'd threatened to do. Why shouldn't people and birds shelter harmoniously together, and so what if the birds splash white blotches all over the fourteenth-century stone floor? What does messy bird shit matter, when Agnès can renovate the house after Po . . . after Po . . .

Frey's breath tickles her eyelashes, his nose next to hers is so close, his "not enough" heart is beating against her hand. The pink, now-golden sun burnishes the armoire and the bedpost, and she hears sounds in the kitchen below. Frey kisses her again, giving her chills down her back, and she is half in and half out of sleep but awake enough to feel his hand slip down her waist and cup her sex. As she twists a little to feel it more, she thinks that yes, this is it. She is experiencing it for the first time. She is reveling in a *grasse matinée.*

She has found the translation in Frey.

Chapter 26

SUNDAY MORNING. SHOULD SHE STAY OR SHOULD SHE GO? The indecision about her departure date is like a chronic illness. Agnès will tell her what to do, but Agnès doesn't know about the recent carryings-on. Yet again, the insightful Agnès may have an inkling. Ilse has already texted Malu and Val that her schedule is unclear.

She rises and dresses quietly, and tiptoes to the door. Tang is at her heels. Her hand twists the knob slowly.

"Come back."

He's squinting because of the strip of sunlight on his face, but there's something else that she can't decipher in his expression.

What is it, what is it in your eyes?

"You're dressed."

"I'm going downstairs."

"Without telling me."

"I . . . It's the morning."

"Miss Lark, come back to bed."

Midnight son is pouting.

The sheets in the peach-colored morning light resemble the folds of fabric on figures in an Italian Renaissance painting. Now the morning luminance dances on Frey's back, just above his buttocks. She locks the image in her mind. The sunlight caressing the sheets, the man in the bed where she was.

"Tang, shhh."

Before she's made up her mind, Frey is out of bed, beside her, slipping her sweater off, unbuttoning her shirt in the front, and unclasping her brassiere from behind. He does it all so quickly, rushing as if the morning will be over in seconds, and it will be, and she wonders how she would translate all these actions into words. The beauty of the sun on the vineyards and the gentle morning heat on her skin give her a deliciously heady feeling that she wants to hold on to forever.

Tang thumps back down on the floor.

Frey pulls her down onto the bed, and she falls into his kiss.

"We'll never be the same now," she says, looking into his intense eyes.

"A truer thing was never said."

As he kisses her on the lips, there's a desperation in his touch, different from before. Maybe it's the daylight. Ouch, he's pulling her hair back and leaning in closer. It's as if he's angry at himself for this, for loving her, this woman from Greenland, and not the woman he should be loving. She knows he won't tell his fiancée.

"Come back to me. Your thoughts and you," he tells her, kissing her fiercely. His sharp stubble scrapes her neck. "I feel like I'm trying to hold on to the sun's rays," he says, "but they keep moving out of reach."

He rolls her over with him on the bed and rocks them both back and forth, and it's as if they're both in a cradle.

"I wish I didn't like you so much," he says, stopping the motion and staring down at her.

"Given the circumstances, I feel the same way."

"I've got something to tell you that will make you like me less." He turns away from her.

"What could be worse than that you're going to be married? Well, that you already are. I suppose that could be worse. A *fait accompli*." She takes a deep breath. "No matter. You'll go back to Paris to inhabit robots, and I'm going home the day after tomorrow."

"Please—" He moves his arm so that her head rests on his shoulder. They both gaze up at the glow of the sunlit ceiling.

"I've got to tell you something whether you leave or not."

"Okay," she says.

He pauses as if he wishes the silence to consume what he is about to say.

"Spit it out." This is what Val would say.

"There's another reason why I'm getting married in August."

He runs his finger along her nose.

"Yes?"

"Caroline is pregnant."

She winces inside, feels herself back away from him, a mile in an instant.

"Ahhh . . ."

Chou-fleur meows in the hall. Tang changes position.

Why did she do it?

"Why didn't you tell me this before? Before . . ."

"I should have."

"It changes things. Everything." She sits up.

He takes her hand, looks at it, and turns it so her palm faces him. He hesitates, then kisses inside her palm.

"Île du Nord!" It's Po's craggy voice from downstairs.

She pulls her hand away and rises from the bed. She throws on her clothes, buttoning her shirt crookedly.

"I'm sorry," Frey says.

"You should have told me before last night."

From the door, she looks back at him in the bed of tossed white sheets. She is the one-night fling, the housekeeper of his father's words, sweeping them from one room into another.

"It was wrong of me," he says. "I thought if I told you, you would never . . ."

"You're right. I would *never* . . ." she says, leaving the room and shutting the door behind her.

Or would I have? she wonders as she steps into the bathroom in the hallway. *Or would I have?* she thinks when she gazelles down the stairs. How successful Frey would be if he could transfer his skill of compartmentalizing to robotic intelligence. How well he does it in his own life: his fiancée and unborn child are in one box, his father is in another, and Ilse in the other. Keep them separate, and everything will work out fine!

She stops on the bottom step and composes herself. Tang trots ahead of her to join his pack. It is strange to see Po at his writing desk inside. He's usually outside at his table under the olive tree in the flush of nature.

"*Bonjour, Po,*" she says.

"Île du Nord."

The dogs lift their noses to her. Can they sense how she feels, a *grasse matinée* gone bitter? Can Po tell?

Of course he can.

"We'll be late for church."

"Church?" she says.

"Come, come," he says, his eyes pleading with her, half expecting her to decline.

He's wearing black pants, a white shirt, and a blue vest that matches his eyes.

"I can hardly walk," he says, standing and limping to the front door, "but the two youngsters in the house are more slothful than I. I expect this of my midnight son, who drags in the morning, I heard him up in the middle of the night. But you, I thought you were a lark." His voice has a fake bravado in it.

"I am . . . a lark," she says, "usually."

"Well, be the lark now and wake my son, 'sluggardized at home, wearing out his youth with shapeless idleness.'" Must be Shakespeare. "Frey," he continues, "wouldn't normally join me in church. He has no faith. But now that I'm a dying man, I have half a hope that he might humor me by coming along. I won't be going up those stairs again until my siesta this afternoon. And by then, which feels a long time off"—and he sighs—"Frey will have to carry me."

She would weep if he weren't looking at her so intently.

"After one glass of red wine," she says, "you'll be running up those stairs."

He chuckles. "I see you've"—his cheeks redden as he stifles a cough—"spied my wines."

He'd caught her peeking at the brick-red caps on the three bottles of wine in the straw basket that he's placed by the door.

"Your tithing?"

"Last week I bought a gut-wrenching bad vintage, Labaye 2013—the label says 'Approach with extreme caution.' It's to cure my friend, Père Clément, of his love of wine. It's working. He says that lately he's been praying for my soul and the soul of the vines. But this week, I'm surprising him with a temporal reward, two bottles of the best wine in the Labaye domaine. Up you go, wake that lazy son of mine."

"I'm not dressed for . . ."

She's wearing blue cotton pants, a light sweater, the shirt she'd not buttoned correctly, and her espadrilles.

"I've heard better excuses. Down here in Provence, the good Lord," and he holds his chest as he coughs, "takes us as we are. *Vas-y*."

She pivots, runs up the stairs, and opens the door that she'd closed so definitively. Frey's focus turns from the sun-striated ceiling to her.

"Church," she says from the doorway. "Your father wants you to come."

He throws off the white cotton covers that set off his dark skin and sits up.

"Ilse," he says, standing. He lifts his bathrobe from the floor. "I was a coward not to tell you before last night."

"You were."

"I'll meet you at church, after I shower."

Before she departs, she glances back at him.

"Ilse, wait."

She closes the door behind her and finds Po in the driveway, beside the passenger door of the canary yellow convertible.

If I had known, would I have? she thinks as she thanks Po when he opens the car door for her.

Would I have, she asks herself, as Po shifts into third gear and drives the car around the enormous oak tree.

Would I have? she wonders, as the wind whips her hair into spirals above her head.

She doesn't know herself anymore.

Chapter 27

"I DIDN'T THINK FREY WOULD JOIN US," SAYS PO, AS SHE AND he hobble, arm in arm, from the small parking area to the church. "Only old people, wrestling with and trying to mitigate the despair of nothingness, go to mass."

Clanging church bells echo and mix with birdsong as they approach. Frey would hear the bells from the house.

Beyond the cypress trees, the bell tower inside its triangle frame looks like an arrow pointing to the sky. For the first time in Provence, Ilse wishes it would rain to reflect her feelings.

The tiny eleventh-century Romanesque Saint-Pantaléon with its sun-dried clay tiled roof sits alone on a promontory not far from the line of tall cypress trees that resemble acolytes in waiting. On its right side, a vineyard is draped like a cape, and an orchard, blooming in white, descends on the left side of their path. A variety of small farmhouses with slanting terra-cotta tiled roofs are scattered randomly across the valley as if they've fallen there from the sky.

At the nave door, Po tells her that the church is named after a Catholic martyr, the son of a rich pagan, who believed that faith was to be trusted over medical advice. He was known as the "all-compassionate" patron saint of doctors, which is why Po had told her on the drive over that it was especially important for him to go to church today.

Once they are inside, it takes a few minutes for Ilse's eyes to adjust to the darkness.

The priest, wearing a long green vestment gown with a rope tie, is sweeping the center aisle with a broom. He smiles when he sees Po, then fixes his gaze on her.

"Whom has God brought me today?"

The priest has a round face and an easy smile. His ears stick out from under thick white hair.

Po introduces Ilse as Île du Nord, then hands Clément the basket.

"Thank you," says the priest, peering into the basket. "Are these for curing me or spoiling me?"

"Curing you *is* spoiling you, or maybe it's the other way around. Which way would God have it?"

"God would have it both ways. Surely, this can't be a worse draught than what you brought last time."

"I'm afraid it is, my friend. When I tried it, I couldn't get the rancid taste out of my mouth for days."

"'Stop drinking water and use a little wine.' Paul wrote this in his letter to Timothy."

"You've used that one before," Po says, and then Clément laughs—or rather he bellows, bending down from the waist, then up, and then down again, and the sound of his guffawing echoes around the small church.

"Yes, yes, Geoffrey. Frail, are we humans."

The church resembles a small cave. Three white-haired women sit upright in the first of—she counts—eight rows of woven rush chairs. A balding man occupies the middle seat in the second row. The dank air reminds Ilse of the smell of her cottage by the sea. There's a stone basin on the left wall and beside that, a small alcove in which a statue of the Virgin Mary stands, her blue dress in folds over her thin body, her head tilted to the side.

Po ushers Ilse into a row of chairs, but before entering, he genuflects deeply and crosses himself, facing the altar. She winces as she watches him struggle to stand.

"One more in," he tells her when she is about to sit, "in case Frey surprises us."

Four churchgoers this morning, and now six. She hopes Frey doesn't show. Po had told her his son had no faith. Frey absolutely should have told her about the baby! Po would be horrified, especially since she knew he'd been scheming to bring them together. She looks over at him, kneeling now, his face in his large square hands.

One of the three women in the front stands. She walks down the aisle with a basket on her arm and hands each of the parishioners and Ilse a paper leaflet. When Po stands and bows to receive his, she winks, a glint in her eye. The French, flirting all the way into their senescence.

Thanks to Frey's recent revelation, Ilse has decided to depart on Tuesday, two days from today, no matter what anyone has to say about her staying.

Shouldn't the priest have placed the wine bottles on the floor, instead of next to the small gold cross at the middle of the altar table?

A bustling sound and voices outside. Ilse turns to see the silhouettes of a woman, a man, and a little girl appear in the sunlit entrance. The glare outside mixing with the dust particles inside forms a halo around the three figures. They slide into the row behind Ilse and Po. The woman looks about Ilse's age. The man holds a chubby-cheeked baby, wrapped tightly in a white blanket. The girl is about four or five with a line of bangs across her forehead. She is dressed in a red, pleated dress. Now they are ten, eleven with the baby.

"Shhh," whispers the woman as she dips her face into the baby's blanket. Her hair shines in the candlelight mixed with the bright daylight from the open door. Now the baby sits on the father's lap. The perfect family. As the mother removes the baby's little white bonnet, she looks up at Ilse. Ilse spins back to face the altar; she's overstepped the boundaries of polite inquisitiveness. The baby's gurgling sounds mix with the priest's voice. The daughter asks to hold the baby.

"*Non, non,*" whispers the mother.

"*Maman!*" she pleads.

"They'll baptize the baby afterward," Po leans over to tell Ilse. "You and I are invited."

Everyone can hear everything in this small echo chamber.

"Mama, can I ring the bell?"

"*Tais-toi,* quiet," says the father.

Clément nods at the father.

When Ilse looks around, the man and his daughter are beside the rope to the right of the entrance door. With her father's help, the girl pulls on the rope. The bells *clang, clang, clang, clang, clang.* Five times.

The priest bows to the altar.

The women in the front row start singing "Kyrie Eleison."

The others join in. The singing is paltry, high, and squeaky, but when Po, and the man, and the woman behind them join, the sound is quite full and good.

It is half an hour into the mass when Ilse hears the throaty exhaust notes of a motorcycle. She tells herself not to turn her head, but she spots a long shadow on the sun-splashed stone aisle.

Po turns to look. He's been waiting for this moment. Now, he can relax. Ilse can feel it in the way he shifts his weight, clears his throat, that now everything is different. Clément raises the round communion wafer. Ilse thinks of the circle of the womb, of the baby growing inside Frey's fiancée.

They don't offer such "thin, perfectly round wafers" in the Lutheran church in Ilulissat that Ilse had attended with her parents and Jann. One of the few times during the year that their minister offered communion was at the midnight Christmas service, which she attended with Jann and Fa. Malu stayed at home, boiling seal meat and baking *kalaallit kaagiat.* At that time of year, the altar is adorned with many slender, tall candles that flicker in the drafts from the windows. With all the reflections in the glass panes, the light looks alive. The communion wafers are bits of bread broken from a loaf of *knaekbrød.*

Jann's memorial service was the last time she or Fa had gone to church. No communion then. Beluga had squeezed in next to her in the front row after she'd gestured for him to join her there. In the Greenlandic culture, when someone dies, friends and family typically celebrate, grateful for the times they've spent together on this earth with the recently departed. But as much as they might have tried, Malu, Fa, and Ilse and community could not hide the intensity of their sorrow. The small red church was packed with Jann's friends, coaches, fans, and a lifetime of soccer teammates and their parents. People stood ten feet deep outside the church, sobbing outright. Ilse's heart aches to think of it.

The French might be surprised to hear her Greenlandic minister telling the parishioners that Jann would be joining those in the underworld, where it was cozy and warm, rather than going up to the skies where it's freezing cold. It was also normal to be told that Jann would reappear as a ghost, and whistle and sing, especially to the children named after him. That was when Ilse determined that if she were to have a son, she would name him Jann.

And in a little over three months, she'll be thirty-six. Frey's unborn child will be twelve weeks more mature in utero.

Père Clément breaks the circle into smaller pieces and delicately places them into a basket. He bows to the altar. The three white-haired ladies queue up in the aisle with their palms cupped upward and receive the heavenly host, as Ilse has heard it is called.

Po scoots out into the aisle, inviting her with his eyes to go before he does. She hesitates, then does as Po expects: she processes down the aisle, all the while feeling Frey's eyes on her. She does not deserve this blessing. The priest says something that she doesn't understand. The communion melts in her mouth on her way back to her row of seats. A sweet, unrecognizable taste. Maybe it has been dipped in wine.

Ilse shuts down the noise in her head, what happened the night before, Po's deathly illness, Frey's dark presence in the back of the church, the surprising news of his child. And for a few sacred moments, as she kneels beside Po on a cushion and listens to his craggy, shallow breath, Ilse is moved by the peaceful setting, by the small, red stained-glass window in the shape of a cross, the hymns, and the twinkling candles.

May Po be healed, she prays. *And please bless Frey's baby. It's not the baby's fault that the father is a coward. May the child be a poet, inheriting all of Po's qualities and carry forth the torch of the past.*

She glances back. As she'd suspected, Frey stands against the stone wall. He catches her eye, but she averts her gaze. Frey does not walk up the aisle for communion. When the priest returns to the altar, Frey slips into the empty chair next to his father.

As the congregation sings "Gloria," Po, sitting back from kneeling position, reaches to take her hand. He offers his other hand to Frey. Po holds both their hands and closes his eyes tightly as if he's using all his energy to be a conduit between the two.

She feels embarrassed holding Po's hand. She wonders when he will let go. Instead of releasing her hand, he does something startling: in a shaking kind of motion, he joins her hand with Frey's hand in front of him.

Time stops. Frey's hand is warm, the same temperature as his father's. She flushes. It feels like a handoff, as though Po, in his infirmity, has decided to give her up for his son. Like a sacrifice. They are in church, after all. If Po knew what she knows, he would not be joining their hands as if in matrimony. She closes her eyes, and it feels as though she's underwater, where everything, including her feelings, is muffled.

Ilse is the first to pull away her hand.

Frey peers around his father at her with a pleading look, and she turns her head to the front.

Maybe it would make Po happy to know that there's a womb-child in their midst to inherit his kingdom. Even though Frey had told her that his fiancée refused to live here, their child would inevitably discover this house, this vineyard, this region, would fall in love with it, like Ilse has.

The baby behind them, who has only gurgled and made delicious baby sounds, now begins to wail, and the echoes reverberate against the stone walls. The mother takes the child outside into the sunlight.

"*Papa, s'il te plaît!*" pleads the young girl, tugging at her father's hand.

They hear the baby crying outside.

"Shhh." The young girl is not allowed to leave.

The priest wipes the chalice with a cloth, drinks the wine from the cup that he has not offered to anyone else.

"Go forth, the mass is ended. Go in peace."

Why does Clément look at Ilse longer than anyone else? Does he know?

The little girl pulls the rope, and the bell rings like the ending of something, rather than a beginning.

They exit the dark church with squinting eyes, and it feels like a rebirth, coming from the dark, and then barely being able to see.

The priest shakes hands with departing parishioners with a laugh, a comment, or a story. When it's Ilse's turn, he asks if she is enjoying her time in the Luberon. She says she loves it, but her response would have felt more authentic before this morning.

The priest tells them to stay for the baptism of the Lambert baby.

Frey will be celebrating his child's baptism before too long.

"You stay, Papa," says Frey. "I need to pick up a few things for lunch. I'm cooking today. Ilse will come with me, won't you?"

"I have to see the look on Clément's face," Po says, "when he tastes the wine that I gave him. I might even have to sit down to share it with him."

"You'll miss my lunch," says Frey.

"We're fast tipplers," says Po.

"Ilse?"

"I wouldn't mind a taste of that wine," she says. Anything to avoid Frey.

"She's turning Provençal before our eyes," says Po, his eyes creasing into moon-slivers. "No, Île du Nord, you go ahead with Frey. I can't let you witness a drunk old man and a priest yelling expletives at God."

"Clément would never curse," says Frey.

"Of course he does, but today, after tasting this Grand Cru, he'll be singing His praise."

"It's time to stop ringing the bells," says the priest, turning to the girl, who runs off around the corner of the eleventh-century church.

Chapter 28

"I'M WALKING BACK," ILSE SAYS TO FREY, ON THEIR WAY TO the parking area.

"That's an hour's hike."

"Fine. I need time on my own."

"It's too far to walk in espadrilles," he says. She doesn't like the disappointed look on his face as his eyes travel from her face to her dusty espadrilles. It's his Parisian self, surfacing like a humpback coming up for air.

"Come with me to the *marché* in Coustellet. It's five minutes away. I'm cooking *morilles à la crème* and an Avignon specialty, *bohémienne,* a tomato and eggplant casserole, for lunch."

He can take his *morilles,* whatever they are, and *bohémienne,* whatever that is, and do whatever he likes with them.

"No thank you," she says.

"I can't leave you here." He's holding out the metallic blue helmet. "How about if I drop you at the house before I go to the *marché.*"

Looking away, she takes the helmet. He's right about her espadrilles.

His face is now solemn, as if someone has died.

Something did die.

She's fumbling with the helmet strap. She's so mad at him, her hands are shaking.

"Let me help," he says.

"I can do this on my own, thank you," she says, finally fastening the strap.

She holds on to the handle at the back of the motorcycle, keeping the space between their bodies, even over bumps.

Wait, she doesn't know this route.

"Where are we going?" she yells out to him.

"Shift in the winds. You can't leave us without seeing the red dirt cliffs of Roussillon."

"I need to go back to the house," she calls out, tapping her fists into his back. "Frey! You're hijacking me!"

Only the air rushing into her face responds, blowing her hair into her mouth. They pass vineyards, fields of poppies, orchards streaming confetti white. Despite her anger, she drinks up the ripe countryside. They climb an orange-red cliff, the color of an Oqaatsut sunset. Vineyards pitch and slope on either side of the narrow road. They stop at the top of the ruddy red cliff in a small bustling village that looks as if it's been sunset-dipped. Most of the structures are the color of this maroon, orange, or mustard-tinted clay. A pack of cyclists arrives behind them, huffing and puffing after the uphill exertion.

Frey removes his helmet and shakes out his hair. She's still on the bike.

"I need to go back."

"You're leaving so soon. I couldn't help myself."

"You can't help yourself in a lot of ways."

"I couldn't let you leave Provence without showing you this village."

She slides off the bike, and he leads her to a bench at the edge of the cliff. He points to the underside of the precipice, where she sees stripes of striking reds, ochre oranges, and mustard yellows.

"And there is our Luberon *bijou*, the Ventoux." He nods to the white-capped mountain in the distance that Ilse remembers Madame Hugot told her was not snow-covered.

"You're the other Luberon *bijou*."

A calico cat with a twisted tail scampers beside them. Even the cats match the yellow-brown color of the rocky cliff.

Frey takes her hand, suddenly, and sinks down on one knee.

"I deeply regret misleading you. It was selfish and shameful. My lady, will you please accept my apology?"

"Your words are fairer than you," she says. She's been reading too much troubadour poetry, and so has he.

In a light whisper voice, he sings the verse of the ballad that he'd sung to her before.

If I were brought to her stronghold
Prisoned by her in some tower,
And daily ate my morsel sour,
Happily, I'd there grow old,
If my desire she granted me!
She should try to do no wrong.
If she made me yearn too long . . .

"And you disparage your father for his medieval ditties," she says. "Anyway, I'm hardly the medieval ideal of purity, and even if you wanted to be, you're not Lancelot."

He stands and bursts out laughing. And he laughs and laughs, uncontrollably. He sits on the red dirt, still laughing.

"I haven't laughed so much, felt like this, in a long time. Thank you, thank you, Ilse."

Against her wishes, she's laughing too.

"*Damn,*" she says, "I wish I'd taken a video of you on your knees."

"We're a strange species, we humans!" he says, standing up, still laughing. "Can you see why I'm putting my mind and heart into robots? Come, let's be friends if we can no longer be lovers."

She smiles a little, then, and nods.

"Let's get some *morilles,* whatever they are," she says.

FREY IS GONE THE following day, Monday, for a meeting in Avignon with one of his work colleagues. When Ilse and Po meet at their usual nine o'clock hour, Po says he's not feeling word-wise. Ilse is losing the ability to distract the Provençal poet from his pain.

"Before I return to my opium den upstairs," he says in a whisper, "I would like to give you something."

"A poem?" she says, surprised at her eagerness.

"Better than one of my useless jingles."

He reaches beside him and bends, not without difficulty, to retrieve something beside him that he now hides in both hands. He opens his palms to her: it's a *boule,* one of his three metal *pétanque* balls.

"One of my favorite possessions, I bestow it on you."

The way Po holds the *boule* out to her with both hands reminds her of the way that Clément offered the wafer to her in church. She receives it.

"This one, marked with the red dot, is the lightest of all three, *un boule tendre,* which limits the bounce back, and increases the chances for a *carreau,* the thing I managed to do on that day when I knocked the Goult team's ball—and myself—out of place."

His hollowed face now looks burdened with wistfulness.

"I thought you might find a use for this *boule* when you meet Frey in Paris, to knock out the other—"

"Po, you'll need this for your next *carreau*. And I'm not planning to meet Frey in Paris."

"You know as well as I do, my truthful friend, that I won't be playing *pétanque* again. But more importantly, why won't you be seeing Frey in Paris?"

"Had he mentioned that to you?"

"No, but he doesn't tell me anything."

"No, Po, I'm not meeting Frey in Paris."

"I'm not convinced." He takes a deep wheezing breath. "As our Buddhist teachers tell us, everything changes, and nothing lasts forever."

A bird in the olive tree above them starts to *twitter, twitter, twitter, chee chee,* then pauses.

"I'm waiting too, blackbird, for the response call," says Po.

"There it is," she says. A shriller note, on an upper branch of the olive tree.

Now the birds sing in unison.

"I detest goodbyes, but I suppose I'll have to survive your departure tomorrow—or not."

"I'll be back, Po, to visit."

She waits for his response like the blackbird had. It's slow in coming.

"In the next few weeks," Po continues, "if you're stuck in translation, tap Agnès for help. She's as fluent in our dialect as anyone. And Frey, though he'll deny that he knows a word, can untangle the more basic vocabulary and expressions. Going forward, Frey should be your resource."

The metal ball in her hand is cold.

Why contact them and not you? she wants to ask, but she doesn't.

THAT EVENING BEFORE HER departure, Frey asks Ilse to dinner, but thankfully, she's already accepted Chloé's invitation to join her for a going away *coupe de champagne* and a *crêpe* at La Crêperie de Maman. It's appropriate that her last dinner in Belle Rivière bookends her first one.

How much more fluent and confident she is when she orders the same delicious *galette au saumon fumé*. This time, she dines and converses with a French friend who will drive her back to the Labayes', saving her the walk through the dark tunnel.

She will say her goodbyes to Carole and Jean-Pierre tomorrow. Jean-Pierre has kindly offered to drive her to the airport. And Carole said she'd come along for the ride, that she wouldn't mind spending a day in Nice. But Ilse knows otherwise, that the six-hour round-trip drive is an extravagant parting gesture.

Tang runs beside her as Ilse climbs the stairs in the hushed house after dinner.

Ilse finds a note on her door.

In large block letters, it reads, "*S'il te plaît, ne pars pas.*" Please don't leave.

She spies a light under the door of Frey's room. She's tempted to knock. It's not a physical craving, but more like the wish to converse with Frey as a friend, maybe even laugh again at them posing as knight and lady. Instead, she stands outside Po's door and listens. Quiet, then a loud cough, another cough. Is there blood on his handkerchief? Does he sense her presence?

"Sleep sweetly," she whispers to the door.

In her room, Ilse stands on the balcony overlooking the moonlit vineyard. She has packed her bag with everything except her nightgown and toothbrush.

She allows Tang to jump up and sleep on her bed. She half expects a midnight knock, is prepared to say a true "no," but there is no tap on the door.

Chapter 29

ILSE WAKES IN THE DARK OF NIGHT TO A BARRAGE OF BARKING. Tang jumps off her bed. Ilse had been dreaming of Inès with her black kohl eyes, dressed in multiple orange-ochre silk scarves. She was running away from Po, who was chasing her. Just before she woke, Po's fingers had caught Inès's ankles, at which point they burst into flames.

Ilse grabs her bathrobe, opens her door. Tang takes off down the stairs. It's Mastiff barking, groaning, and growling at the bottom of the stairs. Frey, in his bathrobe, is in the hallway. Rubbing his eyes, he turns on the hall light.

The door to Po's bedroom is open, and the light is on.

What time is it?

Mastiff won't stop barking.

"Mastiff!" Frey yells at the top of the stairs.

Ilse and Frey sprint down the stairs.

Frey switches the front hall light on.

What?

Po's body is splayed out on the stone floor. In front of Inès's portrait. A stream of blood runs from his head.

"Papa, Papa!" yells Frey, rushing to his side, kneeling, and placing his father's head in his lap.

Mastiff whines. The other three dogs have formed a circle around Po. They're all making strange groaning sounds.

"He must have fallen down the stairs."

"I'll call the ambulance," Ilse shouts, running up the stairs to get her phone. Tang follows closely behind.

"The number is 112!" he calls out. "He's not conscious. Bring down a bedsheet! Or a towel!"

"Yes," she yells from the top of the stairs. In her bedroom, she calls the emergency number. *"Venez, venez, un accident!"* She pulls the sheet from her bed and takes a towel from the hallway bathroom.

Back down the stairs, Frey is bent over his father's head. "Come on, Papa, show some life. Papa, come on." Blood on Frey's hands.

She gives Frey the sheet and towel.

"Why are they taking so long?"

She looks at her phone. "I called four minutes ago."

Frey wraps one end of the sheet around his father's head to form a kind of tourniquet. How can she be thirty-five years old and not know what to do when someone falls and hits his head on a stone floor?

Malu would know.

"I've got his pulse," Frey is saying. "It's slow, but it's going."

Thank God.

"Call Agnès."

She misspells the name as she types. Her hands are shaking. There, got it. No one answers.

Agnès, come! she writes in a text. *Po fell down the stairs.* Agnès had told her to text any time of the night, that she kept her phone on. But she lives forty-five minutes away.

"Call Clément."

"Clément?"

"Clément will bring him around. Clément has a way with him."

There's Agnès's response.

"Agnès and Benoît are on their way," Ilse tells Frey.

Ilse doesn't have Clément's number. In a blur, she texts Agnès to call Clément to come.

"There you are, Papa," Frey says, holding up his father's head. The red spot on the sheet spreads.

"Papa."

Po opens his eyes, then shuts them.

"There, Papa, you're okay. You've hit your head, you silly old man. You'll be fine. The ambulance is on its way."

"*Non,*" Po says, turning his head in a muffled roar. "*Pas d'ambulance!*" He coughs blood, and his face turns from white to red. "*Je n'irai pas à l'hôpital, je n'irai pas.* I won't go to the hospital. I won't go." He coughs. "Son . . ." Blood drips down the side of his face onto Frey's bathrobe.

Mastiff starts barking again.

"Mastiff, stop," Frey yells. The dog has a paw on Po's chest.

Po coughs. He coughs up more blood. Ilse places the towel up to his mouth.

"Mastiff, calm down," Frey says.

Mastiff groans. The dogs stop barking. Tang runs circles around Po, around, and around.

Po is speaking.

"What's he saying?" Ilse asks.

"'*Passant, j'ay dit, suy ta fortune,*' 'Passerby, as I said, follow your fortune,'" says Frey. Po looks like a Sikh, his head in the white, now red-stained turban.

Ilse understands the next line.

"*Ne trouble mon repos, je dors.* Don't disturb my rest, I am sleeping."

"He's quoting Ronsard," says Frey. "Ronsard wrote this on his deathbed."

Po grips his son's hand.

"Better this way, son."

"Ilse, come here, hold his hand. We shouldn't move him." She kneels beside him on the cold stone floor. "I'll get ice. Where the fuck is the ambulance?"

The light goes on in the kitchen. She hears Frey rummaging, collecting ice from the freezer. The dogs continue to moan.

"It's going to be okay, Po," she says. Po opens his red eyes and gazes up at her.

"Île du Nord, don't look so sad." It's a mumble, but she understands.

Sirens. The three dogs run to the door, barking, and scratching at it. Mastiff stays on watch beside his best friend.

Po can't die. He's supposed to die when she's back in her life, when all this will be far away, like a dream.

"Here come the *pompiers,*" she says to him. She wipes the tears from her cheeks. "The doctors will stitch up your head, and Jean-Pierre and Carole will laugh over a Ricard about the great firebrand's clumsiness. Frey is getting ice for your head. You'll be fine. A little crack in the head. My mother would say it might knock some sense into you. Po, come back here. Keep your eyes on mine. Po, Po. Stay with me."

He coughs, blood in his teeth. She lifts his head, wipes his mouth with a clean part of the sheet.

Coughing again, a thick grotesque cough, like the sound of some submerged thing in deep water, a porpoise, caught under, who needs a breath of air.

"Mastiff, give him some air, Mastiff," she says. The dog is pressing in too close.

"Pain is good," he says, his voice a ragged thing. He clears his throat. "No, pain is bad, it means I'm still alive."

He's gazing, his eyes half-open, up at Inès's portrait, and then he turns away and looks at Ilse.

"Île, it is right that you are here now. It is right. Thank you," he rasps, then coughs, more blood. He takes a clogged breath. "Thank you . . . for pointing the way."

"Frey!" she calls, not recognizing the pitch in her voice. She begins to cry, her tears falling on his eyes, on his face, on his cheeks, sallow and gray. "Frey, come back now!"

Car doors slamming. Men's voices. Barking.

Frey saying, "This way. *C'est le bon chemin.*"

And under his gasping breath, Ilse hears Po repeat, "*Oui, c'est le bon chemin.* It's the right way." He closes his eyes.

Frey is back. Two men and a woman wearing bright yellow vests run toward Po and her.

"Frey," she says.

She can't stop the tears.

Frey takes Ilse's place with his father's head in his lap, as she backs off to sit on the bottom stair. She wipes the bloody hands on her bathrobe.

"Don't move his head," says one of the ambulance men.

The ambulance woman puts her ear to his chest.

Frey is leaning down to his father's mouth. "He's not breathing! Breathe, Father, breathe."

Frey looks as pale as his father, perspiration on his brow and his chin. Blood is all over his bathrobe.

The front door open, Ilse can hear a bird singing in the dark, a nightingale.

Sing, nightingale, sing to block out the pain. Sing the poem-songs of the last living troubadour in Provence, sing to his life!

One of the ambulance men administers resuscitation. The woman pumps his lungs. It looks brutal the way they do this.

"He's not breathing," Frey tells them, his hands up to his eyes. He's crying.

They continue trying to pump life into the body. One of Po's hands falls to the side. The hand that wrote poetry, the treasure of Provence.

The three dogs run to the door, but not Mastiff. He continues to make strange groaning sounds. It's Clément. In a brown robe with a rope cord around his belly. Worn brown espadrilles with rope peeling off the bottom. Clément strokes Mastiff to stop the moaning, which is now a loud growl.

"Mastiff, we are with you, Mastiff," says Clément. The dog stops growling.

"I thought so," Clément says, approaching. The ambulance people back off as if they are afraid. Clément, in full authority, places his hand on his friend's forehead.

"He left us willingly," he says, kneeling on the floor and touching his friend's heart. "He is ready to accept his new life."

"No!" says Frey, as if this is the first time he has thought of his father's death. He kneels on the other side of his father. "Father, it's another one of his jokes. He can hold his breath forever."

"Traumatic brain injury," says the ambulance woman.

One of the ambulance men, the one with a beard, steps forward. "I'm sorry for your loss. There's nothing we could have done."

Frey shoots the man a searing *You could have saved him if you'd gotten here faster* glare.

Ilse takes a deep breath.

"Will you please contact his doctor?" says the ambulance man. He's young, maybe twenty-five. He's got one of those open faces that invites a smile. It's a face that hasn't seen many deaths. "We can't leave the premises until the doctor comes to sign his . . . certificate."

Now she remembers the man's face from the day of the *pétanque* game.

"Back off, will you. Give my father some air." Frey's voice is gnarly, changed from anguish to anger. Mastiff starts barking again.

"Agnès and Benoît are twenty minutes away," Ilse says, looking up from her phone. "Agnès gave me the doctor's number. I'm calling him now."

"Mastiff!" yells Frey.

Frey is bent over his father, his hand gripping his father's hand.

"Papa, come back to us, Papa."

The ambulance man hovers over Frey and Po.

"For God's sake, will you wait outside now that you can no longer be of help? Not that you were . . ."

"I'm sorry sir, but we don't have permission to leave until the doctor signs off."

The other ambulance man, the one older and clean-shaven, stands at the doorway. He's seen plenty. Plenty of dying old men and women, who knows, maybe some young ones too. The young woman leans against the stairs, gazing into her phone.

"Please," says Clément, escorting three yellow-jackets toward the kitchen. "I suggest you wait in the kitchen for us to make arrangements with the doctor. You'll find the coffee maker . . ." Clément's voice trails off as he leaves the room.

Frey looks so alone. Ilse resists the temptation to kneel next to him.

"Papa, you had to have it your way, didn't you?" he says, wiping his tears. "You had to die dramatically at Inès's feet, didn't you? Couldn't just go off slowly in your sleep? Everything for Inès. Everything, oh forgive me, Papa, forgive me." He closes his eyes and bows his head over his father's.

"Forgive me for being so stubborn. For not seeing you as an old man on his way out. Forgive me for all the resentment I harbored and continue to carry. Forgive me for wanting to leave you and the life you made for us. Forgive me for hating your poetry, for being jealous of your love for Ummi. You couldn't help that you loved her. His hand is cold," he says, looking up at Ilse. "It was just warm. It was just alive. Yesterday, it was his writing hand."

She gazes up at the stairs, then down at Po. Had Po planned this fall from the balcony above onto the stone floor? He's lying in a place where you would land had you put a leg over the railing. She should not be here. She should be back in Greenland by now. She walks up a few steps of the stairs and sits there, covering her face with her hands.

Agnès and Benoît arrive and melt over the body. They weep. They say their goodbyes. More dog barking as the doctor arrives. He's wearing a navy bathrobe, a stethoscope around his neck. He must be around Po's age. He checks Po for signs of life, or rather, signs of death, fishes a document out of his bathrobe pocket that he signs on a lifted knee, with a pen from his other pocket.

Agnès tells Frey to take the dogs out, they need fresh air, as does he. She wants to be with her brother without the dogs, who are licking his face. Ilse offers to do this, but Frey is pulling the dogs by their collars out the door before she rises from her spot on the stairs. Not Mastiff. Mastiff will not leave Po's side. His chin rests on Po's shoulder. Mastiff refuses to budge, despite the attempts by the ambulance personnel to slide Po's body onto the stretcher. It is Clément who is finally able to coax the robust dog from Po's side. As the two men and woman lift the stretcher and move to the front door, Mastiff jumps up, barking furiously. The dog grabs a part of Po's sleeve, and Po's arm falls, lifeless, from the stretcher.

"Mastiff!" yells Frey, darting at the dog.

Mastiff moans and quiets down.

The firetruck-ambulance drives away with Po, never to return with Po.

The sun is rising.

"Frey, will you and Ilse take Mastiff out of here," says Agnès, in tears.

"Ilse, are you coming?" Frey says. There's blood on the stone floor next to his feet. The bloody sheet is there too.

She hesitates. She's not sure she wants to go with him.

"I'm asking you to come with me." His Parisian voice.

Agnès and Benoît head into the kitchen. Ilse can hear Agnès sobbing, Benoît and Clément comforting her.

Frey holds the door open for Ilse and waits. His gray bathrobe is bloodstained in so many places. Ilse looks away as she joins him.

Mastiff sprints ahead of the pack of dogs.

"Where's he going?" Frey asks.

Frey and she follow the dogs on the still-dark path that Ilse recognizes but that Frey does not know. Frey uses his phone's flashlight.

"I've never taken this footpath, but the dogs seem to know it. It feels like they're taking us somewhere."

She can feel a childlike fear in Frey. Light pink dawn has begun to backlight the Luberon Mountains.

"Where are you going, Mastiff?"

When they finally arrive at Po's hideaway in the vineyards, Frey shines the flashlight on the table and two chairs, then on the cork tree.

"I've seen this tree from afar," he says, "but never ventured inside the vines. I think this is where the vineyard workers come to rest." He touches the bark.

Ilse inhales the heavy and moist scent of the earth. The table and the two chairs look so empty. Mastiff is sniffing wildly around for clues, darting around the tree, pawing at it. He lifts his head, searching the branches above. He jumps up on the trunk.

Watching Mastiff is witnessing grief personified. No more sensitive Poet fingers on Mastiff's forehead, under his chin, along his back. No more walks, no more standing next to Po as he greets his friends, no more keen awareness of Po breathing, sighing, coughing, no more listening acutely to the sounds that a person makes that only a dog can hear, the grumble of a stomach, the inside sensations of good cheer, disappointment, enthusiasm, grief.

"Forget the vineyard workers," Frey says, sliding down to sit at the base of the cork. "This must have been where Father came when he wanted to get away from us. It has *him* written all over it. And Mastiff . . ."

He bows his head and covers his face in his hands.

The birds are singing now, rousing the world, and there's no waking Po.

Ilse pets Tang. The other dogs sit next to the chair that was Po's, as if waiting for him to appear. Carenza has taken off. Independent Carenza. Maybe she's returning to the Basque Country.

Ilse listens to the whistle and the whir, the song of the wind through the vines that Po so loved.

Frey gets up and moves to the chair in which his father sat, his presence so different from the poet's. Frey has striving in him. He lacks his father's rich overflowing gentleness from a life lived in words.

"Mastiff," Frey says, stroking the dog's thick coat, "you knew him better than I, didn't you?" The large dog's tail droops.

Mastiff finally lies down, and Ilse slips from her chair and puts her head on the dog's broad back. And in this small oasis in the middle of the vineyard where Po hid to be fully himself, Ilse weeps for the beauty of the rising sun, for the whistle of the wind and rustling leaves, for the chitter of the blackbirds in the great cork oak, for Minou, and for Malu, for Fa and his blindness, and for Jann, and for all the people who have lost someone, and then her thoughts return to Po, and how the world will be less without him, less poetic, less mystical, less romantic, less tender, less alive, less loving.

Chapter 30

THE STILLNESS IS FULL OF ABSENCE. IT'S SEVEN O'CLOCK AFTER an endless night, and Ilse finds Agnès alone in the kitchen, sitting on a stool, gazing out the window at the terrace. Perhaps she sees her brother at his writing table. The sun enters the room in spokes, and one ray has found a home on Agnès Labaye's long nose.

"Agnès," Ilse says at the threshold of the room. "I'm sorry to bother you."

Agnès turns to Ilse. The sun-spoke now rests on her pale cheek.

"I'm wondering if I should leave as planned this morning. I realize you may like to be alone with your family, and I'm ready to go. But there's also so much to do. If I can be of help, please . . ."

"Ilse," Agnès smiles, blinking away tears, "it seems we Labayes won't let you go."

She takes a dish towel from the stove handle and wipes her tears. "As you can see, I'm devastated. It happened faster than I . . . It would be wonderful if you would stay on another week to help with the funeral preparations. So many people will want to come by the house. The press will be here tomorrow, and they'll be asking for a statement. I realize you keep postponing your trip home."

"Yes, of course," Ilse says.

"*Merci,* Île du Nord, *merci,*" Agnès says as she returns her eyes to the window overlooking her brother's writing table.

When Ilse informs Malu that she will be prolonging her stay another week, rather than express her condolences for Ilse's poet friend, Malu scolds her for missing the annual post office day fair. "And this year, I plan to beat my record!"

Émile sounds relieved that the Labaye family will be reimbursing Ilse for this flight change fee. He tells her that news of the Provençal poet's death is being talked about all over Paris. Because he's Émile, he follows this comment by reminding her about her deadline.

"Émile, I still have a week."

How will she ever re-create the last pages of poems in Po's melodic voice in a week when her mind and heart are deluged with sorrow?

IT'S TWO DAYS AFTER Po's death, and Frey is nowhere to be seen. Ilse doesn't blame him for avoiding contact with her and everyone in the house. The only way she could deal with Jann's death was to sequester herself and Minou for months—taking seaside walks and learning how to breathe again.

Unlike Inès, who wanted her ashes to be scattered in the Mediterranean, Po wished to be buried in the small graveyard on the west side of the Labaye vineyard alongside his troubadour ancestors and their families.

That afternoon, Ilse steps into the roped-off family graveyard. The ancient, crooked, almost buried headstones resemble rotting teeth in the earth's mouth. Po's plot on the crest of the hill has a sunset view. But wouldn't Po have preferred to face east to the sunrise? She and he were the larks.

Ilse sits beside the undug grave. It's a relief that Frey's fiancée has decided not to come to the funeral. Frey told Ilse that he'd suggested that Caroline not make the trip given her condition. But Ilse wonders if Frey made this recommendation because he knew how his father felt about Caroline. Or maybe he was having doubts about his fiancée? Perhaps he disliked the idea of Caroline meeting Ilse.

The breeze stirs a swath of poppies in the nearby field. The delicate flowers have lost their blazing color. Their season is quenched and done.

Come back, Po! Come back so you and I can sit side by side, our minds aligned in the Provençal language, so our hearts can take flight in unison when we listen to that calandra lark chirping in the apple tree over there—so we can stroll barefoot through the vineyard and sit under the great arms of the cork tree.

Sorry, Po, I'll try not to do that again, trying to lure you back. There's a superstition in Greenland that sorrow at a funeral detains a soul's progress to the beyond.

Po was the only person in her life who seemed to appreciate all the sides of her, and this had the powerful effect of making Ilse feel like she'd never felt before—distinct, recognizably unique, someone worthy of the precious company of the last troubadour of Provence.

Po, please come back!

TWO DAYS LATER ON the morning of the Poet's memorial service, Ilse and Frey run into each other in the upstairs hallway. Frey bows his head and apologizes for his silence.

"I had to get ready for today," he says.

"Of course."

He takes her hand and gives it a little swing. Letting it go, he continues toward the stairs, but after a few steps, he turns back to her and smiles gently. Ilse holds that smile in her heart throughout this trying day.

The service, held outside Saint-Pantaléon, is officiated by Clément. The tiny church would never hold the hundreds in attendance. The priest stands with a microphone on a ridge of the rock necropolis where Neolithic graves had been dug into the stone. Émile and Daphné have sent two enormous white chrysanthemum plants, which Ilse learns are traditionally sent for funerals, and which Frey has set on the outdoor makeshift altar. It is the only cloudy morning since Ilse's arrival.

As the crowds gather, Ilse meets Agnès's daughter Muriele, the one who Agnès had said reminded her of Ilse. How could Agnès have made such a comparison—Muriele, with her auburn-brown hair, her dark, perfectly shaped eyebrows, and Agnès's long noble nose. Then again, Muriele dresses as Ilse would dress at home, in black sneakers, long, wide pants, and a much-too-big shirt that must have been taken from Po's closet. She has placed daisies in her hair and behind her ear, and she has a warm smile.

The newborns do the crying for those in attendance. Each cry is like a stab in the still air. When one child cries, the other wails. When Manon calms one of the twins, the other becomes quiet. Ilse imagines that was how she and Jann were, almost twins, feeling each other, being each other.

It is humbling for Ilse to be among these people who have known Po in different parts of his life, for so much longer. Frey reads one of Po's recent poems about seeing light in the dark, Agnès reads a poem from Pierre de Ronsard, one of Po's favorites, and Clément reads from the Bible and supplies the eulogy.

With tears, Clément admits that he's lost his best friend on this earth, and that he will tend the grave and soul of this man as if he were his brother. After that, Clément makes so many jokes about their times together that at one point, amid the laughter, Ilse forgets she's at a funeral. Léon Labaye, a younger cousin who lives in Avignon, plays the rebec, a small, bowed instrument that originated in the tenth century and is thought to resemble a woman's voice. He sings a troubadour song with lyrics from Po, and Ilse has the feeling that if Po were watching, he'd be pleased.

Agnès passes around a sympathy journal with a black cloth cover. Ilse has never seen people as voraciously hungry for a book. Po's friends and admirers wait their turn, and then when they have the book in hand, they turn away from the others to write, as if they are turning to Po. Some write long passages. Many drop tears on the pages.

Frey is calm and gracious as he takes turns embracing friends and family.

At the burial, it's a closed casket; Carole places an open jar of honey beside the coffin. She says that honey connects the soul with soulmates of the departed, and this way, Po may find Inès more quickly. Georges places a *boule* inside should his cousin want to play a game of *pétanque* while waiting in purgatory.

"Purgatory?" Agnès says. "You really think my wonderful brother will spend time there?"

"He might elect to stop there for a Ricard," says Georges.

THE DAY AFTER THE funeral, Georges and the other four elderly men on the Belle Rivière *pétanque* team arrive at the house. One by one, each drops a lustrous white lily into the arms of Agnès, who weeps.

Po is beloved all over France, but especially in Provence. The days following his memorial service are a whirlwind of visits from the Poet's friends and fans, journalists, cousins from Paris, and relatives of Inès's from Marrakesh. The Labaye manor house is overflowing with gifts, flowers, food, and notes. It's nonstop hospitality, which helps distract everyone from missing Po. When Madame Hugot arrives to pay her respects, her suspicious eyes ask Ilse, *And* you're *still here?*

Thankfully, Agnès has hired the neighbor's two teenage daughters to help Frey and Ilse serve breakfast croissants and coffee, baguette sandwiches for lunch, and Moroccan *tagine* for dinner. In her spare time, Ilse collects the eulogies from the local, national, and international newspapers, many with a tombstone in the Arts and Letters sections, honoring the Provençal poet.

It is only in the quiet of the night that Ilse has time to work on the translations.

Gradually, the visits of Po-loving guests begin to ebb, and the house, once so full of the mistral and spring breezes and friends coming and going, now feels lifeless. The swallows and finches that flew in and out and made nests in the corners of the ceiling and windows have had their chicks and flown away. Because Agnès removed the white sheets from the chairs and sofas for the guests, the light airy feeling of the place is now dulled by the dark-colored upholstery. The house is serious.

The saddest sight is Mastiff. He moans through the day and won't eat, not even *le quignon* of a baguette. Inconsolable, he sits by the table under the olive tree, patiently awaiting Po's return.

Chapter 31

MONDAY MORNING, JUNE FOURTH, THE DAY OF ILSE'S DEADline, is misty, dull, and hot, and the Luberons look as if they're fading away. Tang wags his tail as Ilse stands and stretches. She has one more poem to transform from her ungraceful third draft and needs Rumpelstiltskin's magic to conjure titles for six others. She'll be working nonstop through the night.

"I will miss you, Tang," she says as she tickles the dog's sharp chin. Ilse had decided that tomorrow, Tuesday, a week after Po's death, and five weeks since she arrived in Belle Rivière, is the appropriate day for her return home. The most difficult period of time after the funeral is over, and soon life in the Labaye house will shift to a different kind of normalcy. Before going downstairs where she hears people talking, she books her flight. She closes her eyes: it is done.

Ilse finds Agnès in the kitchen organizing Po's papers into piles, one for finished poems, one for first drafts, one for second drafts, and so on. Agnès says that Benoît and she will be moving into the house until things are settled.

Ilse hears someone, she guesses it's Frey, in the pantry, making a pot of coffee, as she tells Agnès about her plans to leave the next day. She's not sure if Frey has heard.

When Frey enters the kitchen with the coffee, Agnès is hugging Ilse. Ilse inhales the sweet smell of her rose fragrance. If she could only smell that scent every day for the rest of her life.

"Oh, Ilse," Agnès says, "you've been an angel to this family. Of course, you'll want to return home. We will be forever grateful to you for the light you brought to Geoffrey and to all of us, especially in his last days. Here, I've been wanting to give you this for a long time."

Agnès slips off one of her gold bangle bracelets.

"So you don't forget us."

"This is too much, Agnès. Really."

"Ilse, your presence has meant more to me and my brother than I think you realize."

Frey is busy with cups and saucers, sugar, and milk.

Ilse slides the gold bracelet onto her wrist. It fits tighter on Ilse's larger wrist than it had on Agnès's, but it dangles just the same.

"I'll give you one every time you visit, so in the end you'll have the set! There's an incentive for you."

Ilse thanks Agnès with another hug. And it occurs to Ilse that she has never given so many hugs to people who aren't family members as she has here in Provence.

No one asks her to stay this time. Agnès turns to Frey. He's focused on pouring coffee into three cups.

"We're all still in shock." Agnès says this as if to excuse Frey's silence.

Had Po conjured it? All of it: the explosion of poppies, Tang's adoration, the vineyard hideout under the cork tree, the troubadour *chansons*, the moonlit nights, Frey's attraction to her and his saber champagne bottle opening, Frey's gentle lovemaking, and her *grasse matinée* that made her think of the possibility of a future together? Yes! She and Frey were ingredients that Po had blended to create an elixir of love. It was all illusion!

Now that the magician was gone, Ilse would regress to her old dismal self. Frey had changed back to the man she had first met at the table under the olive tree: the suave, brittle Parisian, caring more about the coffee than about the news that Ilse is leaving.

"I'll take you to the airport," he says.

He *had* heard.

"Thank you, Frey," Ilse says, "but you're needed here. And Jean-Pierre has offered to drive me."

"I want to take you—"

"Frey," Agnès interrupts, "Ilse is right, I can't let you go. Uncle Fadoul is arriving late tonight from Marrakesh to pay his respects."

"I was wondering where he's been." Frey hands Ilse a cup of coffee. "Fadoul is our mother's brother. The last time we saw Fadoul was five years ago. I would have insisted on taking you, but—now I'm grounded."

Is Frey relieved to forgo the unwieldy burden of the airport goodbye? She can't tell. The only thing she knows is that soon she will be replacing her dusty and worn lavender espadrilles with her waterproof boots.

ILSE WORKS ON PO'S translations in her room, taking frequent breaks to help Agnès in the kitchen with washing the coffee cups and saucers. *Note to self: tell Frey to buy a dishwasher for this house.* When Ilse returns to her room after the afternoon kitchen cleanup, she notices a white box wrapped with a pale blue ribbon on her bed. She opens it to find a French-blue sundress. How cheerful! It has a square neck and pockets on either side of the skirt. No note. Is it from Frey? It must be from Agnès.

She rushes to try it on. A little tight around the waist; she must suck in her stomach, but otherwise it's fine. Tonight may be the only night she can wear it. In an Oqaatsut summer, it's rarely hot enough to walk around without a sweater. She doesn't care, she'll wear this dress to Tipsy's with four sweaters.

Another surprise. On her desk, she finds a blue envelope on which her name is scrawled in elegant handwriting. Inside is a handful of euros and a note:

Ilse,

This is for both flight changes.

You will always be welcome in the Labaye home as part of our family. Thank you for the gift of your spirit.

You filled Geoffrey's last days with light.

Ilse counts five hundred euros. She will leave half the euros in the envelope, since Émile had reassured her that Éditions Elsevier would pay for the first flight change. She wishes there had been only one flight change.

Chapter 32

"SHHH," ILSE WHISPERS TO TANG AS SHE LIFTS HER ROLLER bag across the threshold of her room and into the hallway. She blows Po's room a kiss and creeps down the stairs, holding the railing the way she'd seen Po do it in his last days. She needs the support. She was awake until two in the morning reworking a few impossible-to-translate words in the last poem in the collection. Finally, with a deep sigh, she'd clicked the send button. She doesn't want to be finished with this project! After all this time, she feels she's finally captured Po's voice, his timbre, and the rhythm that he deemed so important. Now she must leave it behind.

There's a noise downstairs. It's a door, slamming with the wind.

Tang at her heels, she slips down the stairs.

For a moment, she thinks Po is already up, waiting for her at the table on the terrace. She imagines his white poet's shirt glowing in the soft morning sun, his face focused, his right arm fluid.

She stands before the portrait.

Are you with him now, Inès?

Somehow, she doubts it.

It's the kitchen window shutter that's banging.

She hears tires on the sandy driveway outside. Why isn't Mastiff downstairs, barking at the new visitor? He is probably asleep in Frey's room, dreaming of Po. She kneels to pet Tang and to say goodbye. She snaps a photograph of her companion who made her feel welcome on her first day at the Labaye house.

She drops down to hug the dog. "We had a good time here together, didn't we? Didn't we?" She wipes her eyes as she stands. His ears perked, the copper-colored dog is looking up at her. He must feel her forlornness, or else sense her departure.

"Don't make any noise, Tang. Please do that for me."

At the front door, okay, she lets Tang out with her. He'll wake up the house if she doesn't. She leaves the door ajar.

She wishes Carole and Jean-Pierre would keep their voices down.

The dog does a little dance around the car.

"Goodbye, Tang. Stay here. Take care of Frey."

She looks up at the house. Frey's room faces this way. She sees something move. Is that him, risen to watch her depart? No, he sleeps late. It's the shadow of the cypress, tall and graceful, like Frey.

Goodbye house. Goodbye Tang. Goodbye Po, Geoffrey Labaye, goodbye Frey, goodbye the vineyard and your welcoming vines, and the wine that taught me about the Provençal soil, and the sun-smiling days that gave me inner warmth. Goodbye Agnès and Benoît, and your daughters and your daughter's daughters, and the future female troubadour poets.

"I tried to bring a cup of coffee," says Jean-Pierre when Ilse rounds the car, "but Carole here wouldn't let me. She doesn't believe in coffee to go."

"But I did bring you a *pain au chocolat* just out of the oven!" Carole says, as she gives Ilse the warm pastry and touches her hand, holding it there for a moment.

3.

A Rainbow for Ilse

Only the spirits of
the air know,
what I will meet behind
the mountain,
but I still drive my dogs
further forward,
further forward,
further forward.

—KNUD RASMUSSEN

Chapter 33

"NO SCHNAPPS FOR ME," ILSE SAYS TO VAL, COVERING THE TOP of her mug. "On deadline."

Ilse has been hired to translate a crime thriller by a best-selling English author into Danish for a big fee. Ilse has never translated a thriller, but after Provençal poetry, this should be a snap. Language takes second place to plot, and the sentences are concise and unnuanced.

"Brrrr, my body isn't used to the wind chill," she tells Val, who looks to Ilse more beautiful than ever with her wild black hair outlining her luminous face.

"You've been gone too long: it's hot as Hades today. All I can say is that you're lucky you missed the rain. Everyone is *sialliliuppua*."

"Translation, please."

"You really have forgotten us!"

"I've never heard that word before!"

"Hello. It means 'surprised by the rain'!" Val sips her coffee. "It's been raining nonstop for the last two weeks. I've never seen or heard more frogs around this place. Everything is wet, soggy, and slimy." She makes a frowning face, sticks out her tongue.

"That doormat will tell you what you missed." Val nods in the direction of the mud-caked entryway. "And we're getting more rain at the end of this week."

"Fast-moving clouds, take me back to Provence," Ilse says, peering out the white salty windows.

"You said you missed us!"

"You, yes, Minou, yes, Fa, yes, Malu, hmm, but the damp cold, no." She rubs her hands together.

"Wake up, Ilse, it's almost summer solstice! Here, the schnapps will help remind you where you are."

"It's too early, and I've got a full day of work."

Last night, she caught herself dreaming in Provençal.

"Po, aren't you proud of me?" she'd asked him aloud when she woke that morning.

Of all the translations she's completed in her career, Ilse feels most proud of *The Provençal Poet*. Thanks mostly to the intimacy she and Po shared, Ilse can say that for the first time, she's experienced the mysterious alchemy of being a conduit for a masterpiece. She lay upon the Poet's soul, or more likely, he'd lain upon hers. Theirs was not a physical relationship, but it may have been the sexiest thing she has ever experienced.

She feels weepy when she thinks of the days when she was deeply immersed in Po's singing words. Since she's been back, upon waking, or during her walks, or just before sleep, she catches herself humming the melodies that Po trilled to her. It's her way of creating a new pattern in her old life.

Another thing: she's no longer as content as she had been, working and sleeping alone out on the tidal island off the mainland in her sea captain's cottage; she misses the feeling of belonging to the tight community of Belle Rivière.

Val is wearing the kohl eyeliner that makes her look like an Egyptian queen, her eyes wider and larger than they already are. The shirt under Val's apron is a midriff, and a quick glance shows her slim waistline. Her smile is bright today, and it's the first time in all her and Ilse's years together that she seems, yes, cheerful. It's so not *Val* to be cheerful.

Is it because of Beluga?

"Well, we missed you, Ilse."

We.

"Donny especially. Your mother, painfully. She stopped in once a week, then twice a week, then three times a week. She told me and everyone in town that she was adopting me as her new daughter. At first, it was kind of nice, Ilse, given that, as you know, my mother is still addicted to online gambling. She loses every penny I give her. But at least when my mother visits, she buys a coffee and a cake."

Val rounds the corner of the counter and takes the swivel stool next to Ilse. She leans on the counter with both of her sharp elbows, coffee cup in her hands.

"Ilse, your mother is cheap!"

"Tell me about it!"

"She came in here with her own coffee in that old green thermos, telling me that I could never make coffee that was strong enough. And she took the best seat, the one you're in. She *did* bring me my mail, yes, twice a week, but then she'd start complaining to all my customers about her backbreaking work. I've spent precious hours trying to think of how to get her to stop coming here. Now that you're back, you've got that job. I'm surprised she's not here by now."

"I told her to hold her horses, that I've got to work all day today, and that I'll come home for dinner tomorrow night. She leaves me alone when I tell her I'm working to pay the bills. How's Fa been?"

"His eyes are pretty bad these days, Ilse," Val says, twirling the stool, then sitting again.

"Malu told me."

"But I mean *really* pretty bad. Since you've been away, I've watched him struggle even with the small step at the entrance, to come in. He uses his hands to navigate around the counter. Duggan's been ferrying him around. As much as we give Malu a hard time, it's been tough on her."

Ilse wants to reach over and hug her friend and weep a little about time passing. But she knows that Val will push her off and say, "Ilse, get a life!"

Has five weeks in temperate Provence warmed Ilse's heart?

Ilse wants to ask.

About the other thing.

The wind blows open the door. Ilse swivels to shut it.

"You can leave it open for now. You may think it's cold after where you've been, but it's perfectly warm for the rest of us. And it's not raining! Thank goodness we still have three months of delicious, warmer weather and daylight before it turns in the other direction."

Warmer weather means forty degrees Fahrenheit.

Val refills Ilse's coffee cup and her own. Ilse sips, the taste bitter and sour at the same time. Frey would spit it out. Po would appreciate its "otherness." Malu is right, her own rotgut is better. And to think that Ilse hadn't noticed before Provence.

"Okay, Ilse, so tell me."

"I'll start with the vineyards, because the grape leaves are as green as your eyes, no, sorry, let me look."

Val opens her eyes wide.

"No, your eyes are greener. Val, I have to say, the life there is . . . what you'd expect on the other side of paradise. Or maybe it's this side of paradise! It's all sides of paradise."

"Come on, my fairy-tale lover," Val says, standing and placing her hands on her hips. Ilse catches sight of her belly button with the gold ring in it. Val is so cool.

"I think it's the refracted light there," Ilse continues. "I need someone to give me the scientific explanation, it's some kind of multi-electron process, oh, who knows? Whatever the reason, the colors of the sky, the mountains, and the landscape mutate and blend throughout the day. It's an incantation of color. Val, stop looking so exasperated."

"This is how people talk when they're head over heels in love," Val says as she rearranges the salt and pepper shakers on the counter.

"I am . . . I mean, I was," Ilse says. She feels like crying, *she misses Po,* but she takes a deep breath instead. "As I told you, my poet friend died, and yes, you could say all the colors of his countryside passed away with him, but now they're in me, too, and in everyone who knew him."

"You're still in love. I see it in your sad eyes."

Ilse nods.

The wind howls outside, and Ilse feels a cold draft through the door.

"And then there was his son," Ilse says, sipping the bitter coffee. She tears open another packet of sugar and shakes the contents into her cup.

"I'm finally getting the *real* story."

"We had a thing, but now I'm thinking that it really was his father . . ."

"*A thing*," repeats Val. "Will the word person please be a little more specific?"

"We got romantic, but it felt misplaced. The more I think about it, the *liaison* really was with his father, and the word-worlds we inhabited together. We laughed, we played, we dangled in delight, but we also probed layers of deep meaning in just about every one of his words. We enjoyed each other's company, every bit of each other. His words brought us together, fused us into another being, like a lit-from-inside new person."

If she'd met Frey without his father, she doubts that they would have ended up in the same bed.

"Hold that thought," says Val, as she runs to the kitchen. "Buns are ready."

Ilse looks at her phone.

Another text from Frey. *How goes?*

Since she's been back, Frey has been sending tidbits of *hello*s, *how are you*s, *missing you*s, three words max. Ilse's colleague, Bea Fugue, had once referred to this kind of communication as "breadcrumbing," the act of sending brief, flirtatious, but noncommittal signals. The one from last night was an amazing four words: *Have I lost you?* Ilse had been tempted to respond *Yup, you lost me.*

Val's back.

"So, what happened to the son romance?"

"When his father died, everything changed. Oh yes, and by the way, he's getting married in August, and his fiancée is pregnant."

Val whips her head of hair around to face Ilse.

"You sure know how to pick 'em!"

"It was the Poet's, his father's fault. He used secret sorcery to bring us together."

"And then . . ."

"Po died, and the enchantment evaporated. And here I am, home again. Enough of me. What about you, Val, what gives your skin the color of the Luberon sun?"

Val smiles, again. She's never smiled so much!

"You inspired me, Ilse. I'm going to get away, too."

Ilse was right. It's happened.

"Nice, Val, you deserve a getaway. Tell me where?"

Ilse hears voices outside and turns toward the window.

"There he is," says Val, standing, to look out. "Spot on, wanting to be the first to greet you."

Val pulls the rope curtain tie from the window and uses it to cinch her thick, wavy hair. Val does everything with a spontaneous flourish.

Ilse pushes the now-hanging curtain back to look. Two men are walking on what looks like the surface of a muddy, jagged cratered moon. Ilse recalls the wave of cliffs of Roussillon, the rich burnt sienna color of the clay.

"Just about every day," Val says, sipping her coffee, "Donny drags one or two of his brothers, last week all of his brothers, in here, sometimes they're here twice a day, which isn't so bad, I tell you, and he asks me the same question, 'When is Ilse coming back?' He proudly shows my customers the postcards you sent him. You probably don't realize the impact your postcards have had on my life. They gave your postal-delivering mother another twice-then-thrice-weekly excuse to come here."

"But Val, before the Qannik brothers get here, tell me where you're going—on vacation." She asks too quickly.

"We're going to . . . meet his family."

They must be visiting Beluga's errant uncle, the one he'd once mentioned who lived in a hut in Estonia on the Baltic Sea.

Ilse hears a shout. It's Donny.

"Ilssse, Ilssse!" Ilse hears his deep voice through the open door.

Val darts into the kitchen to prepare for the arrival of her customers.

"Donny!" Ilse says, standing to greet him.

Donny jumps to hug her and almost knocks her down. His smile is so wide, she wants to hold it in her memory for the rest of her life. Most people, even villagers who know each other well, shake hands when they see each other. Donny is the exception.

"Ilssse," he lisps, his arms wrapped tightly around her. "She's home!" he yells to Ingun, a few feet behind him. Ingun is the oldest of the Qannik brothers. Just before she left for Provence, he'd returned from Copenhagen, where he'd been for three years pursuing an engineering degree. Ingun had always been the serious Qannik, but now he has a grin on his ruddy face.

"Thanks to our town crier here, the whole place knows you're home, Ilse," says Ingun, shaking hands with her. How different this formal greeting is from the delicate, soft, three-cheek kisses of Provence. "I'm surprised there's not a parade of small crafts motoring down the coast right now with horns and drums to welcome you."

Ilse smiles, at the same time feeling an ache as she gazes down at the gold bracelet that Agnès gave her. She's remembering her first sip of coffee on the small balcony overlooking the purple mountains. How her heart had jumped at the sight of such a view.

Val returns with a brimming mug of coffee for Ingun and a hot chocolate for Donny.

Ingun takes a sip.

"Hits the spot. Thanks, Val. Ilse, I'd have to say that I'm glad you're home, if only to get Donny off my back. He's been pestering all of us daily. He wanted to be the first to see you."

"Donny, you *are* the first," says Ilse. "If you don't count Val."

"I don't count," yells Val back in the kitchen.

Donny seems bigger than before, stronger, and broader. Everyone is bigger here than the people she'd met in Provence.

"So, you're growing a beard, Donny?"

He stands taller. "D'ya like it?"

"It's very handsome, but you're handsome, no matter what."

"Do you have some good stories for us from *la belle* France?" asks Ingun.

"I was just telling Val about the vineyards almost as green as her eyes, and the ever-present sun. I think it was the sun, most of all, that filled the soil of . . . the soil of my soul."

"She hasn't changed," says Ingun, shaking his head and sipping the coffee. "Talking about soil and soul in the same sentence."

Donny takes a postcard Ilse had sent him from the back pocket of his jeans. It's crinkled and bent, but Ilse recognizes the windmill in Goult, and she feels a pang in her chest.

On a motorcycle ride with Frey, he'd driven up a steep, bumpy cobblestoned road to show Ilse this seventeenth-century windmill on top of the world. The mistral almost blew them off the hilltop. That was the day he'd told her that he often made wrong decisions when the mistral was blowing, one of them being leaving Belle Rivière for Paris. Ilse knows that he would have left Belle Rivière no matter what.

"You should see our motorboat," Ingun is saying. "Donny's taped every postcard you sent to him inside the windshield. I can barely see out."

"I want to see what Ilssse saw," says Donny.

"That was kind of you, Ilse, to think of Donny while you were away on your adventure," Ingun says. "Val!" he calls out, turning toward the kitchen. "What's she doing back there for so long?"

This time he shouts louder. "How about saying hello to your regulars?"

"Buzz off, Ingun," she yells from the back.

She appears with a tray of plates and a powdery confection that smells like raspberry Danish coffee cake.

That smile again, unlocked, free, easy.

"Come on outside," she says to Ingun, sashaying beside him in her loose-below-the-belt frilly apron.

They sit at one of the two small tables on four dark green plastic chairs. The chairs are usually stacked in the inside corner near the coat hooks. Because of the gale-force winds that can arrive at any moment,

Tipsy's clients know to bring the lightweight chairs inside with them when they pay the bill.

"You had a good time. I can tell," says Ingun.

Ilse nods. Malu used to say that everything Ilse did in her life was written on her face. Maybe if Ingun looked hard enough, he would see Frey's face, and Po's, and the manor house with pale blue shutters surrounded by vineyards. He might smell the dry scent of thyme.

"And you got your work done?"

Ingun is the most intense. When he puts his gaze on you, it's hard to look away.

"It was a tight deadline," she says. She sighs deeply and closes her eyes. "But yes, I got it done on time."

"Here comes Duggan," says Val, and then, pointing to the sky, "Is that a rain cloud over Paakitsup Inlet?"

"Lightning. Did you see the flash?"

"I did," yells Donny. He grabs Ilse's hand.

"It was sunny just a few minutes ago," says Ilse.

"The way you talk," says Ingun, "it's as if you've been gone like I was, for three years."

"Ingun, give her a break. She's got jet lag."

"Well, look who's here!" It's Duggan yelling from a few feet away.

If Duggan were an instrument, he'd be a tuba.

"Hello, Duggan," Ilse says, rising from her chair.

"Back from the Riviera and into the rainy season," Duggan shouts, thumping Ilse on her back, almost knocking her off balance. He's wearing a Rodebay Fish Company baseball cap. He's cut his hair. It's no longer in his hippie ponytail but falls from the cap in gray strands an inch above his shoulders.

Duggan looks older. The lines on either side of his mouth are deep, and a small pouch of flesh hangs a little below each cheek. Had she been gone only five weeks? Or perhaps she hadn't looked at people closely enough before she left. Ingun brings Duggan a chair from inside.

"Good trip?" Duggan asks.

She nods.

"Bring us back any little snow globes with French people raising their snobby French noses?"

"I do have a souvenir for you and Mary. I'll bring it by tomorrow when I visit my parents." When Ilse bought scented soaps for Malu, Mary, and Val at the Belle Rivière *marché*, the kind woman behind the stall gave her four dish towels as a going-away present. If Ilse had stayed, she thinks, longingly, this woman would have been one of her pals.

"Your cat caused a lot of mayhem in here. Did Val tell you that in the same morning, she ate my crowberry cake and spilled my coffee?"

"Minou is now the prisoner in the post office," says Val.

"Behind bars," says Ingun.

"Poor Minou! I'm going to rescue her tomorrow."

"She earned her keep by eating a bunch of mice in the beginning, but after she scared them all away, she started terrifying my customers. One thing she loved to do when I turned my back was to fly down this counter and topple the coffee cups. She also liked to lick my *kalaallit kaagiat* batter. We started calling her T-Rex."

We.

"Now the storm's over Sikuiuitsoq Fjord," says Duggan, shading his eyes with his cap from a bright splinter of the sun. "I give it ten minutes to get here."

"I bet you ten kroner it passes to the east of us," says Ingun.

Betting on the weather is an Oqaatsut pastime that would never exist in Provence. Take that back. She's sure the Provençals bet over the number of days the mistral whips up their paradise.

"I want a rainbow for Ilssse," says Donny, looking up at Ilse.

"Maybe, Donny, maybe," says Ingun.

"How much you want to bet that Donny gets his rainbow over the bay?" says Duggan.

"Another coffee," says Ingun.

"Can't you guys raise your stakes a little?" adds Val. "How about betting a whole cake?"

"A coffee is as much as I'll bet," says Duggan. "Rainbow or a rainfall, which one, Ingun?"

Ilse laughs.

"Bet's off!" says Ingun, looking at his phone. He stands. "We don't have time to watch a storm cloud. Come on, Donny, we've got to get up to Uummannaq in an hour. By that time, we'll have had both rain and a rainbow."

Why is everyone in such a rush? Weather forces behavior here.

"I'm guessing that it's hailing in Uummannaq," says Duggan.

"Since when does it hail in June?" says Ilse.

Duggan looks over at Val and Ingun.

"Ilse, how long did you say you were away?"

"I said the same thing," says Ingun. "Let's go, Donny."

"Bye, Ilssse. I'm so glad you're back."

Ingun's yelling something from the dirt path outside Tipsy's.

"Lover Boy Donny's insisting we bet on a rainbow!" they hear him shout. "We'll bet a *kalaallit kaagiat*—on a rainbow! See you this afternoon, Val!"

Ingun is making a double trip to Tipsy's?

It's almost summertime, and all the routines are changing.

"*Kalaallit kaagiat* coming right up," cries Val. She dashes inside to the kitchen.

"Thanks for looking after my parents, Duggan," Ilse says.

"Speaking of bets, we were placing bets that you wouldn't come back, Ilse, that you'd fallen in love with someone over there. It was an easy bet since you kept delaying your return."

"Who won that bet?"

"Come to think of it, Beluga did. He predicted you'd be back this week, in fact."

She shakes her head.

"And you thought I'd be gone for good?"

"Not for good, but for the summer at least. I'm glad I lost *that* bet."

"How much?"

"A single malt at Naleraq Bar."

"High stakes."

"So now that Donny's gone, you can tell us. Who was the lucky guy?"

"I fell in love, yes," she starts. Anything she says now will be all over town. "With a village, with a way of life."

"Poor Oqaatsut," says Val, returning outside. "In competition with a village in Provence, France!"

"We've got more characters here"—Duggan stands, places five kroner on the table, and tips his cap—"than in any French village."

Before she knows it, he's striding across the rock-strewn stretch ahead of them toward the Rodebay Fish Company. He disappears around the bend.

She and Val are alone again.

"Iluuna Lusa will be here any minute, then the Oqaatsut coffee klatch," says Val, running to the back.

Ilse brings the empty cups to the kitchen.

"Val . . ."

"Almost out of coffee grinds. Just enough till closing hour."

"Let me run out and get more for you."

"Don't bother. I'll ask Ingun to pick some up on the way back this evening. Another subject, Ilse, what are you gonna do when Donny asks you to marry him?"

"What?"

"He's asked Ingun to help him buy a ring."

"No way! Surely his brothers have set him straight."

"They've tried. You know how stubborn Donny can be. Maybe next time you see him, you can reinforce the friendship thing."

"I guess I shouldn't have signed off the postcards with 'Love, Ilse.' "

"Maybe."

Val's phone dings.

Val scrolls through the text. How can her fingernails be so perfect, a heart painted on each one? Po would enjoy writing about her. Her exotic, strong features remind Ilse of Inès—in the photograph, not the portrait.

"Val, before Iluuna comes in, this trip you're taking . . ."

"Yes?" She looks up from her phone.

"Beluga and you . . ."

"What? Oh, Ilse, you *have* been away too long."

"Why? I thought . . ."

"Yes, I guess it's true, before you left, Beluga and I started out like revved engines, the two of us like hungry wolves. We were sex-crazed . . ."

Ilse winces inside.

"Too bad it lasted ten days. I appreciated how original he is, he's a fast thinker, he challenged me all the time, made me consider things upside down and sideways, shook my mind up like a martini. And he was sweet to Caroo. Sometimes, I thought he was more sweet on her than on me. It became clear pretty fast that we're too different. In the way my people talk, he's a land spirit, and I, I'm the sea, fluid and moving."

Val spreads her arms and floats them up and down as if she's a ray skirting the ocean floor.

"And then, Ilse, I've got to say, after a while, we both decided the only thing we had in common was you. And I grew tired of him saying 'Ilse does this,' and 'Ilse says this,' and 'Ilse this,' and 'Ilse that.' I began to feel like the third party when it was just the two of us. He tried; I'll give him that. But the poor man, sort of like Donny, he just can't get over you. At about the same time as this was going on, something else began to brew."

"Brew?" Po's word game.

"I suppose, more like percolate."

Val uses the stool to step on the kitchen counter to pull a jar of sugar from the top shelf.

"Percolate like this." Val shakes her hips.

Ilse laughs.

"Val, you should have been an actor," Ilse says, laughing. "You build suspense in everything you do."

"Ilse, of all people, couldn't *you* tell? You, with those keen eyes and ears of yours."

"You're killing me . . . Ingun? But I thought he was with . . ."

Val winks and does a shoulder shimmy.

" 'Was' is the operative word."

"Of course! He's never looked spryer. And you look radiant."

"My ancestors say that when two people fall in love, their hearts leap from one to the other. That's what happened with ours and keeps happening. Wait, look over there."

Ilse turns toward the craggy ledge of inland rock.

"No, over there," Val says, pointing.

A rainbow. It sprawls over the bay from one end of the spit of land to the other; it's an arch as big as Ilse's ever seen, and the colors are getting brighter.

"Donny's wish come true, and Ingun and he get a *kalaallit kaagiat*," says Val. "And here comes Iluuna."

But Ilse has her eye on the rainbow. It will be gone so quickly. And it is.

Chapter 34

ILSE WAKES TO A CRASH IN THE MIDDLE OF THE DAYLIT NIGHT. It's August 1, two months since she's been back, and as Malu has said to her more than once, it's the most unseasonably rainy summer in thirty years. Meteorologists are concerned that the deluge has accelerated the already world-threatening retreat of Greenland's glaciers, speeding the meltdown of compressed snow more than one hundred thousand years old.

Another crash. Then a thud.

She removes her eye mask. Dim daylight peeks through the blackout shades in her bedroom.

Minou jumps off the bed.

"Minou, come back!"

Mr. G wouldn't make so much noise. When she reaches over to snap up the blackout shades to let the midsummer light in, her bedside lamp tips over and falls to the floor. She picks it up, but it falls again. That's strange. She checks her phone for the time. Four in the morning. A gust of wind through the poorly insulated walls makes Madame LaRoche's curtains billow.

After the two crashes, it's oddly quiet. Sitting up in her bed, Ilse grabs her knees, and listens.

The sound of water gushing. No way! Her bed is tilting to one side.

She's guessing that the wooden stilt on the right side of the house has finally rotted through, especially after all the rain. Her nightmare come true, what Fa has always warned her of: her cottage is being swept into the sea.

She jumps out of bed. Madame's full-length curtains are an inch deep in water. Water is gushing into the corner of the bedroom!

She grabs her phone and the attached charger from the outlet and calls 112. No one answers. How can no one answer the national emergency line? She presses the number again, is put on hold.

"What's your emergency?" It's an automated voice.

"My house is flooding! Help!"

She barks her response when the recorded voice asks for the address in a calm nasal-drip kind of way.

"Hurry!"

She calls the owner of the house, who lives in Copenhagen, and leaves a message for him in Danish as she looks out the window at the rain-pelted sea.

Bathrobe on.

Turn off the electricity, cut the main circuit breaker. Malu had once given her a printed-out checklist of what to do in a storm. Ilse remembers the circuit breaker part, but never bothered to find out where the circuit breaker was. Must be in the cellar. The cellar is full of the owner's stuff, corroded with five or more years of mold and mildew. Anyone would die breathing that air.

The bedroom floor is now two inches under seawater. A hissing sound. It sounds as if the surf is rushing below her. And the water is rising fast.

Minou has jumped on the bed. She meows.

Ilse catches her floating boots and pulls them on. They're only partly soaked, but they're freezing cold.

"Minou, let's get out of here!"

When Ilse reaches the front door with Minou in her arms and pulls it open, the cat jumps out into the muted predawn light.

Where'd she go?

"Minou!" Ilse steps out into the rain. The rays from the low-lying sun make the sea and sky appear dreamlike. It's light enough for her to see that one side of the house is tilted over. Just as she thought, one of the four stilts on which the house rests has collapsed. Panic rises inside her and fills her from stomach to head.

She dashes through the mud to the hatch door of the cellar. With her phone flashlight on, she peers down the steps. The sea has taken possession of the cellar: briny water is ceiling high and creeping up the concrete stairs. So much for turning off the electricity. From this angle, it looks like the other three stilts on which the house rests may slip underwater soon.

Back inside the house, she trips on her way upstairs. The stairs slant to one side. Into a large canvas duffle bag that she takes from her office closet, she throws her laptop, power cord, the manuscript she's working on, and Po's favorite *pétanque boule* that she uses as a paperweight. From the window, the sea looks strangely calm, as if taking her house down requires none of its energy.

"Come on, Mr. G, if you're around, let's blow this joint."

She hasn't heard Mr. G since she's been back from France. He must have been bored without her here. Or else he knew the place was doomed. Ghosts know these things.

Down the stairs, in her bedroom again, the water is now up to her lower calves. She stuffs her wallet and passport, the silver chain necklace her father had given her at her graduation from university, plus jeans, shirts, a sweatshirt, and her bright-blue Provençal sundress into the duffle bag. She's wearing Agnès's bracelet. In her bathroom, she throws personals into a toiletry bag.

She hears a pop. She could be electrocuted! She pulls her rain jacket from the hook on the front door and throws it on as she runs out of the house. She stands near the gate. Another pop of electricity.

This is when she calls Beluga. When she sees the sparks.

He picks up. Thank goodness.

"Beluga, my house is falling into the sea! Yes, I'm outside. Yes, I've called 112. There are actual waves splashing on the front steps.

"Oh, Beluga. One of the stilts is gone, you always told me to bolster it, but . . . I didn't listen."

Why hadn't she prepared for a night like tonight when she knew this would happen, had even been half expecting it?

Minou jumps up into her arms and knocks her phone with Beluga on the other line into the water at her feet. *Damn!* Where is it? She dips down with Minou in one arm and whips her hand around in a freezing, muddy puddle. Got it. She wipes it off. The light flickers. It's raining hard again now. Everything is gray and opaque.

She rubs the phone dry on the inside of her now wet bathrobe.

Minou scrambles out of her arms and is gone.

Beluga's booming voice on the phone. "Whatever you do, whatever you just realized you forgot, Ilse, listen to me, do not go inside the house. No matter what. The electricity could kill you. I'll be over as soon as I can get there."

"My phone is going dead," she says, her voice cracking. She shakes the phone. Throws it into her duffle bag, pulls up the hood of her jacket.

She had always thought that her life would have moved on before the sea pushed her out. Maybe this is the reason she felt safe and comforted in France—in the tides of vineyards instead of the undertow of the sea. The smell around her is thick with sea salt and seaweed. She unsticks loose grass from the back of her leg.

The duffle bag that she received as a door prize at a translator convention in Nuuk is durable, but it's not waterproof. If this downpour continues, and if the rainwater gets in through the zipper, in a half an hour her laptop will be soaked and stop working. Why didn't she grab an umbrella?

She blinks the rain from her eyes. She can barely see, but what she beholds is surreal: her home is sinking into the sea, one leg of it at a time. Already, the water is midway up to the bedroom window on the first floor. She wishes she'd taken down the curtains, Madame LaRoche's curtains, among her favorite things in the world. And her red silk scarf! Now she thinks of all the other things she should have taken. Her heart sinks when she remembers Beluga's father's compass. She'd taken it all the way to France and back. How could she have forgotten to grab it from where she'd propped it up on her bedside table? Her bedside table had been the first thing to fall. How stupid and sleepy she'd been when she threw her belongings into the bag. She should have thrown the things she wanted to keep out the window. Instead of standing here, witnessing her life sinking into the sea, she'd be running around the perimeters of the house collecting her belongings. She'll rent a metal detector to find Beluga's father's compass, that's what she'll do. It would be near the remnants of her desk. But by then, the wooden desk will have floated out to sea.

Where to find shelter from the interminable, dousing rain?

"Minou!" she calls out. "Minou!"

If only she'd taken the photo book her mother had given her of her and Jann's childhood years, and her school ring that she'd waitressed for a summer to pay for.

Oh, who cares about anything? She has her cellphone, her laptop, Po's *boule,* and Minou. All the rest will become part of the kelp-rich seabed.

"Is this you, Madame LaRoche?" Ilse says to the house. "Is this you telling me from the sea that I must change my life?"

It happened so quickly. With a slight *whoosh* noise, and a bunch of electrical sparks, like a child's pitiful fireworks display, now only two stilts hold up the captain's cottage. It is almost beautiful, the house on its side in the swirling sea, the tinkling sound of the glass breaking.

The emergency coast guard should be here by now. She could have still been sleeping inside, and her bed, with her in it, could have been swept out to sea!

The barely visible moon is playing peek-a-boo in the daylight, and the seawater—*no way!*—is pouring into the second-floor windows. Gushing in. Soon the floors will collapse. Where is Beluga? The rescue teams? She is here, alone, at the end of the earth, at the end of time. Where is Minou?

"Minou!" she calls out.

She backs farther away from the house. The sea might drag her in. She might trip and be electrocuted by a stray electrical cord. What if something happens to Minou?

"Minou!"

The sea-facing bedroom wall collapses. There goes the kitchen!

She can see the refrigerator. Everything will be used for something in the sea world. The broken glass from the windows will turn up years later, soft and pearly.

Finally, a siren. What good will a siren do for a drowned house pulled out to sea?

Will the whales have use for anything? They're too noble, too grand to succumb to the trifling details of humans. She wonders which sea creatures will make homes of her books. How long does it take for a water-saturated book to disintegrate into sea-smothered nothingness, for the glue to melt, for the pages to fall out, for the ink to smear? How long is the life of a drowned book?

The floorboards and the walls could be a good shelter for little creatures. The octopus might like to slink along a metal bed frame. Some diver, centuries from now, will find her copper teapot and comment about such a funny contraption. What in the world did that ridiculous species use this for?

Soon nothing will be left, not a vestige, not a trace of her life. Except for her.

Her boots sink into the wet, peaty mix of weather-stunted bushes and mud. Not even a utility task vehicle will get through this stuff. She should call off the coast guard. There's nothing to do now, nothing to see but the sea.

"Jann!" she says, looking up at the looming black clouds. "Where is the rainbow?

"Jann," she says, "where am I going?"

A shout in the distance.

"Beluga?" she calls out.

Nothing.

It was the wind. The sea and the wind and the rain. She can't see anymore for the rain, and now the tears in her eyes.

She sits on a rock near her gate.

"Minou!"

Malu will say *I told you so.* The town will say *I told you so.* The only one who won't say it is Beluga because he's too kind to say it.

She won't stay with Malu and Fa. No. Maybe she can ask Émile for a short visit to Paris, this time to meet Zoë Gaudet. Émile said the prolific author has a book coming out in the next few months. And Gaudet, bless her, has told Émile that she wants Ilse to translate her again. Maybe if the translation of Po's book does well, she can convince Émile to pay for another trip. Anything to get out of here.

"I'm going to Paris," she announces to the rain.

Luckily, she was late with her rent payment this month. She'll use the money for a cheap top-floor studio apartment in Paris if Émile doesn't ante up.

The black clouds in the brooding sky grow thicker, but the water around the house is glowing. What's that blue light in the reeds over there? It flickers on and off, on and off.

Through the opaque mist, she spots a yellow slicker in the distance.

Finally.

She stands.

It's Beluga.

Who else is so tall? Squinting, she can see his same old felt hat that provides no cover from the rain.

The relief she feels is physical from her head to toes. Griffin, Beluga's sheepdog-Rottweiler mutt, is tail-wagging, a wet-mop-come-alive beside Beluga.

"Oh, Beluga," she says, wiping the rain from her face as he approaches, "you're the only one! Thank you!"

"Are you all right?" he says, bending down to look into her eyes. "You must have had a fright." She would have expected him to give her a hug as any friend would have done in such a situation, but he keeps his distance.

"I can't find Minou." She holds back her tears.

"Guaranteed she's watching from a place that's drier and safer than where we're standing. When I bring Griffin back to my quad, we'll go on a search."

"I heard the siren a few minutes ago."

"Don't expect Gwen to be able to get through this mud, even with her four-wheeler. I had to abandon my UTV back at Rasmussen Ledge. Gwen and her team are probably stuck in the mudflats between here and the dock. In the last few weeks, any vehicle that's tried to ford that lowland pass has been mired for hours. I can't get through to Gwen. I'll try again now."

Gwendolyn Solodak, chief of the joint Arctic Command, is responsible for patrolling the coastline from Ilulissat to Upernavik.

Beluga shakes his head. "No phone service."

There's nothing Gwen and her team could have done anyway.

"I called the utility to shut off your power," he says, after clicking off with Gwen. "What do you want me to salvage? There's no danger now that the electricity is off."

Griffin licks her hands.

"There's nothing to save."

With Beluga's weight, whatever is left of the foundation could collapse under him.

She won't tell Beluga that his father's compass is now in the tight grasp of one of the six species of octopus that inhabit these seas. She'd be glad to share her treasure with an octopus. What other creature has three hearts?

"I rushed out here to help you salvage the stuff you love. Make me feel useful."

"Thank you, Beluga. I have what I need." She points to her soaked duffle bag. "I know I should have seen this coming."

Standing side by side, they watch in silence for a few minutes.

There's a bird call, Po would know it. So would Jann. She guesses a Lapland bunting by the high-pitched *trrrrr.* There's the answer, maybe from its mate. It's the dawn of morning in a night sheathed in light. It's when, as a child, she believed the sprites came out to play, chasing one another through the hoary seagrass.

Both speak the same thing at the same time.

"I haven't—"

"You first," she says.

"I haven't had a chance yet to say 'welcome back.'"

She'd learned from Malu that Beluga had recently returned from Skagen, Denmark, where he'd been for the last three weeks. He'd been hired to manage a distribution of gantry cranes from containers to the port, which they were enlarging to accommodate cruise ships.

"Thanks for not saying 'Welcome home.' "

"You needed a flooded house to remember me." He smiles slightly and winks.

Not true, she's about to respond, but their conversation is interrupted by cracking and ripping sounds.

It resembles the sound of an iceberg calving off a glacier in the icefjord.

"Stand back!"

There go the rest of the walls. The house is now at a full tilt and falling over, slow motion, into the water. Who was the dreamer who built such a ridiculously frail wooden house so close to the swirling seaside coast? Wood panels drift away. The sea is a snake swallowing the mouse of a house. The wood foundation is too large to swallow in one gulp.

Snapping, popping sounds.

"I thought they turned off the power?"

"Residual electricity in the wires."

There it goes, there goes the house that the sea captain built, that she lived and worked in, that she ate and drank and slept in, that she isolated herself in, was chilled to the bone in, that Minou snuggled beside her in, that Mr. G galloped up and down the stairs in, where she hoarded the memory of Jann.

The lopsided house slides a few more feet, then entirely into the now foamy froth. As if to wave a final goodbye, Madame LaRoche's pink taffeta curtain flaps in the wind from a broken window. The house is down, collapsed, and flattened into the sea.

Smoke rises in the aftermath.

"The whole house. Beluga!"

"The whole house. 'Earth to earth, ashes to ashes, dust to dust,' " Beluga says.

Stroking Griffin, who is the height of her hand, makes her feel better.

"If you hadn't shown up, I don't know what I would have done."

"You would have been as you are now, calm and resolute."

"Resolute about what?"

He doesn't answer. He's gazing at the empty space where the house stood.

"Tell me again why you chose to live here?"

If she can't cry, she'll laugh. Instead, she sighs deeply. "Cheap rent, and . . . I guess after Jann's death, I wanted to be on my own."

"An island living on an island."

One day, she'll tell Beluga the nickname that Po had given her. "*You* should talk. Your island is your plane, a moving island."

Another spark out of the water.

Voices in the distance.

"Thank you, Troy," she says, taking his hand.

It's a spontaneous impulse.

But now it feels awkward. She pulls her hand away.

"What did you call me?"

"Troy. It's your name, isn't it?"

Griffin barks and bolts in the direction of the flatlands, sending mud flying.

Ilse hears a woman's voice, then a man's, then another's.

"It's Gwen," Beluga says.

"Get back!" Gwendolyn's voice on a megaphone. Flashlights brighten the dark part of the house that lies on its side in the sea.

"Now she tells me!" says Ilse, under her breath.

"Hello, Ilse," Gwen says. "Tough night, eh?" She steps up on a rock that makes her the same height as Beluga.

"While you've been stuck in mud," Beluga is telling Gwen, "we've been watching the sea rob Ilse of all her stuff, and now she's fled the scene of the crime."

"The sea is a woman, is she, Beluga?" Gwen eyes him sideways, like he's gone a little deranged. Greenlanders don't easily stomach metaphors.

For a second, Gwen reminds Ilse of skeptical Carole.

"How did you get here before me?" Gwen asks. "It took five of us to push our UTVs out of the lowland mudflats. The pass is at least a foot deep in sludge."

"I came by way of Rasmussen Ledge. I tried but couldn't get through to you." He kicks the heel of his boot against a rock to clear it of mud. "What's the matter with your GPS?"

"What's the matter with *you*? If you'd joined our volunteer squad, I'd have had you as my guide."

Another voice, then another. A small group of Gwen's crew approaches from the direction of the harbor.

"Calm down, Griffin. It's okay."

"My contact at Nukissiorfiit Energy says you called to turn the power off. Yes," she tells a man on her team, "the house is gone."

Into the sea. A part of the black tarp that patched the roof flutters. The waves tug at it, consuming it.

"We'll try to drag out as much as we can." Gwen's on her phone. "Yes, four more UTVs as soon as you can, via Rasmussen Ledge. Whatever you do, avoid the lowland pass between the harbor and here. GPS sucks out here in the flood zone."

Chapter 35

In the distant ripples of water, Ilse catches sight of the oval mirror that hung on the wall in her upstairs office, washed clean of the pale, dolorous face that's been reflected in it for the last five years. She peers into the thick brown muck for Beluga's father's shiny, round compass, berating herself again for leaving it behind.

Papers float in the up pressure of air, a flurry of them. They're like white doves taking wing. Now they tumble-swing down—pages of the Gaudet manuscript with sentences and expressions that troubled her, or those she'd printed out because she loved them enough to save them.

Words erased, ink smeared, the paper will soon be white seaweed. Thankfully, the recordings of Po's voice, reciting his poetry, are on her phone. For safekeeping, she'd also sent them to Émile.

Gwen's voice rises above the cries of the gulls. She's directing the rescue team to pitch ropes over the edges of the wood foundation. The crows and the gulls circle overhead scanning the sea's debris. The refrigerator on its side and the cast-iron stove stand like bastions against the swelling tide.

"How are you holding up?" Beluga asks.

"Remember when I texted and asked if you knew where you were going?" she says.

He nods.

"Well, now I *really* don't know."

"You're going to my house to dry off, that's where you're going. You're shivering, and you've seen enough."

"There's nothing to save," she says. "Tell Gwen not to bother."

"You can't leave a house underwater like they did sunken ships a century ago."

"Pollutants?"

"Particulate matter, radon, lead, toxic adhesives in furniture and appliances."

"We should be living in *igluits* or *tupiqs,* like Val's ancestors."

She regrets having said Val's name.

"I've got to help Gwen, or I'd take you to my house. Duggan will give you a lift in my quad." He lifts the phone to his ear.

"But Duggan's in Ilulissat—"

"He spent last night at my house. He does that occasionally when he and I have a late drink at Tipsy's."

Late drinks at Tipsy's?

"Please don't bother Duggan," Ilse says, her teeth chattering from the cold. "I can easily walk there."

"Duggan never sleeps. You're freezing, and it's too far to walk to my house. I'll tell him to meet you at Rasmussen Ledge, where I left the UTV." Before Ilse can protest again, he's giving Duggan directions and telling him the keys are in the ignition.

"Beluga, get over here!" Gwen is calling.

Waving goodbye to Ilse, Beluga departs with his characteristic dip, it's almost a curtsy, and splashes over to Gwen. Griffin follows closely behind.

What a mess.

Frey's wedding is two and a half weeks away. The thought comes to her out of nowhere.

"Minou!" Ilse calls, jumping over a fast-flowing stream. "There you are!"

Ilse lifts the fur-soaked cat. Through her wet bathrobe she can feel

Minou's heart beating fast. With the cat in her arms, and her tears mixing with the next downpour, she turns from her sunken captain's house and starts jumping from one sodden pillowy moss patch to another to Rasmussen Ledge. Ten minutes later, shivering with cold, Ilse sees the headlights of the UTV.

"Hop in, and your wet rat, too," Duggan yells.

She slides into the vehicle. Duggan's yellow slicker, or maybe it's his knee-high black rubber boots, smells like fish.

"I heard the siren," shouts Duggan, starting the engine. "You knew it was going to happen, Ilse. Time was up."

"I suppose so. Wait, before we go, please, one last look."

From the high point on Rasmussen Ledge, she stands to see Beluga's silhouette in the distance. With ropes attached to the UTVs, the coast guard team is hauling submerged parts of the house from the sea.

She hears Gwen's powerful voice, and the yells of others: "Down here!" "No, get that side!" "Pull harder!"

Finally, she sits hugging her knees to keep them from shivering. "Thanks, Duggan. I'm ready to go."

Duggan guns the engine and Minou falls out of her arms, then settles on Duggan's lap.

He pushes Minou off. "Your wet rat is too wet for me."

"She's a cat!"

Whenever Ilse is with Duggan, she feels the need to defend herself.

"Looks like a rat to me. Domestication of animals—the first tyranny on earth."

"This cat works for her food! I consider her my roommate."

He squints into the rain-splashed windshield as though he hasn't heard her.

Torrents are lashing them sideways. It's as if someone above is pulling curtains made of rain across the sky. She gathers the wet Minou in her arms again.

"Here, take this," Duggan bellows, reaching into the cargo box at the back of the UTV and tossing a thick red wool blanket onto her lap. "I grabbed this before I left Beluga's house."

"Thank you," Ilse says, burying herself and Minou in the coarse blanket. They would never use anything so scratchy as this in Provence. It smells like cigarettes, which is slightly better than the fishy smell of Duggan's waterproof gear.

Duggan is leaning forward to peer out the windshield.

"Should we stop and wait for this downpour to pass?" she asks.

"No time for that. If I don't pick up my truck at the harbor in Ilulissat where I left it last night, with all this rain, it will be *in* the harbor."

"Thanks for coming to get me, Duggan."

He slaps the wheel.

"What anyone would do!" he yells above the engine noise and the rain. He's squinting again. "Don't want to be around when your ma finds out."

"She'll heap blame on me for years to come. Not for risking my life, but for scaring her to death. She'll be at work in two hours, and since the post office is gossip central, she'll be one of the first to hear about this."

Duggan coughs up a brittle laugh. "Mary goes to the PO now instead of paying for a subscription to *The Ilulissat Eagle*."

Ilse grabs on to the side of the UTV and holds Minou tightly as they veer around a spit of land overlooking the sea. She spots an enormous iceberg with two huge arches in it. Even in the daylit dawn, half-blinded by the rain, the bright white majesty of icebergs never ceases to amaze her. The arches remind her of a poem that Po had written about le Pont du Gard, the ancient Roman aqueduct bridge. The iceberg is probably hundreds of thousands of years older than the first-century bridge.

"Hope you didn't lose too much," Duggan yells over the sound of the engine. "If you did, Dhruv Shugnut owes you." Dhruv Shugnut is the owner of Ilse's cottage.

"I think I signed a clause indemnifying him against loss due to flooding. At the time, I'd have done anything for cheap rent. I also got a sea view."

"Well, you sure got that, didn't you?" Duggan yells. "Shame on

Shugnut. Never put a penny into that place. Collected your rent all the same. Playing a waiting game with the sea, he was, and hoping for the house to collapse, so he could collect the insurance."

"I don't have much. I guess that's a good thing."

"Every lease has got a built-in warranty for habitability."

Warranty for habitability. Po would like the rhyme-sing of the words.

They swerve again, this time heading inland, and Ilse falls hard against the side of the quad. "Sorry about that!" he yells. "It's hard to see out here."

Finally, they arrive at the gravel-strewn path that leads to Beluga's house. Thank you, Eva Sorrell, Gravel Goddess of these parts. Leave it to Beluga, the only person in Oqaatsut to use gravel for the passage leading to his house.

"Thanks, Duggan," she shouts over the sound of the motor. She's got Minou secure under one arm, her duffle bag in the other. "Please leave me here. You've got to get back to the harbor."

"I'm taking you all the way in," he yells. What a long track to a house! Ilse had been many times to Beluga's previous high-pitched kit house closer to the harbor, but not to this new one farther inland that he'd built himself and finished last summer, working day and night.

"What I don't get is why you and he live out here in the wilds like this!"

Everything Duggan says is emphasized because of his failing hearing and subsequent booming voice. He's shaking his head.

"People could say the same about you: 'Why would Duggan Nielsen live all the way up here, above the Arctic Circle, if he could live anywhere in the world?' "

As she asks this, she feels a pang in her heart.

"What do you want me to do? Close up the fish shop my great-grandfather started when Ilulissat was only a trading post? Some people think it's nothing to erase a family's history."

He clears his throat.

Through the rain, she can see it now: Beluga's house. While her rental cottage was out in the wide-open sea and sky, his is lodged between boulders. One of Beluga's pastimes is scavenging other people's odds and ends. Last summer, he'd told Ilse that he'd found a metal roof intact on the side of a road down in Nanortalik. He'd split the roof into three parts and flown them up to Oqaatsut. She imagines Frey's raised eyebrows, seeing this house with its concrete base and metal roof. Po might appreciate its brutalist architectural features.

She opens the heavy oak door.

"Down you go, Minou."

It's nice and cozy-warm inside. Minou scrambles out of her arms.

"Duggan, come in to get warm."

"As I said, I've got to get my truck out of the lot at the harbor. Ilse, you have a good sleep here, and I'll see you tomorrow."

"It's *already* tomorrow!" She's begun to speak as loudly as Duggan.

Duggan is climbing back into the UTV.

"Thank you, Duggan!" Ilse yells out. "And thank you for bringing the blanket!"

THE FIRST THING ILSE notices inside Beluga's home is the fresh smell of the birchwood walls. Beluga must have flown the wood in from Denmark.

At the entrance, she hooks her dripping wet jacket over the musk ox antler on the back of the door. Removes her boots and wet socks. Her feet are freezing! She runs, her eyes adjusting to the darker interior, to the bathroom. She'd needed to pee for what feels like hours. Nice, clean bathroom, everything in its place. An electric toothbrush? She locks the bathroom door, drops her soaked, mud-hemmed bathrobe and nightie on the floor, turns on the shower, and yes, hot water, thank you very much, feels her body melt in the warming shower.

"Beluga won't mind if I use his bathrobe," she says aloud, stepping out. It's plaid flannel and hits the floor in layers when she stretches her arms into it.

She passes through the kitchen, where Minou is lapping up water left in a bowl for Griffin. Ilse is relieved to see that there are two bedrooms, one beside the other, one with a king-size bed (he would need a king size), and the other with twins. In both rooms, the beds are covered with white down comforters. Everything appears spotless and fresh-looking.

A refrigerator reveals much about its owner. Beluga's is empty except for two six packs of Grønland Ice Cap beer, a box of Istanbolly feta cheese, a roll of salami, a loaf of rye bread, a container of shrimp, one of reindeer soup, and a yogurt. She takes out a beer and the cheese. It's a little early in the day for beer, but she's had a tough night. She opens the cabinet to find a box of crispbread rye crackers. She brings the cheese, crackers, and beer to the pinewood coffee table in the living room, sits down to her picnic, and looks around. A fireplace made from what look like boulders splits the living room in two. A sofa and two chairs, also made of birchwood, occupy one side, and a dining room table and four chairs the other. A rusted scythe, probably one of Beluga's great-grandfather's farm tools, decorates the wall above the mantel on the living room side. A copper bucket is filled to brimming with chopped birch branches.

Cool. A tall tin sculpture occupies the corner near the window. Despite the metallic material, it has curves, and now she realizes the tin pieces form the shape of a man. A Norseman at ease, if there ever were such a thing. One of the parts reaches up to the ceiling and disappears as if it's entering the roof. Perhaps an artist friend gave it to him. Or maybe Beluga is the artist?

She gravitates to the books on the coffee table. *The History of Saqqaq People's Customs and Rituals.* A leftover from his days with Val. She pictures Val here, on this brown, woolly sofa, her long legs dangling over the side. She wonders which girlfriend sewed the red-and-white gingham curtains in the kitchen that make the place look so cozy. That wouldn't have been Val.

Beside this book, no way! A French dictionary? Under the dictionary is a book titled *French Literary Greats,* and under that, *Medieval French Poetry.* Passages have been underlined, and small notations in a kind of stick shorthand fill the margins. She places the books down when she hears a scurrying in the bedroom. The telltale sound of a mouse. She gets up.

"Minou, your dinner awaits."

Instead of chasing the mouse, Minou jumps onto Beluga's king-size bed.

"No, no, Minou, not with your muddy paws! Have some manners! Now look what you've done." Paw marks dapple the white comforter. Ilse ups the cat and returns her to the floor. The cat pounces back onto the king-size bed.

"You were definitely a queen in another life," Ilse says.

She lets Minou stay. The comforter is already mud-splattered, and Beluga won't mind.

Ilse's legs feel suddenly heavy. She'll wash the comforter later.

Back in the living room, she takes a few sips of beer, then lies down on the sofa.

It's a deep sleep; she's in a seabed made of floating pages, but the words are decomposing, and the letters are jumbling, and she's telling herself all the words have been lost, and she no longer has a job.

Chapter 36

THE SUN IN HER EYES, ILSE SITS UP ON THE SOFA. SHE NOTICES the empty bottle of beer and the untouched cheese and crackers. The sour taste after sleep. That's right. She's in Beluga's bathrobe. She doesn't remember covering herself with this plaid wool blanket.

What time is it? She reaches into the bathrobe pocket for her phone. Where's her phone?

The crickets are making a racket! At the sea captain's house, her morning orchestra was composed mostly of gull cries, geese jabbering, eagles piping, and hawks' high-pitched *keeeeeeee-ar*s. It would be almost impossible to hear a cricket over such a clamor.

Po had told her, almost in tears, during one of their last times together, that the one thing he loved most about where he lived was the arrival of the *cha-cha-cha* rattle of the cicadas, heralding the thick deliciousness of summer. He'd told her that the cicada rhythm informed much of his poetry. She wonders if Po is listening to the cicadas now.

The branches on a small glen of stunted birch trees outside wave at her through the window. Her home on the seaside is all horizontals. It's unusual to glimpse a small grouping of birches, even though they're short and spindly. This huddle of silver-gray greenery is shielded from the wind by the boulders and rocks beside it. In Provence, harmony is achieved by a delicate and achievable balance of horizontal and vertical. Will she be forever comparing her life to what she experienced in France?

Where is Minou?

"Minou!" she calls out in a panic.

"There you are," she says when the cat pops her head up from the blanket at the end of the sofa.

After stroking Minou for some time, remembering the calamity of the night before, Ilse rises and walks into the kitchen, where she finds her phone in a bowl of salt. Nice way to salvage a drenched mobile! Thank you, Beluga. The phone is plugged into an outlet. Two o'clock in the afternoon? She shakes the phone. It's not like her to sleep through the morning. Ten messages await her: seven from Malu, one from Val, and one from Frey. *It's working!* She checks to see if the video she took of Po reciting his poetry still plays. She closes her eyes, and tears creep down her cheeks as she listens to the grainy, yet soft, low-gentle Provençal tones.

She rubs her eyes, then opens the text from Frey. *When are you coming to visit? It's hot in Paris.*

Not bad timing.

Then another text, again inviting her to come see him. Two weeks before his wedding? That's untenable, ridiculous—even if she has nowhere to live because her house fell into the sea!

The whirring sound, she discovers, is the dryer in the kitchen closet.

She peeks into the open door of Beluga's room. The bed has no comforter.

A knock at the front door.

Minou hisses, then scampers into the kitchen when Ilse opens the door.

Beluga, in his wet, yellow slicker, in the doorway.

"You knock to enter your own home?"

"Didn't want to barge in on you."

She thinks of Frey and his insistent raps on her door, the way he entered the room as if he had a right to do so.

"So it wasn't a nightmare after all?" she says.

He shakes his head.

He stands on the threshold, as if he's afraid to move.

"How're you doing?" he asks.

"Groggy, but grateful." She raises her cellphone. "Thank you." She hesitates. She's about to call him Beluga but catches herself in time. "Thank you, Troy, for salvaging me, my home, and my phone."

"I didn't exactly salvage your house."

She nods, then gazes down at the bathrobe that she's wearing.

"I made myself at home."

"Looks like you did just fine," he says, finally removing his slicker.

Griffin shimmies, shakes, then sits at Beluga's feet as he removes his boots.

Minou hisses from the kitchen.

"I must have seen a hundred rainbows this morning."

"Where?"

Ilse is always sorry to miss a rainbow.

"Over your drowned house. I can finally understand why you liked it there. When the rain paused for a few minutes, the clouds held the colors, and then the rainbows kept coming. More rain is expected tonight."

"Troy! I could have drowned last night."

"You're a good swimmer. I remember that from school."

"I wouldn't have drowned, would I have? I mean, the house wouldn't have suctioned me down during a deep sleep?"

"Too shallow. And, Ilse, you're a fighter. You tend to go against the current and do just fine."

Fine? She's homeless. Thankfully, she has a paying job, which is more than many in her village can say. Yesterday, Émile had told her about a new collection of poetry, this one by a Parisian who had specifically requested for her to be his translator. The pay is good, and the timing jibes with her schedule; she's almost finished with the crime thriller for the English publisher. And then there's the forthcoming Gaudet. Still, she thinks she'll decline the poet. It feels like a betrayal to translate another poet so soon after Po's death. And she'd never be able to evoke the depth of feeling that she felt she'd brought to *The Provençal Poet*.

"Stay here as long as you wish, Ilse, until you figure out your next home. I've cleared off the desk for you. I'm working in Maniitsoq today, got to leave in an hour. I'll be back tomorrow morning. You know that Val's uncle is in the real estate business. He'll find you something when you're ready. An apartment in Ilulissat might suit you right now. Though knowing you, you may wish to rent a houseboat."

"Very funny. How can I thank—"

"By continuing to call me Troy. I'm beginning to like my given name. I haven't heard it in so long. If you don't mind, I'm going to take a hot shower. I'll keep Griffin with me."

"But your robe."

"Not necessary," he says, as he leaves the room, Griffin tagging behind. Griffin's devotion reminds her of Mastiff's to Po.

He's back in the living room.

"I hope you don't mind if I put your clothes in the dryer."

She has a faint memory of dropping her nightgown and bathrobe in a wet pile on the bathroom floor.

"You've thought of everything," she says. "Thank you."

He takes a slight bow as he departs the room. Ilse calls Minou out of hiding. The black cat curves around Ilse's legs, then lies down in the slice of sunlight near the window.

How she misses Po.

To distract herself from bursting into tears, she studies the painting hanging on the wall near the kitchen. It's a watercolor of an island scratched in ink in a sea of blue. Islands are never landlocked; they grow whatever they like, why not poppies, or lavender, for that matter; they attract all kinds of fauna, why not full-throated nightingales, and wild boars; and because they're on their own, they can do whatever they like.

So go ahead and cry, for heaven's sake.

And she does.

THE NEXT MORNING, ON opening the front door for Minou, Ilse finds a basket, and in it, a thermos of coffee with a splash of milk, just the way she likes it. No way! Two miniature bottles of schnapps and two similar-size bottles of Grand Marnier—thank you, Val—two large slices of *kalaallit kaagiat,* and a note written in Val's poor handwriting in Greenlandic: *You are brave, Ilse. I'll fetch you at 10 o'clock. Malu will be at your house, or what* was *your house. Love, Val.*

It's already nine-thirty. Here in this cozy, warm, secure house, all Ilse wants to do is sleep. The last thing she needs is a "told you so" scolding from Malu. She pours a dash of the schnapps and a few drops of the Grand Marnier into the coffee and sips. It tastes horrible.

Out the window, the clouds are brooding, deciding whether they should dump another deluge onto the battered coast. She spots a large Arctic hare. Its snow-white fur stands out against the rain-blackened boulder and rocks beside the house.

Her phone rings. It's Frey. Now he actually wants to speak to her! He's probably still got the pre-wedding willies. She doesn't pick up: it wouldn't feel right to talk to Frey with Beluga in the house.

In a duffle bag underneath Val's basket, Ilse finds a pair of brown suede pants, how chic, a pair of rain pants, purple! Two long-sleeved T-shirts, a fisherman's cable-knit sweater, several pairs of lacy black underwear—so Val—a sheer undershirt, a silk negligée, and two pairs of wool socks. All from Val's cool clothing and underclothing repertoire.

Ilse finishes the coffee and the delicious, sweet bread, then dons Val's clothes, squeezing into her friend's suede pants and the waterproof outer layers. On her way out, she slips one of the bottles of schnapps into her jacket pocket.

Ten o'clock sharp, and there's Val's bright red ATV, headlights shining through the gray. It's begun to drizzle. Ilse slides in. Val is wearing a dark green slicker and a bright green rain hat. Her thick black hair is pulled back in a braid. She is beautiful in the rain.

"Just so you know," Val says, as she swerves right and left around the potholes, "your mother was crazy with fear for you when she heard about the house. I know I don't have to tell you this, but by now she's substituted anger for her deeper feelings of caring and concern. I've told her to go gentle on you."

They skid, get stuck in the mud, almost do a donut.

"If we can get to Rasmussen Ledge, Val, we can leave the ATV there and walk the rest of the way. That's what Beluga—"

"Have no fear, Ilse Erlund, I know how to get there."

They splash through a large pool of water, then another one. When the ATV finally gets traction, Val accelerates and the mud spins out from the wheels and splatters Ilse in the face. They're taking the faster coastal route to Ilse's captain's house, not the inland route to Rasmussen Ledge. Somehow, Val gets them there; she even maneuvers her ATV close enough so Ilse can see a remnant of the front gate and the abandoned site of the lost-at-sea cottage. In the gray light, the place Ilse called home looks like the end of the world.

Ilse remembers the poem by Robert Frost asking whether the world would end in fire or ice. *Mr. Frost, you got it wrong. The world will end in water.*

It's high tide.

Ilse swipes the steamy windshield.

The land that is visible near the deranged-looking picket fence is a miry combination of brown, gray, and black, and where the house was, submerged in a foot or more of seawater, are the bald head of the refrigerator and the metal top of the black cast-iron woodstove, along with some floating wooden beams. The few bottom steps of the stairway have survived.

"Stairway to heaven," Ilse says.

"You're taking it pretty well," Val says.

"Thanks to your schnapps and Grand Marnier delivery this morning, and the cake. It was even warm! And your clothes. Thanks, Val."

After devouring Ilse's home, the winded sea still looks hungry.

"Why won't the rain stop?" Ilse says.

"Ingun told me that Beluga is leading a grassroots commission to monitor the melting ice cap. The measurements these days come mostly from satellite imagery, and according to Beluga, they don't tell the real story. I mean look at all this water! If the world wants to keep its land intact, it's got to pay attention to our ice fields! Ingun, by the way, is Beluga's greatest fan."

"Beluga never talks about himself or about what he's up to," Ilse says.

"Even when we were . . . intimate," says Val, "he didn't tell me about this commission."

Ilse is grateful that Val has chosen the word "intimate" rather than other words in Val's more colorful descriptive vocabulary.

In the distance, Ilse spots Malu, stabbing at the mud.

Val puts on the brakes and tells Ilse she'll join her after she drives the ATV onto a drier ridge about fifty feet away.

Ilse steps out and stumbles through the sludge toward her mother. Malu is holding a black plastic garbage bag in one hand and what looks like a fireplace poker in another.

"Malu!" Ilse calls.

"I got your pots and pans!" Malu shouts when she sees her daughter.

As Ilse approaches, her mother is crouching down, peering into the foot-deep water, moaning, "The waste, the waste!"

"How about a hug?" yells Ilse across a gully forming into a stream.

Malu jabs at the rain-dappled pits of silt-water.

"A hug!" Ilse repeats. Ilse pulls back the hood of her slicker, so her mother can see her face.

"Come over here!" Malu shouts, standing and lifting her face. Her cheeks are ruddy from the morning's exertion. As Ilse had expected, her expression is reproachful.

Ilse jumps over the gully. Malu and she have so much outerwear on, their embrace hardly feels like human contact. Malu smells of something sweet, sugary, like donuts, maybe from Val.

"This is the one day I'm glad Fa can't see," Malu mutters as she continues to nudge the glop.

"All he says is 'Thank God, Ilse is safe.' Praying to God. What's the use? A waste of breath, that's what. Scavengers! Buzz off!" With her poker, she takes off after the seagulls that are alighting on the refrigerator. Malu is a crow in her shiny black slicker.

"Malu!" Ilse wails.

"This chair is fine," Malu says, returning breathless and lifting a broken wooden chair for Ilse to see. "Only one lost leg."

One lost leg caused her house to fall.

"Not sure if you want to keep any of this stuff," says Val, approaching and opening a bag to reveal the contents. Ilse spots the owner's mud-caked blue-and-white dishes. Most of them are cracked or in pieces, probably from falling off the shelf when the house started to teeter.

"Give it to me," says Malu. "I've got glue for that."

Val hands over the bag, which Malu places alongside two other black plastic bags nearby. Malu has a splatter of mud on her chin, which makes it look like she's got a beard.

"Malu, don't lift these heavy bags," Val says. "Ingun and his brothers will be back here in a few hours from Sisimiut to help you."

Since Ilse has been in France, she notices that Val has become protective of Malu.

Val wipes her eyes, squinting into the distance. "That Beluga out there?"

Malu and Ilse pivot to see the silhouette of the man in the distance. Ilse had not seen him in the heavy mist and drizzle.

"He hasn't stopped since I got here at six o'clock this morning," Malu says. "Lifting things and waiting for me to give him a thumbs-up or down."

His figure looks lonely against the backdrop of the welted, gritty sea.

"I'm not throwing away this perfectly good lampshade," Malu is saying. The stained shade is punctured in three places.

"Most of this stuff came from the dump, and to the dump it will return," says Ilse.

Malu peers through the rain at her daughter.

"Too highfalutin for your old life here, are ya now?"

"Sorry, Ilse, I've got to get back to the shop," says Val. "Duggan's probably outside, swearing under his breath. This morning, he said he wanted you to stay at his house until you find another home. Iluuna said the same thing. Everyone sees this disaster as a chance to have you as their guest. It's sweet, Ilse, how much this place loves you."

"Thank you, Val, my pal."

She watches Val stride in her kind of sultry way toward her truck and hop in lightly.

"That's a girl I respect," says Malu.

"Her ATV nearly lost a wheel on the way here from Beluga's house."

"Yes, Val knows the way to and from his house," says Malu. "By heart."

Malu gives her daughter a meaningful sidelong glance.

To change the subject, a skill Ilse had almost forgotten after her weeks with Po, she tells her mother what Val had just told her during their bumpy ride, that Val's uncle had found her a short-term rental above Jessie Jonkuk's shop in Ilulissat. And that Ilse is trying to work out a trip to Paris to meet another author.

"I thought this disgrace would bring you to your senses," Malu sneers.

"The cottage was a rental, Malu. It's not my house."

"Exactly. Look what you have to show for yourself." She points to the torn lampshade.

"Malu, is this your way of making me feel better?"

"It's my way of making you smarter."

Malu skewers a floating towel.

Ilse imagines how Po would have responded to Ilse, whose tears are now mixing with the raindrops. Po would have sung her a poem-song about tasting rain teardrops.

"Malu," Ilse says, "I'm smart enough to tell you that I'm tired of your blame and criticism! Look at me! Malu, look at me!"

Ilse opens her arms and looks around her.

"Can't you see that I've had a nightmarish night? Can't you understand that what I need is compassion, and not your disapproval and your anger?"

Malu looks up from the black rag of a towel that she'd been shaking out.

"You've brought this on yourself, Ilse Erlund!"

"I guess you didn't hear me. Malu, stop blaming me for everything! Stop!"

"You should have been like your bro—"

"And stop comparing me to Jann! Jann is dead! Don't you know it by now? Jann is dead!"

The wind blows the hood of the slicker off Malu's head. Her narrowed eyes are slits in the windblown rain.

"How *dare* you!" Malu's lips cinch together.

"No, how dare *you*! How dare *you* blame me for being alive when Jann is dead. I won't be the dumping ground for all your frustrations and your anger in your life. I'm sick of it. It's over!"

"I am your mother, and you are superior to no one here!" Malu says, flinging the towel into a pile next to her. She about-faces and marches like a soldier in the direction of Beluga.

The bone-whittling wind has picked up. Ilse sees something red swirling around her boots. She bends down and reaches for Madame LaRoche's muddy red silk scarf. She holds it up to the gray flint of a day and then buries her face in it. "Oh, Madame!"

Chapter 37

It's August 11, and Frey is on the phone, telling Ilse that the bookstore window on the corner of boulevard Saint-Germain and the rue du Four is plastered with copies of the English translation of *The Provençal Poet*.

"You're the buzz!" he says.

"You mean your father is."

Émile was supposed to send her ten copies as soon as the book was out in the world. Invisibility has its drawbacks. Then again, it takes a while for the mail to get to Ilulissat.

"Who's talking about it?" Ilse asks.

"Of course, my friends, but also, people in the bookstore. I overheard one woman say that when she read the poems, she could feel the Provençal air caressing her face."

"How lovely! How does it look? More importantly, how does it read?" Frey's English is good enough to know.

"I've only read the first section, and you've done it, Ilse. You captured Papa's spirit. I would argue that the poem about *les bories* is better in English than in French. I wept while I was reading it, as if I was experiencing it all over again."

The person whose opinion matters most to her is not Émile, or Frey. It is Agnès. She will text Agnès that afternoon.

As she tells Frey about her toppled house, she recalls the Poe story "The Fall of the House of Usher." She'd translated it from English into Danish back in school. In the story, the house splits in two, then sinks into a lake. But that was a Gothic horror story!

Damn! How she would love to jump back to Provence, to that time and place when she felt more alive than ever before, so effervescent that her skin tingled because she was in it. Thanks to Po, she'd fallen in love with herself as much as with him and Frey. How free and smart and daring she'd felt. How sexy and beautiful.

"Now you have no excuse. Hop on a flight tonight."

"What are you saying, Frey? Your wedding—it's a week from today, right?"

His decisiveness in telling her what to do is his way of covering up his irresolution about his wedding. She doubts the AI he's building vacillates like he does.

EIGHT DAYS LATER, it's Sunday, midmorning, the day after Frey's wedding. On her trek back from Tipsy's to Beluga's house, she imagines Frey and Caroline exchanging vows, the confetti crowning their heads as it's thrown outside the church doors. It's too bad that her dream of being together with Frey in the paradise of Provence and Paris is over, but a part of her is relieved. From the beginning, her feelings for Frey have been confused. She wonders if she'd loved Frey's French life more than she'd loved him. Or whether she'd been trying to translate her love for Po into feelings for Frey. Or whether she'd been trying to translate to please Po by pretending to love Frey. Then again, maybe she loves Frey more than she cares to admit.

What does it matter anyway?

In the end, Frey is married now. Ilse was merely a convenient stopgap—that's the word she's been seeking. It is defined as a temporary way of dealing with a problem, which in Frey's case was his uncertainty about his marriage.

More rain clouds. Please, no more rain! There's so much moisture in the air that the sky looks iridescent, white with all the colors of the seasons, the pale greens of summer combined with the bluing ice of winter.

Her phone vibrates.

It won't be Malu.

She and Malu haven't talked since their fight at the site of the end of the world; Malu, gritting her teeth and gripping that blackened towel in her rubber gloves. Stubborn Malu would never unthink that her daughter was ungrateful, unworthy of her respect, a silly person, throwing her life away on something as irrelevant as literature.

It's Frey.

She hesitates. What the heck? The man got married yesterday.

"Frey?"

"*Bonjour, Ilse.*" There's urgency in his voice.

"Frey, congratulations. You're married!"

"No, Ilse, I'm in Paris. I got a flight out of Boston."

"What?"

"I flew here last night. It's crazy. Of course, I've been an idiot."

"Why? What happened?"

"Ilse, you and Papa are the only ones who could possibly understand. I became paralyzed! I was in the back hallway of this simple island church, the light from the window striking the floor in front of me, and the priest told me that it was time for me to stand at the altar and wait for my bride. I couldn't move. After some time, Agnès came to find me. She thought I was having a stroke. She tried to help me out of my stupor, tried to get me to move my legs. But they wouldn't budge. It was an out-of-body experience. All I could think about was Papa, and then you, and the time we had together. You know how much I've struggled with this decision. Well, it's hardly been a decision. It's been a responsibility."

"Frey," she says, stunned. It's all she can say.

"When I could finally move, I found Caroline alone in the robe room in the church, and there she was, looking so beautiful and so sad in her wedding dress, her face a pleading question mark. I told her I would be the best father, but that I would not be the best husband."

How heart-wrenching for this woman. Everything planned, everything perfect.

"I think the thing that caused my paralysis was just before the service, I overheard Agnès practice reading the poem that she planned to recite at the wedding, the poem my father dedicated to you, one of the last ones he wrote. I think it's more passionate than any of the love poetry that he wrote to my mother. It is fresh, and it flickers with heat. And the feelings expressed in that poem were something that suddenly, I wanted. It was what Papa was telling me over and over again. It was his poem that paralyzed me. Yes, it was horrible for Caroline. I know I should have figured this out earlier. If I had only listened to Papa, to my feelings about you.

"So, meet me here tomorrow? In Paris. I'll pay for your airfare, of course."

Her house falls into the sea and Prince Belle Rivière asks for a rendezvous in Paris. Yes! Frey's summoning her to Paris reeks of rebound decision making, but really, now that Ilse no longer has a home and has told off her mother, she can hop on a plane to Paris and live the life of a Parisian translator! There, she'll meet Zoë Gaudet, and the two of them will spend their afternoons at the Café de Flore discussing the written landscape of love and desire. She can hardly believe it! On the weekends, she and Frey will take the fast train down to Belle Rivière and have picnics with Agnès and drink pastis with Carole and watch the sunset from the little balcony of Le Cercle overlooking the purple Luberon Mountains.

The vineyards appear in her vision. Also, endless rows of sweet-smelling lavender, which should now be in bloom or else just at the end of their bloom. And the cicadas will be serenading loudly to females, and Ilse will recognize Po's language inside their *cha-cha-cha* sounds.

She's ecstatic at the thought of trading in this, her trudge through these muddy flats, her face dripping with rain and fog, for Provence's sun-kissed land.

"But Frey, I thought we both agreed that after your father died, the magic had—"

"I was trying to convince myself that that was true. I was getting married, for heaven's sake!"

"Wait, Frey."

She had ventured off her rock-hopping path into a marshy area and without realizing it had stepped into a sinkhole! This was new territory for her. She'd heard about the silt mud shores to the north of her house, and how dangerous they were. She'd never encountered a sinkhole. She remembers Duggan telling her that sinkholes, or bog holes, as they were often called, can be open tunnels, weedy arteries that lead to the sea. Those who fell in, like Ollie Olson had, held their breath and then, if they were able, swam sideways and out, that is if they could hold their breath that long. Only if you were actually *in* a sinkhole could you tell its depth and width.

Beluga had warned her to stay on the rocky path.

Her boots are sinking!

Oh no!

When she tries to step out, she sinks deeper. If she stays still, she stops sliding.

"Frey, I'm in a sinkhole! I'm going to have to call you back. I've got to get out of here. I just lost a boot! I'll call you back!"

"What's a sinkhole? I've never heard of a sinkhole."

"Oh my God."

She hangs up.

If she yelled out, no one would hear her. The exertion could make her sink deeper. She sees a patch of stunted dwarf birch a few feet away and a large rock a few feet from that. If she can shimmy over to the mound of dwarf birches and the rock, she might be able to hoist herself out, using the rock as ballast. She maneuvers toward the rock, but as she does so, she sinks a foot deeper. She tries again and falls in another six inches.

Sempiternal though sodden towards sundown, suspended in time.

Even now, T. S. Eliot haunts her!

If only I could be suspended in time, not mud!

She sinks another foot! She's up to her waist now. She will die in a sinkhole, and no one will know. They'll find her rubber boots before they find her bones, but that may be a decade from now. She holds her phone over her head. She'll call Beluga. As she makes the motion to press his number, she slides lower. Up to her chest. She tries to calm herself, stop herself from hyperventilating. If she can just get a hold of that rock. It's a foot away. Another wriggle in the thick brown noose of wet earth. She closes her eyes. She's touching distance from the stone. She throws her phone onto a crowberry shrub not far from where she is. She'll need both hands to get the leverage. One more squirm. Almost there.

Got it! It's slippery but will have to do. She takes a deep breath. Pushing down on the rock, she imagines that she's a breaching whale, and with a deep breath, she hurls herself out onto the mealy, muddy ground nearby.

"*Damn*. That was a close call!" she says aloud as she looks down at her mud-caked jacket, pants, and one booted leg. "I just lost one of my boots to a sinkhole. And I almost lost myself."

She chokes back tears as she picks up and wipes off her phone and walks one-booted back to the path. It's raining again. She removes her other boot and her mud-oozing socks and walks barefoot.

That's it. This was a sign. She'll book the next flight to Paris.

She hears the high-pitched grind of a motor. It's Duggan in Beluga's UTV.

"Barefooted, with one boot?" he yells, stopping the vehicle.

"I lost the other in the sinkhole back there." She points and bursts into tears.

"Hop in," Duggan yells.

"Thank you, Duggan. But I'll get the seat filthy," she says, still crying. "I'm a mess."

"You can thank Mary, who wanted me to drop off a basket of food for you at Beluga's house. Beluga let me use his quad. Where did you lose your boot?"

"I almost lost my life." She can't catch her breath. She wipes mud from her neck. It's hard to believe that she'd almost sunk into the salivating mouth of the earth.

"Where was it?" He digs deep in his pocket and hands her a crumpled handkerchief.

"Thank you, Duggan," she says, wiping her tears. The stitched cloth smells like the lavender soap she'd given Mary.

She points.

"Behind that clump of dwarf birch. Thank goodness there was a rock nearby."

"Up farther north, they call them suck holes."

"Where would it have sucked me?"

"Bowels of the earth. Some go down fifty, one hundred feet."

Now she really needs the handkerchief.

Duggan slides out of the seat of the quad slowly, holding his lower back. He's scrabbling around for something in the cargo box. He returns to the passenger-seat window with a long-armed tool.

"I knew I could count on Beluga to have a boot grabber!" he yells out, happy for his find. Frey would not be able to imagine such an instrument. "Why the heck did you go off the rock path?"

"I was distracted. I was on the phone."

"That trip to France really turned your head upside down," he says. His wet gray hair doesn't move when he shakes his head.

She slips from her seat and follows him.

"Stay in the quad!" he hollers back at her.

"Over a few feet to your right," she yells. "Be careful, Duggan! Right there!"

"See it!" Duggan bends his tall body over the boggy spot.

"It's a stick, not your boot!" he shouts. "Nothing! Might have sunk all the way down."

Her rain boots, one of her last possessions, and she's lost one. She resists more tears as the rain douses her face.

"Got it!"

For an old man with a sore back, he jumps nimbly through the patchy bog back to Ilse in the quad. He throws the slime-seaweed-choked boot into the cargo box and removes something blue.

"Thank you, Duggan, thank you." She wipes more tears on his lavender-scented handkerchief.

"Thank Beluga's pipe grabber clamp. And you can thank Mary for this." He places a basket covered with a large blue cloth on her lap. He starts the engine as Ilse removes the blue cloth.

"She's like that, Mary," he yells over the motor. "She always knows when someone needs comfort. A few fishcakes and some fries. A container of my favorite seal stew in there too."

"That's so thoughtful."

The windshield wipers swiping is a comforting sound.

"All of Oqaatsut is feeling for you: Ilse, almost pulled out to sea, now almost yanked into the depths of the bog. I'm glad Beluga has an extra room."

The whole town knows she's at Beluga's.

When they arrive at Beluga's house, Ilse slides out of the quad, wearing one boot and hugging the other. Her feet are numb. She tries to wipe the mud from the seat with her slicker.

"I'll take care of it later, Ilse. You go in and take a hot shower."

"I'll return your handkerchief after I wash it, Duggan. I may need it a little while longer."

Po had a handkerchief like this.

"Keep the handkerchief, Ilse. Mary sews me a few a year."

After another round of gratitude to Duggan and to Mary for the basket, Ilse dumps the seaweed and blue-green scum from the suck hole out of her boot to the side of the gravel pathway and takes refuge in Beluga's house. Minou trots into the main room to greet her.

"You smell river-scampy!" she says to her cat. "But, I suppose, so do I." She sits on the stool just inside the door to remove her mud-sullied pants, socks, boot, and jacket, and hurries into the shower. Even her hair is viscous with mud.

After showering, she shares Mary's fishcake with Minou and wonders how long her cell phone's coverage would have lasted in the mud. She would have suffocated long before that.

She takes another bite of the fishcake.

Her phone flashes. It's a text from Émile, telling her about the disastrous wedding, and that luckily for her and the Labaye family, it was too late for Daphné Solenz to call off the marketing plan for the poetry collection.

Minou slithers around her legs.

"The rest is yours, Minou," she says.

She pictures the shape of Frey in the serene Nantucket church, paralyzed in the vestry, the priest and the father of the bride encouraging him, pleading with him, trying to understand him, while his daughter waits. Waiting in white. Frey would be brooding. They're touching up the cheeks of the bride, they're straightening her veil, they're telling her that this is normal, typical even, the groom taking a little pause to let the beauty of the moment sink in. "Do you think he's having second thoughts?" the bride-to-be is asking. Her father is saying, "No, no, he's just taking his good old time," but meanwhile, the father is thinking *I will kill that bastard if he doesn't take my daughter down the aisle.*

What does Frey say when the priest and the father press him, and then, when the mother of the bride, Daphné Solenz, Émile's boss, gets involved? Does he say *I'm sorry,* and then slink out the back door of the church with wilting shame? As he slips into his car, does he bow his head to avoid catching the eyes of the guests who are arriving late?

She looks at her phone. No call back from Frey. He must not have believed her when she said she had fallen into a sinkhole. She must not have conveyed how dangerous it was.

It all fits together so perfectly: Ilse's life in Paris was set in motion from the instant she'd watched the stylish Madame LaRoche sashay into the classroom and heard her first melodic French words. She looks over at the red scarf that she'd washed and placed on the back of Beluga's desk chair. She thinks back to the solemn moment when Po had joined her hand with Frey's that day in church. *Po's and her dream had come true.* Goodbye to Malu and her anger and complaints. Goodbye to winter's dark monochrome and the chill of snow and ice, the slush, sleet, and the rain-flooding spring, the gluttonous sea, and houses that smell of mildew and surrender to the tides. Goodbye to suck holes.

Paris in September. What could be more ideal?

"Minou, don't worry. You're coming with me this time."

She composes the text to Frey. *Find me yours on October 1st.* Is it too quick? That's when the lease for her apartment expires. Too bold? Too romantic? She doesn't care. She sends the text.

Frey's immediate response is music to her ears. In preparation for Minou's arrival, he's bought a pink tufted cat bed. He's also begun arranging two book-signing parties, one at his apartment on rue de Grenelle and the other at Shakespeare and Company on the Left Bank. Both will be opportunities for her to meet his friends and colleagues and to celebrate her work as a translator.

Over the next weeks, the intimacy and intensity of their communication increases. Frey continues to praise her work and sends texts and photos of himself at iconic spots in Paris holding up *The Provençal Poet*. The captions read *Someone is missing in this photo.*

Chapter 38

At the Disko Arts Festival in Ilulissat on the first Saturday in September, Donny is wearing his baseball cap backward, and his face is not big enough to contain his smile. The festival grounds on this crisp, bright day are packed with people standing at booths, in lines for ice cones, playing games, or watching the puppet show. Donny, Beluga, and Ilse are moving hips and shoulders to the beat of Björk, the Icelandic singer, who has made a special trip north to celebrate circumpolar artists. It's been a perfect day, beginning with lunch at Disko Bay Beach with a Tipsy-to-Go lunch basket. Val Barker is an entrepreneur.

Ilse can feel the sunburn on her face after half an hour at the Greenland version of a beach, which involves wearing a down jacket and wool hat, sitting on a rocky cliff overlooking a jagged coastline, and spotting whales while listening to the booming, cracking, rumbling splashes of icebergs birthing from the nearby glacier. While the sound was a thrill in her childhood, now it's an unwelcome reminder of planetary doom.

While Donny is in line for an iceberg cone, Beluga leads Ilse to a grassy spot just outside the white tents. The red-and-white flags are flapping wildly.

"I wanted to tell you . . . Wow, those flags will be frayed in no time . . ."

"Yes?"

"That I read your poetry translation."

"What?"

"I don't read much poetry, but the writing is really good. The feelings of this man stayed with me for hours later, the tenderness. It's still with me. It's like I saw directly into this guy's heart, and felt his grief, but also his joy at being alive. I'm wondering if I was also catching a glimpse into your heart."

"Troy, how did you—"

He jingles something in his pocket. "Your mother gave me her copy. I'm waiting for my own in the mail." Ilse's copies arrived only the week before.

"When you saw my mother, did she say anything about me?"

"She said you two had had *some words*."

Why does everyone feel they have to protect Malu?

"Did she say it was my fault?"

Beluga lifts his hands.

"I liked the last poem best, the one dedicated to you. That line about the gray, ice-pearl-luster eyes. They're yours. You made an impression on this French poet, Ilse."

"I'm a different person thanks to him."

He turns toward her; his normally calm, gentle brown eyes are now intense.

"How so?"

She scans the festival grounds: people laughing, eating cake, dancing to the beat of Björk.

She taps her heart. How to put it in words? She takes a deep breath.

"After Jann's death, I was a jagged island in human form. I was living a kind of nameless, unsung dirge. I felt oppressed, restless, and ungrateful, but . . . thanks to the Poet . . . I feel lighter, less adrift in the sea. In the literal and figurative sense! And I'm singing."

Beluga is like Po. He leaves room for her speaking to catch up with her thoughts.

"I'm singing life," she continues. "I mean, I'm living life like a song. No, I *am* the song. Yes, that's it. I'm the song."

"I can see that about you, Ilse," says Beluga, nodding slowly. "Since you've been back, you *are* a song of yourself!"

It's a wondrous and rare thing when a person confirms who you are, unalloyed. Or at least, when a person has the decency to let you think you know who you are.

Ilse wipes a tear from her face.

Val, and Caroo, her daughter, are walking toward them.

"What was his son's name?" Beluga asks.

"Frey, short for Geoffrey," she says. As she says his name, she can feel the slight tug on Beluga's heart, like the one she felt when she thought about Beluga and Val together.

"You . . ."

"Yes?"

"You got to know each other?"

She can't bear to look at Beluga's face.

"Yes—"

"Where've you been, you two?" Val says, grabbing Beluga's arm.

Val's wearing a green-and-blue beaded top and her green feather earring in one ear, and all that green makes her enormous kohl-lined eyes look like emeralds. Beluga says hello to Caroo, and she responds with a grin.

"Come over to my table. It needs some love," Val says, leading them to her red-and-white tent celebrating the Saqqaq culture. Val is selling beaded necklaces and intricate beaded shirts that she and her four aunts have made by hand.

Beluga, who can spot whales, eagles, polar bears, you name it, from vast distances, finds Donny and Ingun among a large group at the balloon pop booth and corrals them to Val's table.

"So, Beluga," Val says, "Ilse's birthday is coming up. September eighth, right? Aren't you going to buy one of these for her?" She points to one of the more extravagant three-tiered beaded necklaces.

"I wwwwant to buy one for Ilssse," says Donny.

"You can both buy one for her," says Val, "and I'll make sure the necklaces go together."

"You're ruthless, Val," says Beluga.

"When a woman makes a sale, she's ruthless; when a man does it, he's a good businessman. We'll start with you, Donny. Choose your favorite."

"Ilssse, put it on!" Donny is saying, holding up the blue tiered necklace.

It is long enough to slip over her head. With her handheld mirror, Val shows Ilse the necklace with the large heart-shaped turquoise stone at its center. Ilse knows Val won't charge Donny for it.

"Thank you, Donny! I love it," Ilse says. She won't let the sea swallow *this*.

"Your turn, Beluga," says Val.

"Eyes shut," Beluga tells Ilse.

Ilse closes her eyes. The next thing she feels is another layer of cool beads around her neck. She shivers as Beluga's hand brushes her ear.

"Wait," he says. His fingers glide along the back of her neck. He's hooking the clasp.

"There," he says.

"Ilssse, open your eyes!" yells Donny.

Donny holds the mirror up so that Ilse can see Donny's many-stranded blue beaded necklace with Beluga's choice, a carnelian semi-precious stone necklace. The orange color of the gemstone reminds her of the ochre cliffs of Roussillon.

"Val was right," Beluga says. "Donny's necklace and this one look great together."

Ilse fingers the two necklaces, intertwining them.

Donny is pulling Ilse and Beluga to a nearby kiosk selling guided hiking trips.

"I www-want to do this with you and you," he says, pointing at each of them and smiling.

The trip, scheduled for the first week in October includes two overnights in different rustic huts on Uummannaq Mountain after eight-hour days of hiking around the Uummannaq Fjord. No electricity, no plumbing. Picnics are provided. Donny looks at Ilse with pleading eyes.

Beluga looks at Ilse for approval.

"I think I'll be in Paris, Donny."

Donny drops his hands, pouts, and turns away.

"To Paris, really, Ilse?" says Beluga, with a surprised look. "You haven't told me about that."

She shrugs. "I've been preoccupied, to say the least . . ."

"Is that why you signed for only a month's rental above Jessie's store?"

How does Beluga know this?

Donny is asking the woman at the booth about what to pack for the hiking trip.

"It's a temporary place for me and Minou to dry our paws. Anyway, I don't think I could live longer than a month in town."

"If you can't handle a month in the titillating town of Ilulissat, how will you fare in the City of Light?"

"So, Ilssse, are we going on the trip?" Donny asks, waving the brochure.

"I'm not so sure, Donny. But I'll take the brochure so I can think about it," says Ilse.

"I've been looking for you three!" It's Ingun. "Come on, this is Björk's encore, then Olrik will be DJing."

"Ingun, over here!" Val calls out. She's already on the dance floor. She waves her arms.

The music is thumping. Pulling Ilse's hand, Donny runs with her into the middle of the throng. Ilse copies him as he kicks up his legs in a kind of cancan, one leg up, then another. Beluga dances nearby with Jessie, who owns the *tupilak* store beneath the one-bedroom apartment that Ilse has rented. With Beluga's back to her, Ilse notices his straight dark hair that curls at the nape of his neck and his broad shoulders that carried the weight of supporting his two younger sisters and his mother after his father died. They were the family of his childhood, but he cared for them as if they were the family he'd created.

Donny swings Ilse again, and she bumps into Duggan and Mary, who are doing a kind of waltz step to the rock-and-roll music.

"Sorry!" says Ilse.

Here come Val and Caroo and Ingun to join them.

Val on the prowl catches Donny's hand and makes a threesome a foursome with Ingun and Caroo. Caroo hops up and down as if she's on an old-fashioned pogo stick. Now Donny is swinging Ilse. Donny looks so happy. Yikes, she almost fell over on the last spin.

When a slower song comes on, Beluga taps Donny's shoulder and says, "It's my turn." Donny shakes his head, but Val takes his hand, so that he turns to dance with her, Caroo, and Ingun.

Beluga smells of pine, and his hand is cool and dry. He places his cheek on Ilse's, and she feels thrilled in a way she had not expected. The music melts around them, and she imagines Po describing the melody as being in the form of a willow tree, with branches swaying to a lazy breeze.

Beluga is a fine dancer; his legs move lightly under his tall frame. Ilse wishes the languorous song would last, just as she wishes this day would continue.

Who knows how long she'll be here, in this dance, in this town, in this country, and she lingers on Beluga's shoulder longer than the music. She will miss festivals like this and will miss Donny and the pine smell of Beluga and the way he just laid his cheek to her cheek in such a simple and easy way.

On their way home in Beluga's truck late that night, fires of green and orange rip across the darkened sky. It's rare to see the aurora borealis in early September. Beluga stops the car, and the two slip out to watch the dance of colors. Now immense green ribbons are pluming and painting the sky pink, orange, and red. The color-shapes unfurl, stretch, and undulate, whisper-roaring through her and Beluga.

And Jann is with them.

Chapter 39

IT'S QUIET IN THE FURNISHED RENTAL ABOVE THE *TUPILAK* store. No winds howl through the windows, no surf slides, gushes, sucks, and slurps around the foundations. Ilse doesn't hear the Jurassic screeches of seafowl, or the booming reports of icebergs calving from glaciers across the way.

She doesn't miss her mildew-scented, always-damp clothes, not that she has any clothes anymore. Nor does she listen for Mr. G stampeding the stairwell. Mr. G wouldn't like this apartment: it's too airtight, too clean, too new.

In her *tupilak* store, Jessie Jonkuk sells figures carved from the bones of walruses, reindeer, and musk oxen; knives, jewelry, and knitting needles; and other odds and ends that tourists buy. Ilse isn't keen about living over a store that uses animal bones as decorative objects, but Val's uncle has told her it's the only furnished rental in the area.

When it's not foggy as it is now, Val's uncle told Ilse that she'll be able to see seals on the shores of Disko Bay from one window, and from the other, the mouth of the twenty-four-mile-long Kangia Icefjord, stuffed with massive icebergs. On a clear day, he'd elaborated, you can see the rough outline of Baffin Island across Baffin Bay. Yeah, right. On a clear day. He's a good salesperson.

Ilse prefers Beluga's house, where, as at Po's, nature felt at home, inside and out. Everything in his house felt as solid as Beluga. What she liked most of all was the owl that hooted her to sleep. Three hoots, a stop, four hoots. Stop. Three hoots. Owl haiku.

Ilse needs the short-eared owl—she'd spotted it the prior evening—to help her fall asleep tonight. Her mind returns to Donny's fallen face when she said she couldn't join him for the hike, followed by the confusion in Beluga's face. She's also tormented by Malu's silence. Has Val replaced her as the recipient of her mother's daily texting? Will she and Malu ever speak again? And what about Fa? How can Ilse spend time with Fa if Malu won't let her inside the house? Too bad the best sorter in the country can't sort out her relationship with her daughter. Too bad her daughter the translator can't understand her mother's language.

First things first: Donny. She'll find a hiking expedition in the next few weeks before she flees to Paris. That's what she'll do! She checks out the brochure with the photographs of the cheerful little huts on Uummannaq Fjord. This is the kind of adventure Ilse loves. Horse around outside all day, and then cozy up in front of a fire in a small rustic hut, and sleep like a bear.

Her phone's ring startles her. Who could be calling at 11:39 at night?

Frey.

"Hello, Frey. Everything okay?" It's 3:39 A.M., Paris time.

"I'm thinking of you, and I'm wondering why you aren't here in Paris with me right now."

She turns on the light.

"Sorry?" she says, not quite getting his meaning.

"I'm asking why you haven't come over by now?"

After their last conversation, Ilse had texted him that she had needed more time to think things over.

"Ilse, I need you here now. I told you that I'd pay for your flight."

It occurs to her that he'd never offered to come to Oqaatsut. Not that she's ever invited him. Frey and Oqaatsut? Ilulissat would be more palatable for him. Who doesn't swoon over icebergs?

"Why the rush?"

"Caroline has come back to Paris. She's returned to work here and has decided to have the baby here rather than in Boston, where her father lives."

"What does that have to do with us?"

"She'll be tempting me again, like she does so well."

He goes on to recap his fun time that night in Paris with champagne flowing and dancing at clubs, and how she'll love it there. Half listening, she spots on the bureau in the corner of the room the small bouquet in a ceramic vase made from Greenlandic clay that Beluga had brought for her when he helped her move into the apartment two days ago. As Frey talks on, she rises from the bed and carries the vase to her bedside table. A handful of deep purple saxifrage jiggle as she walks. It's as if the flowers are giggling. A few white Arctic poppies, all proud and upright, and a bunch of delicate light-blue harebells accompany the saxifrage. Beluga had added a spray of pink-gray heather. Three tall grasses in there too, one with a shirred leaf, and, what? A sprig of knotweed, mostly favored by reindeer. Not many people would find a stalk of knotweed worthy to place among these wildflowers. And he must have had to search far and wide to find the princess of the bouquet, the dwarf magenta-colored *niviarsiaq*.

"Is that right?" she says after Frey tells her about the new AI assistant he's installed in his apartment.

The delicate bouquet of nature's bounty contrasts with the stridency in Frey's voice.

"What's the AI's name?"

"Rose."

"Why Rose?"

"Why not Rose?"

She touches the lively petals of the *niviarsiaq*, which means "young girl" in Greenlandic. The combination of textures and colors in the bouquet is exquisite. She brings one of the tall grasses from the vase into bed with her and feathers her face with it.

"I'll have Rose get you a flight for tomorrow."

What's that in his voice? It's as if he's anticipating an easy "yes" from her.

"Frey, I need more time to think about this."

"I don't understand what's keeping you from jumping on that plane tomorrow. There are no mud sucks, if that's what you call them, here in Paris."

Frey has installed Rose the robot; now he wants to do the same with Ilse.

She hears a noise on Frey's side of the phone. Is he kicking off his fine Italian leather shoes? She pictures Beluga's mud-splashed work boots, and what a welcome sight they were the night of the flood. She thinks of the way Beluga dips his robust frame, so modestly and yes, that's it, reverently, every time he says goodbye to anyone. Rather than dressing up in fancy nightclub frocks, she's happy in Jann's slouchy, comfortable gray Shetland sweater, and her loose pants, not unlike the ones Po wore around his house.

She surprises herself and Frey with a laugh.

"You're laughing."

"Frey, you've just walked out of a wedding. *You're* the one who needs time to think. Let's talk next week."

"I need you here now!"

He's a petulant child.

"Stop, Frey," she says, glancing again at the small bouquet. One of the cool tall grasses falls from her fingers onto her neck. The fresh frond reminds her of Beluga's fingers brushing against her ear as he tried to fasten the beaded necklace that she's still wearing.

She sits up in her bed and takes a deep breath.

"Frey, please listen to me now."

"All I can hear are the words of my father's poems in my ear. About you, Ilse."

"Frey, please listen. We both know something we've never talked about. It's that deep down, or not even so deep, we're different, too different for us ever to be happy together. I'm a spiky milkweed seed pod, and while I may be an appealing blue-violet color, I'm still a wildflower. And you, Frey, you're a cultivated rose from a historic French garden. We came together as a love wish for your dying father."

"I can't hear you that well. You're breaking up."

Minou jumps off the bed.

"That's right, Frey. We're breaking up. Frey, can you hear me now?"

"Barely."

"Frey, I congratulate you on making the crucial life decision not to marry the wrong woman. But"—and Ilse takes another deep breath—"I'm not the right woman either."

"Ilse—"

"I wish you all the best, Frey, I really do."

"I thought . . . I thought you felt differently," he says. His tone is suddenly cold.

She says nothing.

"Goodbye, I guess, then," he says.

"We will always share those last days with your father."

"Goodbye."

He clicks off first.

When she does too, she runs to the window, opens it, and thrusts her head out.

"Goodbye, Provence!" she yells into the rainy, dimly lit night.

"Minou, that was a dream that almost came true," she tells her cat, as she settles back in bed. "But it was the wrong dream, and now I've finally woken up."

She turns off the light and to quiet her thoughts and beating heart, she prays for Jann. Jann wouldn't have liked Frey. And she also prays for her father's eyesight, and for a host of other things including Caroline Solenz for believing in such a man.

And for the first time ever before falling asleep, she rolls around two names on her tongue—Ilse, and Troy—and she thinks about how his large hands would feel around her waist.

Chapter 40

TROY BELKE DOESN'T NEED TO RING THE BELL. ILSE HAS BEEN looking out the open window to catch the first sight of him and Griffin as they walk up the road to her building's door: Troy in his wrinkled felt hat, with the slight bounce in his stride, and Griffin trotting beside him.

She squints to see better. Troy is carrying two brown paper bags and a box in his arms. He had offered to bring dessert. If that's dessert, it's in a big box.

"Come on up," she calls down to them.

It's a misty night but still warm for September 8, and she's prepared halibut that she bought fresh from Duggan that afternoon and potatoes and atrociously expensive green beans from the farmer's market. A bottle of white wine that Eva Sorrell had sent over as a housewarming-birthday gift is chilling in the refrigerator.

And here's a surprise. That morning, Malu had dropped off a round, white wool crocheted tablecloth. It's her mother's impressive handiwork. On a plain, unstamped post office card, she'd written *For Ilse. Happy birthday. I hope you like it. Fa misses you. Come home for dinner next week.*

That's a first. The word "happy" in a communication from Malu. Does "Happy" in "Happy birthday" count?

"Fa misses you" leaves out Malu missing her. Why should Fa suffer Ilse's absence? Fa! She misses his silent, stoic hugs. She'll go home and do what she loves to do with Fa: accompany him out to the fjord, where he'll carve a hole in the ice to fish. And while he waits patiently to catch dinner, she'll put her ear to the ice and listen to the gurgling language of the undersea.

Ilse will accept Malu's handmade tablecloth as her apology.

Ilse has placed the tablecloth over her desk, and—thank you, Malu—it has transformed her workplace into an inviting dining room. For Ilse's special night, Val has lent her two crystal wineglasses, a gift from a customer, and Ilse sets these on a tray.

She'll start the evening with a glass of wine on her rooftop, to which she has access via a pull-down ladder outside her apartment door. The roof is painted gunboat gray and houses her brick chimney and a drainpipe. For most Greenlanders, if the temperature outside is warm enough, a little or a lot of damp mist is no reason to stay indoors.

Troy is joining her for dinner to celebrate her birthday and her receipt of the Carlisle Translation Award, an American literary prize that Émile had told her about the week before. The award is given annually to a literary translator who has made "an outstanding contribution in literature in English by masterfully recreating the artistic force of a book of consummate quality." It's the only prize for a translation into English that includes an evaluation of the source language text. It's a prize recognizing both her *and* Po.

She's been invited to accept the award that fall at a conference in Tucson, Arizona! Émile says he'll pay for the airfare and hotel. The gathering includes a *declamación*, a performance featuring the recitation of literary translations from memory. Would she have the guts to sing one of Po's poems? For Po, maybe she'll do it!

Another thing to celebrate: sales figures for *The Provençal Poet* in the UK and the United States are better than expected. Émile is pleased. Ilse won't ask whether Daphné Solenz, publisher, and mother of the abandoned bride, is pleased.

Ilse's phone rings. It's Bea.

"Bea!"

"Ilse! *Joyeux anniversaire! Et aussi, félicitations!* You did it! You won it! If there's anyone who deserves this award, it's you! They write that your imperceptible hand can reach into the heart. But I still don't believe translators should be invisible."

Ilse laughs. "We'll have to fight over that later, Bea. Right now, I must be visible. Someone and his dog are at my door."

"Someone more special than me?"

"Special in a different way."

Bea laughs. "Will my Nordic friend be experimenting with *un grand* French kiss tonight?"

"Birthdays only come once a year."

"Joyeux anniversaire, mon adorable amie. Profites bien."

Minou hisses from under the bed when Ilse opens the door for Troy and Griffin.

"I shouldn't have brought Griffin," Troy says, his honey eyes tentative. "I didn't think." He replaces his hat on his head, turns sideways, and is about to leave.

"Of course you should have brought Griffin. Come in. Minou will get over it. She's frightened by Griffin's size, as we all are at first."

Ilse shows them around the one-bedroom apartment. Troy places his hat, the large box, and two bags on the kitchen table.

"Are you moving in?" she says.

"I wish," he says, removing marshmallows, chocolate bars, graham crackers, and a small box of birthday candles from the bag. "What's moving in is a cold front. Everyone at the grocery store is talking about it. That's why I brought a fireside dessert."

"Perfect! Then let's go to the rooftop terrace to enjoy the last moment of summer. Then we can come down and make a fire to start the fall season."

Griffin barks from below as the two climb the ladder to the roof. In a few round trips, Ilse carries the wineglasses, a blanket from her bed, and the white wine bottle, and Troy brings up the mysterious box and the other large brown paper bag.

Too bad the flat roof surface is wet, but who cares. She's wearing jeans, and the blanket is thick. And look, there's a line of pink on the horizon.

Troy removes a bottle from the bag.

"No way! Champagne!"

She bites her lip remembering the last time she'd had champagne. How gallant was Frey, severing off the top with his saber and Napoleonic swagger.

Troy pours the bubbly into the two wineglasses and bows a little. He lifts his glass high and pauses.

She laughs at his formality.

"Congratulations on work well done and now acknowledged."

They clink glasses, and the fizz tickles her nose as she sips.

"Delicious," she says.

"Now for this," he says, pulling out a rectangular something wrapped clumsily in brown paper.

What?

It's the book jacket of the American edition of *The Provençal Poet*—framed! The cover artist had captured, rather translated, using pen and ink and watercolor, the Provençal poet's table and two chairs under the olive tree with the lavender Luberon Mountains in the background. On Po's table, a pen and paper rest, at the ready. Just as it was.

This is also for you, Po, she says inside herself.

Troy has added a lavender-colored mat inside the frame.

"Here it is, without the jacket, if you'd like another copy," he says, reaching into the paper bag. "I have my unharmed copy at home."

"Troy, how thoughtful you are."

"And here's a second toast: Happy birthday, Ilse. This has been quite a year for you."

They sip in unison.

She hugs the frame to her, then flips through the book. The words *les Bories* catch her eye. She hadn't told Frey about her birthday. She knew so much about Frey; his birthday was March 5, yet she didn't think he knew the date of hers. He knew the year she was born—that would be relevant to him—but her birthday? He'd never asked.

With another small formal bow, Troy hands her the box. It's as if he's been watching a video of Po's chivalric manners. Bowing is not a typical thing to do in her country.

"Open it when I'm gone. I don't want to see your face if you don't like it."

"No, I'll open it right now."

"Drink more bubbly, then."

"I don't need to do that."

She pulls off the paper bag and the newspaper wrapping to reveal a stone sculpture in the shape of a humpback whale.

She looks up at him quickly, then down at the sculpture in her hands.

"You carved this?"

He nods.

"You've got the eyes just right—and the tail and the grooves, and the curves of the flukes are in perfect proportion. It's beautiful, Troy. How did you get it to be so smooth?"

"A lot of sanding."

She reaches over to him and kisses him on his cheek. "Thank you."

Her heart feels full.

"Wait. I've got something else for you."

"Not another thing!"

"I ran out of brown paper, so you'll have to close your eyes and open your hands."

As she holds out her hands, she thinks of when she received communion in Saint-Pantaléon, with Po standing behind her.

The object now in her palms is also round, but weighty like a large, thick coin.

"May I open my eyes now?"

"Only if you can tell me what direction you're facing."

Of course!

"It's your father's compass!" she says, her eyes still shut. How did Troy ever find it?

"You haven't told me what direction you're facing."

"North, true north," she says, and she opens her eyes.

"You may need it for when you're in Paris."

"I'm not going to Paris."

He looks confused.

"The Paris thing didn't work out."

Troy pauses. He looks like he's about to ask a question but doesn't.

"No Paris," she confirms.

"Another toast, then," Troy says, lifting his glass. He's hiding whatever he's feeling by looking westward to the coast. "To the flood!"

"What?" she blurts out. "To losing my life?"

"No." He quickly turns to smile at her. There's a twinkle in his eyes. "To gaining it."

The rain begins to fall in heavy drops. The pink-white sky turns gray, the wind whips around them, and they see a streak of lightning in the west over Baffin Bay. And then it thunders. They hear Griffin bark down below, and they take the blanket and the other things down the ladder and into her apartment.

"Troy," Ilse calls from where she's standing, at the window. It's lightning while it's snowing. "Come look. This is crazy. I've never seen thundersnow in September." White dusts the streets and the rooftops of the colorful houses.

Inches apart at the window, they watch the lightning zigzag behind the pirouetting snow. She feels the tension, not from the electrons in the bottom of the clouds pulled down by the positive charges on the ground, but from Troy's proximity. She remembers a line by the fifteenth-century Indian poet, Kabir, that Po had read to her: *Paper would turn to flame if I touched it in an ecstatic mood.*

"I'm glad we abandoned our rooftop picnic, or else we'd be the roasted marshmallows," says Troy.

Griffin barks at the next lightning flash. Minou hisses from the kitchen.

"This isn't fair to Minou," he says.

Breaking the intensity, Troy leaves her side to slip a leash on Griffin. He ties the leash to the latch of the front door.

"Now Minou can relax a little."

Griffin strains at the leash.

Troy builds a fire in the cast-iron woodstove using the logs that Jessie provided Ilse for the first month of the rental, and Ilse prepares the potatoes and halibut in parchment paper with lemon and white wine. As she sprinkles *herbes de Provence* that Agnès had dried in the sun and had pushed on Ilse the day before she left—*oh, Agnès!*—Ilse hums a little tune, something from the Poet's repertoire.

"I've never known you to be a singer, Ilse," says Troy, poking at the fire. "What's that song?"

She hadn't realized she was singing.

"Something I picked up from my friend the Poet. Do you like it?"

"I love it."

"After dinner, I'll sing it to you in Provençal."

"I'd like to hear more about your month in France," Troy says, joining her in the kitchen.

Could he detect the print of Frey on her skin? Could he envision Frey's shoulder where she had laid her head so comfortably? But if Troy looked closer, he would see that the deepest part of her had not been touched. The connection between her and Frey was almost preposterous, a concept more than a reality, something that she wished to believe in as much as when as a little girl, she wanted to imagine that the grit in her waking eye was a grain of sand dropped by the sandman.

After dinner, they sit on the red-and-white rug with the KAK Greenland Football Association logo at its center that Jann had given her the first time he'd been named the MVP. Gwen had found it in the swirling waters near Ilse's house the night of the flood and had recently returned it to Ilse, washed clean. Troy begins roasting marshmallows. For skewers, they use sticks that Troy had pulled from shrubs near his home. He leans forward to prod the flames with the poker.

The room has grown cold. Ilse pulls a glowing roasted marshmallow off his stick, places it and a piece of chocolate between the graham crackers, and offers it to Troy's lips.

He bites into the chewy, fluffy chocolate dessert and closes his eyes.

"Your turn," he says, assembling and offering hers. They laugh as she drops most of it on Jann's sweater.

"Here comes Minou," Ilse says. "Her appetite for sweets is greater than her fear of Griffin."

Troy lights a birthday candle in the fire and sticks it into a marshmallow and brings the dancing flame to Ilse's face.

"A wish," he offers. The illumination is bright between them.

She closes her eyes, wishes—shhh, it's a secret—and blows out the candle.

Troy asks her to read aloud one of the reviews of her translation.

"Not tonight," she says. "Po's the one who should receive these accolades, not me. About his translation of Pushkin's *Onegin,* Nabokov said, 'I'm the thorn to his rose.' "

Troy looks at her in that way of his of gazing from some distant place.

"When I read this book, Ilse, I began to see that two can equal one."

He pauses, his eyes with those thick black eyelashes on hers.

"The way you coaxed this man's words, converted his feelings into another language, is a love story that I aspire to. I'd be lying if I didn't tell you that I envy it."

"That's exactly how I felt about Po's love for his wife!" Ilse says. Frey felt the same thing. "But Troy, that is what I learned in France. It's what Po taught me, that there's always enough love, that it's infinite, even beyond death."

The rain slashes at the window sideways. And a little panic rises inside Ilse. Then she relaxes: she doesn't need to board up the cracked windows of the sea captain's house!

"So, Ilse Erlund, brilliant translator who has made an outstanding contribution to literature, tell me. How would you translate this?"

And Troy leans over and cups her chin in his large hand and kisses her on the lips, and as they kiss, Ilse's birthday wish is granted. Minou darts out from the kitchen and crawls on Ilse, and Griffin barks, and they laugh, and despite the dark clouds outside, a glimmer of the setting sun darts into the room for a moment as a last farewell to the day and makes everything golden.

And in this moment, even the award-winning translator Ilse Erlund thinks to herself, *There are no words for this.*

Acknowledgments

As Ilse discovered, it is often difficult to express deep feelings with words. So it is now as I thank my agent, Michael Carlisle, who threw me a solid line when I was swirling in uncertainties. Michael brought Penguin Random House editor Susanna Porter into my writing life, who not only edits with sensitivity and an acute sense of what makes a page turn, but read this: she accompanied me to Ilulissat, Greenland, and to the settlement of Oqaatsut, where there are more Greenland sled dogs than people—so that we could live in the novel! Thank you, Susanna. You and I are always on the same page. If that isn't enough, Michael led me to Bogaards Public Relations, where Paul Bogaards, Stephanie Kloss, and Heather Brown continue to provide wise and thoughtful counsel, support, and guidance in the fast and fluid world of publicity. Thank you, Michael, for being a part of and assembling this brilliant team and for our shared love of Provence! I'd also like to thank Diane Zinna for an encouraging early reading of the novel and Galya Morrell, an Arctic explorer, who regaled me with the stories about the Greenland way of life.

I am grateful to you all.

Credits

Illustrations on title page and part title pages by John Eric Oberbeck

Page 147, excerpt from the poem "Twilight" by Guillaume Apollinaire, translated by A. S. Kline.

Page 259, excerpt from a poem by Knud Rasmussen, engraved on the statue of Knud Rasmussen in Charlottenlund, Copenhagen, translation by Nanna Kaalund.

About the Author

Elizabeth Birkelund started her career in the editorial department at *European Travel & Life* magazine, then turned to freelance writing as a monthly personal finance columnist for *Cosmopolitan* magazine. She has written for over fifteen publications, including *Glamour*, *Self*, *Working Woman*, and *Victoria*. She is the author of two novels, *The Runaway Wife* and *The Dressmaker*, which has been published in England, Germany, and Russia.

Facebook: @ElizabethBirkelundAuthor

X: @e_birkelund

Instagram: @elizabethbirkelund

About the Type

This book was set in Fournier, a typeface named for Pierre-Simon Fournier (1712–68), the youngest son of a French printing family. He started out engraving woodblocks and large capitals, then moved on to fonts of type. In 1736 he began his own foundry and made several important contributions in the field of type design; he is said to have cut 147 alphabets of his own creation. Fournier is probably best remembered as the designer of St. Augustine Ordinaire, a face that served as the model for the Monotype Corporation's Fournier, which was released in 1925.